Items should be returned on or before the last date shown below. Items not already requested by other borrowers may be renewed in person, in writing or by telephone. To renew, please quote the number on the barcode label. To renew online a PIN is required. This can be requested at your local library.
Renew online @ www.dublincitypubliclibraries.ie
Fines charged for overdue items will include postage incurred in recovery. Damage to or loss of items will be charged to the borrower.

Leabharlanna Poiblí Chathair Bhaile Átha Cliath
Dublin City Public Libraries

Dublin City
Baile Átha Cliath

Rathmines Branch Tel: 4973539
Brainse Ráth Maonas Fón: 4973539

Date Due	Date Due	Date Due
		2 0 AUG 2014

WHAT CAME BEFORE

Max and her flock are genetic experiments. Created by a mysterious lab known only as the "School," their genetic codes have been spliced with avian DNA, giving them wings and the power to soar. What they lack are homes, families, and memories of a real life.

After escaping from the School, the flock is hunted by Erasers, agents of the School who can transform into terrifying wolf creatures, and Jeb Batchelder, the man they once thought of as a father. Despite the targets on their backs, though, the flock is desperate to learn about their individual pasts, and their inquiries lead them to Washington, D.C., where the Erasers are waiting and Fang is seriously injured!

Rushing Fang to the hospital, the flock meets Special Agent Anne Walker of the FBI who's interested in learning everything they know about the School. In exchange for information, Agent Walker offers Max and her "siblings" a safe haven in her home — even going so far as to enroll the lot of them in a proper school!

But are Max and the others really cut out for a "normal" life? School crushes and jealousies are hard enough to deal with, but there are Erasers circling, a duplicate Max and, most concerning of all, Max keeps having visions of herself turning into the thing that she hates most! Is domesticated life turning the flock soft…?

CHARACTER INTRODUCTION

MAXIMUM RIDE

Max is the eldest member of the flock, and the responsibility of caring for her comrades has fallen to her since Jeb Batchelder's apparent death. Tough and uncompromising, she's willing to put everything on the line to protect her "family."

FANG

Only slightly younger than Max, Fang is one of the elder members of the flock. Cool and reliable, Fang is Max's rock. He may be the strongest of them all, but most of the time it is hard to figure out what is on his mind.

IGGY

Being blind doesn't mean that Iggy is helpless. He has not only an incredible sense of hearing, but also a particular knack (and fondness) for explosives.

NUDGE

Motormouth Nudge would probably spend most days at the mall if not for her pesky mutant-bird-girl-being-hunted-by-wolf-men problem.

GASMAN

The name pretty much says it all. The Gasman (or Gazzy) has the art of flatulence down to a science. He's also Angel's biological big brother.

ANGEL

The youngest member of the flock and Gazzy's little sister, Angel seems to have some peculiar abilities — mind reading for example.

ARI

Just seven years old, Ari is Jeb's son but was transformed into an Eraser. He appears to have a particular axe to grind with Max.

JEB BATCHELDER

The flock's former benefactor, Jeb was a scientist at the School before helping the flock to make their original escape.

MAXIMUM RIDE

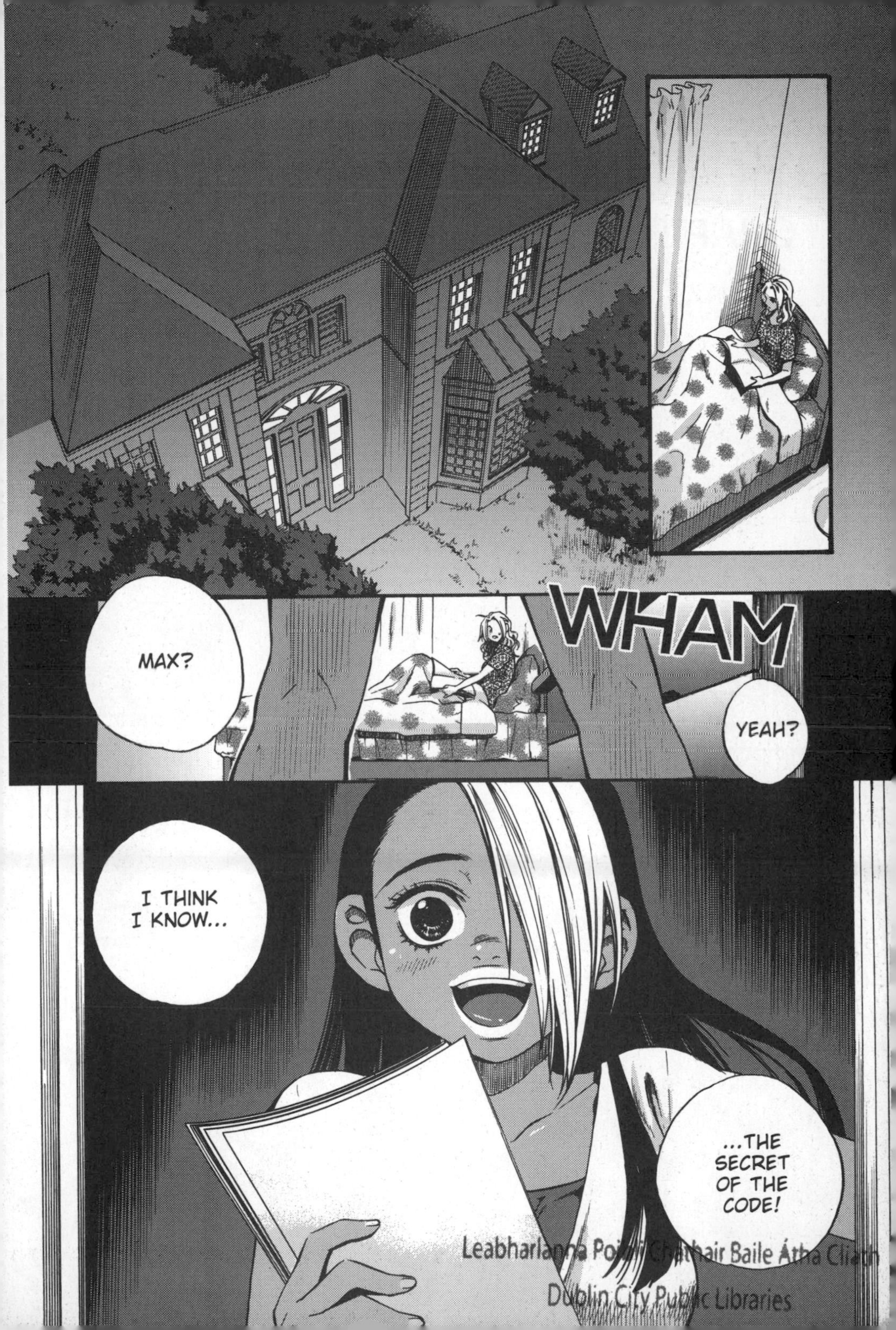
MAX?
WHAM
YEAH?
I THINK I KNOW...
...THE SECRET OF THE CODE!

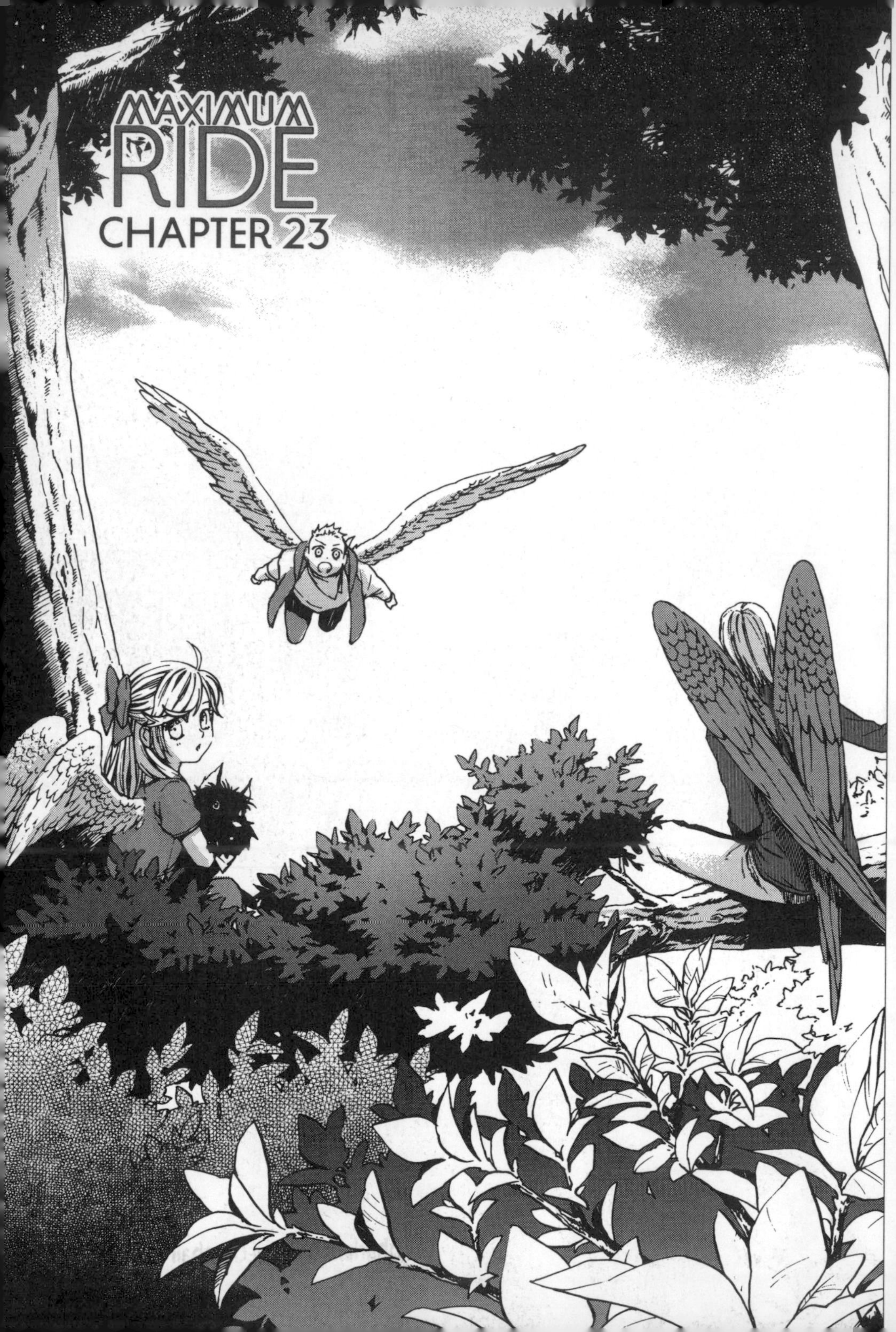
MAXIMUM RIDE
CHAPTER 23

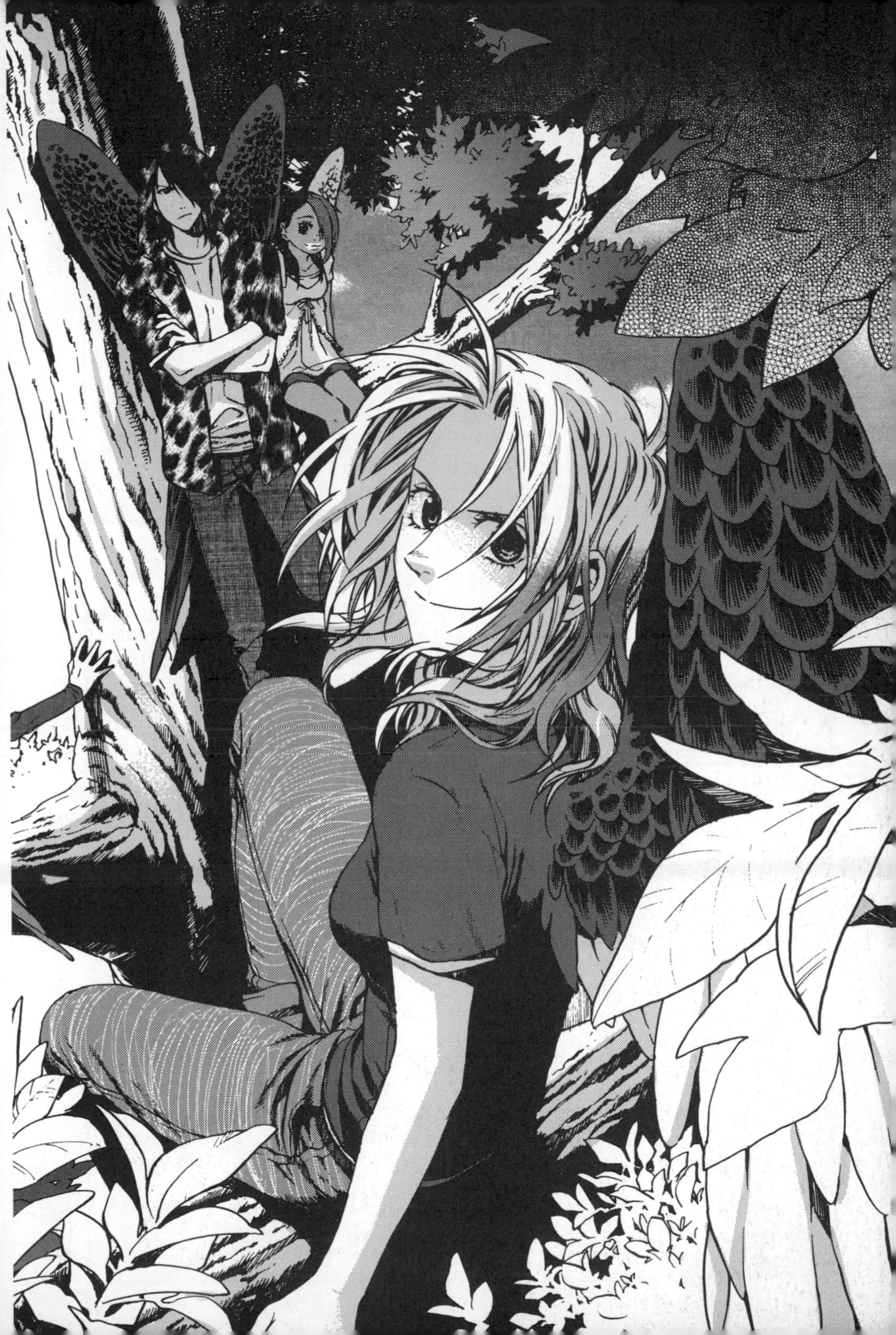

I THINK IT'S FROM A BOOK.

DO TELL!

I MEAN, OKAY, IT COULD BE SOME COMPUTERIZED CODE, IN WHICH CASE WE'LL NEVER BREAK IT.

BUT I THINK THEY WANT US TO BREAK IT—WANT *YOU* TO BREAK IT, AS PART OF YOUR TESTING.

YEAH, I GUESS I'M FAILING THIS PARTICULAR TEST.

NOT YET.

THERE'RE STILL A COUPLE OF THINGS WE HAVEN'T TRIED. LIKE IF THE NUMBERS ALL RELATE BACK TO A BOOK.

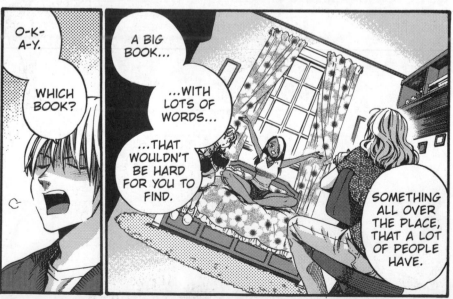

O-K-A-Y.

WHICH BOOK?

A BIG BOOK...

...WITH LOTS OF WORDS...

...THAT WOULDN'T BE HARD FOR YOU TO FIND.

SOMETHING ALL OVER THE PLACE, THAT A LOT OF PEOPLE HAVE.

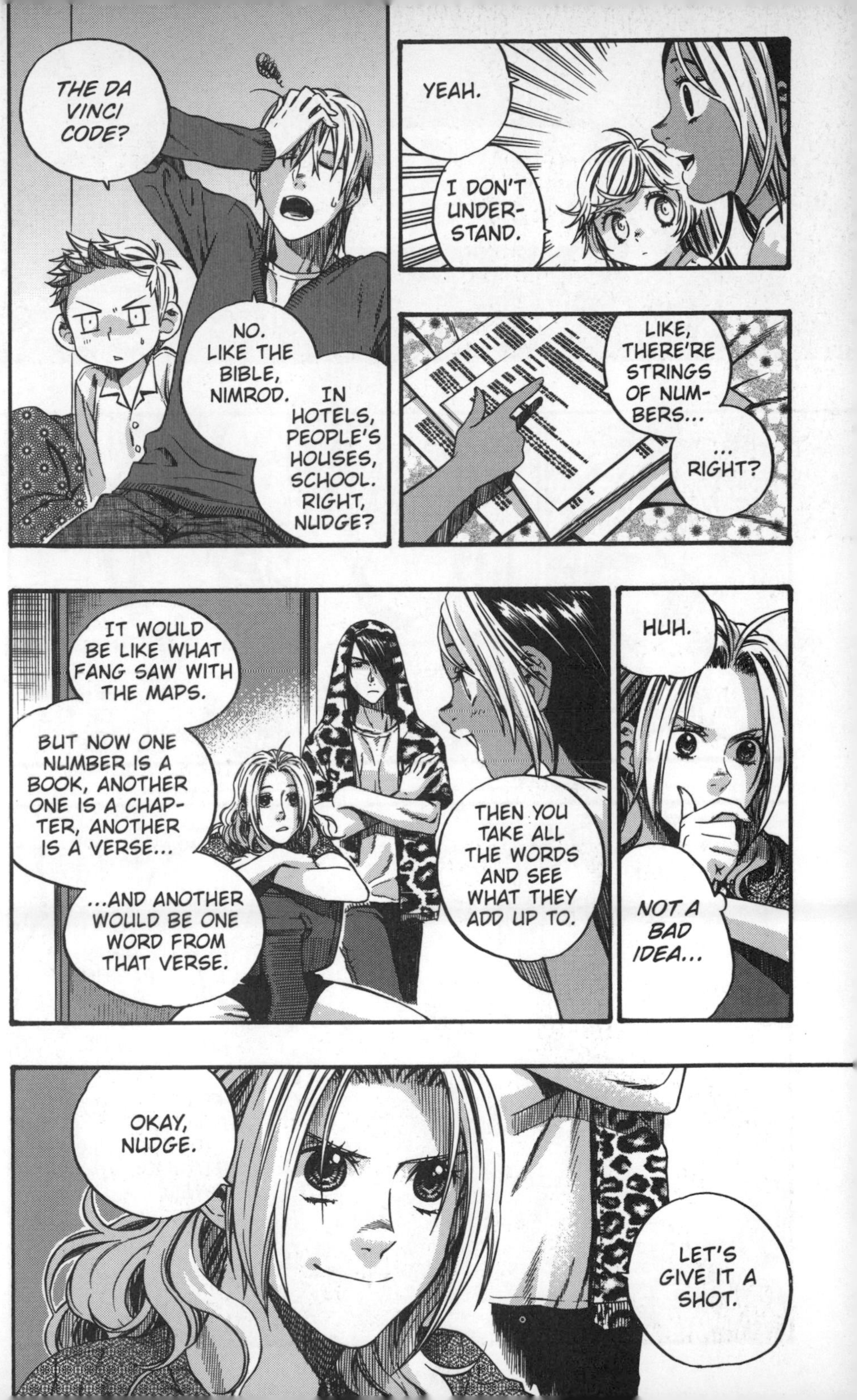
THE DA VINCI CODE?
NO. LIKE THE BIBLE, NIMROD.
IN HOTELS, PEOPLE'S HOUSES, SCHOOL. RIGHT, NUDGE?
YEAH.
I DON'T UNDER-STAND.
LIKE, THERE'RE STRINGS OF NUM-BERS...
... RIGHT?
IT WOULD BE LIKE WHAT FANG SAW WITH THE MAPS.
BUT NOW ONE NUMBER IS A BOOK, ANOTHER ONE IS A CHAP-TER, ANOTHER IS A VERSE...
...AND ANOTHER WOULD BE ONE WORD FROM THAT VERSE.
THEN YOU TAKE ALL THE WORDS AND SEE WHAT THEY ADD UP TO.
HUH.
NOT A BAD IDEA...
OKAY, NUDGE.
LET'S GIVE IT A SHOT.

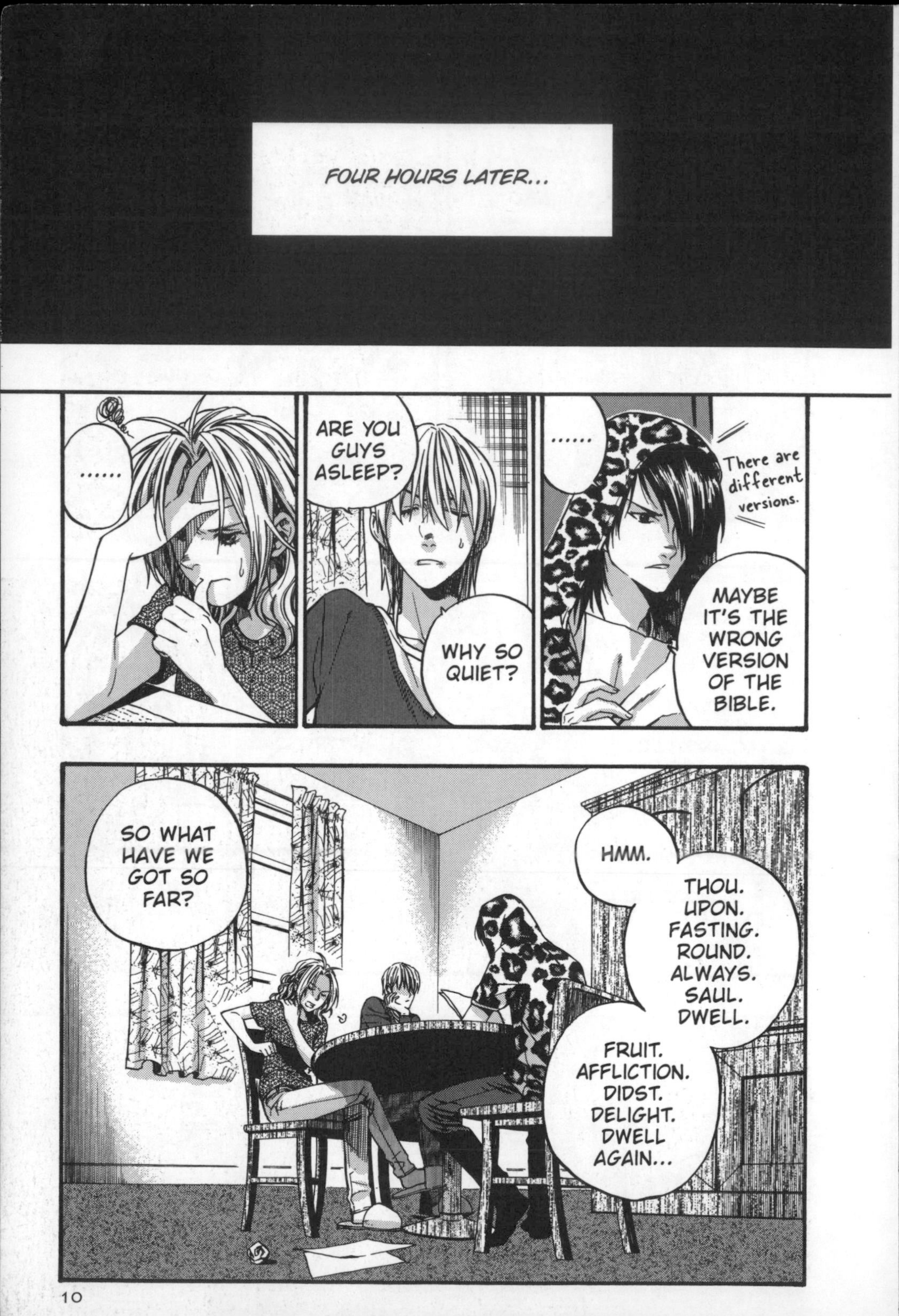
FOUR HOURS LATER...
......
ARE YOU GUYS ASLEEP?
WHY SO QUIET?
......
There are different versions.
MAYBE IT'S THE WRONG VERSION OF THE BIBLE.
SO WHAT HAVE WE GOT SO FAR?
HMM.
THOU. UPON. FASTING. ROUND. ALWAYS. SAUL. DWELL.
FRUIT. AFFLICTION. DIDST. DELIGHT. DWELL AGAIN...

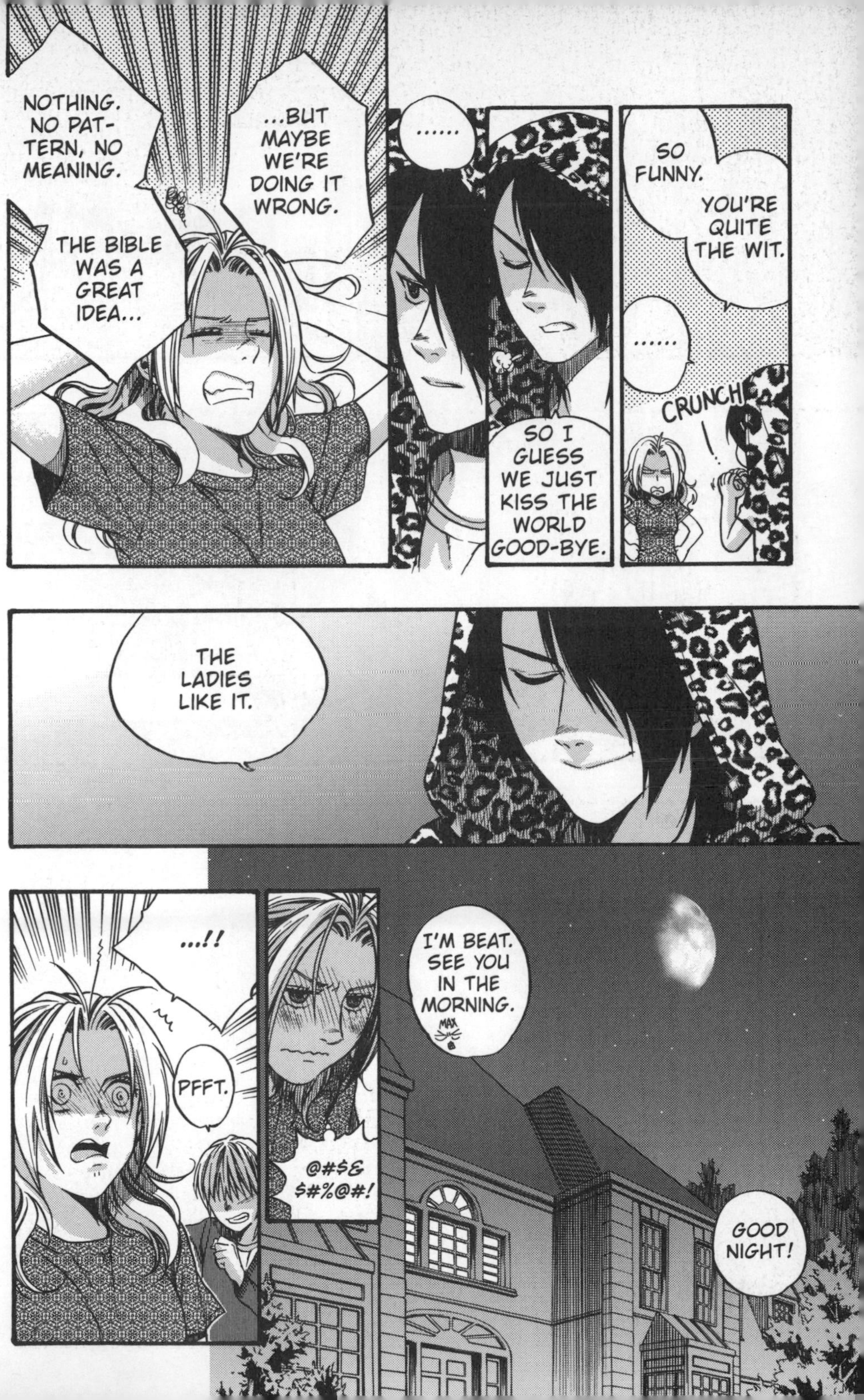
NOTHING. NO PAT-TERN, NO MEANING.
THE BIBLE WAS A GREAT IDEA...
...BUT MAYBE WE'RE DOING IT WRONG.
......
SO I GUESS WE JUST KISS THE WORLD GOOD-BYE.
SO FUNNY.
YOU'RE QUITE THE WIT.
......
CRUNCH
THE LADIES LIKE IT.
...!!
PFFT.
@#$& $#%@#!
I'M BEAT. SEE YOU IN THE MORNING.
MAX
GOOD NIGHT!

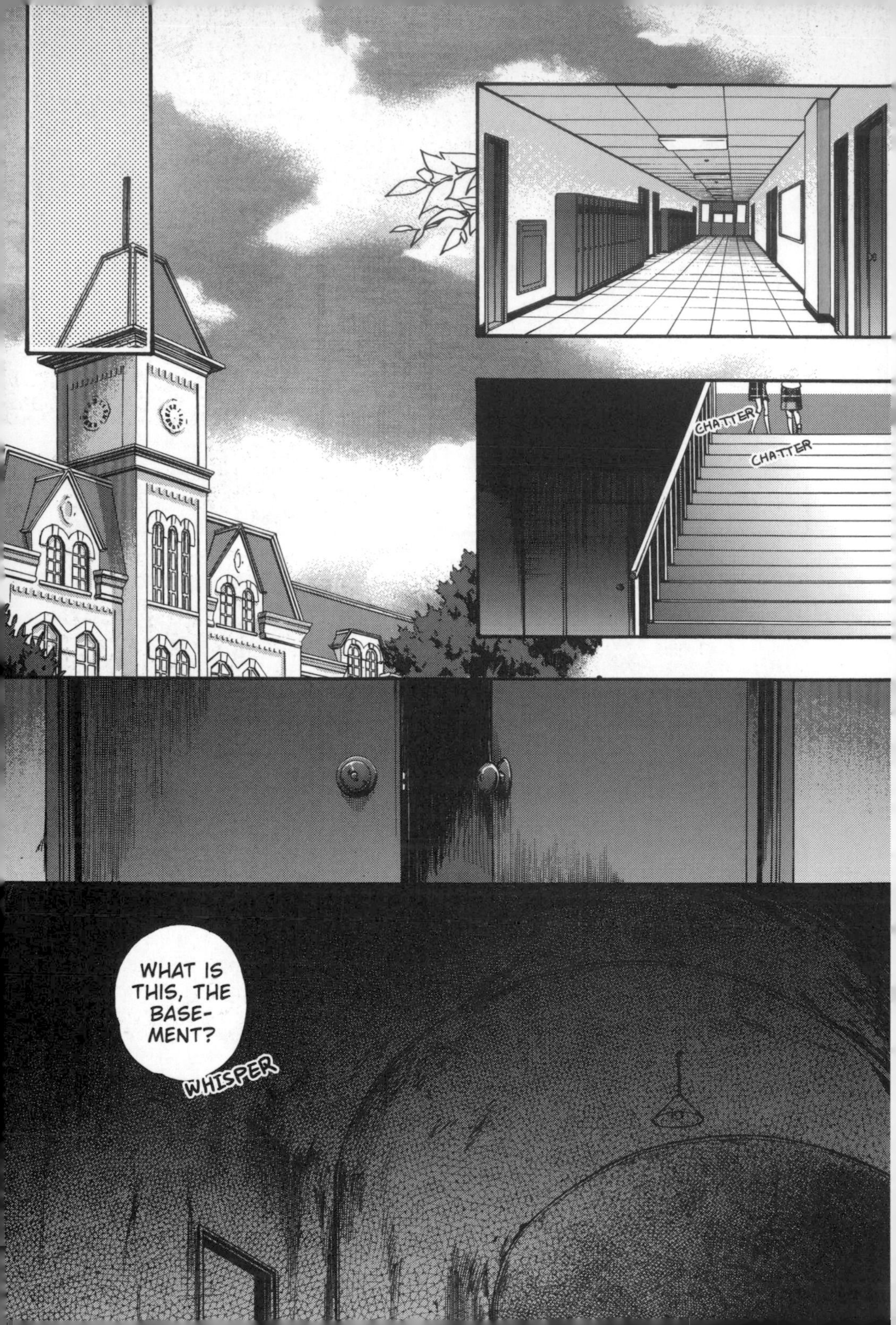
CHATTER
CHATTER
WHAT IS THIS, THE BASE-MENT?
WHISPER

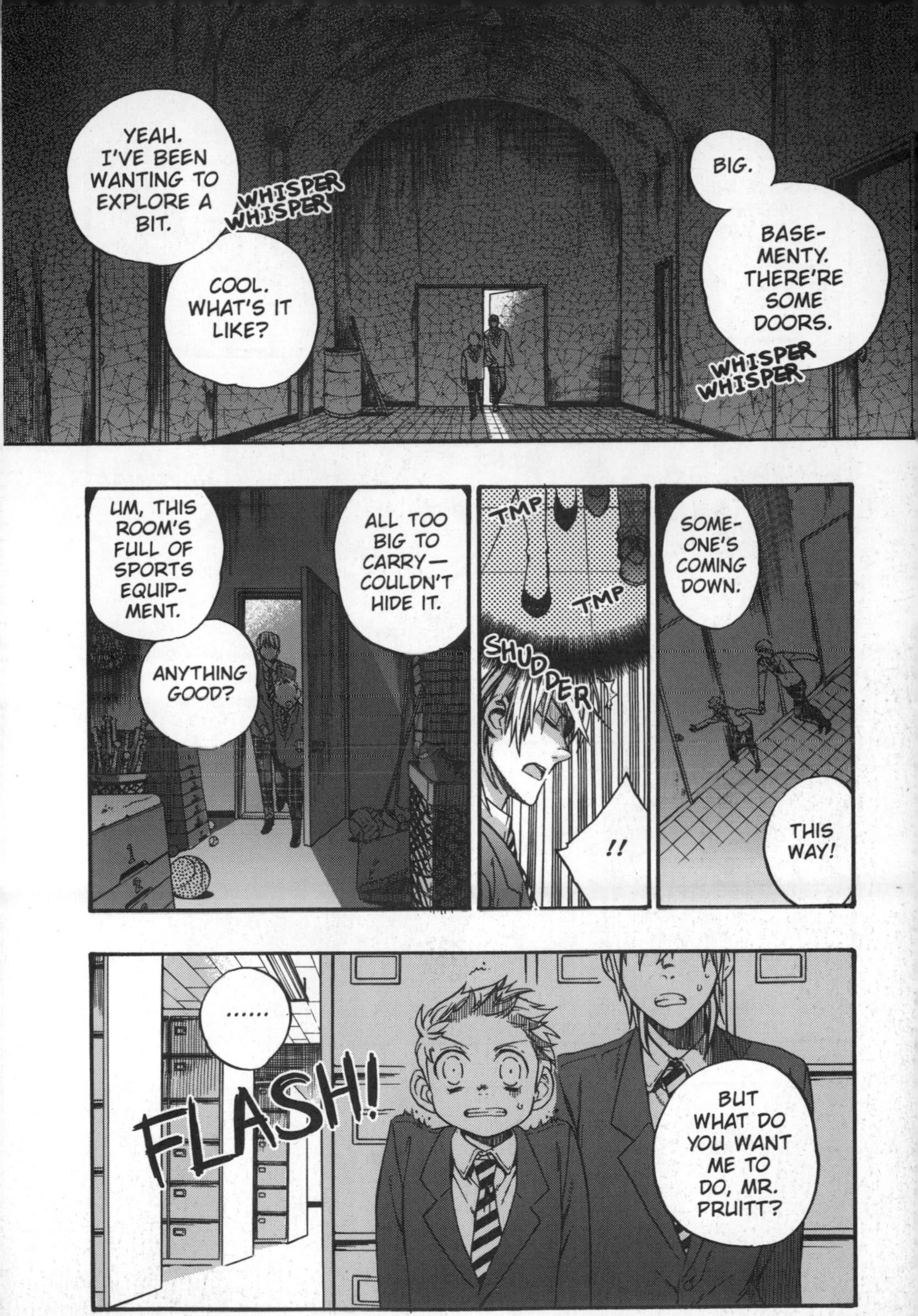
YEAH. I'VE BEEN WANTING TO EXPLORE A BIT.
WHISPER WHISPER
COOL. WHAT'S IT LIKE?
BIG.
BASE-MENTY. THERE'RE SOME DOORS.
WHISPER WHISPER
UM, THIS ROOM'S FULL OF SPORTS EQUIP-MENT.
ANYTHING GOOD?
ALL TOO BIG TO CARRY—COULDN'T HIDE IT.
TMP
TMP
SHUDDER
!!
SOME-ONE'S COMING DOWN.
THIS WAY!
......
FLASH!
BUT WHAT DO YOU WANT ME TO DO, MR. PRUITT?

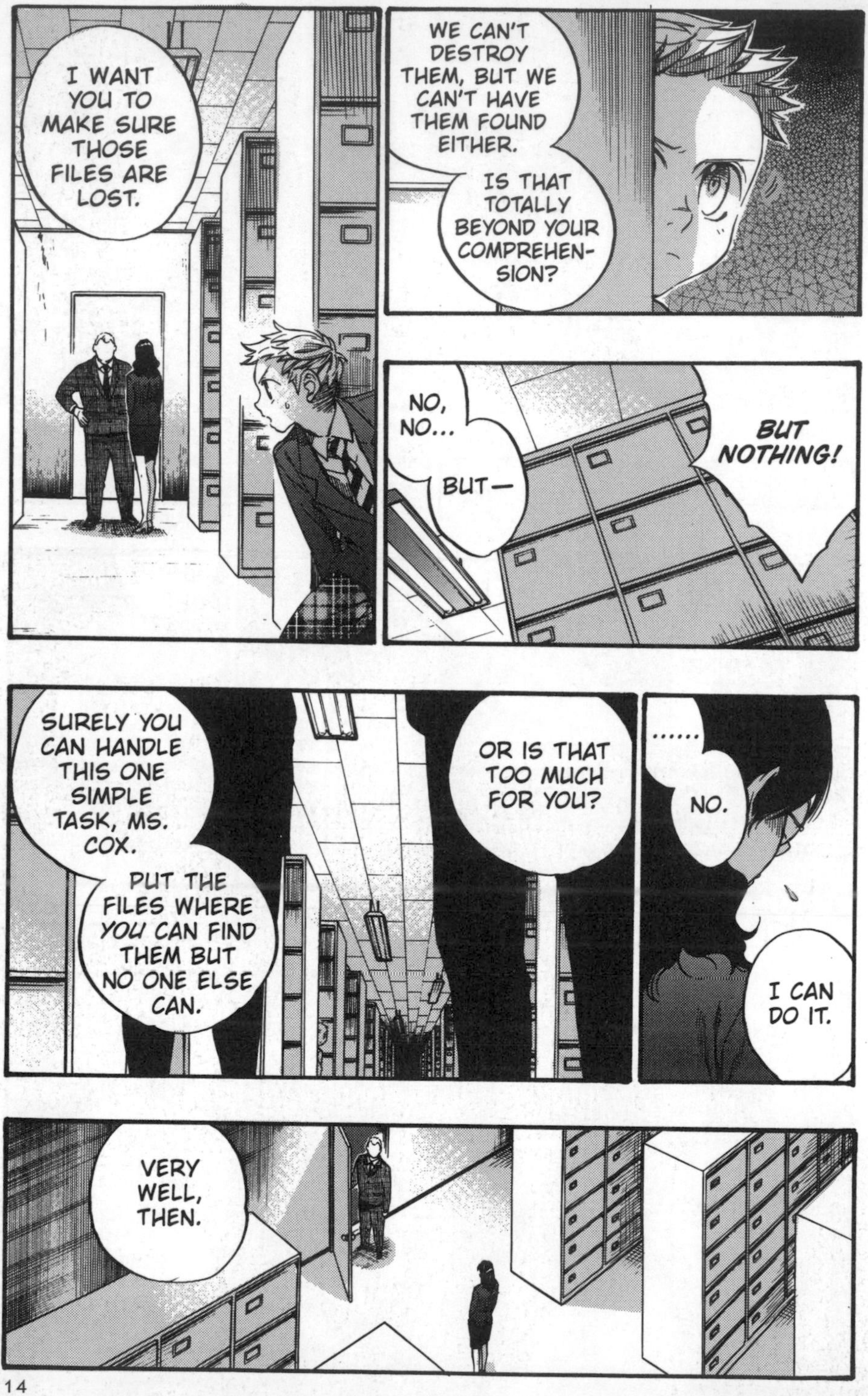

I WANT YOU TO MAKE SURE THOSE FILES ARE LOST.
WE CAN'T DESTROY THEM, BUT WE CAN'T HAVE THEM FOUND EITHER.
IS THAT TOTALLY BEYOND YOUR COMPREHENSION?
NO, NO...
BUT—
BUT NOTHING!
SURELY YOU CAN HANDLE THIS ONE SIMPLE TASK, MS. COX.
PUT THE FILES WHERE YOU CAN FIND THEM BUT NO ONE ELSE CAN.
OR IS THAT TOO MUCH FOR YOU?
......
NO.
I CAN DO IT.
VERY WELL, THEN.

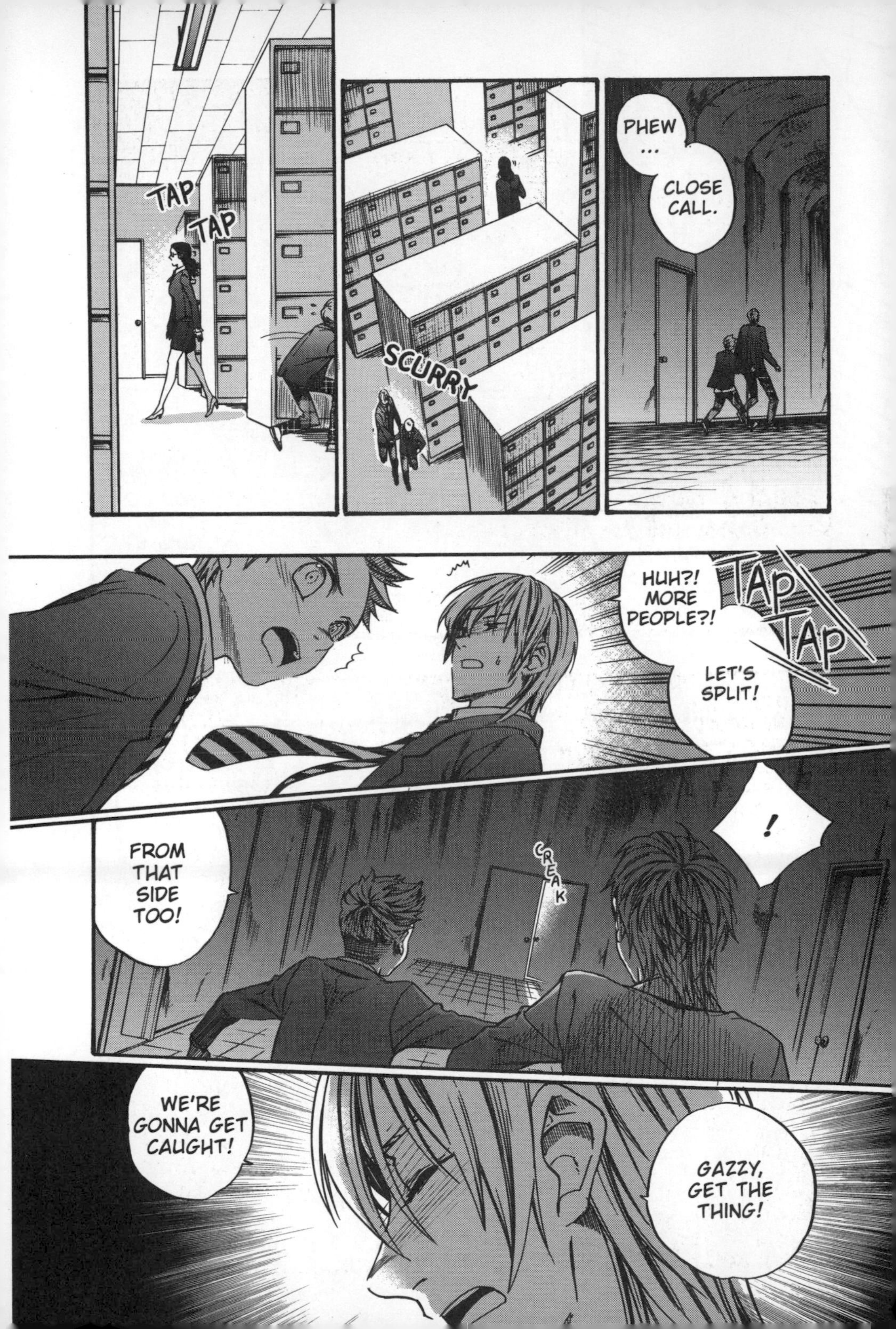

TAP
TAP
SCURRY
PHEW ...
CLOSE CALL.
HUH?! MORE PEOPLE?!
TAP
TAP
LET'S SPLIT!
FROM THAT SIDE TOO!
CREAK
!
WE'RE GONNA GET CAUGHT!
GAZZY, GET THE THING!

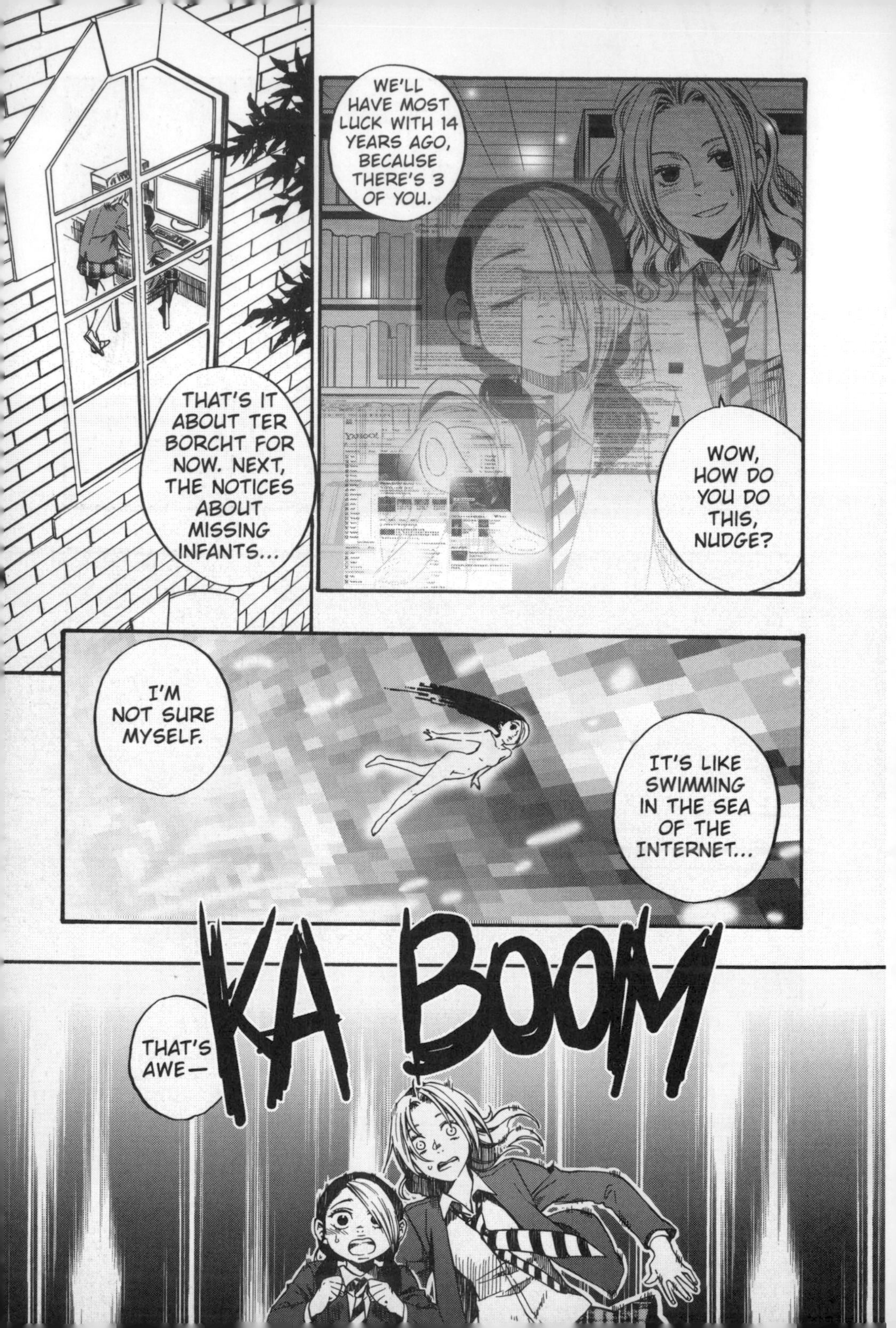
THAT'S IT ABOUT TER BORCHT FOR NOW. NEXT, THE NOTICES ABOUT MISSING INFANTS...
WE'LL HAVE MOST LUCK WITH 14 YEARS AGO, BECAUSE THERE'S 3 OF YOU.
WOW, HOW DO YOU DO THIS, NUDGE?
I'M NOT SURE MYSELF.
IT'S LIKE SWIMMING IN THE SEA OF THE INTERNET...
THAT'S AWE—
KA BOOM

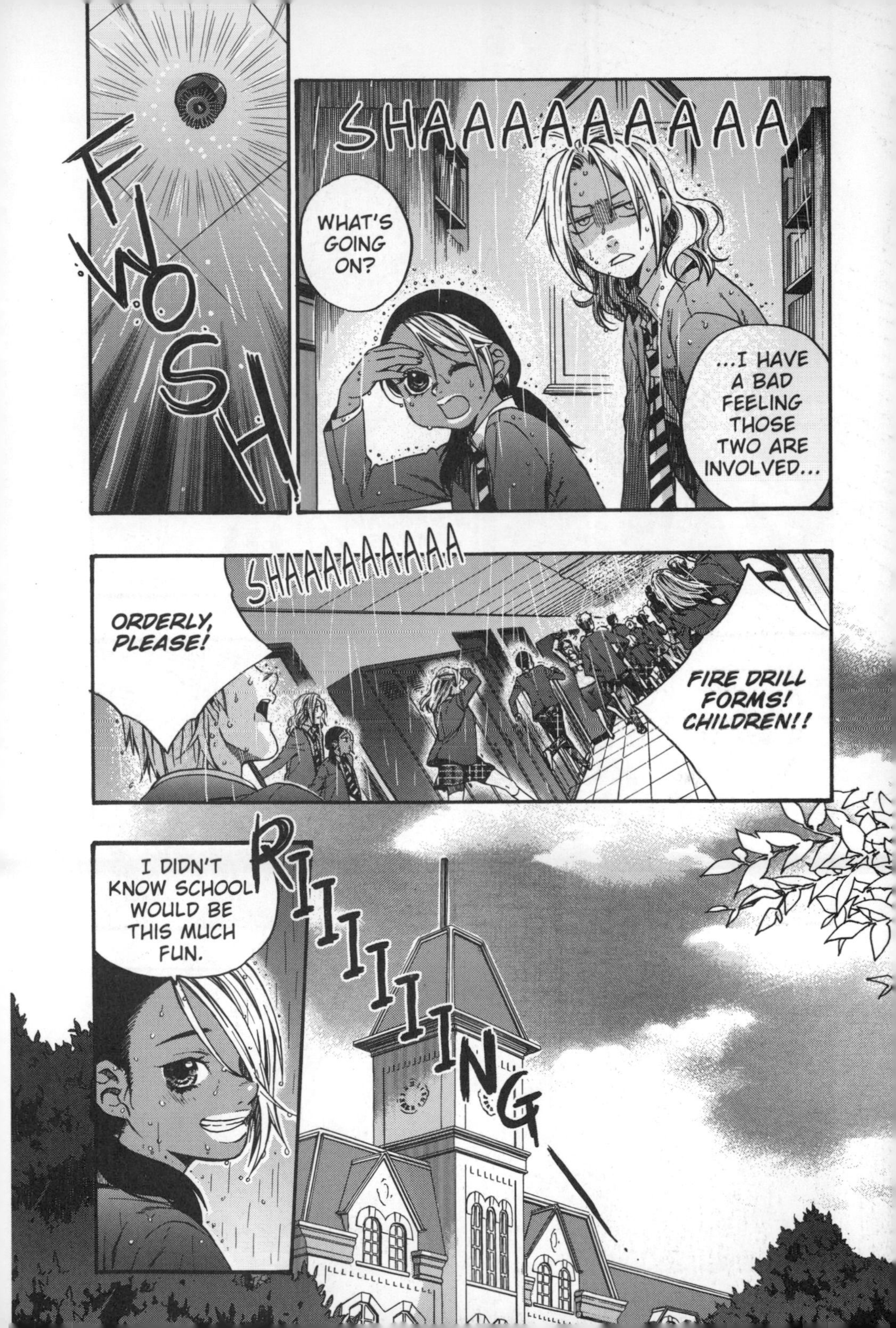
FWOSH
SHAAAAAAAAAA
WHAT'S GOING ON?
...I HAVE A BAD FEELING THOSE TWO ARE INVOLVED...
SHAAAAAAAAAA
ORDERLY, PLEASE!
FIRE DRILL FORMS! CHILDREN!!
I DIDN'T KNOW SCHOOL WOULD BE THIS MUCH FUN.
RIIIIIING

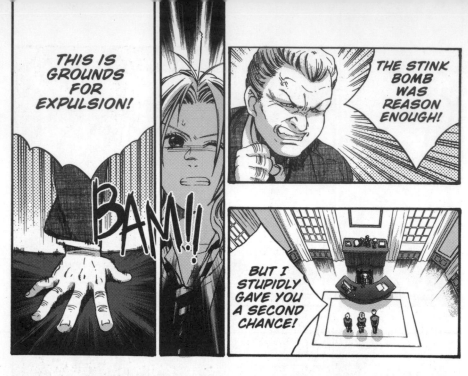

THIS IS GROUNDS FOR EXPULSION!

BAM!!

THE STINK BOMB WAS REASON ENOUGH!

BUT I STUPIDLY GAVE YOU A SECOND CHANCE!

YOU'RE NOTHING BUT A BUNCH OF STREET RATS!

VERMIN!

VERMIN? THAT'S A NEW ONE...

MY BROTHERS DIDN'T DO THE STINK BOMB!

YOU NEVER PROVED IT!

NOW YOU'RE ACCUSING US AGAIN WITH NO EVIDENCE!

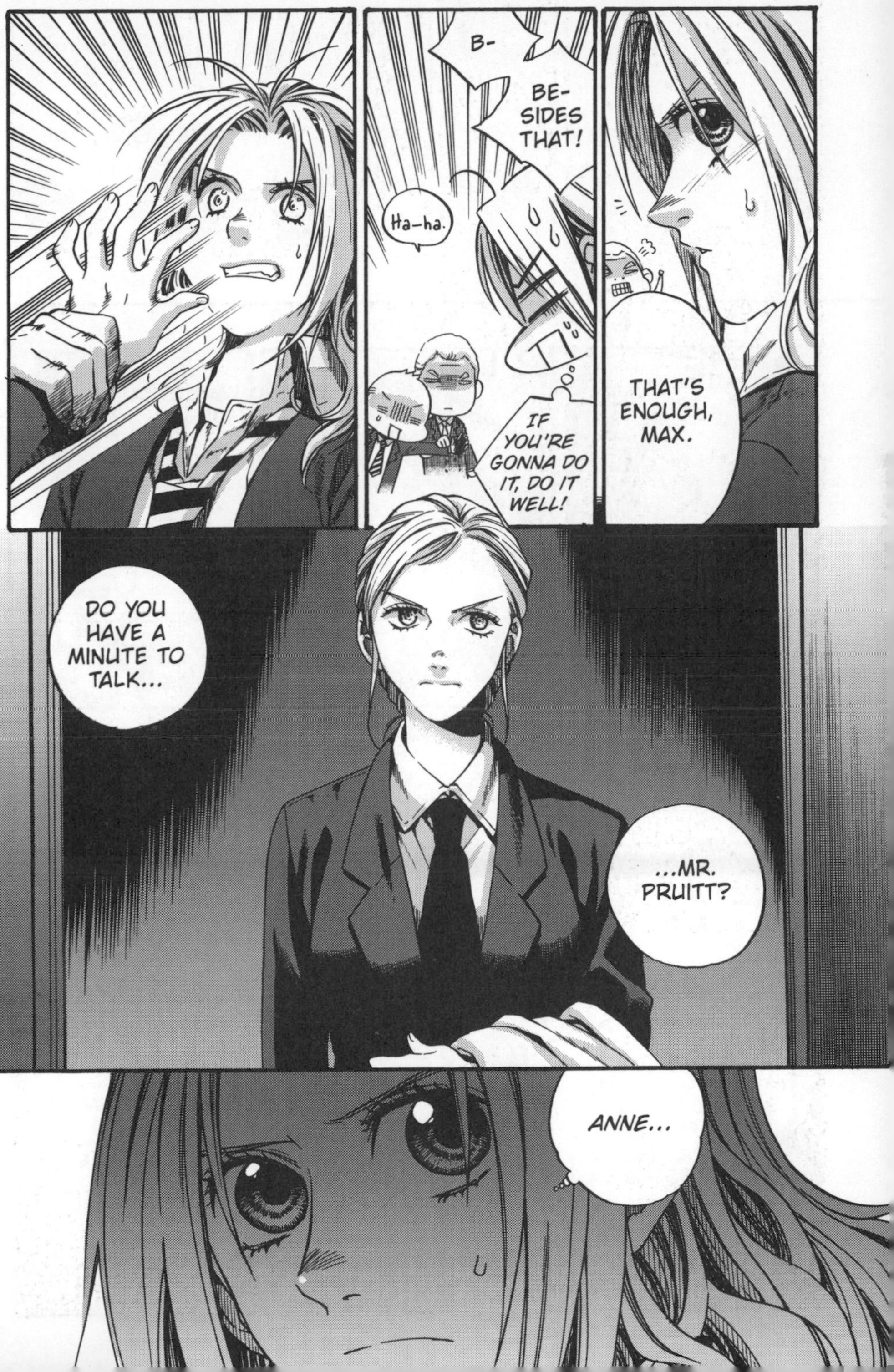
B-
BE-SIDES THAT!
Ha-ha.
IF YOU'RE GONNA DO IT, DO IT WELL!
THAT'S ENOUGH, MAX.
DO YOU HAVE A MINUTE TO TALK...
...MR. PRUITT?
ANNE...

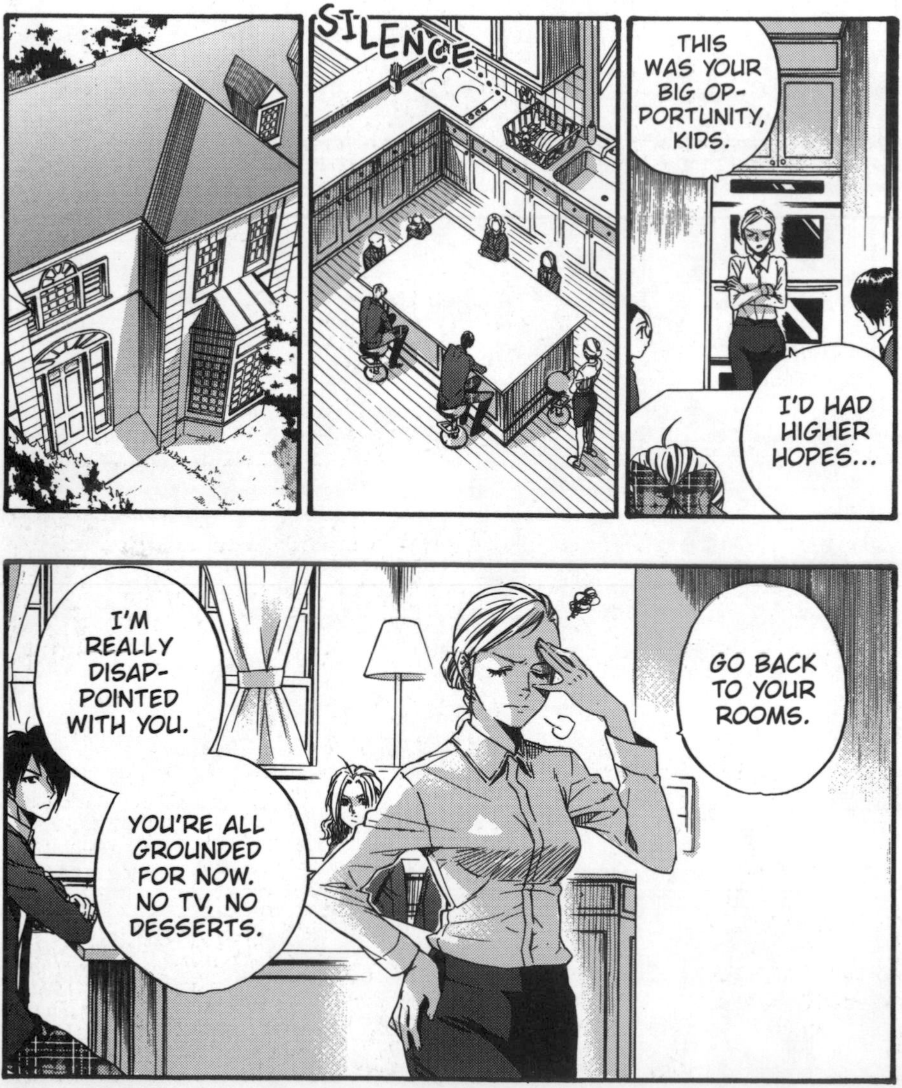
SILENCE...
THIS WAS YOUR BIG OP-PORTUNITY, KIDS.
I'D HAD HIGHER HOPES...
I'M REALLY DISAP-POINTED WITH YOU.
YOU'RE ALL GROUNDED FOR NOW. NO TV, NO DESSERTS.
GO BACK TO YOUR ROOMS.

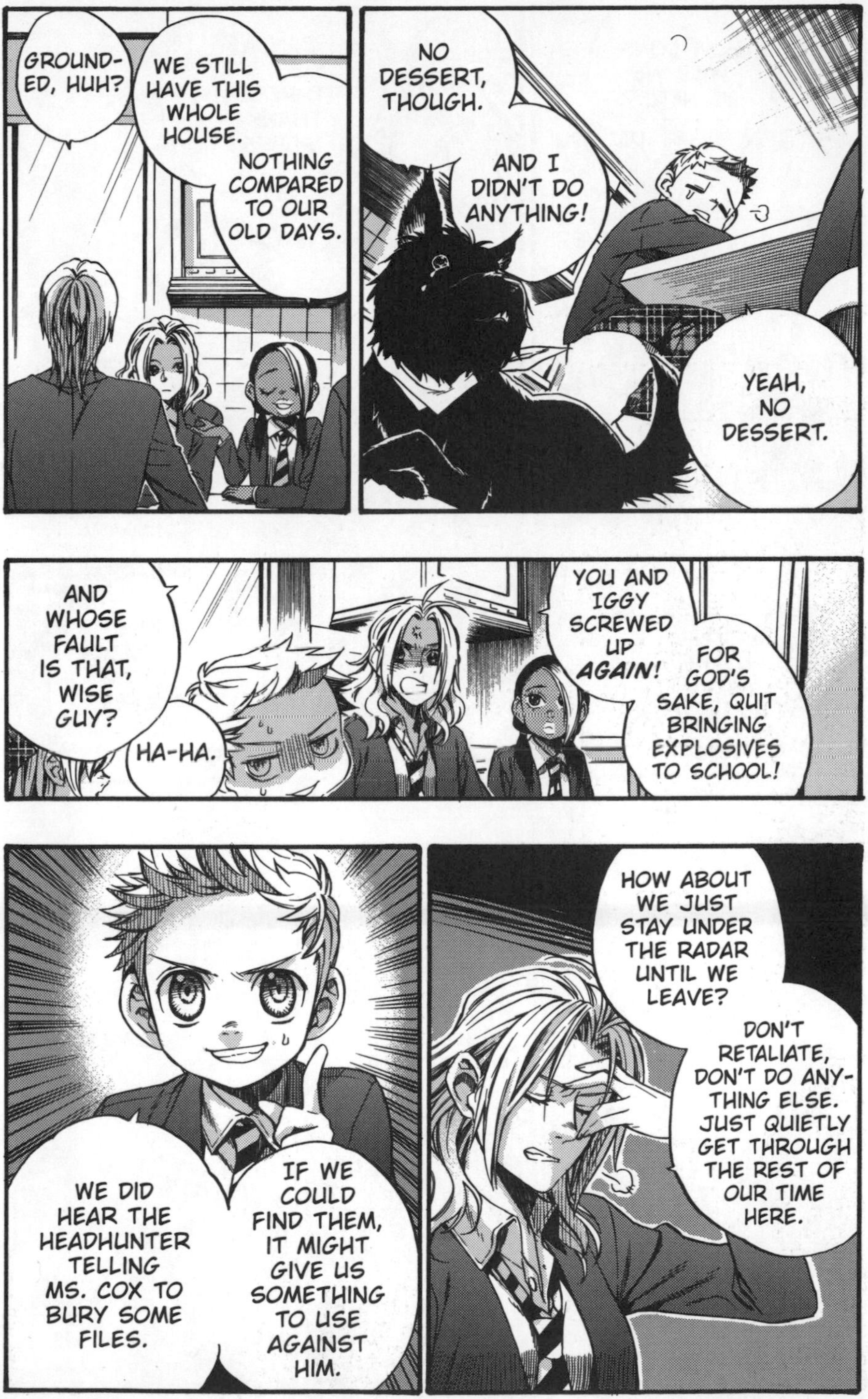
GROUND-ED, HUH?
WE STILL HAVE THIS WHOLE HOUSE.
NOTHING COMPARED TO OUR OLD DAYS.
NO DESSERT, THOUGH.
AND I DIDN'T DO ANYTHING!
YEAH, NO DESSERT.
AND WHOSE FAULT IS THAT, WISE GUY?
HA-HA.
YOU AND IGGY SCREWED UP *AGAIN*!
FOR GOD'S SAKE, QUIT BRINGING EXPLOSIVES TO SCHOOL!
WE DID HEAR THE HEADHUNTER TELLING MS. COX TO BURY SOME FILES.
IF WE COULD FIND THEM, IT MIGHT GIVE US SOMETHING TO USE AGAINST HIM.
HOW ABOUT WE JUST STAY UNDER THE RADAR UNTIL WE LEAVE?
DON'T RETALIATE, DON'T DO ANY-THING ELSE. JUST QUIETLY GET THROUGH THE REST OF OUR TIME HERE.

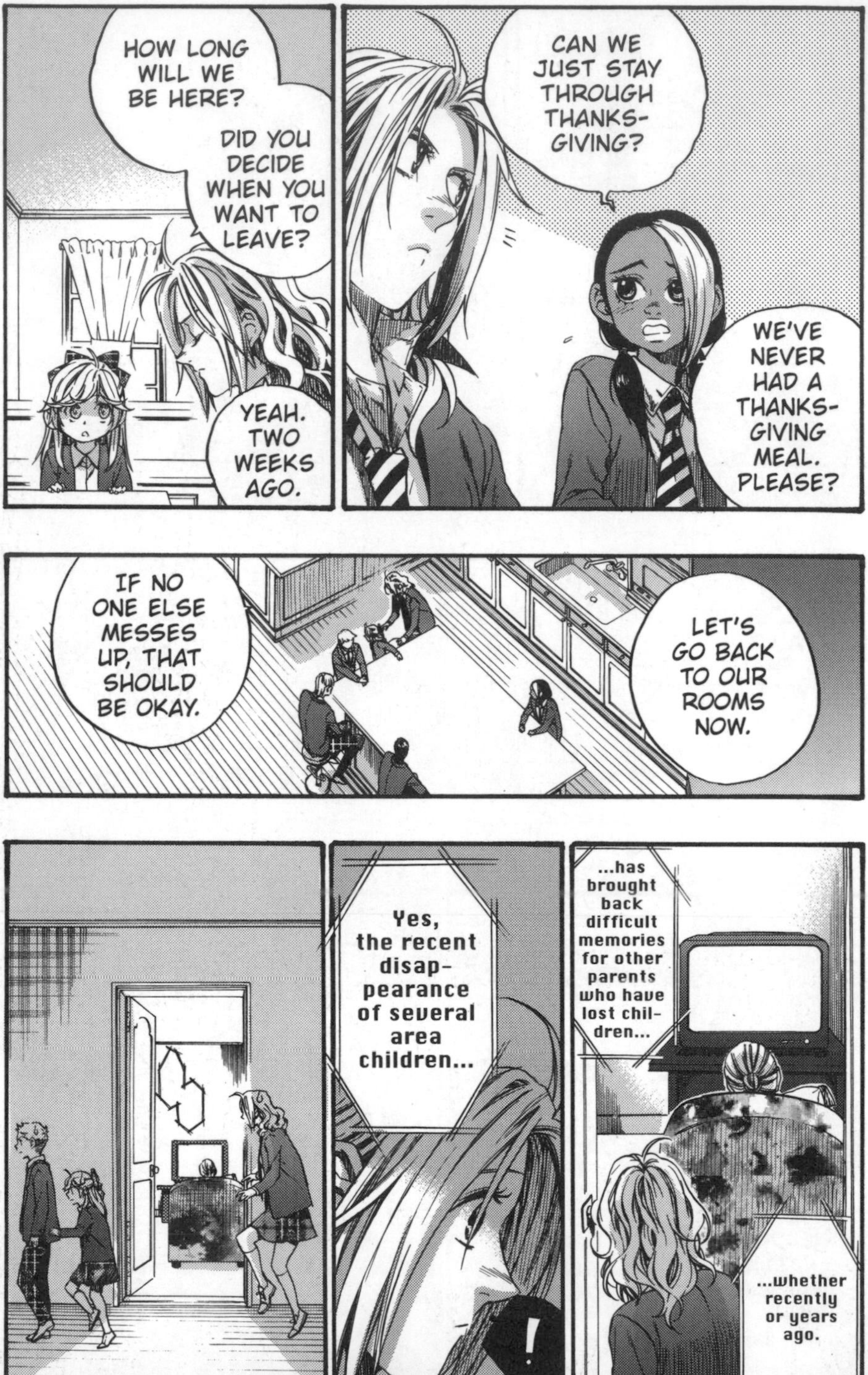
HOW LONG WILL WE BE HERE?
DID YOU DECIDE WHEN YOU WANT TO LEAVE?
YEAH. TWO WEEKS AGO.
CAN WE JUST STAY THROUGH THANKS-GIVING?
WE'VE NEVER HAD A THANKS-GIVING MEAL. PLEASE?
IF NO ONE ELSE MESSES UP, THAT SHOULD BE OKAY.
LET'S GO BACK TO OUR ROOMS NOW.
Yes, the recent disap-pearance of several area children...
...has brought back difficult memories for other parents who have lost chil-dren...
...whether recently or years ago.
!

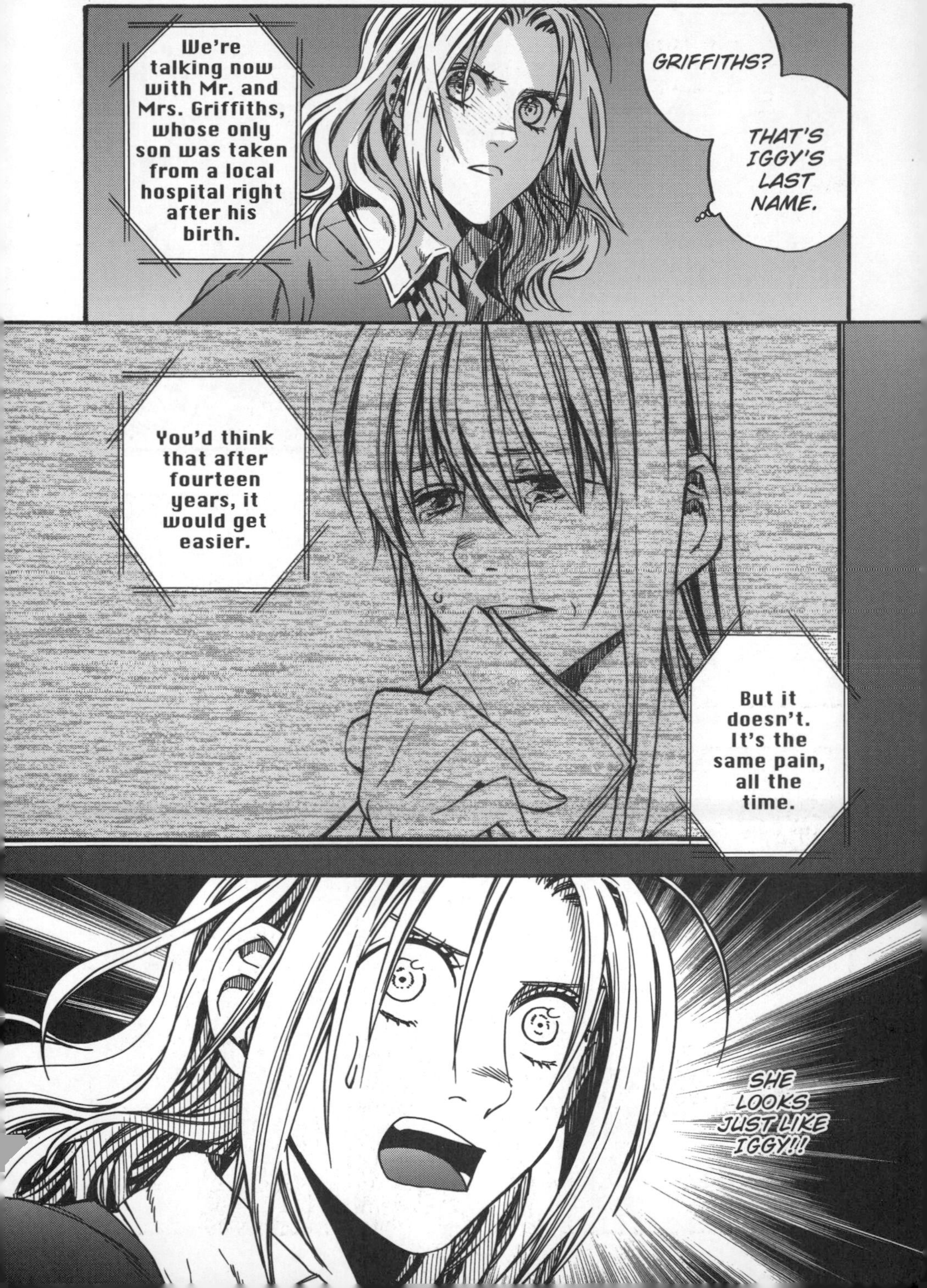
We're talking now with Mr. and Mrs. Griffiths, whose only son was taken from a local hospital right after his birth.
GRIFFITHS?
THAT'S IGGY'S LAST NAME.
You'd think that after fourteen years, it would get easier.
But it doesn't. It's the same pain, all the time.
SHE LOOKS JUST LIKE IGGY!!

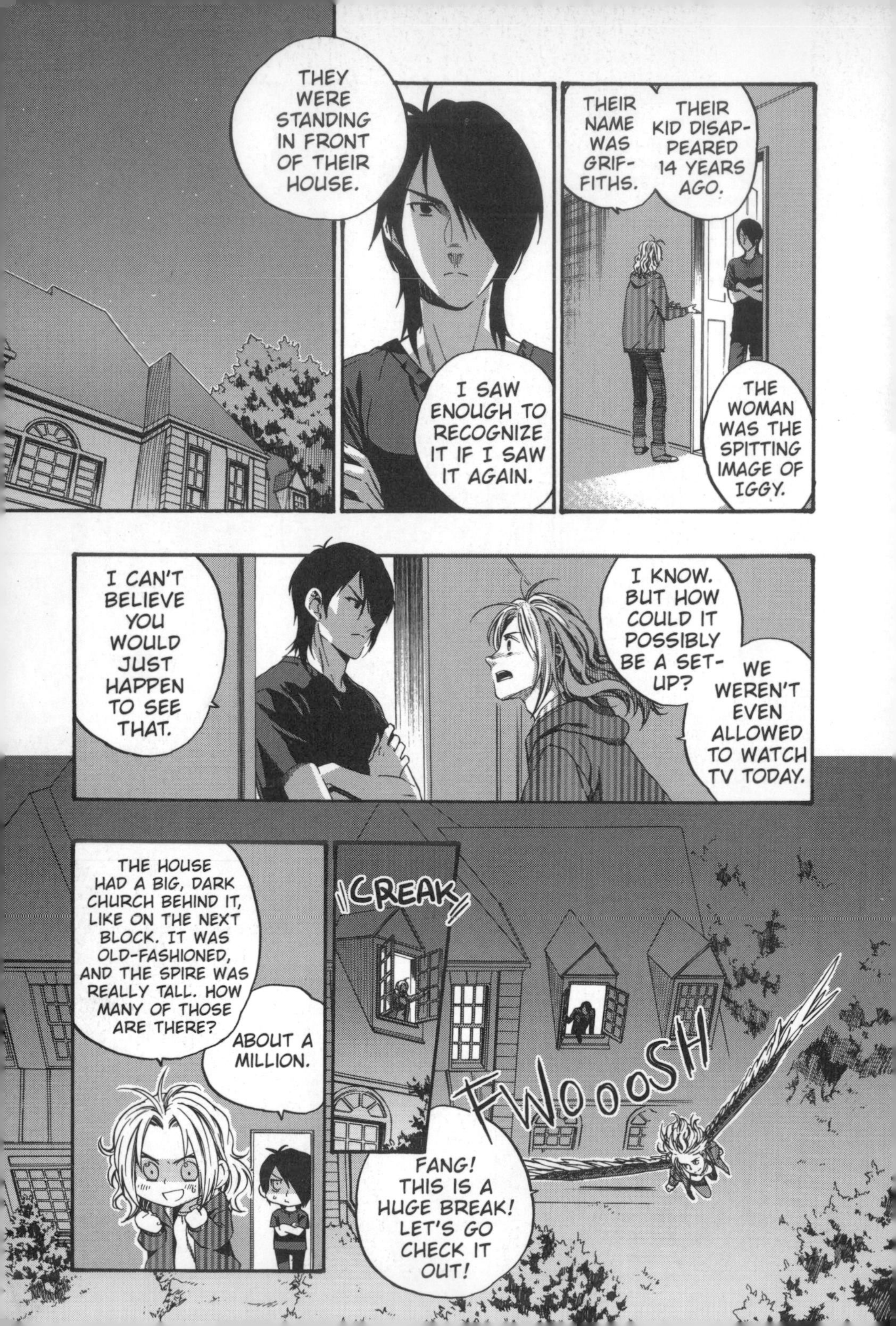
THEY WERE STANDING IN FRONT OF THEIR HOUSE.
I SAW ENOUGH TO RECOGNIZE IT IF I SAW IT AGAIN.
THEIR NAME WAS GRIF-FITHS.
THEIR KID DISAP-PEARED 14 YEARS AGO.
THE WOMAN WAS THE SPITTING IMAGE OF IGGY.
I CAN'T BELIEVE YOU WOULD JUST HAPPEN TO SEE THAT.
I KNOW. BUT HOW COULD IT POSSIBLY BE A SET-UP?
WE WEREN'T EVEN ALLOWED TO WATCH TV TODAY.
THE HOUSE HAD A BIG, DARK CHURCH BEHIND IT, LIKE ON THE NEXT BLOCK. IT WAS OLD-FASHIONED, AND THE SPIRE WAS REALLY TALL. HOW MANY OF THOSE ARE THERE?
ABOUT A MILLION.
FANG! THIS IS A HUGE BREAK! LET'S GO CHECK IT OUT!
CREAK
FWOOOSH

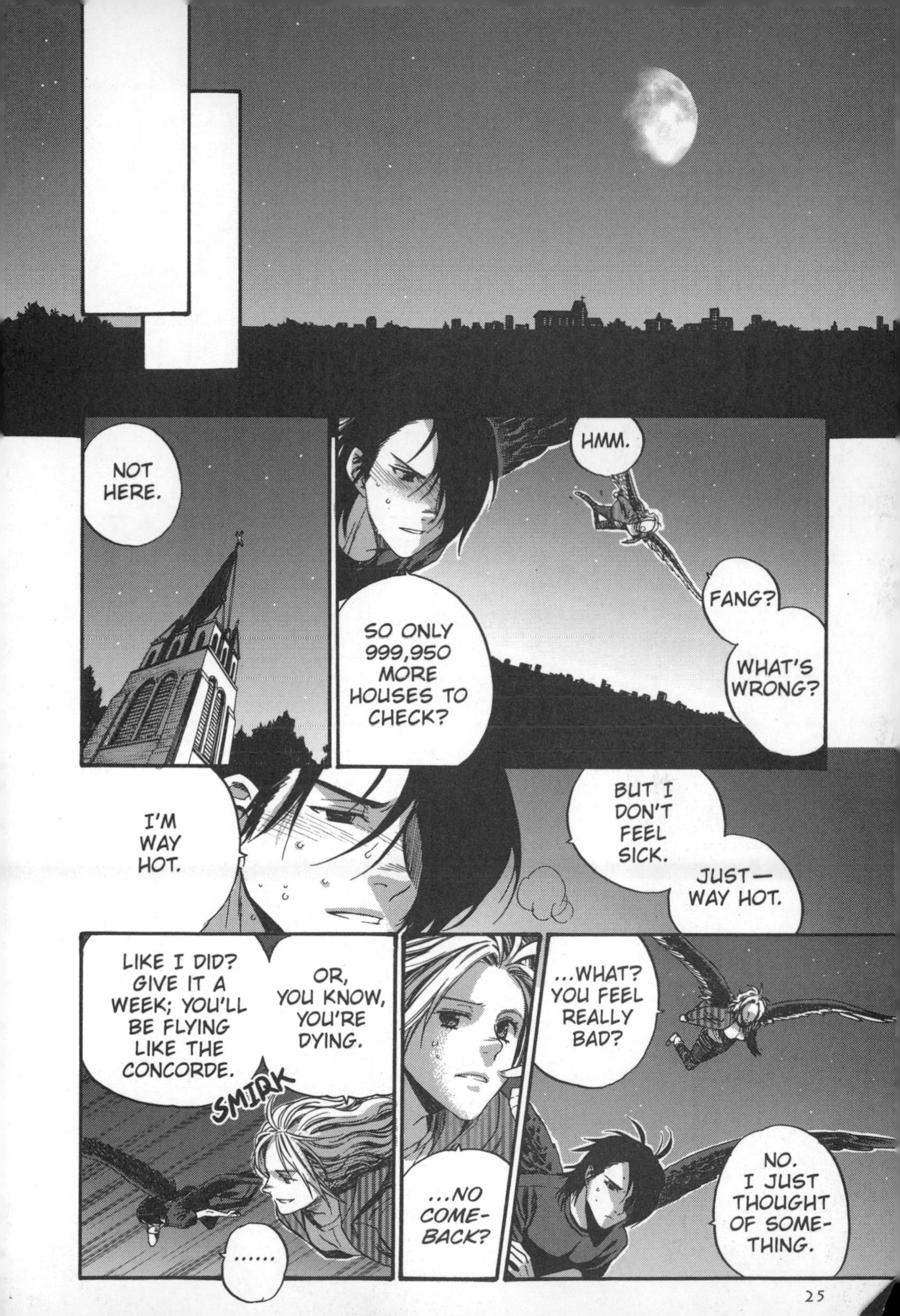

NOT HERE.
HMM.
SO ONLY 999,950 MORE HOUSES TO CHECK?
FANG?
WHAT'S WRONG?
I'M WAY HOT.
BUT I DON'T FEEL SICK.
JUST— WAY HOT.
LIKE I DID? GIVE IT A WEEK; YOU'LL BE FLYING LIKE THE CONCORDE.
OR, YOU KNOW, YOU'RE DYING.
SMIRK
......
...NO COME-BACK?
...WHAT? YOU FEEL REALLY BAD?
NO. I JUST THOUGHT OF SOME-THING.

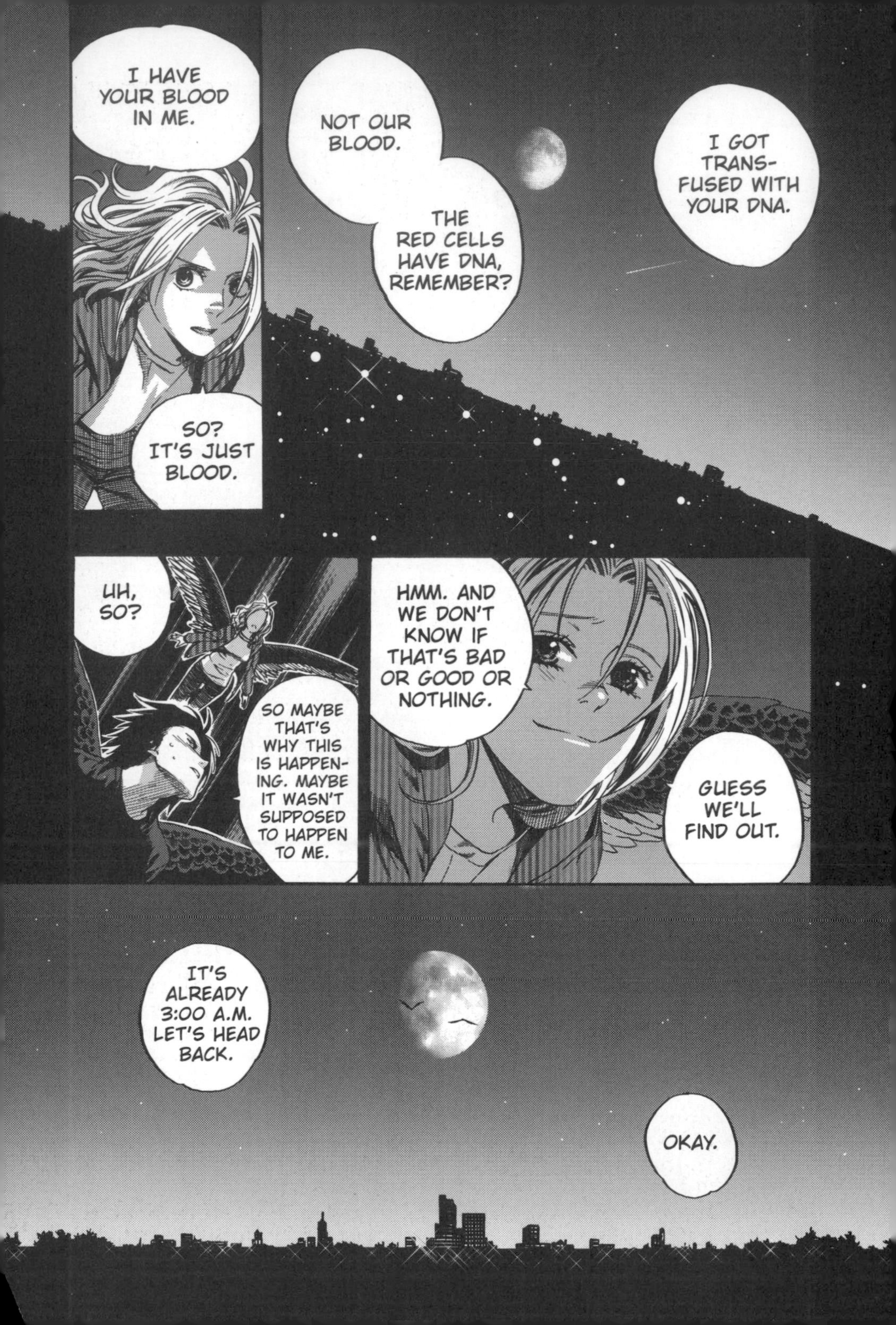
I HAVE YOUR BLOOD IN ME.
SO? IT'S JUST BLOOD.
NOT OUR BLOOD.
THE RED CELLS HAVE DNA, REMEMBER?
I GOT TRANS-FUSED WITH YOUR DNA.
UH, SO?
SO MAYBE THAT'S WHY THIS IS HAPPEN-ING. MAYBE IT WASN'T SUPPOSED TO HAPPEN TO ME.
HMM. AND WE DON'T KNOW IF THAT'S BAD OR GOOD OR NOTHING.
GUESS WE'LL FIND OUT.
IT'S ALREADY 3:00 A.M. LET'S HEAD BACK.
OKAY.

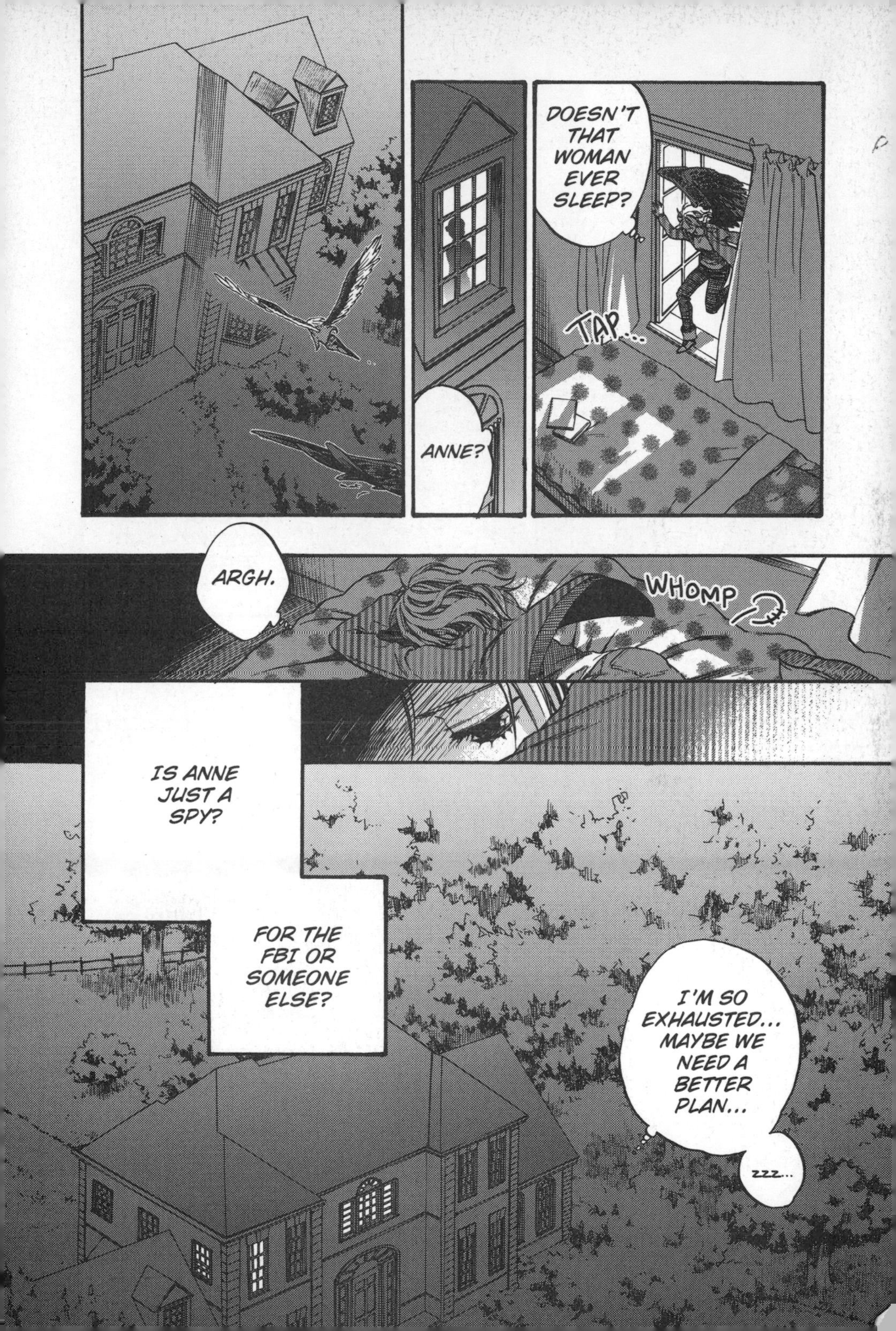
DOESN'T THAT WOMAN EVER SLEEP?
TAP...
ANNE?
ARGH.
WHOMP
IS ANNE JUST A SPY?
FOR THE FBI OR SOMEONE ELSE?
I'M SO EXHAUSTED... MAYBE WE NEED A BETTER PLAN...
zzz...

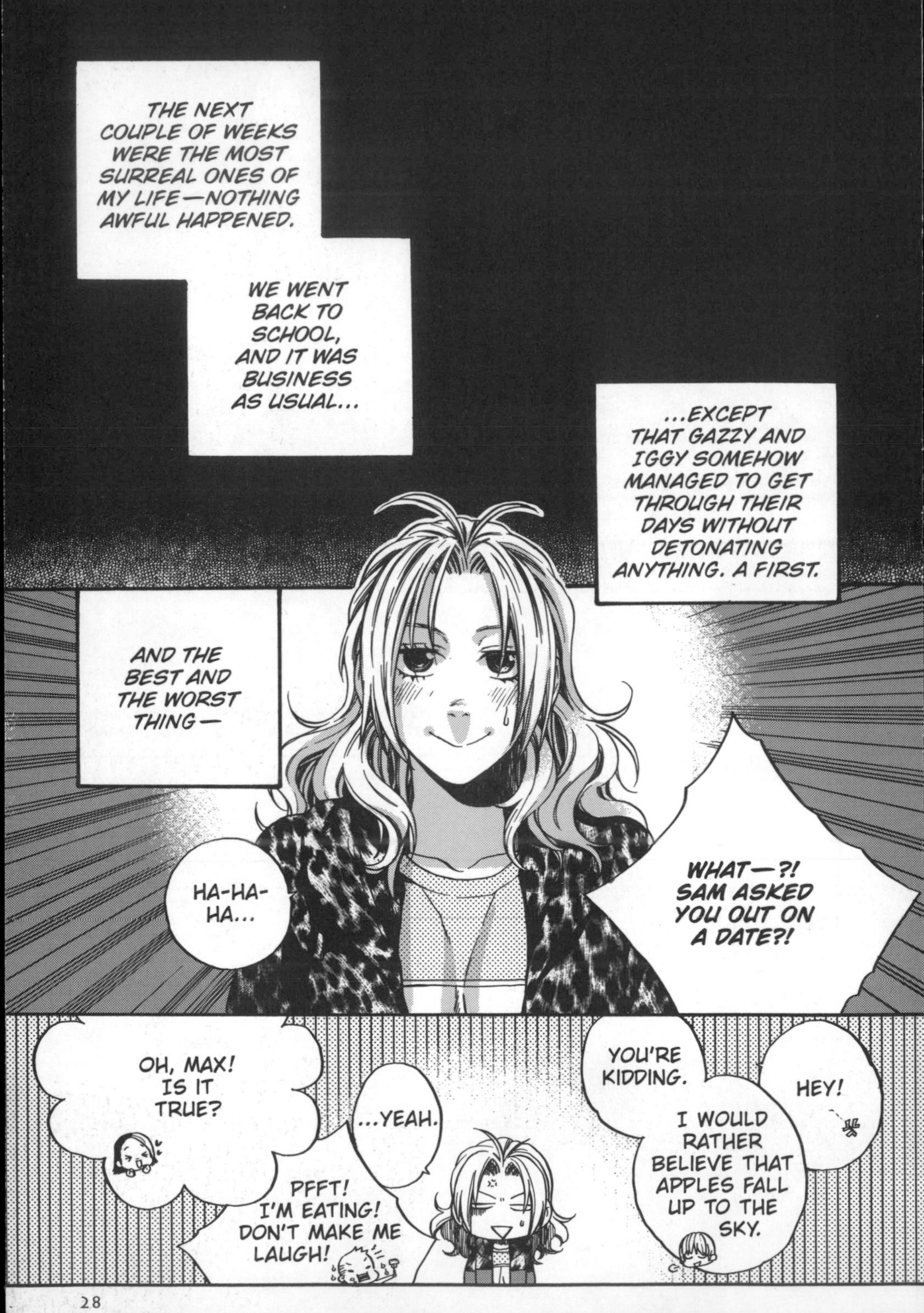
THE NEXT COUPLE OF WEEKS WERE THE MOST SURREAL ONES OF MY LIFE—NOTHING AWFUL HAPPENED.
WE WENT BACK TO SCHOOL, AND IT WAS BUSINESS AS USUAL...
...EXCEPT THAT GAZZY AND IGGY SOMEHOW MANAGED TO GET THROUGH THEIR DAYS WITHOUT DETONATING ANYTHING. A FIRST.
AND THE BEST AND THE WORST THING—
WHAT—?! SAM ASKED YOU OUT ON A DATE?!
HA-HA-HA...
OH, MAX! IS IT TRUE?
...YEAH.
PFFT! I'M EATING! DON'T MAKE ME LAUGH!
YOU'RE KIDDING.
HEY!
I WOULD RATHER BELIEVE THAT APPLES FALL UP TO THE SKY.

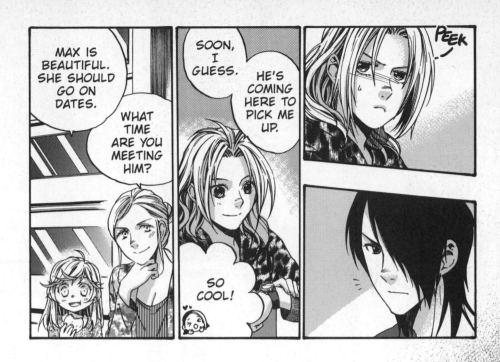

MAX IS BEAUTIFUL. SHE SHOULD GO ON DATES.

WHAT TIME ARE YOU MEETING HIM?

SOON, I GUESS.

HE'S COMING HERE TO PICK ME UP.

SO COOL!

PEEK

DING DING

THAT SHOULD BE HIM.

......

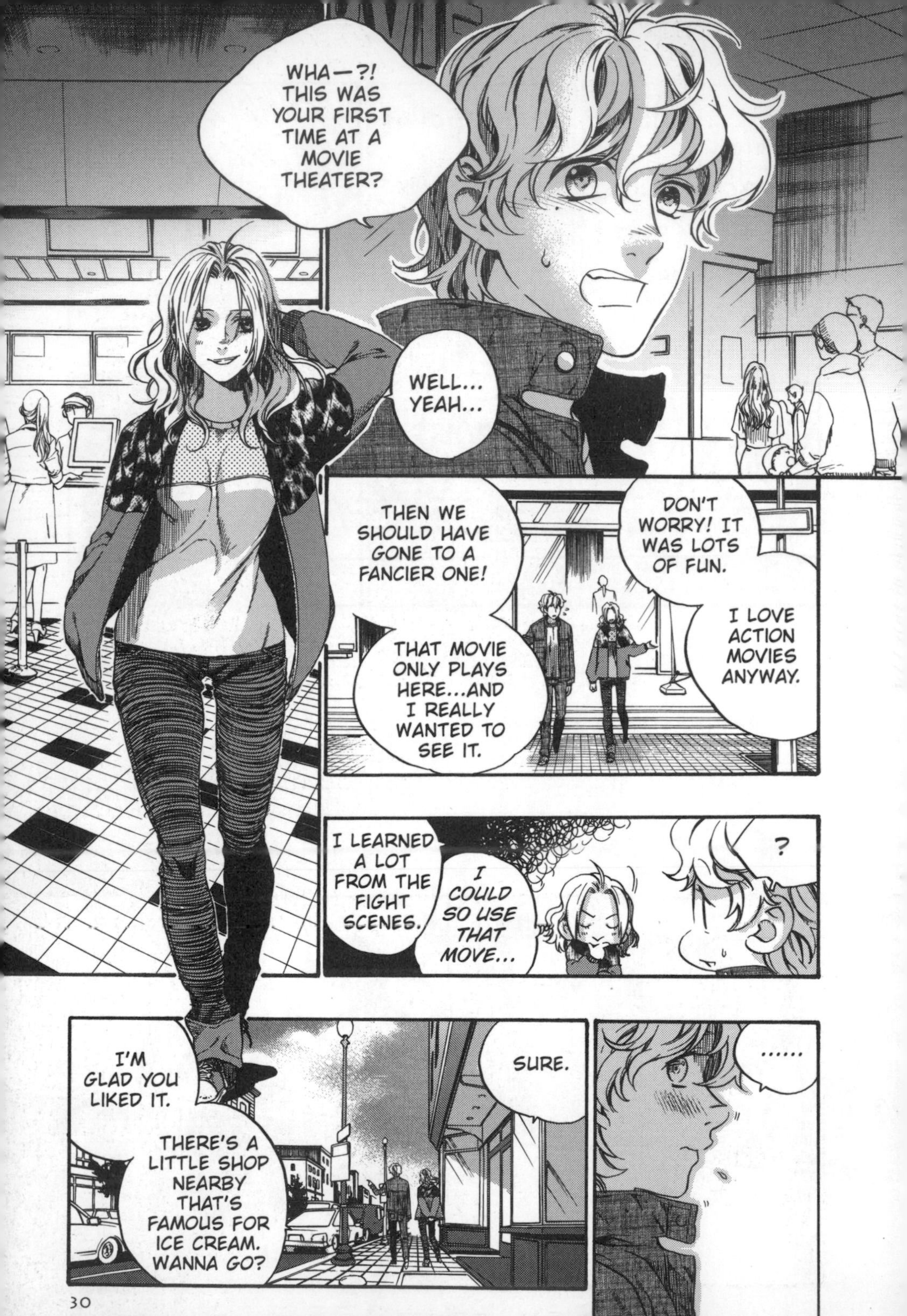
WHA—?! THIS WAS YOUR FIRST TIME AT A MOVIE THEATER?
WELL... YEAH...
THEN WE SHOULD HAVE GONE TO A FANCIER ONE!
THAT MOVIE ONLY PLAYS HERE...AND I REALLY WANTED TO SEE IT.
DON'T WORRY! IT WAS LOTS OF FUN.
I LOVE ACTION MOVIES ANYWAY.
I LEARNED A LOT FROM THE FIGHT SCENES.
I COULD SO USE THAT MOVE...
?
I'M GLAD YOU LIKED IT.
THERE'S A LITTLE SHOP NEARBY THAT'S FAMOUS FOR ICE CREAM. WANNA GO?
SURE.
......

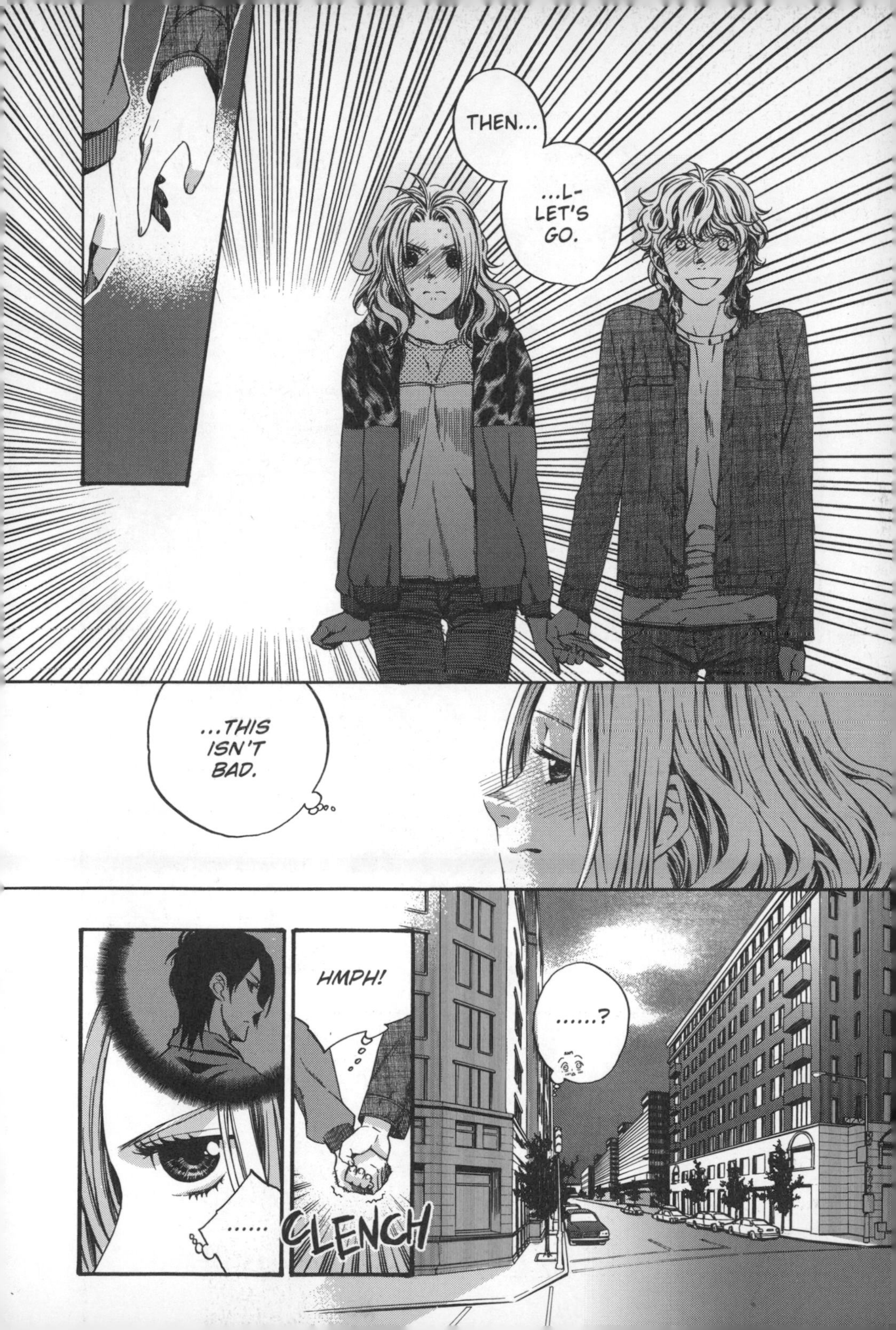
THEN...
...L-LET'S GO.
...THIS ISN'T BAD.
HMPH!
......
CLENCH
......?

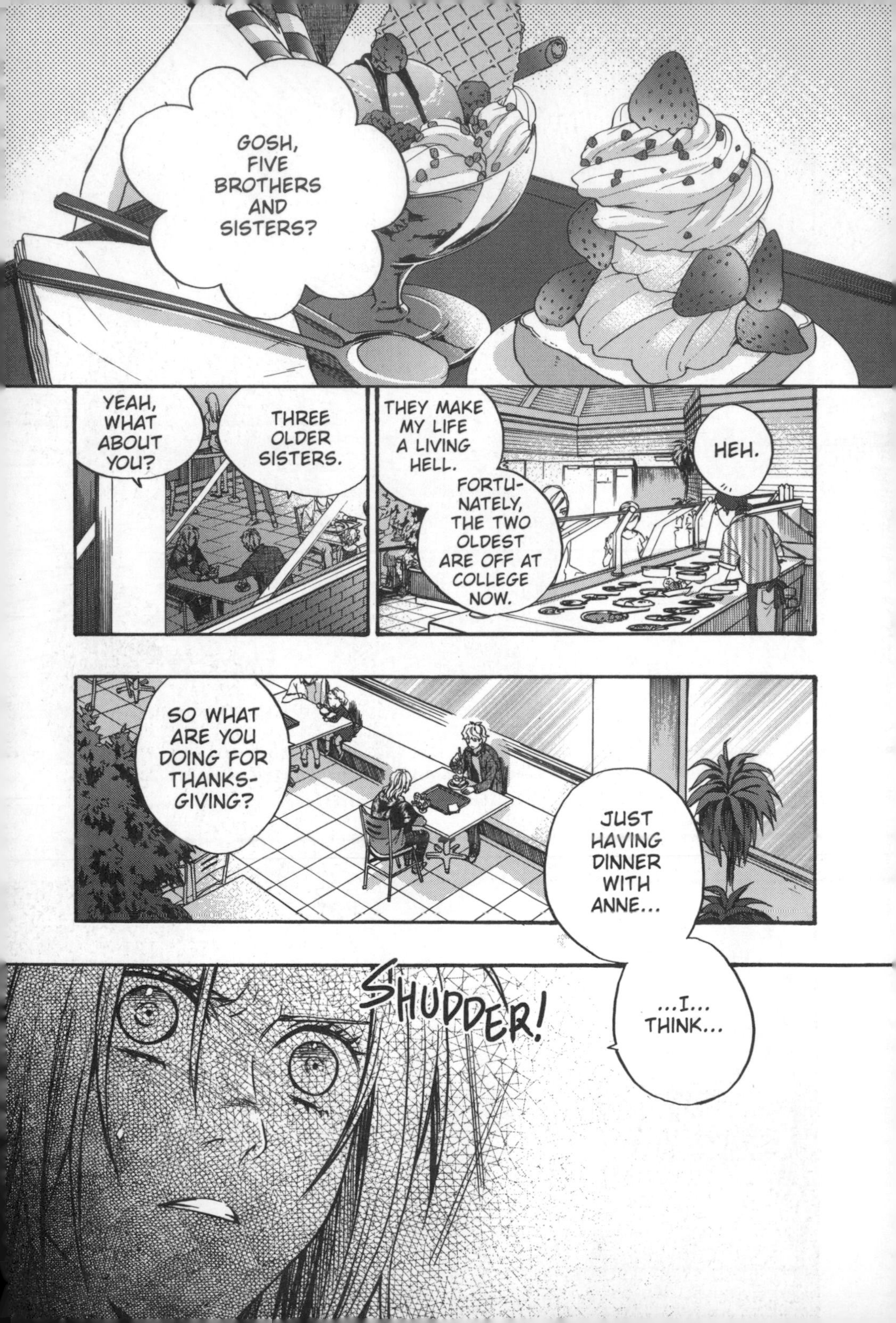
GOSH, FIVE BROTHERS AND SISTERS?
YEAH, WHAT ABOUT YOU?
THREE OLDER SISTERS.
THEY MAKE MY LIFE A LIVING HELL.
FORTU-NATELY, THE TWO OLDEST ARE OFF AT COLLEGE NOW.
HEH.
SO WHAT ARE YOU DOING FOR THANKS-GIVING?
JUST HAVING DINNER WITH ANNE...
SHUDDER!
...I... THINK...

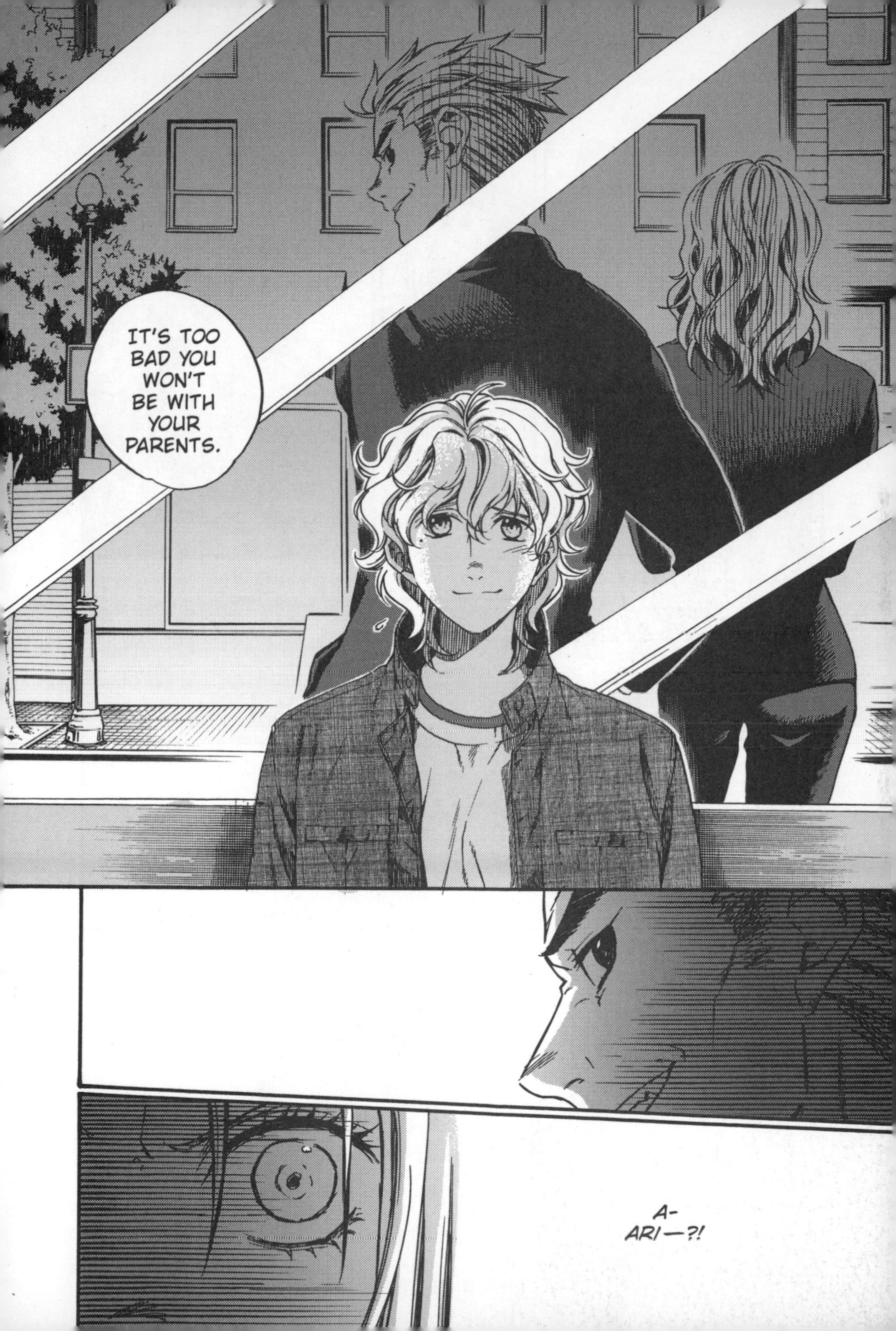
IT'S TOO BAD YOU WON'T BE WITH YOUR PARENTS.
A- ARI—?!

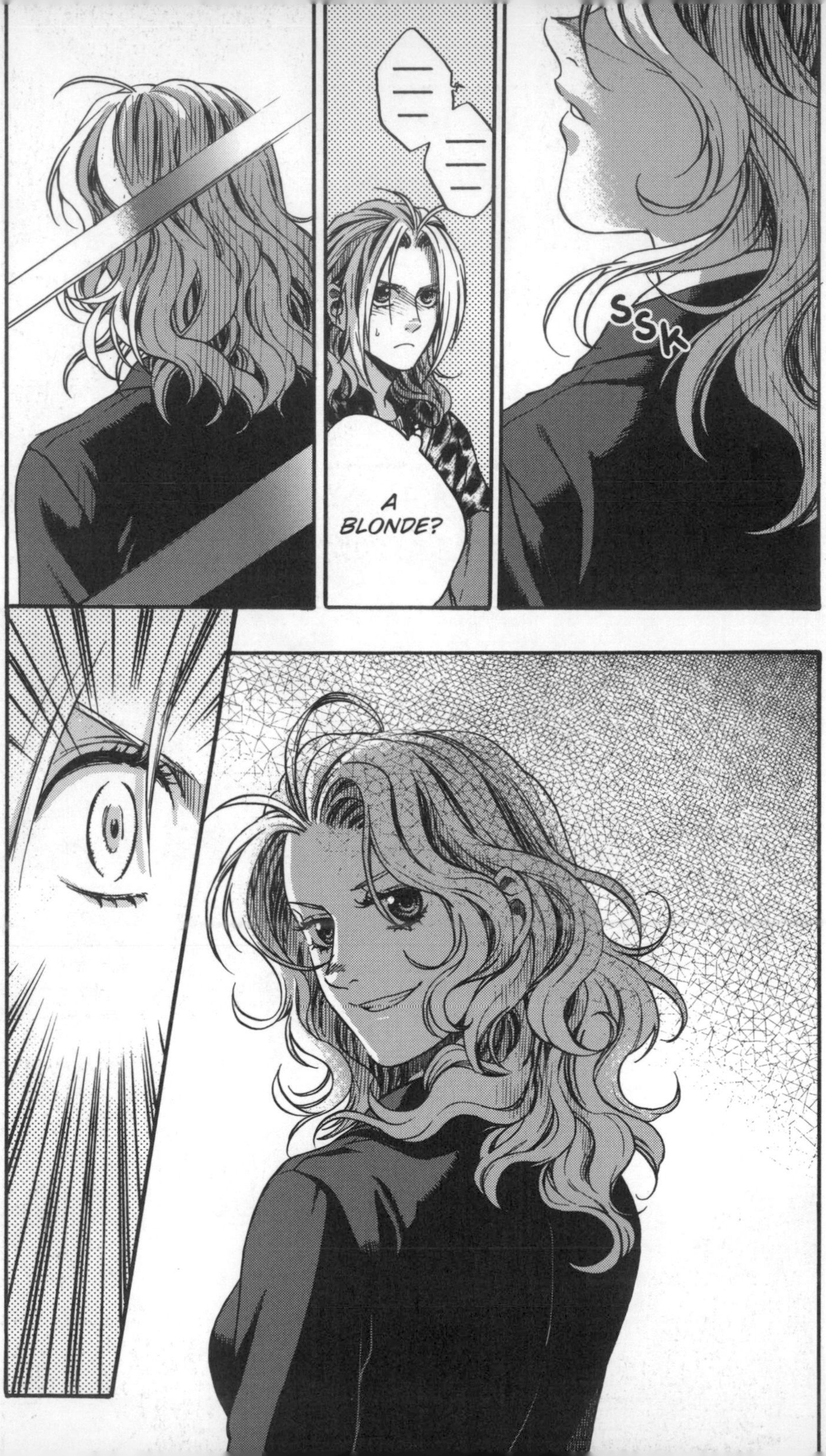

A BLONDE?
SSK

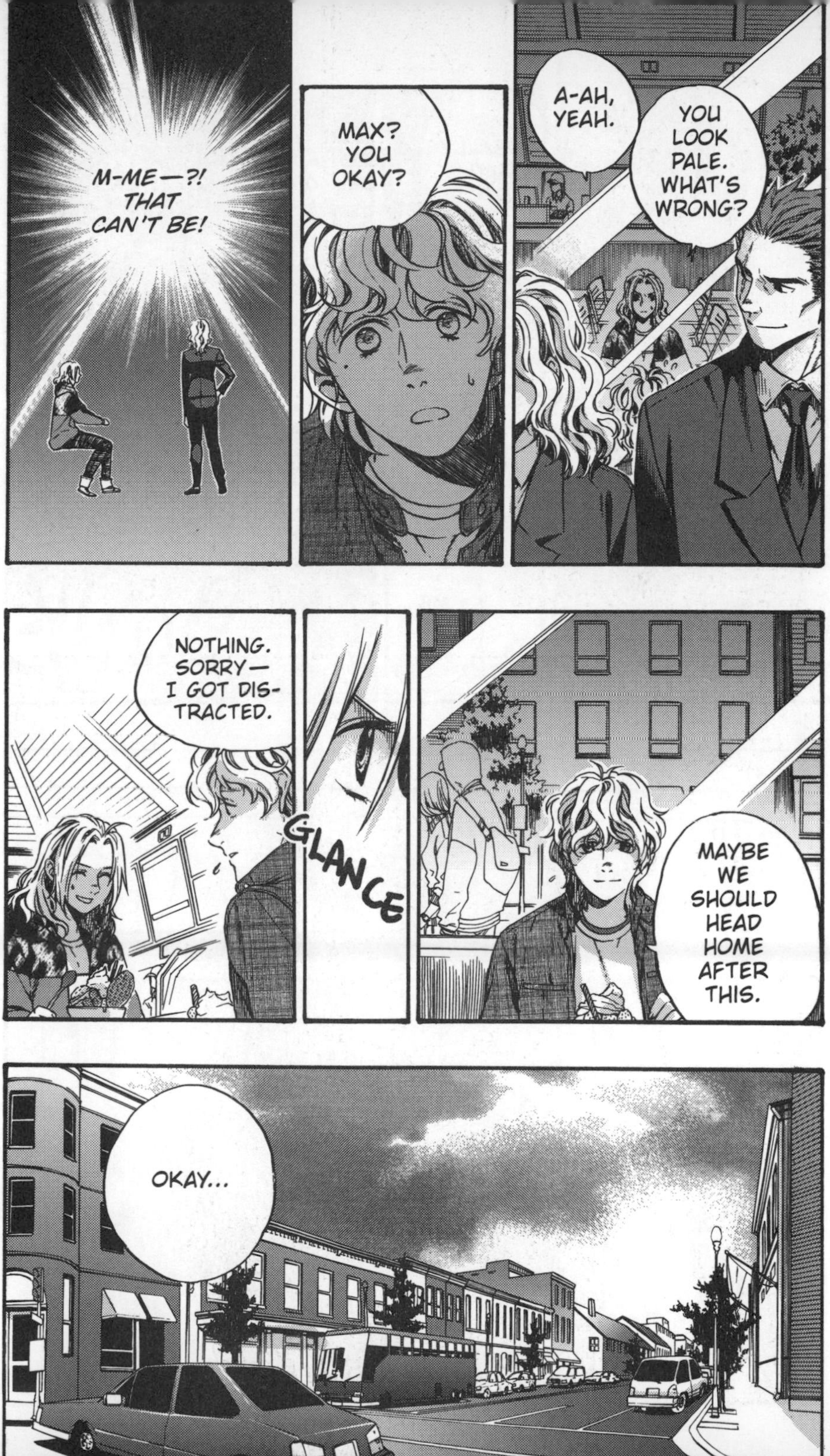
M-ME—?! THAT CAN'T BE!
MAX? YOU OKAY?
A-AH, YEAH.
YOU LOOK PALE. WHAT'S WRONG?
NOTHING. SORRY— I GOT DIS-TRACTED.
GLANCE
MAYBE WE SHOULD HEAD HOME AFTER THIS.
OKAY...

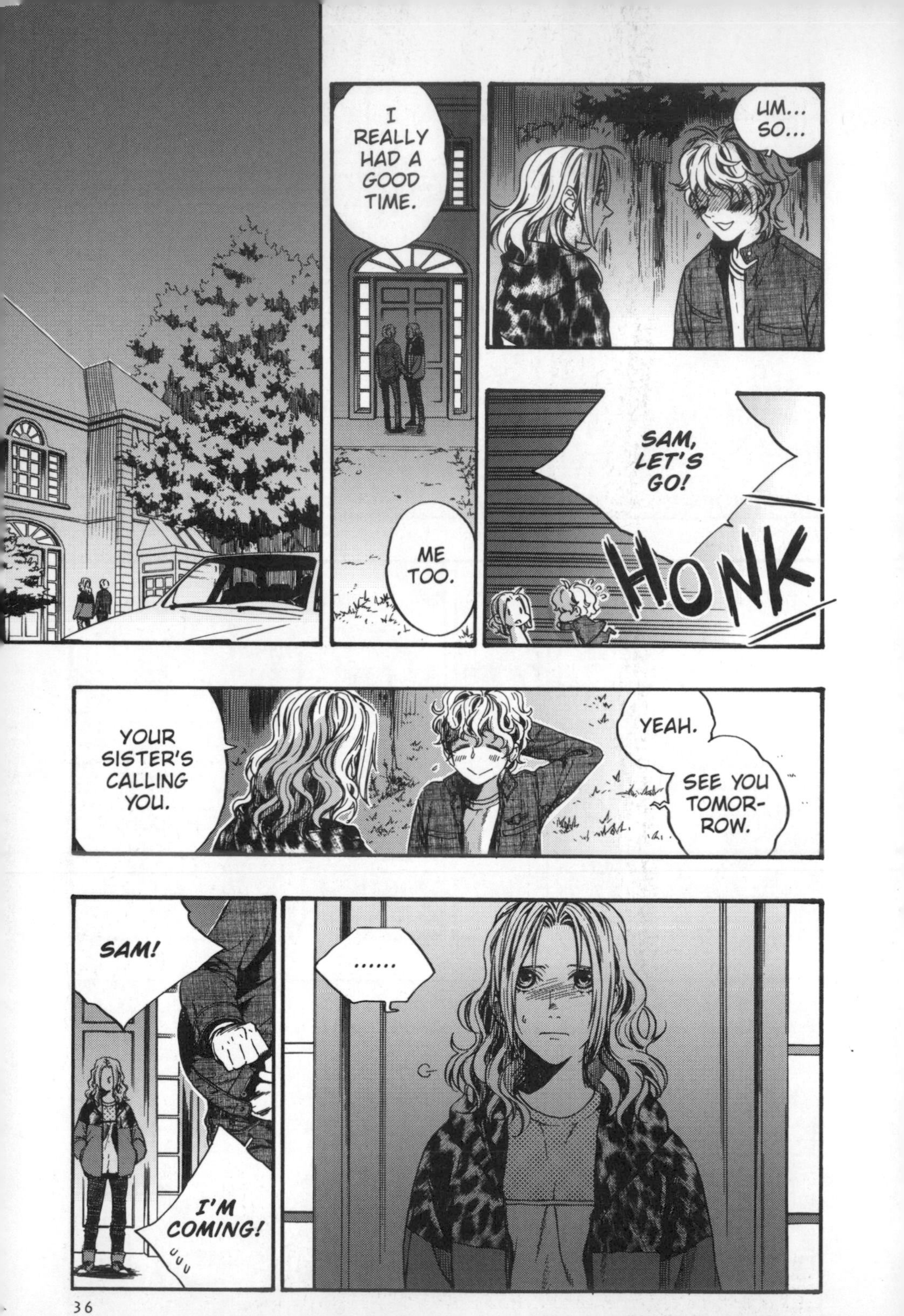
I REALLY HAD A GOOD TIME.
UM... SO...
ME TOO.
SAM, LET'S GO!
HONK
YOUR SISTER'S CALLING YOU.
YEAH.
SEE YOU TOMORROW.
SAM!
I'M COMING!
......

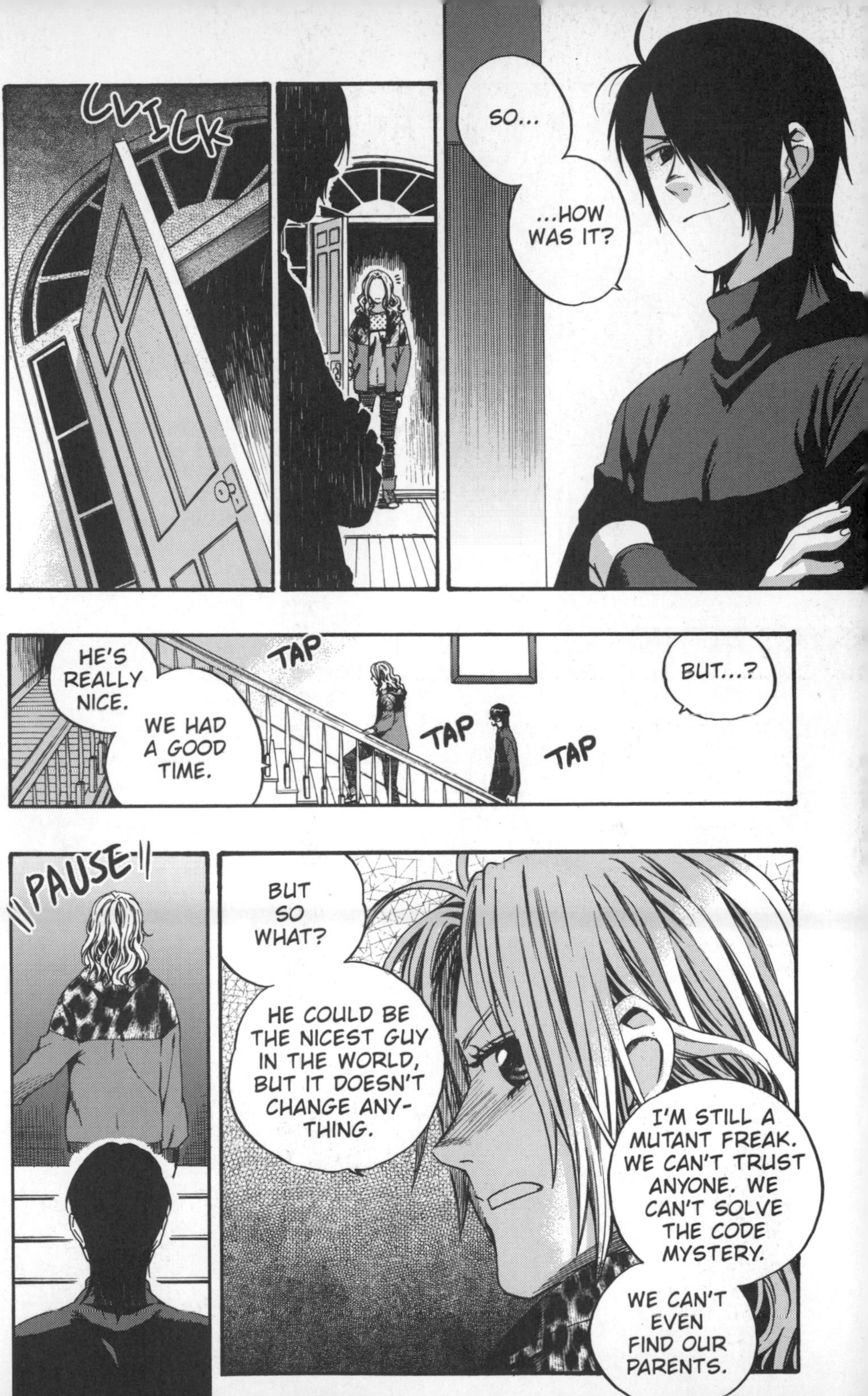
CLICK
SO...
...HOW WAS IT?
HE'S REALLY NICE.
WE HAD A GOOD TIME.
TAP
TAP
TAP
BUT...?
PAUSE
BUT SO WHAT?
HE COULD BE THE NICEST GUY IN THE WORLD, BUT IT DOESN'T CHANGE ANY-THING.
I'M STILL A MUTANT FREAK. WE CAN'T TRUST ANYONE. WE CAN'T SOLVE THE CODE MYSTERY.
WE CAN'T EVEN FIND OUR PARENTS.

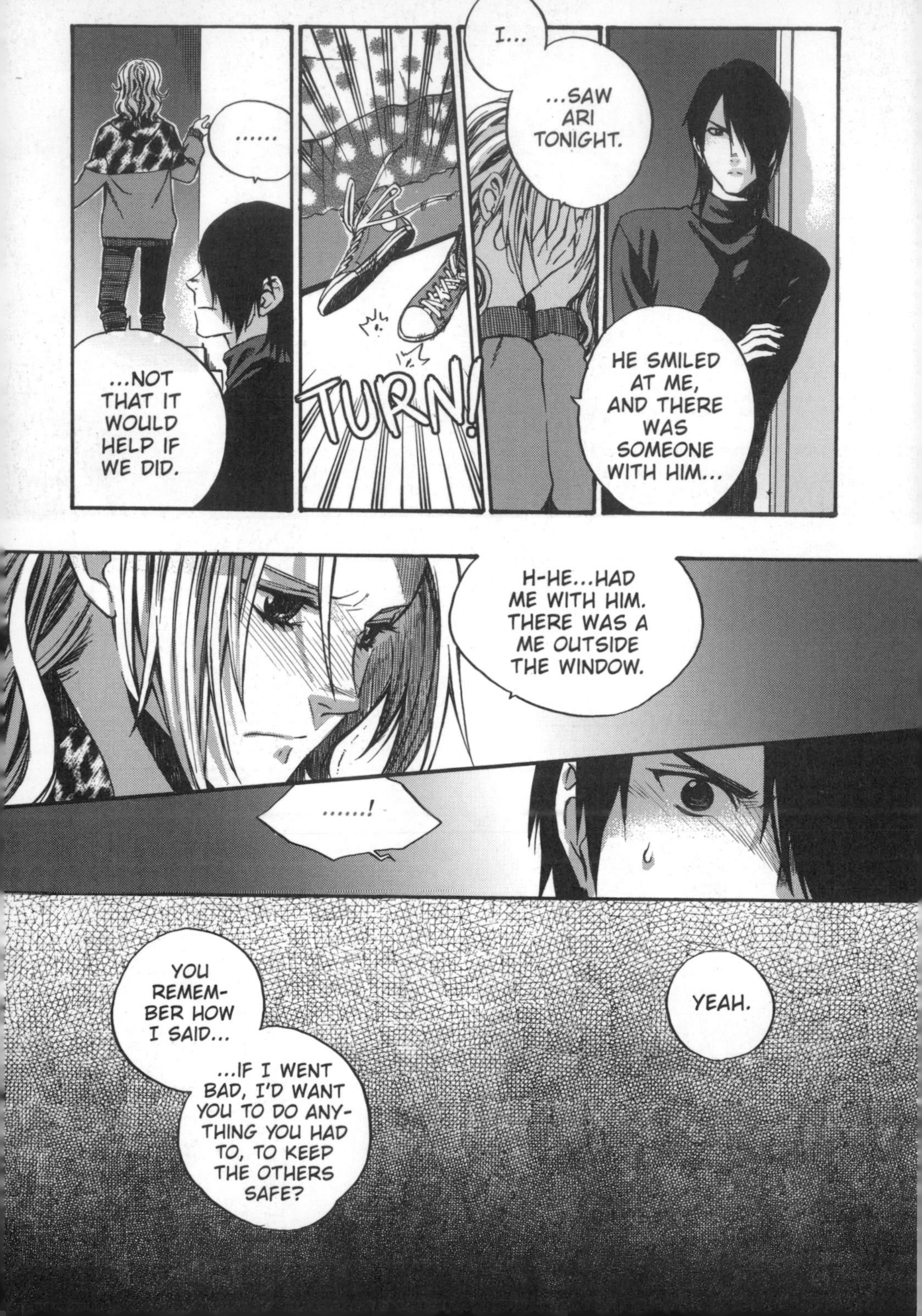
......
...NOT THAT IT WOULD HELP IF WE DID.
TURN!
I...
...SAW ARI TONIGHT.
HE SMILED AT ME, AND THERE WAS SOMEONE WITH HIM...
H-HE...HAD ME WITH HIM. THERE WAS A ME OUTSIDE THE WINDOW.
......!
YOU REMEMBER HOW I SAID...
...IF I WENT BAD, I'D WANT YOU TO DO ANYTHING YOU HAD TO, TO KEEP THE OTHERS SAFE?
YEAH.

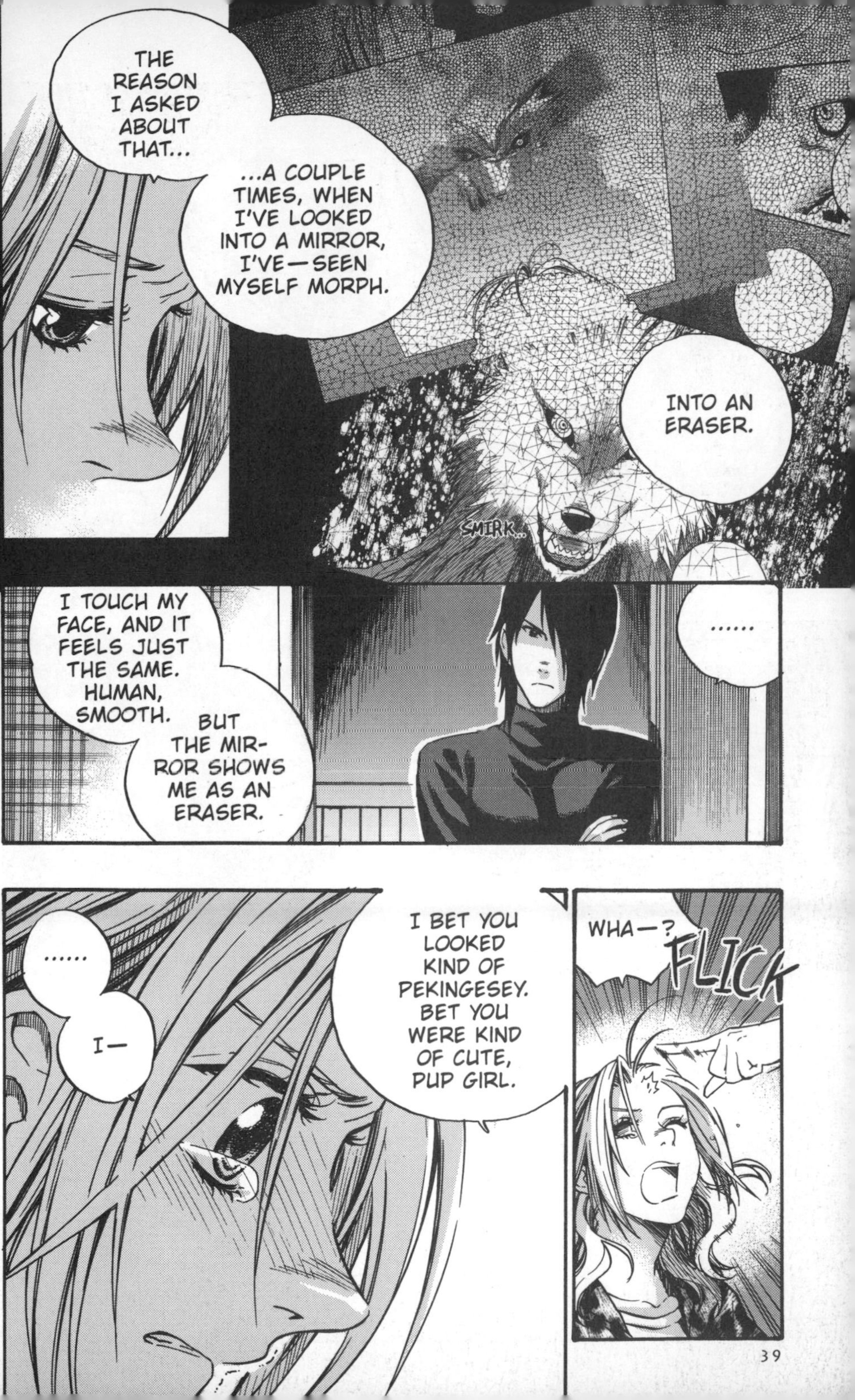
THE REASON I ASKED ABOUT THAT...
...A COUPLE TIMES, WHEN I'VE LOOKED INTO A MIRROR, I'VE—SEEN MYSELF MORPH.
INTO AN ERASER.
SMIRK...
I TOUCH MY FACE, AND IT FEELS JUST THE SAME. HUMAN, SMOOTH.
BUT THE MIRROR SHOWS ME AS AN ERASER.
......
......
I—
I BET YOU LOOKED KIND OF PEKINGESEY. BET YOU WERE KIND OF CUTE, PUP GIRL.
WHA—?
FLICK

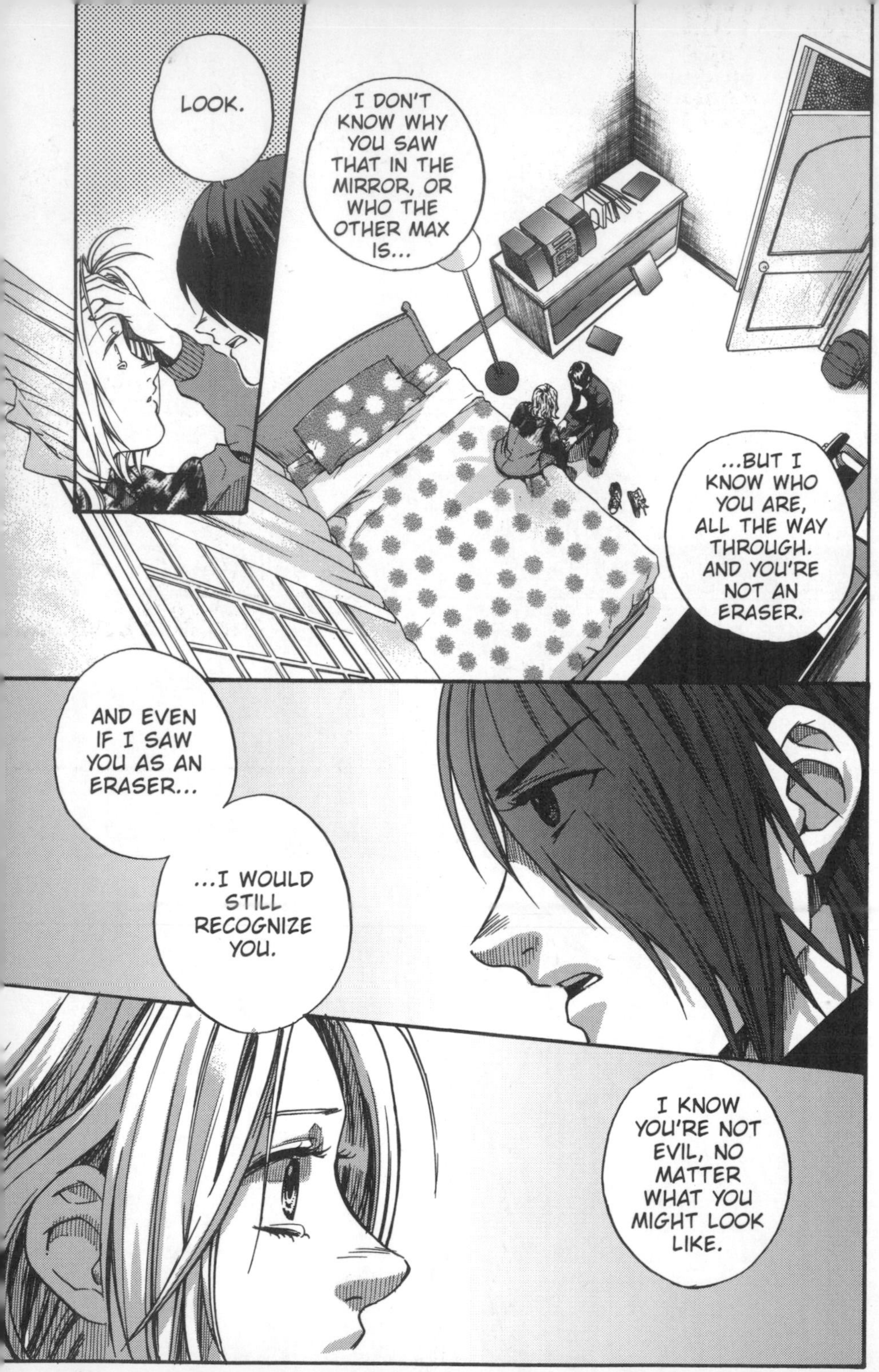
LOOK.
I DON'T KNOW WHY YOU SAW THAT IN THE MIRROR, OR WHO THE OTHER MAX IS...
...BUT I KNOW WHO YOU ARE, ALL THE WAY THROUGH. AND YOU'RE NOT AN ERASER.
AND EVEN IF I SAW YOU AS AN ERASER...
...I WOULD STILL RECOGNIZE YOU.
I KNOW YOU'RE NOT EVIL, NO MATTER WHAT YOU MIGHT LOOK LIKE.

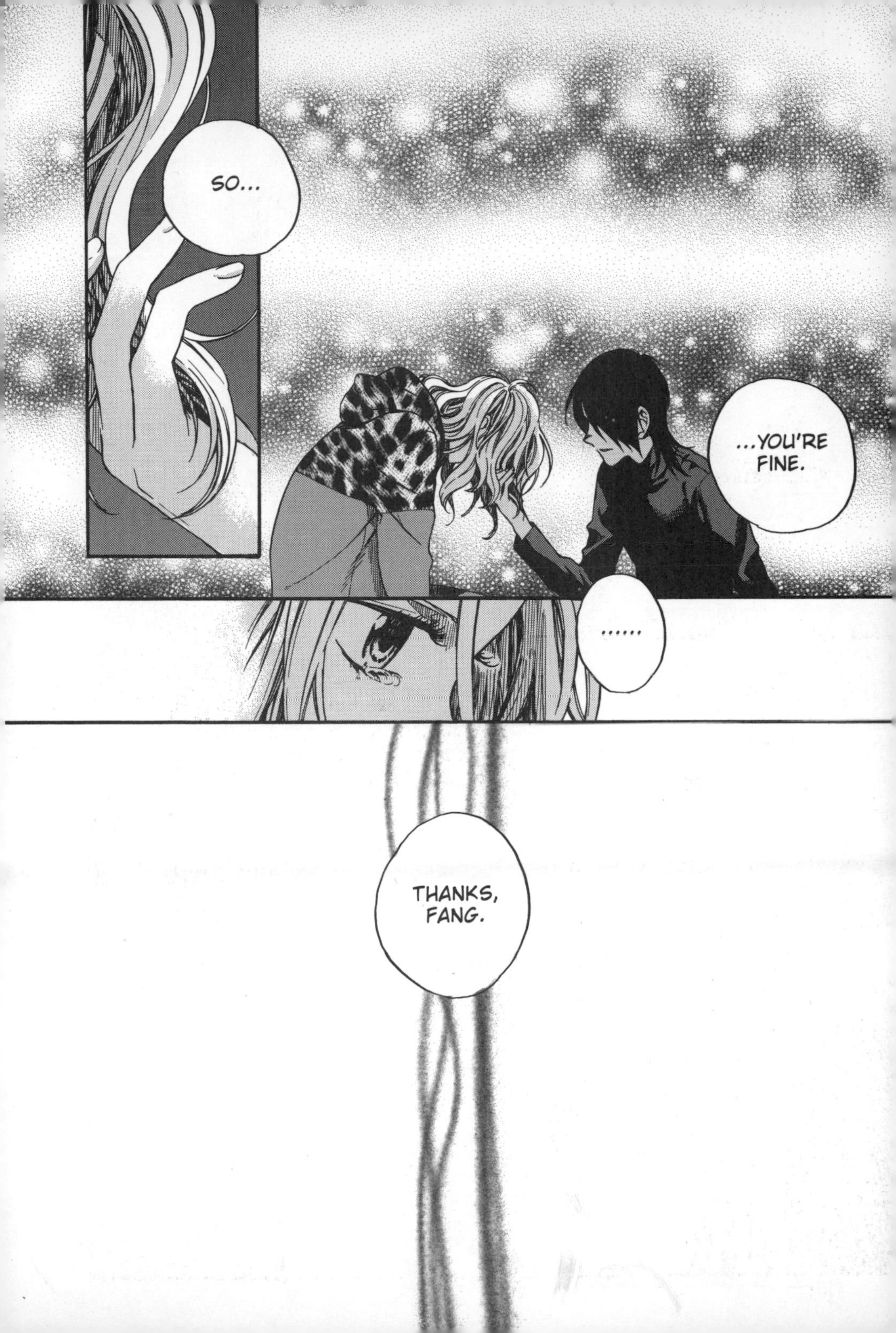
SO...
...YOU'RE FINE.
......
THANKS, FANG.

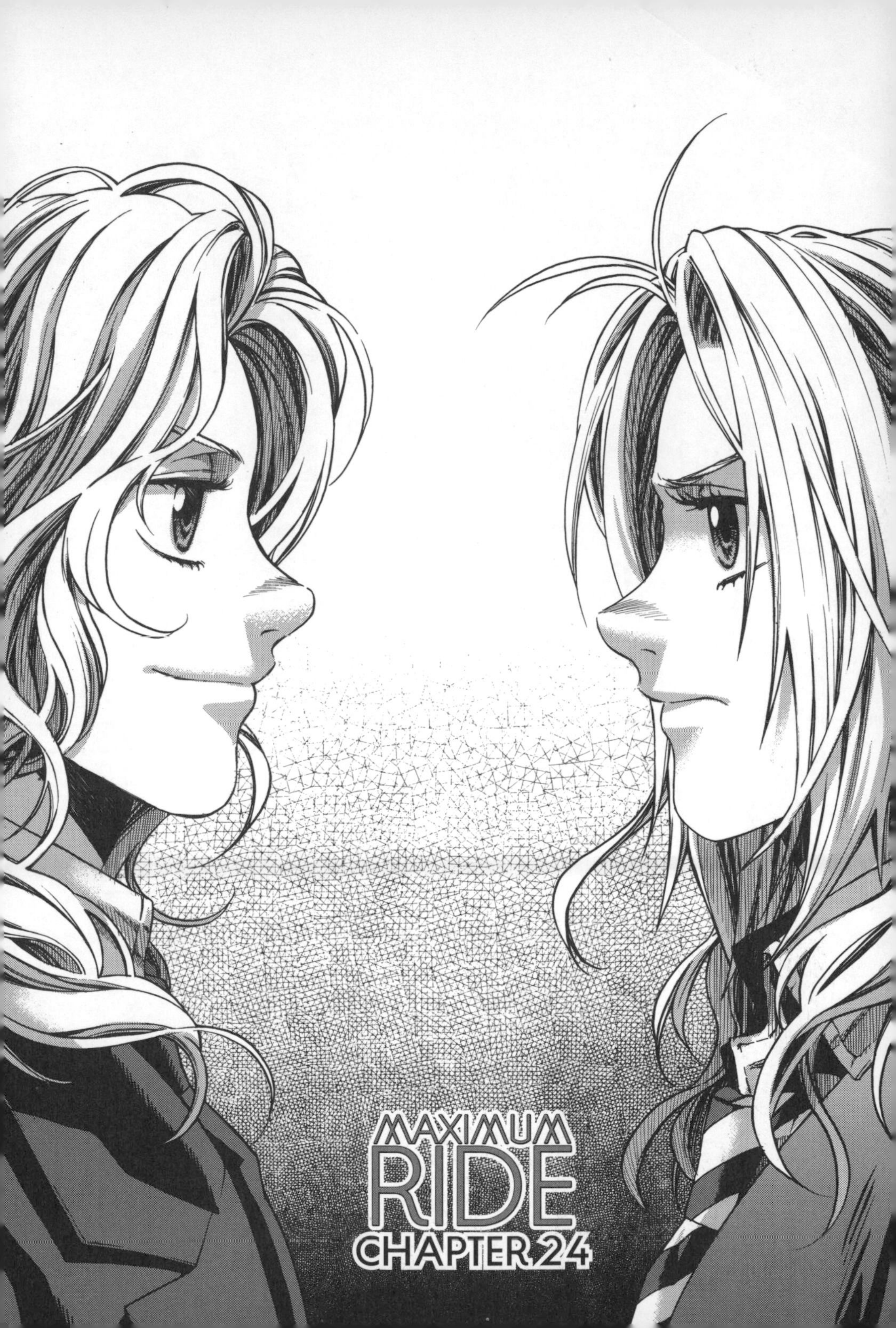
MAXIMUM RIDE
CHAPTER 24

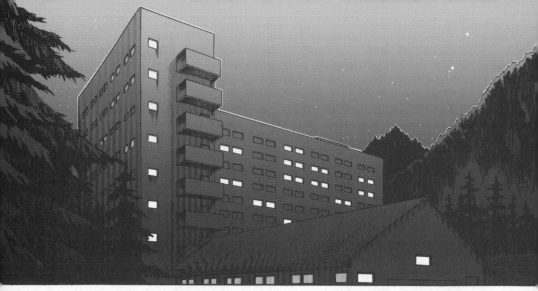

PLEASE.

IT ISN'T TIME YET...

...ARI.

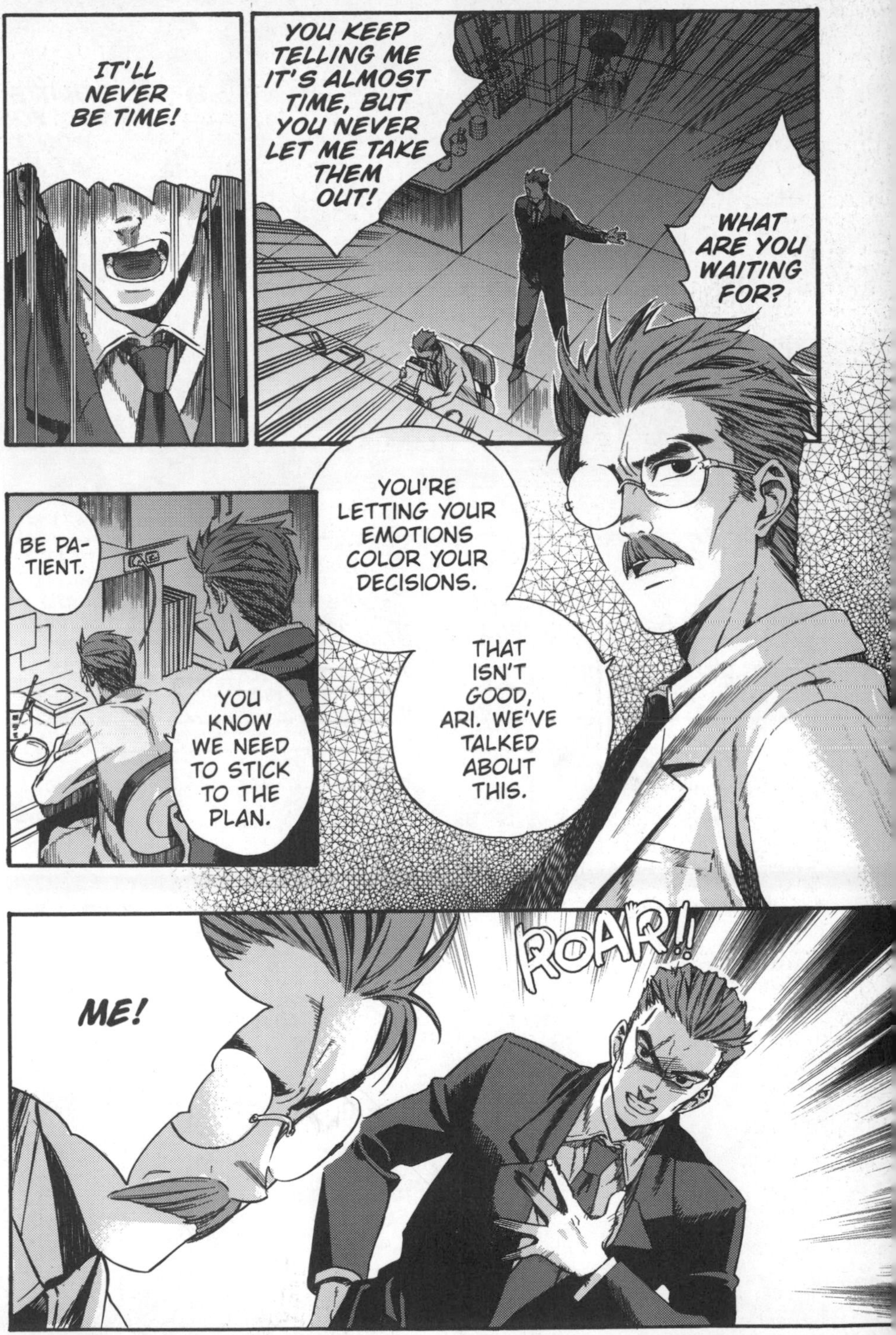
IT'LL NEVER BE TIME!
YOU KEEP TELLING ME IT'S ALMOST TIME, BUT YOU NEVER LET ME TAKE THEM OUT!
WHAT ARE YOU WAITING FOR?
BE PA-TIENT.
YOU KNOW WE NEED TO STICK TO THE PLAN.
YOU'RE LETTING YOUR EMOTIONS COLOR YOUR DECISIONS.
THAT ISN'T GOOD, ARI. WE'VE TALKED ABOUT THIS.
ME!
ROAR!!

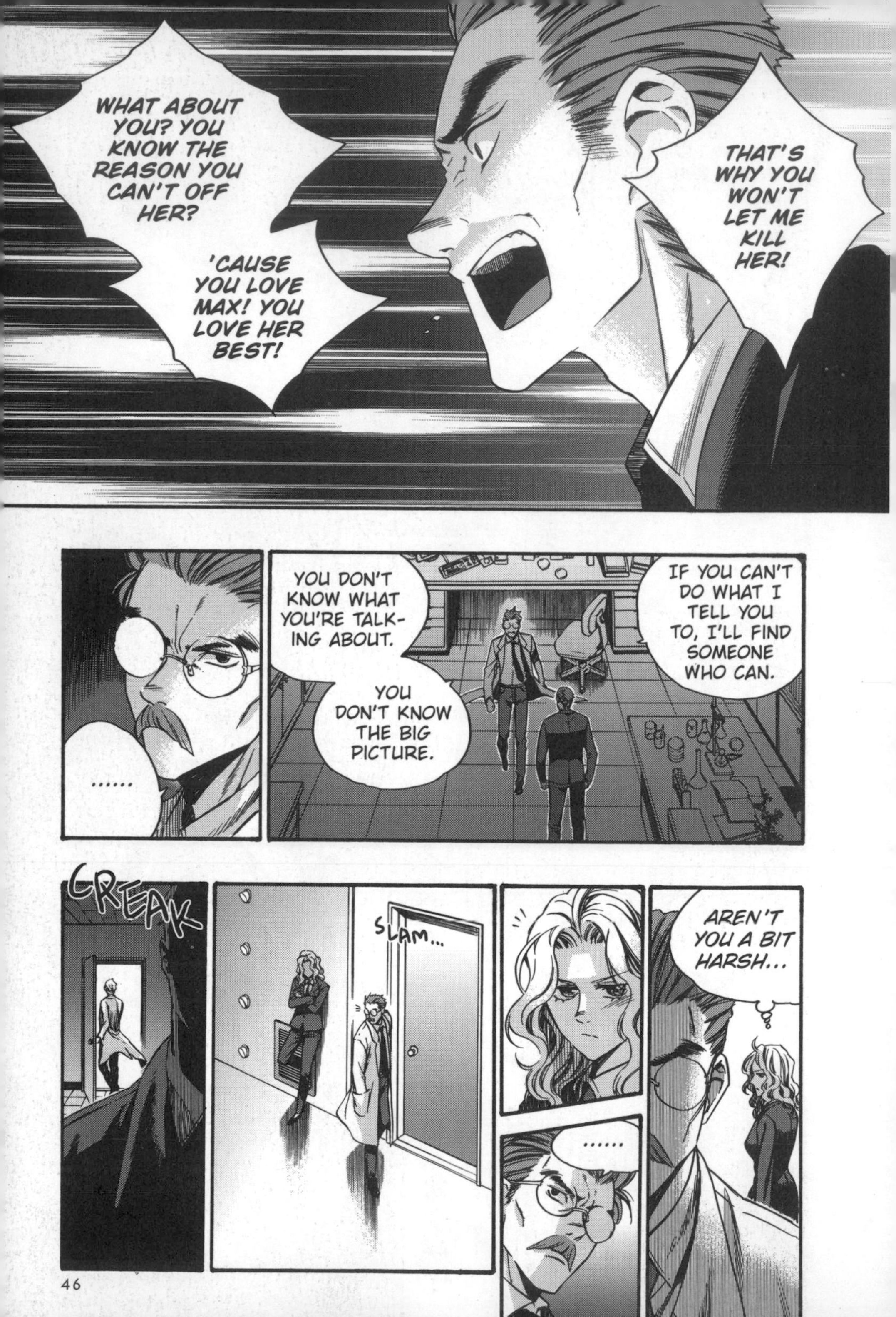
WHAT ABOUT YOU? YOU KNOW THE REASON YOU CAN'T OFF HER?
'CAUSE YOU LOVE MAX! YOU LOVE HER BEST!
THAT'S WHY YOU WON'T LET ME KILL HER!
......
YOU DON'T KNOW WHAT YOU'RE TALKING ABOUT.
YOU DON'T KNOW THE BIG PICTURE.
IF YOU CAN'T DO WHAT I TELL YOU TO, I'LL FIND SOMEONE WHO CAN.
CREAK
SLAM...
......
AREN'T YOU A BIT HARSH...

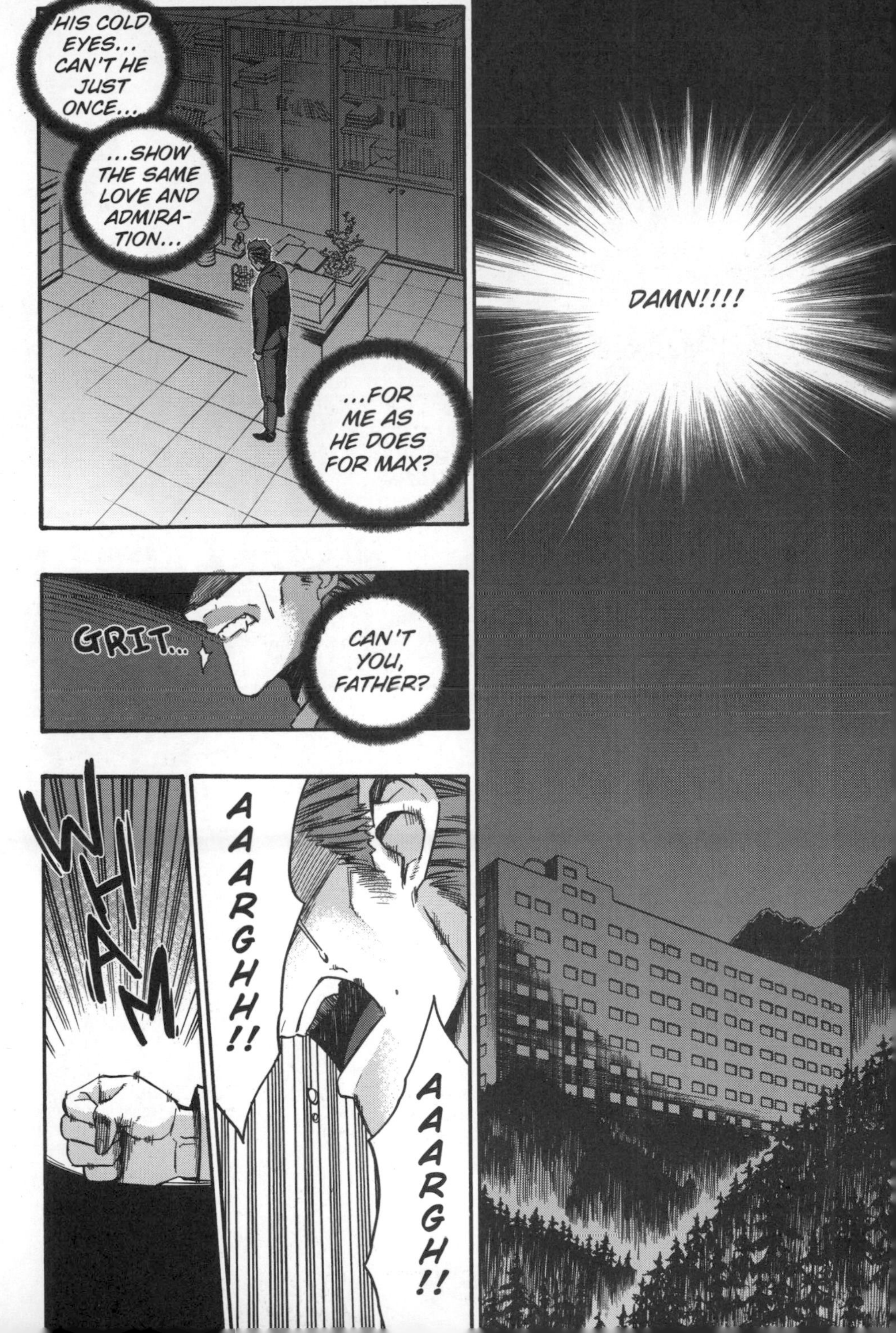
HIS COLD EYES... CAN'T HE JUST ONCE...
...SHOW THE SAME LOVE AND ADMIRA-TION...
...FOR ME AS HE DOES FOR MAX?
GRIT...
CAN'T YOU, FATHER?
WHAM
AAAARGHH!!
AAAARGH!!
DAMN!!!!

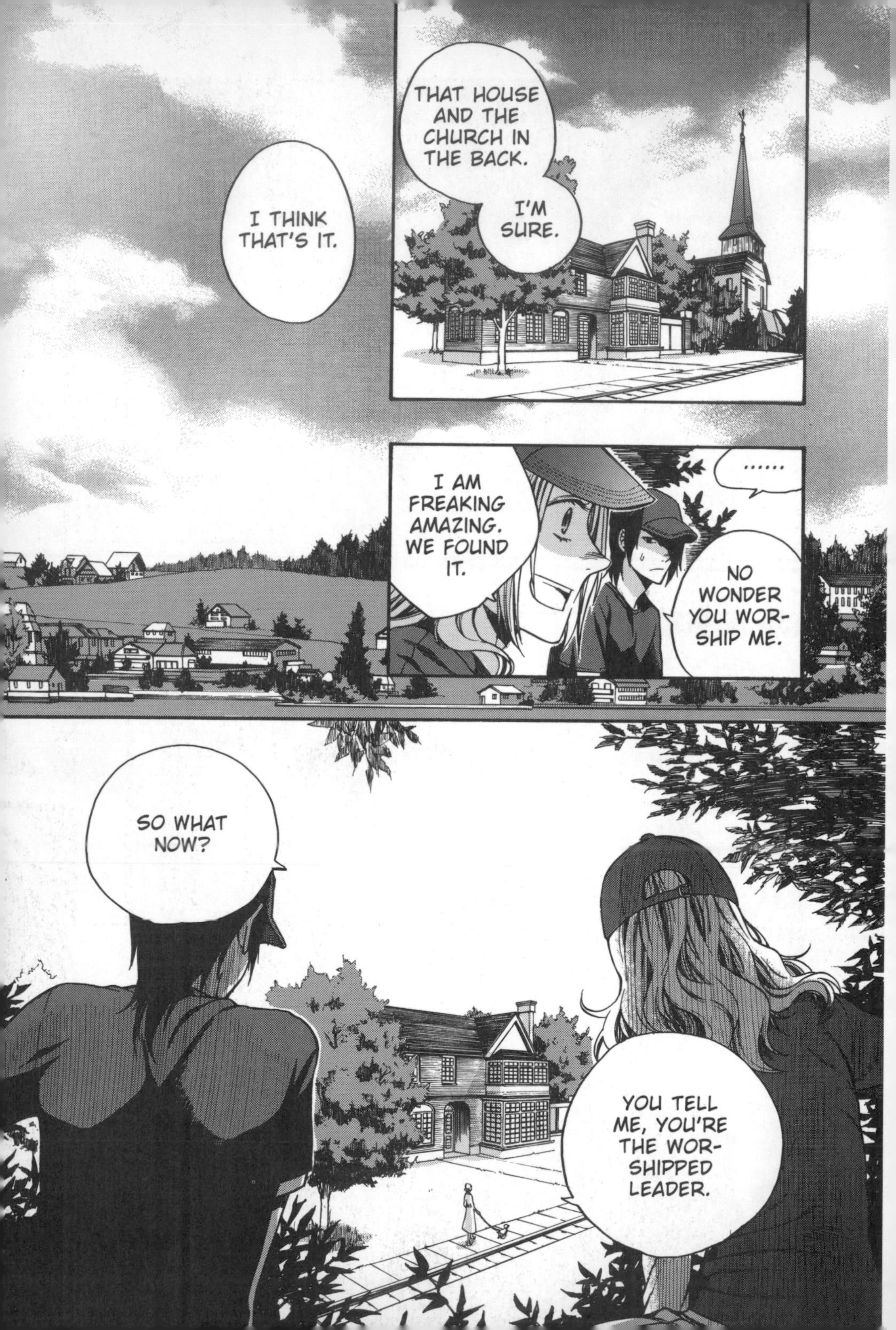
I THINK THAT'S IT.
THAT HOUSE AND THE CHURCH IN THE BACK.
I'M SURE.
I AM FREAKING AMAZING. WE FOUND IT.
......
NO WONDER YOU WOR-SHIP ME.
SO WHAT NOW?
YOU TELL ME, YOU'RE THE WOR-SHIPPED LEADER.

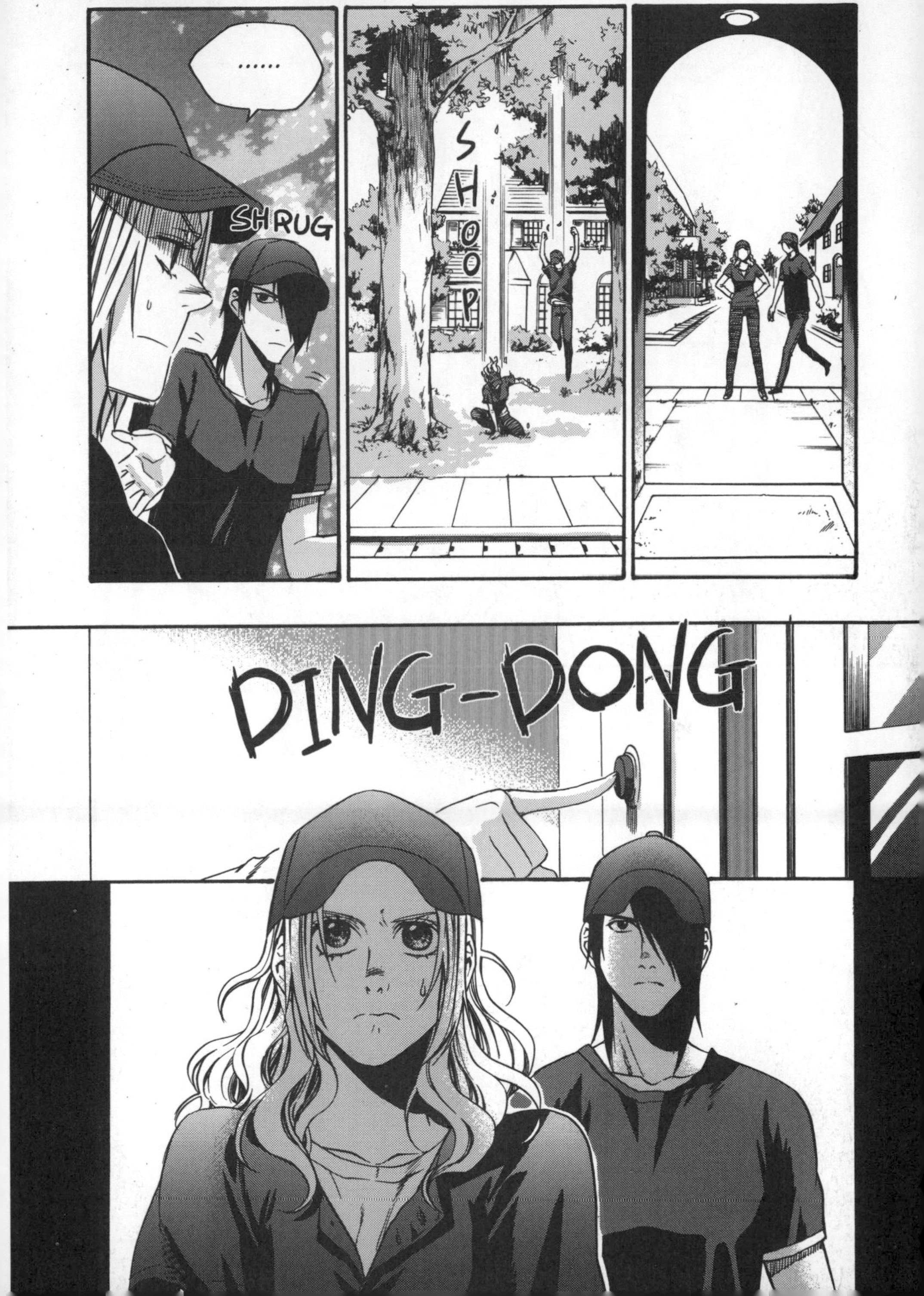

......
SHRUG
SHOOP
DING-DONG

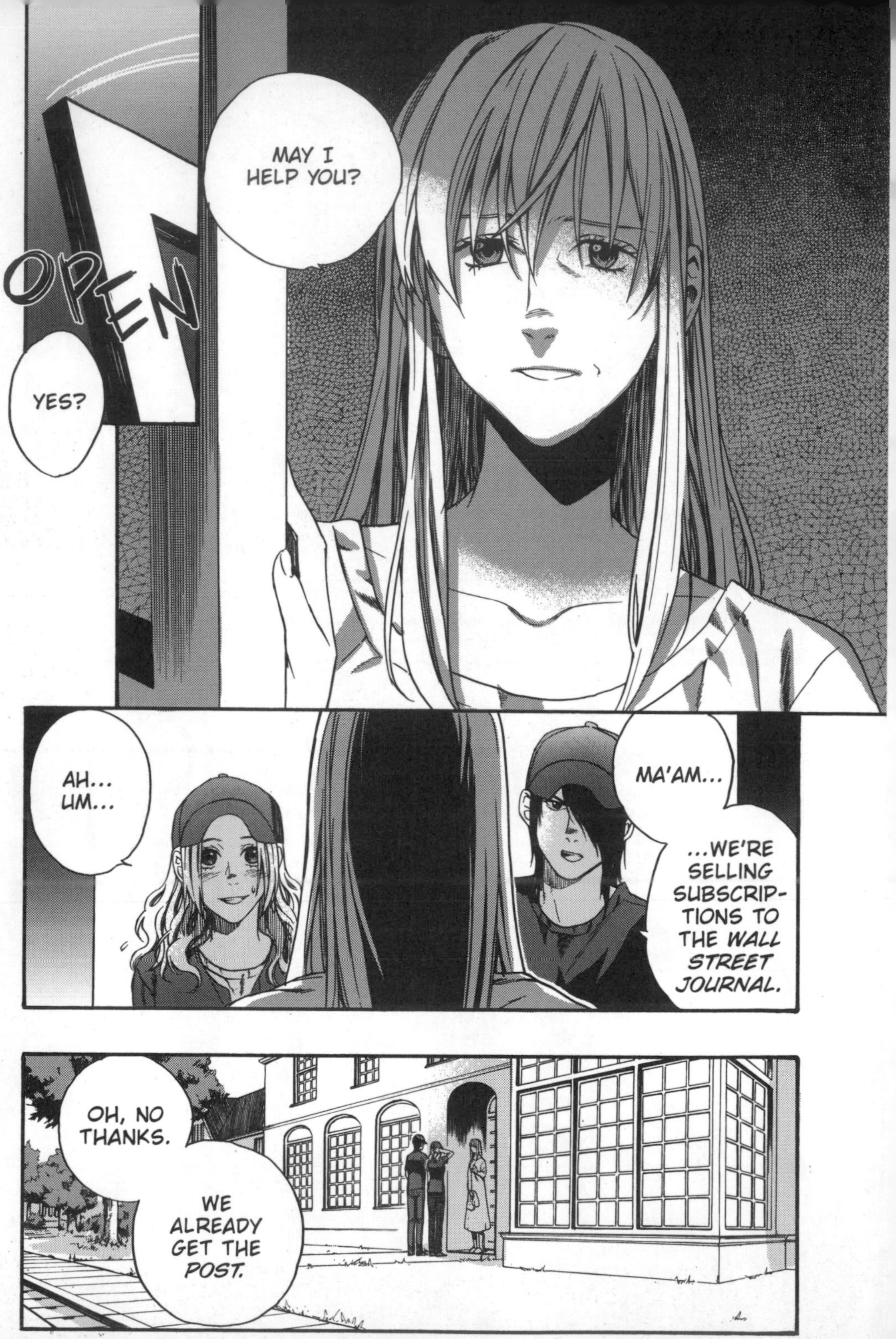
OPEN
YES?
MAY I HELP YOU?
AH... UM...
MA'AM...
...WE'RE SELLING SUBSCRIPTIONS TO THE *WALL STREET JOURNAL*.
OH, NO THANKS.
WE ALREADY GET THE *POST*.

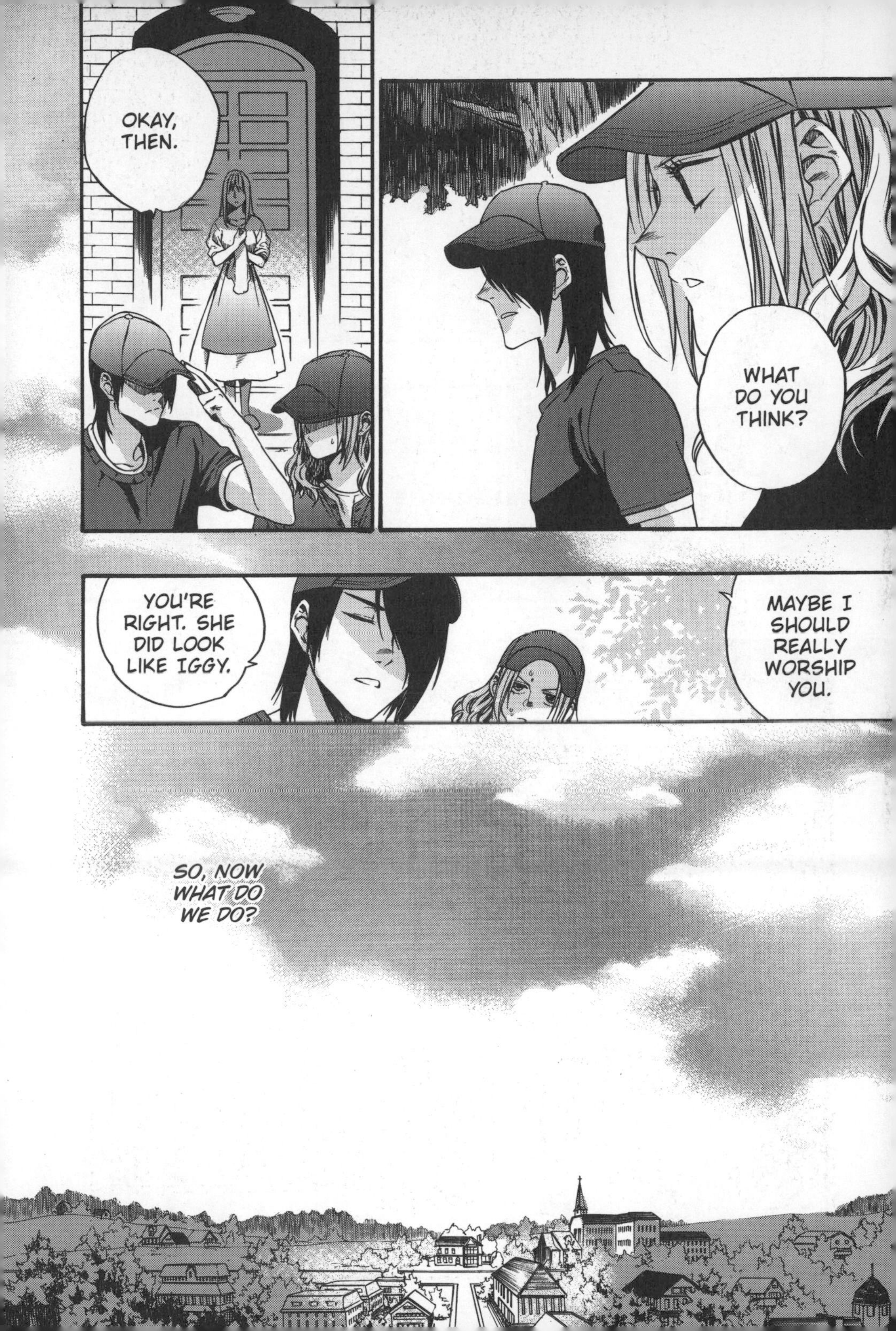
OKAY, THEN.
WHAT DO YOU THINK?
YOU'RE RIGHT. SHE DID LOOK LIKE IGGY.
MAYBE I SHOULD REALLY WORSHIP YOU.
SO, NOW WHAT DO WE DO?

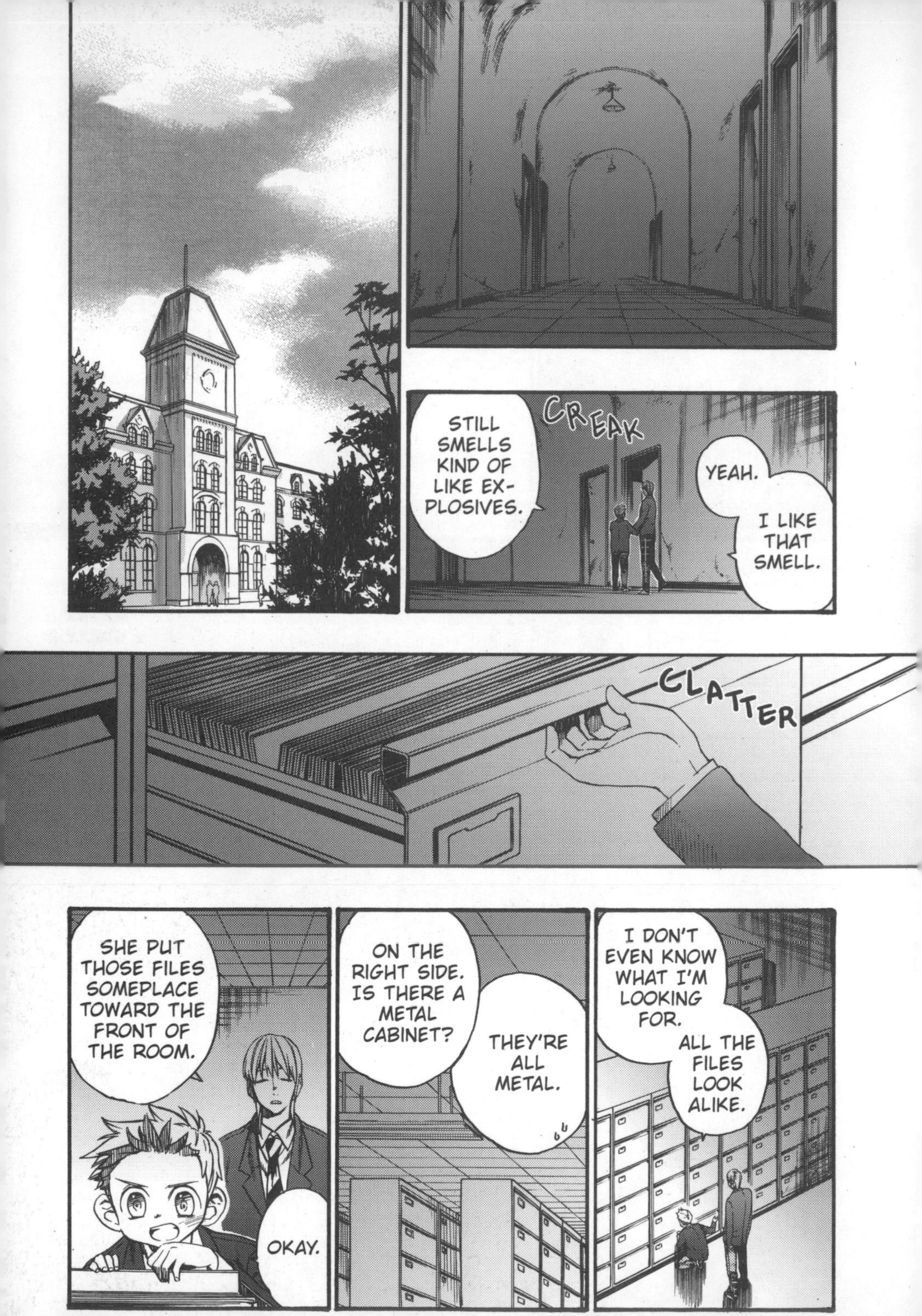
STILL SMELLS KIND OF LIKE EX-PLOSIVES.
CREAK
YEAH.
I LIKE THAT SMELL.
CLATTER
SHE PUT THOSE FILES SOMEPLACE TOWARD THE FRONT OF THE ROOM.
OKAY.
ON THE RIGHT SIDE. IS THERE A METAL CABINET?
THEY'RE ALL METAL.
I DON'T EVEN KNOW WHAT I'M LOOKING FOR.
ALL THE FILES LOOK ALIKE.

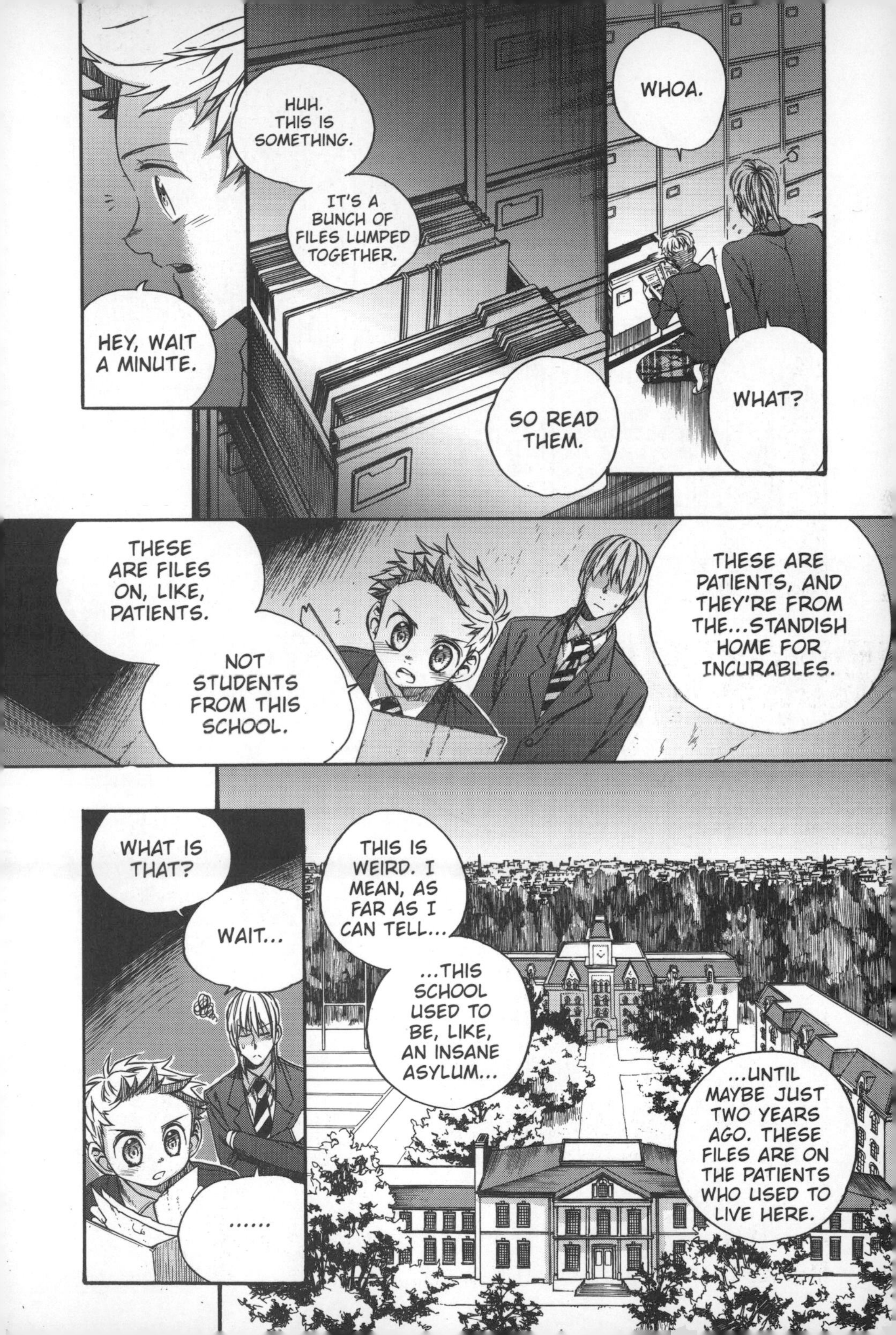
HEY, WAIT A MINUTE.
HUH. THIS IS SOMETHING.
IT'S A BUNCH OF FILES LUMPED TOGETHER.
SO READ THEM.
WHOA.
WHAT?
THESE ARE FILES ON, LIKE, PATIENTS.
NOT STUDENTS FROM THIS SCHOOL.
THESE ARE PATIENTS, AND THEY'RE FROM THE...STANDISH HOME FOR INCURABLES.
WHAT IS THAT?
WAIT...
......
THIS IS WEIRD. I MEAN, AS FAR AS I CAN TELL...
...THIS SCHOOL USED TO BE, LIKE, AN INSANE ASYLUM...
...UNTIL MAYBE JUST TWO YEARS AGO. THESE FILES ARE ON THE PATIENTS WHO USED TO LIVE HERE.

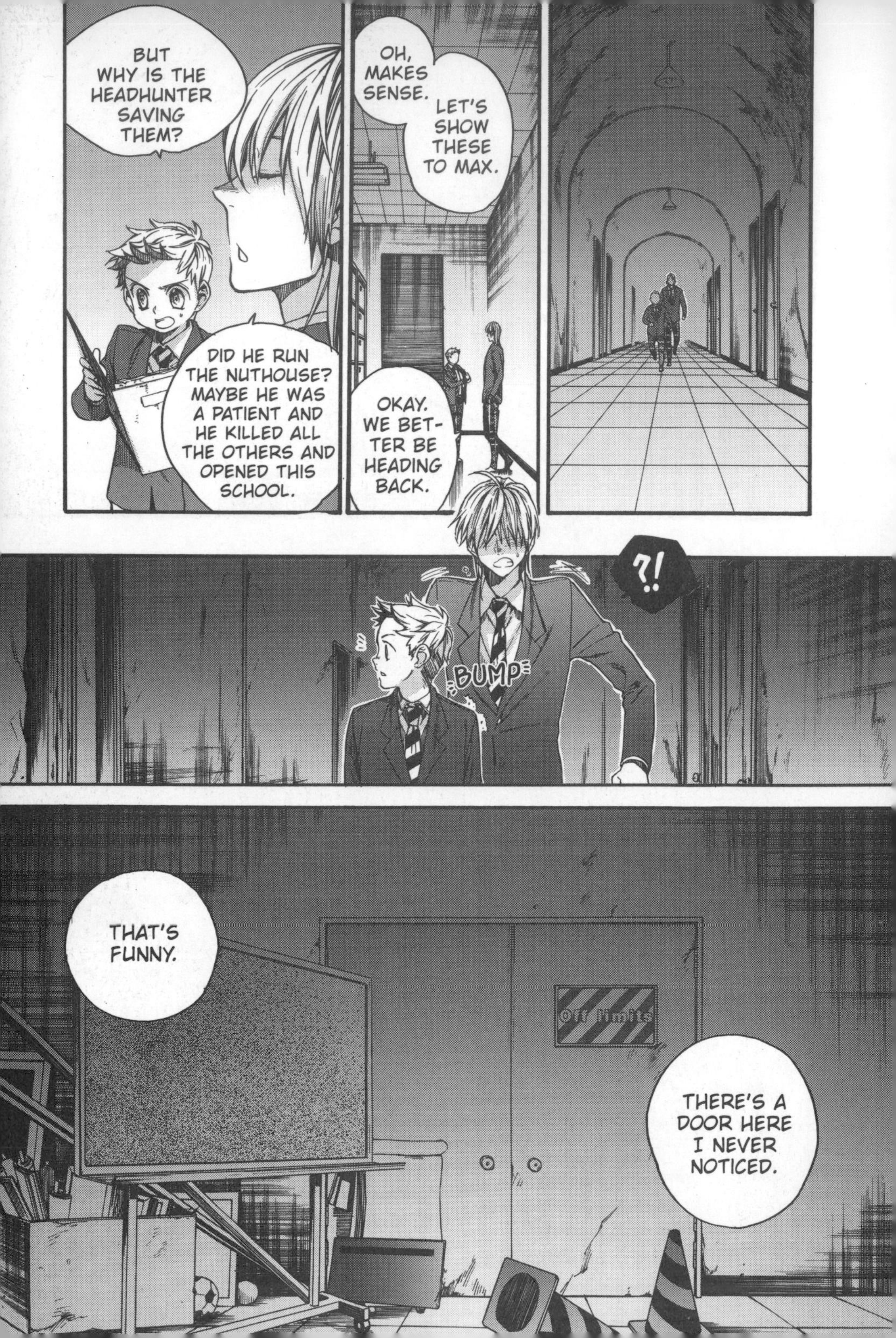
BUT WHY IS THE HEADHUNTER SAVING THEM?
DID HE RUN THE NUTHOUSE? MAYBE HE WAS A PATIENT AND HE KILLED ALL THE OTHERS AND OPENED THIS SCHOOL.
OH, MAKES SENSE.
LET'S SHOW THESE TO MAX.
OKAY. WE BET-TER BE HEADING BACK.
?!
BUMP
THAT'S FUNNY.
Off limits
THERE'S A DOOR HERE I NEVER NOTICED.

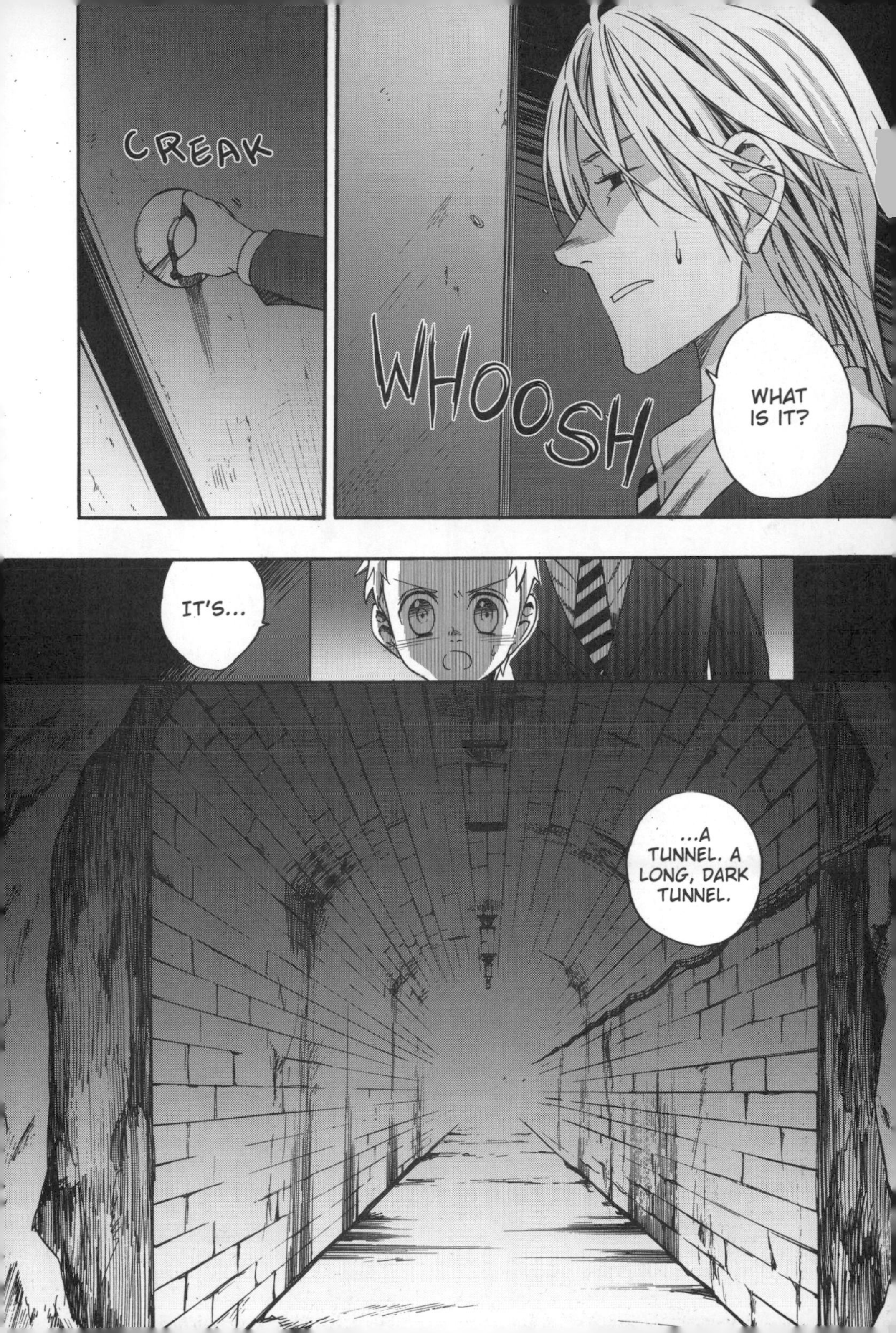
CREAK
WHOOSH
WHAT IS IT?
IT'S...
...A TUNNEL. A LONG, DARK TUNNEL.

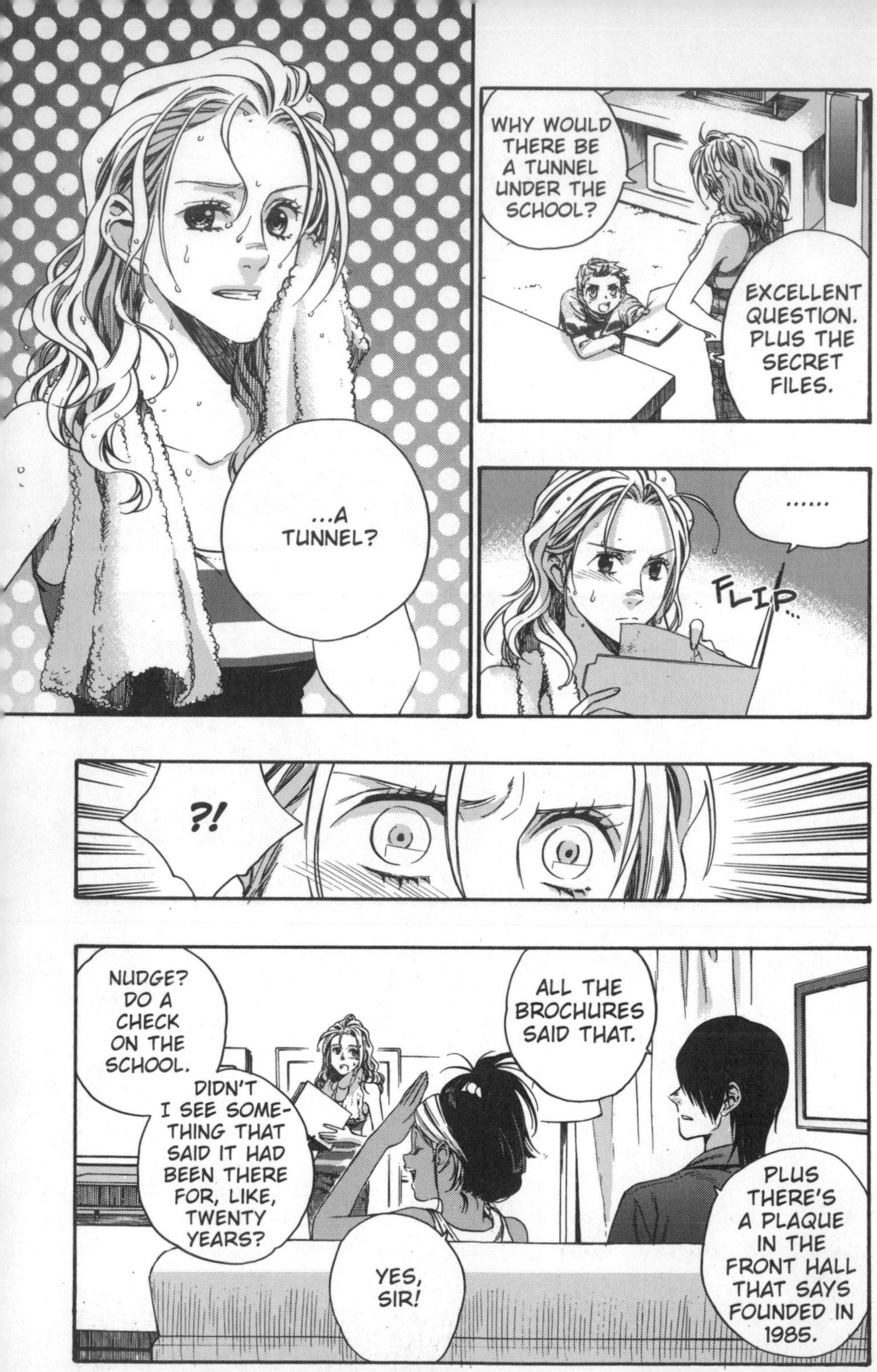
...A TUNNEL?
WHY WOULD THERE BE A TUNNEL UNDER THE SCHOOL?
EXCELLENT QUESTION. PLUS THE SECRET FILES.
......
FLIP...
?!
NUDGE? DO A CHECK ON THE SCHOOL.
DIDN'T I SEE SOMETHING THAT SAID IT HAD BEEN THERE FOR, LIKE, TWENTY YEARS?
YES, SIR!
ALL THE BROCHURES SAID THAT.
PLUS THERE'S A PLAQUE IN THE FRONT HALL THAT SAYS FOUNDED IN 1985.

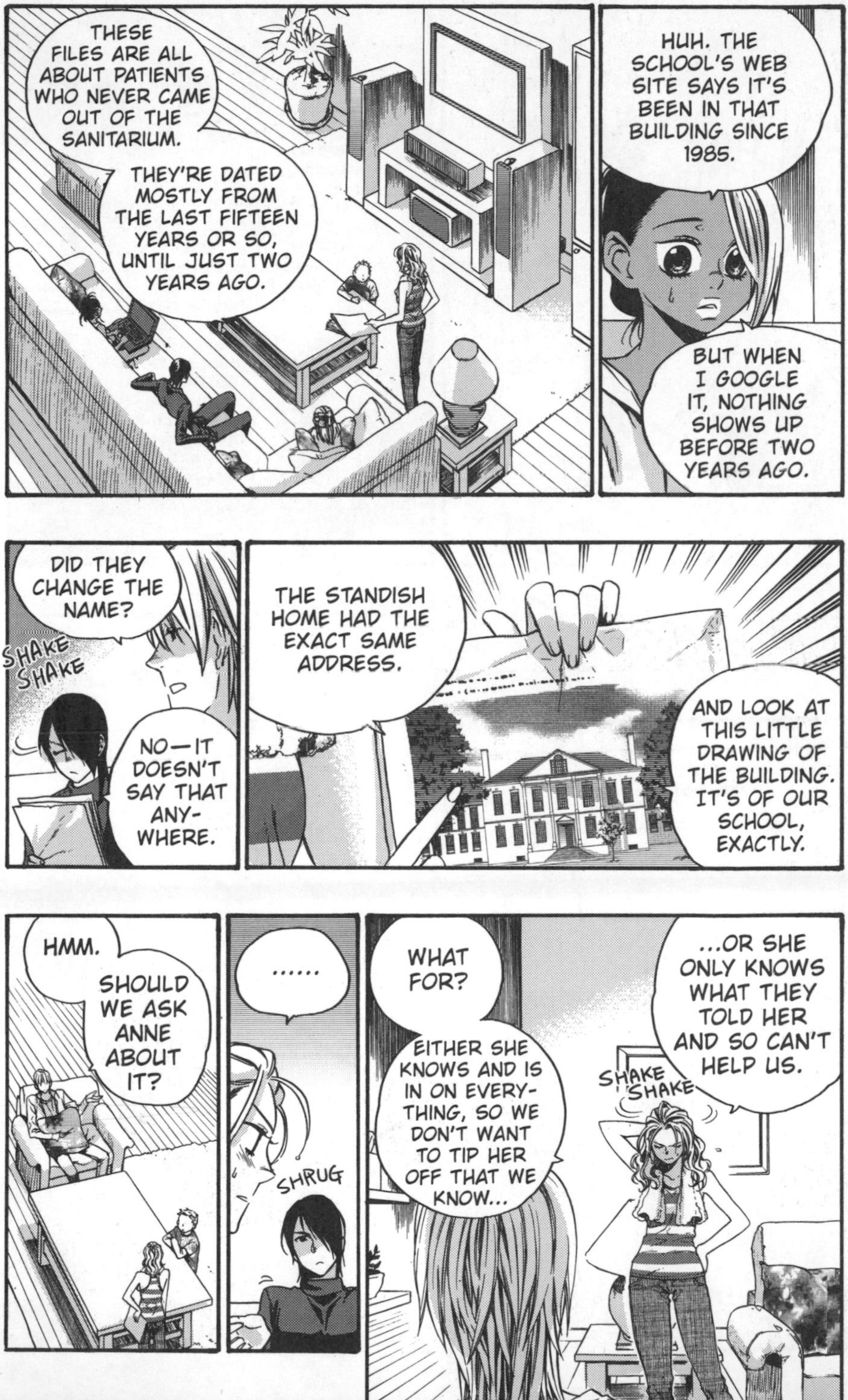
THESE FILES ARE ALL ABOUT PATIENTS WHO NEVER CAME OUT OF THE SANITARIUM.
THEY'RE DATED MOSTLY FROM THE LAST FIFTEEN YEARS OR SO, UNTIL JUST TWO YEARS AGO.
HUH. THE SCHOOL'S WEB SITE SAYS IT'S BEEN IN THAT BUILDING SINCE 1985.
BUT WHEN I GOOGLE IT, NOTHING SHOWS UP BEFORE TWO YEARS AGO.
DID THEY CHANGE THE NAME?
SHAKE SHAKE
NO—IT DOESN'T SAY THAT ANY-WHERE.
THE STANDISH HOME HAD THE EXACT SAME ADDRESS.
AND LOOK AT THIS LITTLE DRAWING OF THE BUILDING. IT'S OF OUR SCHOOL, EXACTLY.
HMM.
SHOULD WE ASK ANNE ABOUT IT?
......
SHRUG
WHAT FOR?
EITHER SHE KNOWS AND IS IN ON EVERY-THING, SO WE DON'T WANT TO TIP HER OFF THAT WE KNOW...
...OR SHE ONLY KNOWS WHAT THEY TOLD HER AND SO CAN'T HELP US.
SHAKE SHAKE

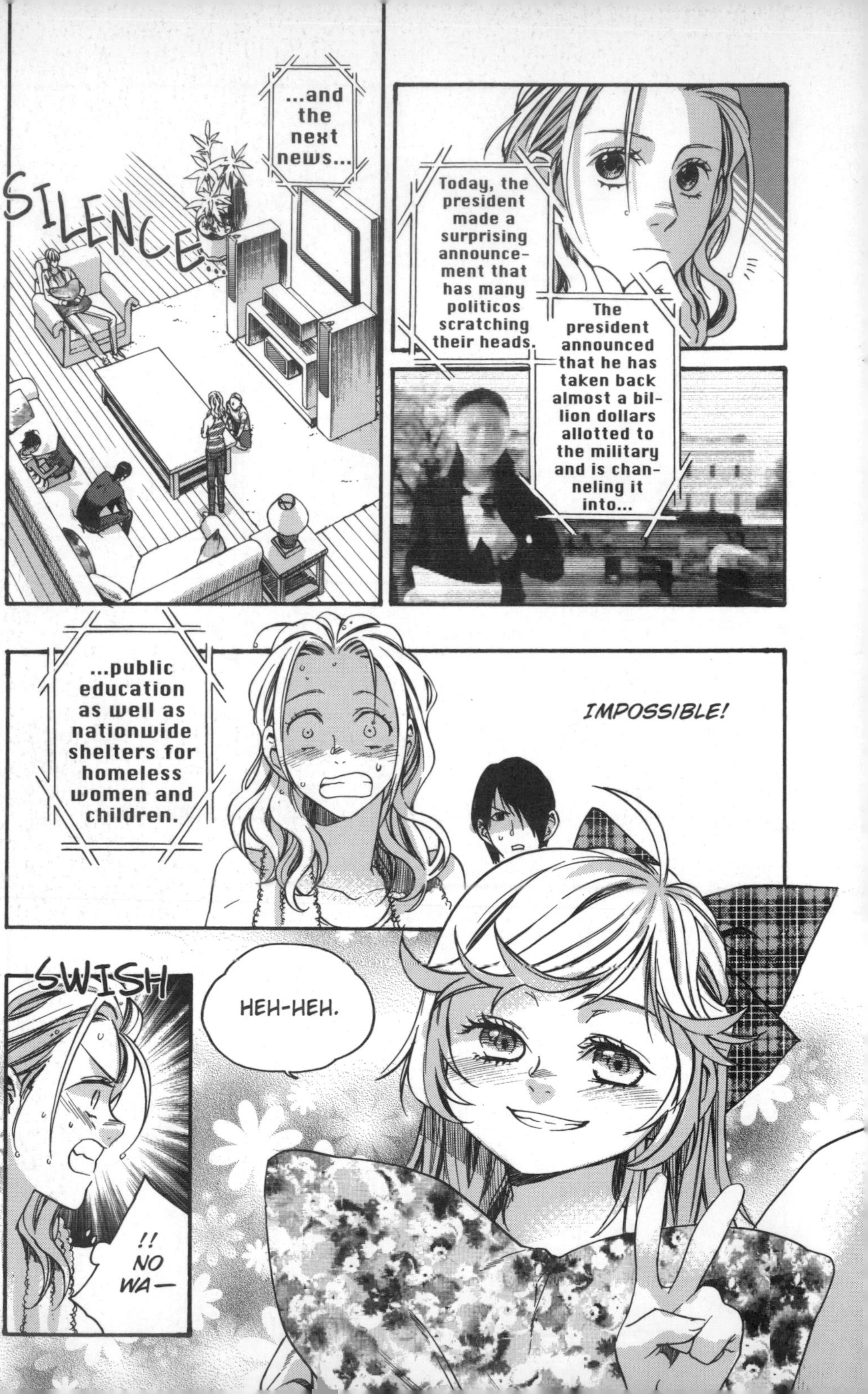
SILENCE
...and the next news...
Today, the president made a surprising announcement that has many politicos scratching their heads.
The president announced that he has taken back almost a billion dollars allotted to the military and is channeling it into...
...public education as well as nationwide shelters for homeless women and children.
IMPOSSIBLE!
SWISH
HEH-HEH.
!! NO WA—

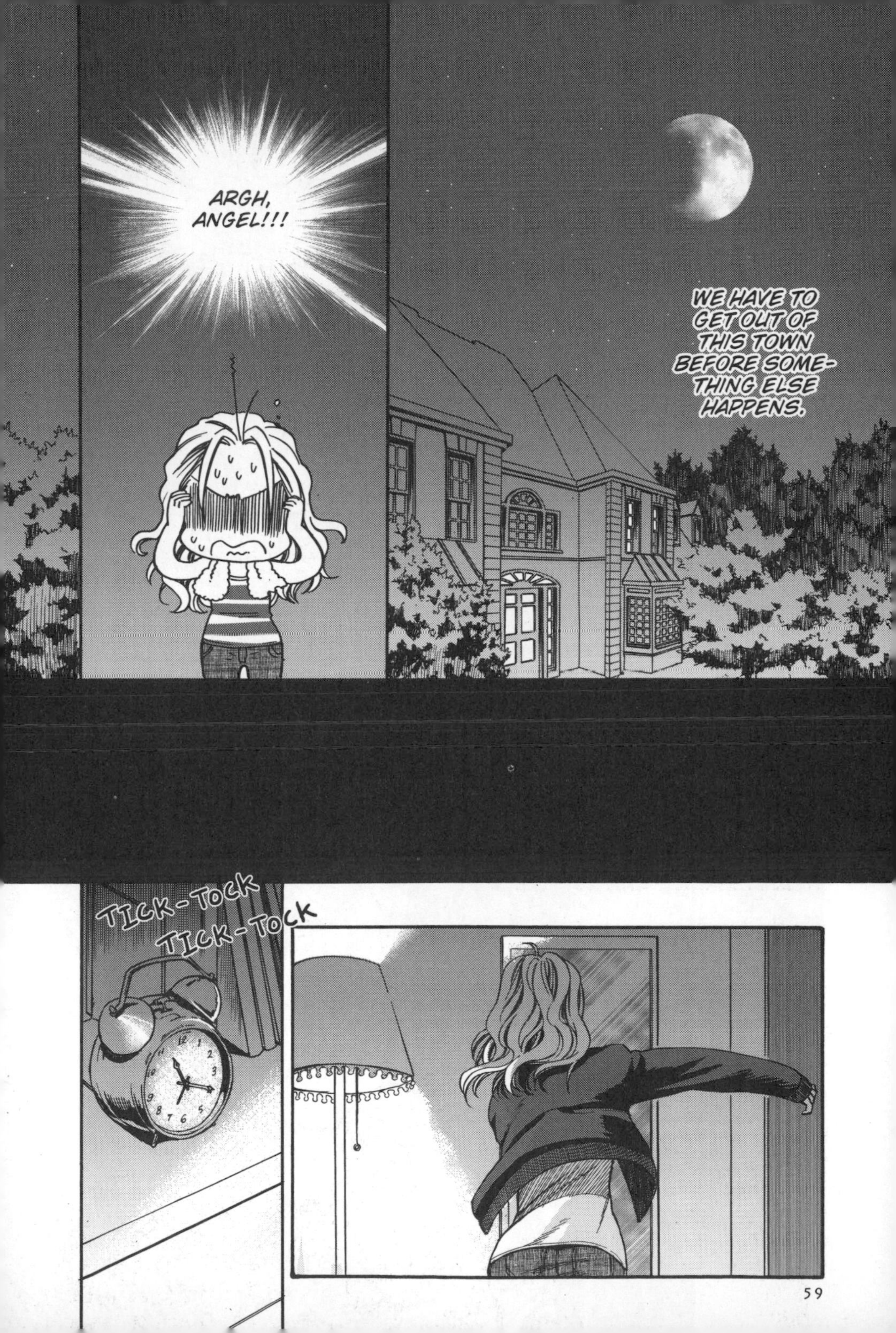
ARGH, ANGEL!!!
WE HAVE TO GET OUT OF THIS TOWN BEFORE SOME-THING ELSE HAPPENS.
TICK-TOCK TICK-TOCK

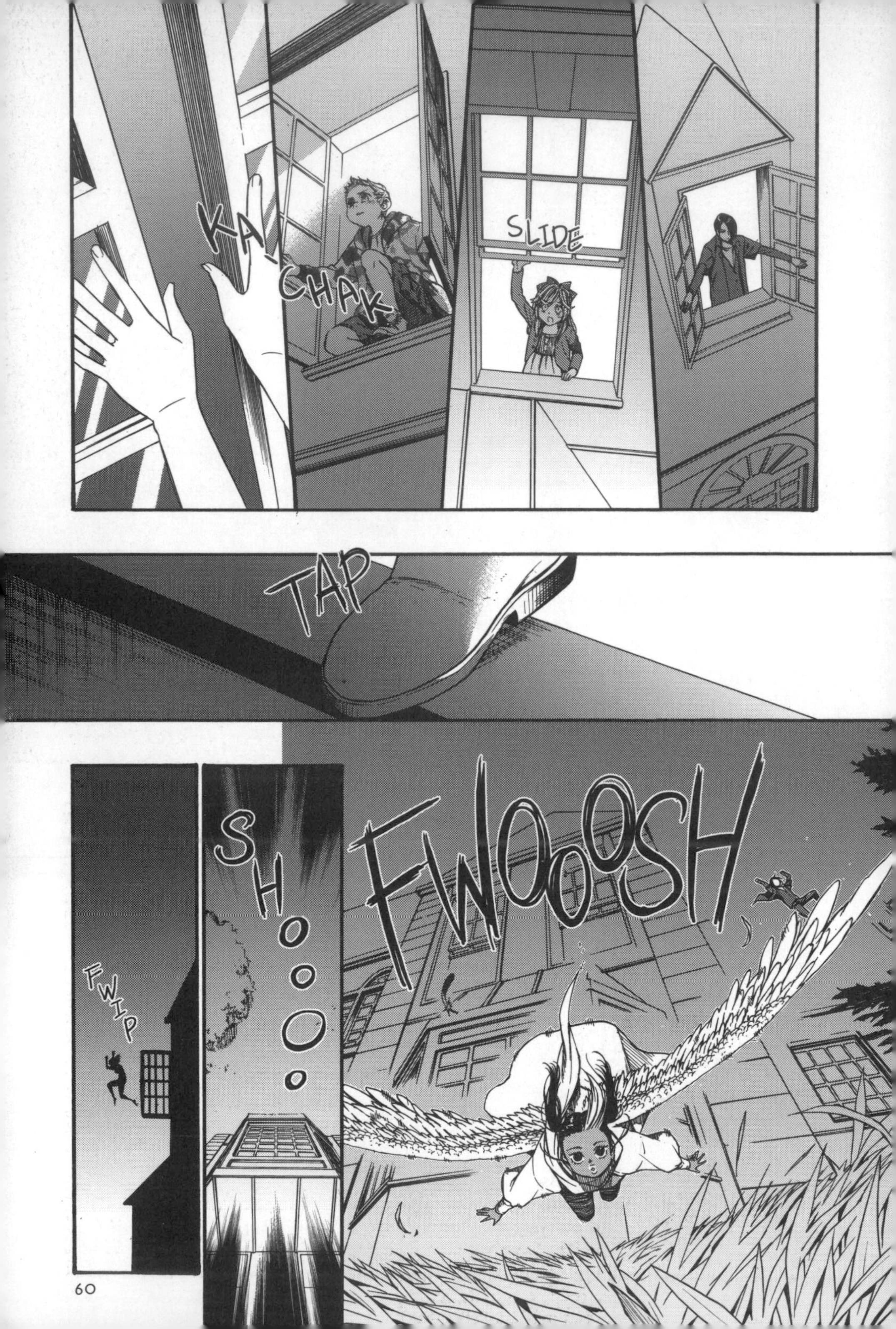
KA-CHAK
SLIDE
TAP
FWIP
SHOOOOO
FWOOOSH

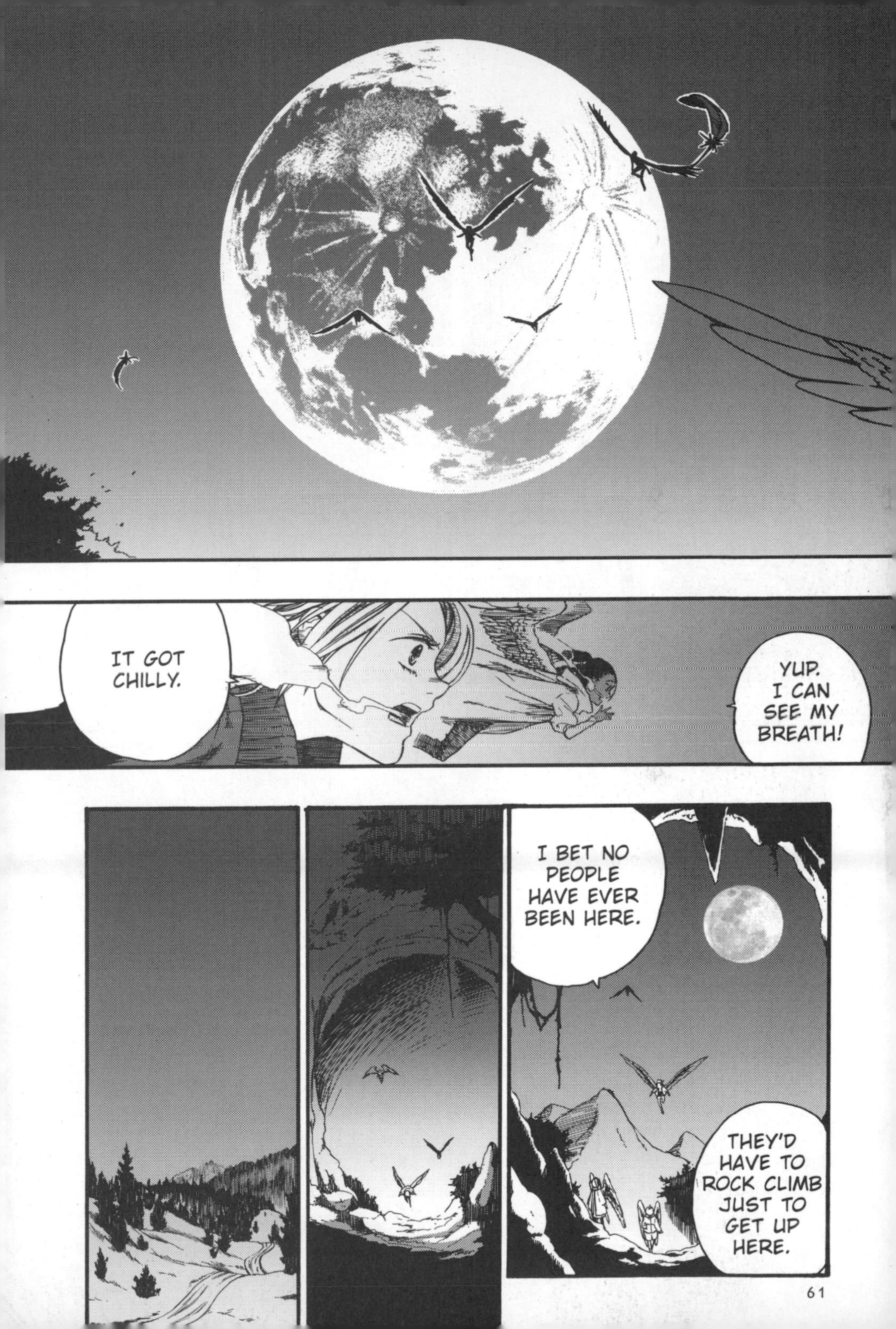
IT GOT CHILLY.
YUP. I CAN SEE MY BREATH!
I BET NO PEOPLE HAVE EVER BEEN HERE.
THEY'D HAVE TO ROCK CLIMB JUST TO GET UP HERE.

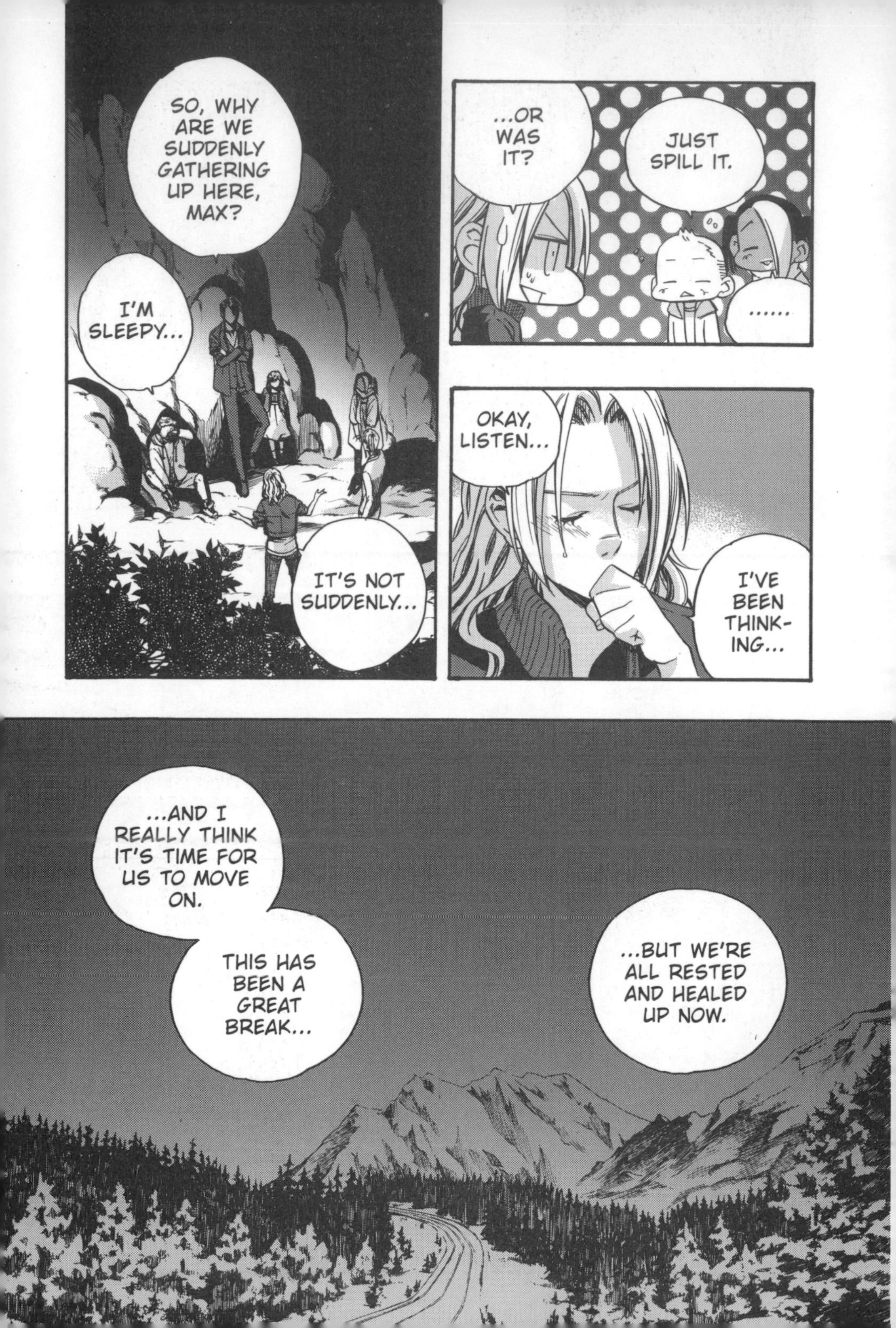
SO, WHY ARE WE SUDDENLY GATHERING UP HERE, MAX?
I'M SLEEPY...
IT'S NOT SUDDENLY...
...OR WAS IT?
JUST SPILL IT.
......
OKAY, LISTEN...
I'VE BEEN THINKING...
...AND I REALLY THINK IT'S TIME FOR US TO MOVE ON.
THIS HAS BEEN A GREAT BREAK...
...BUT WE'RE ALL RESTED AND HEALED UP NOW.

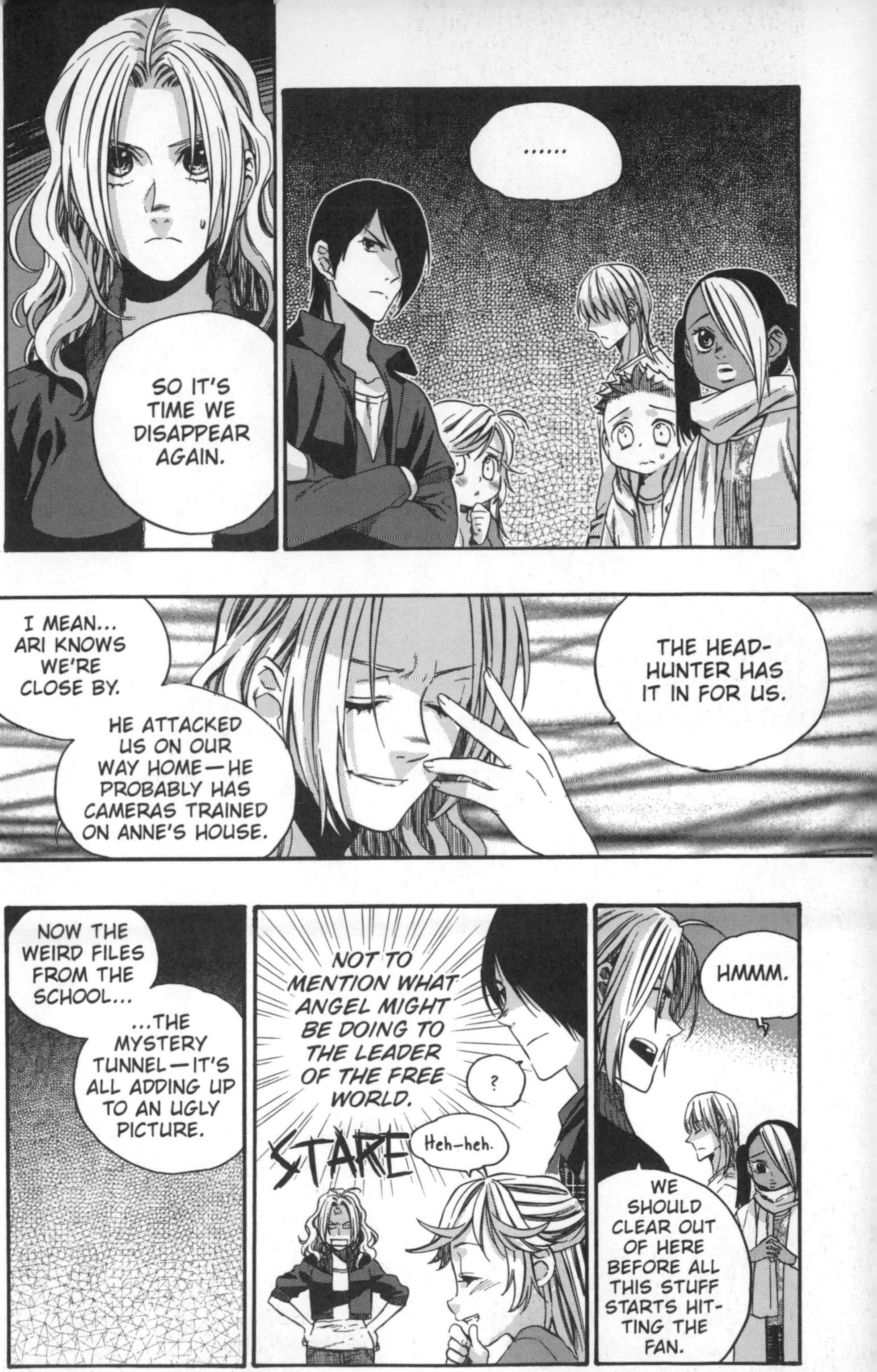

SO IT'S TIME WE DISAPPEAR AGAIN.
......
I MEAN... ARI KNOWS WE'RE CLOSE BY.
HE ATTACKED US ON OUR WAY HOME—HE PROBABLY HAS CAMERAS TRAINED ON ANNE'S HOUSE.
THE HEAD-HUNTER HAS IT IN FOR US.
NOW THE WEIRD FILES FROM THE SCHOOL...
...THE MYSTERY TUNNEL—IT'S ALL ADDING UP TO AN UGLY PICTURE.
NOT TO MENTION WHAT ANGEL MIGHT BE DOING TO THE LEADER OF THE FREE WORLD.
?
STARE
Heh-heh.
HMMM.
WE SHOULD CLEAR OUT OF HERE BEFORE ALL THIS STUFF STARTS HIT-TING THE FAN.

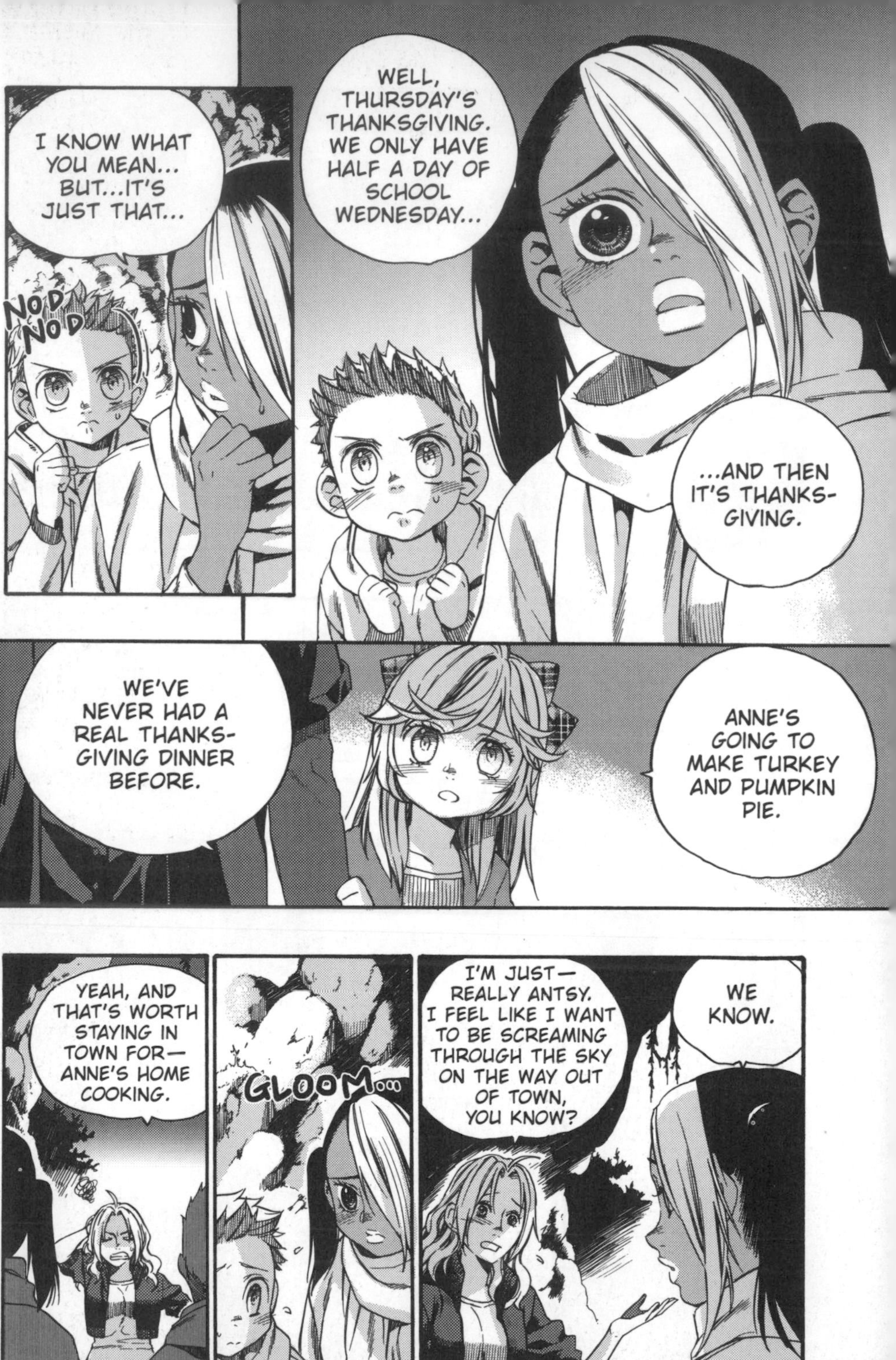
I KNOW WHAT YOU MEAN... BUT...IT'S JUST THAT...
NOD NOD
WELL, THURSDAY'S THANKSGIVING. WE ONLY HAVE HALF A DAY OF SCHOOL WEDNESDAY...
...AND THEN IT'S THANKS-GIVING.
WE'VE NEVER HAD A REAL THANKS-GIVING DINNER BEFORE.
ANNE'S GOING TO MAKE TURKEY AND PUMPKIN PIE.
YEAH, AND THAT'S WORTH STAYING IN TOWN FOR— ANNE'S HOME COOKING.
GLOOM...
I'M JUST— REALLY ANTSY. I FEEL LIKE I WANT TO BE SCREAMING THROUGH THE SKY ON THE WAY OUT OF TOWN, YOU KNOW?
WE KNOW.

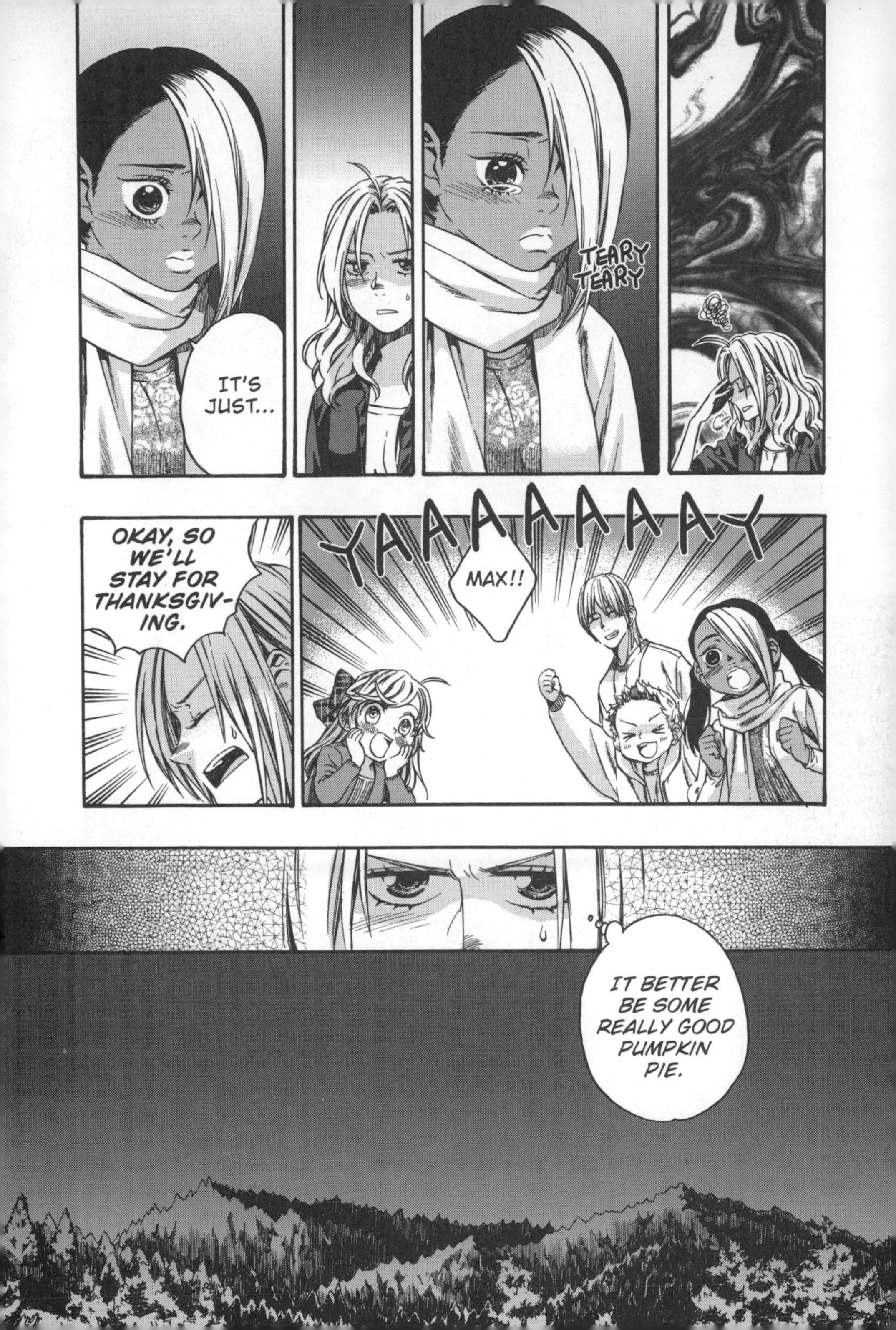
IT'S JUST...
TEARY TEARY
OKAY, SO WE'LL STAY FOR THANKSGIV-ING.
YAAAAAAAY
MAX!!
IT BETTER BE SOME REALLY GOOD PUMPKIN PIE.

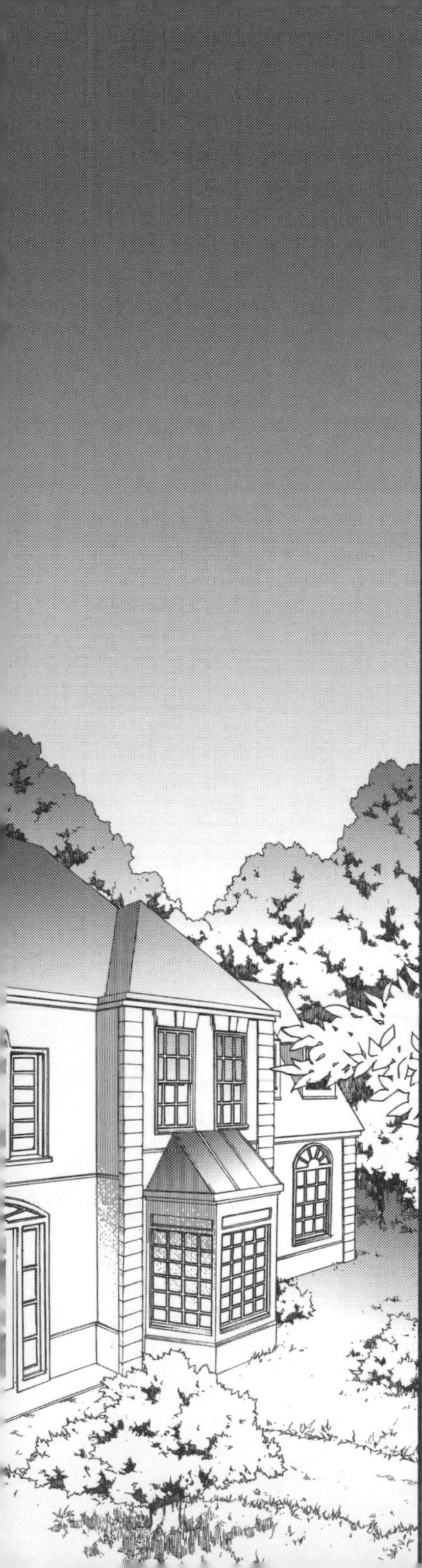

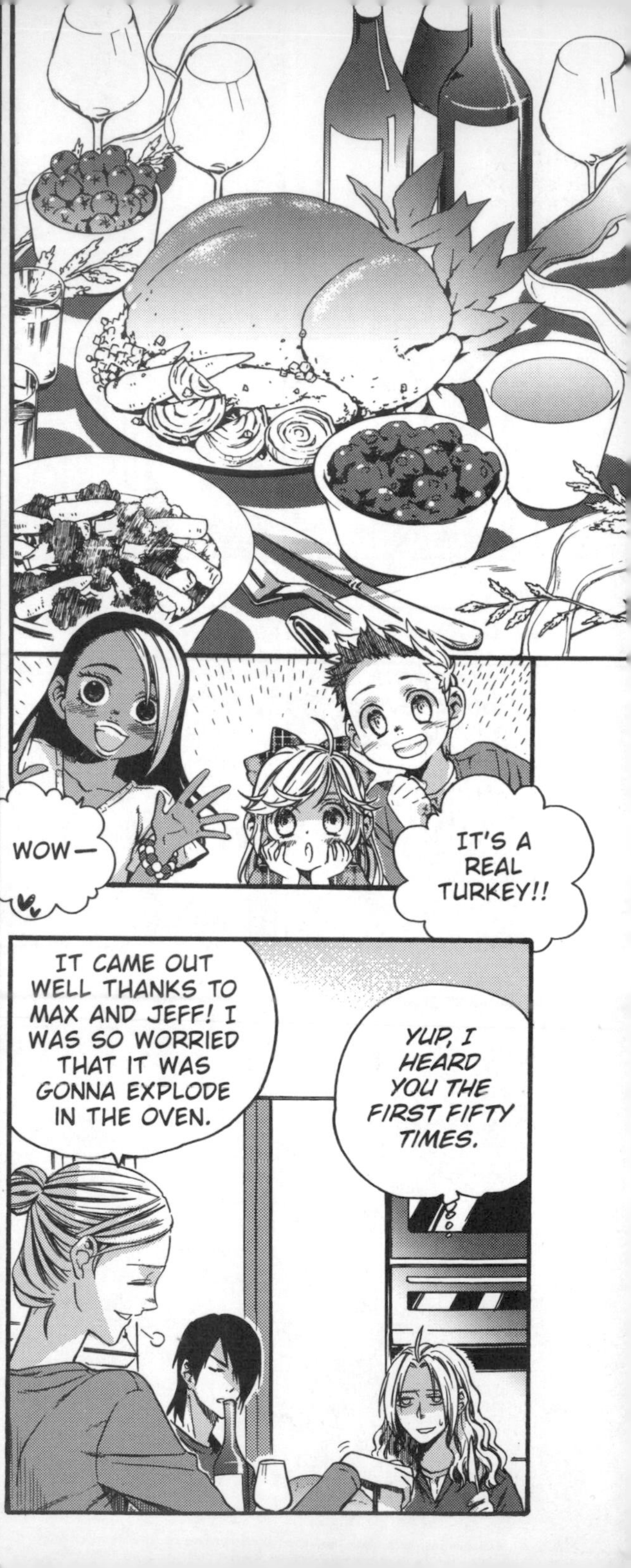
WOW—
IT'S A REAL TURKEY!!
IT CAME OUT WELL THANKS TO MAX AND JEFF! I WAS SO WORRIED THAT IT WAS GONNA EXPLODE IN THE OVEN.
YUP, I HEARD YOU THE FIRST FIFTY TIMES.

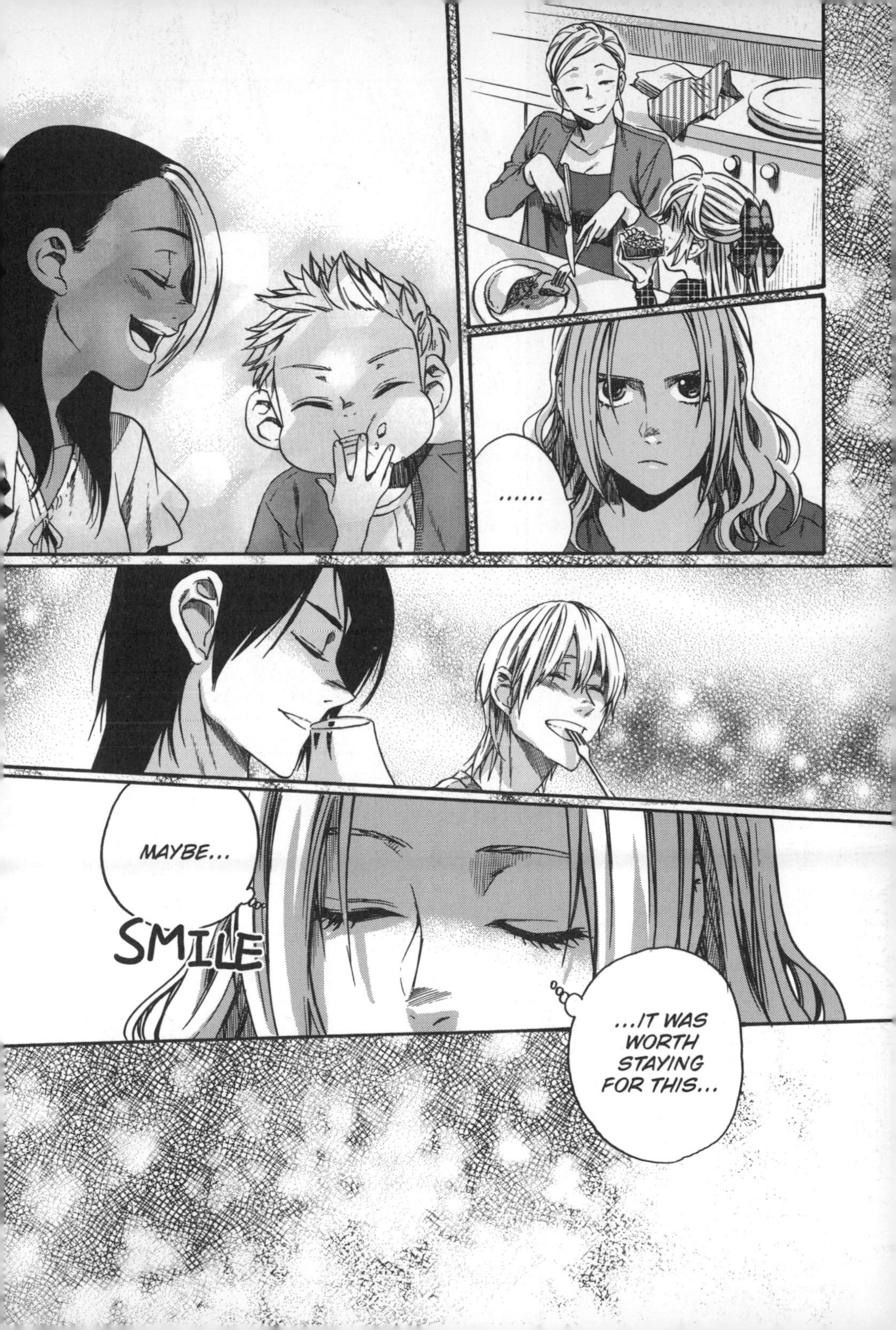
......
MAYBE...
SMILE
...IT WAS WORTH STAYING FOR THIS...

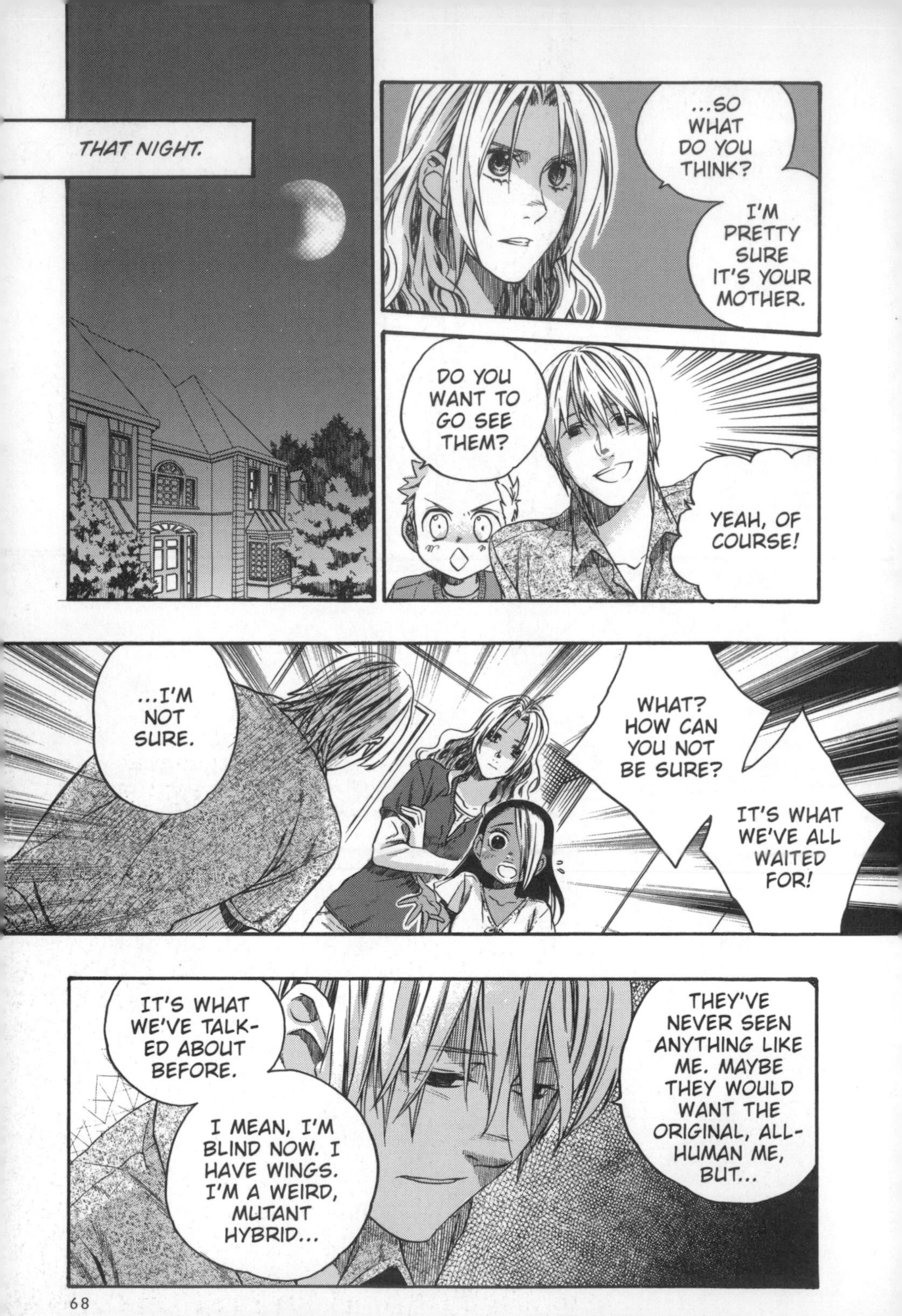
THAT NIGHT.
...SO WHAT DO YOU THINK?
I'M PRETTY SURE IT'S YOUR MOTHER.
DO YOU WANT TO GO SEE THEM?
YEAH, OF COURSE!
...I'M NOT SURE.
WHAT? HOW CAN YOU NOT BE SURE?
IT'S WHAT WE'VE ALL WAITED FOR!
IT'S WHAT WE'VE TALK-ED ABOUT BEFORE.
I MEAN, I'M BLIND NOW. I HAVE WINGS. I'M A WEIRD, MUTANT HYBRID...
THEY'VE NEVER SEEN ANYTHING LIKE ME. MAYBE THEY WOULD WANT THE ORIGINAL, ALL-HUMAN ME, BUT...

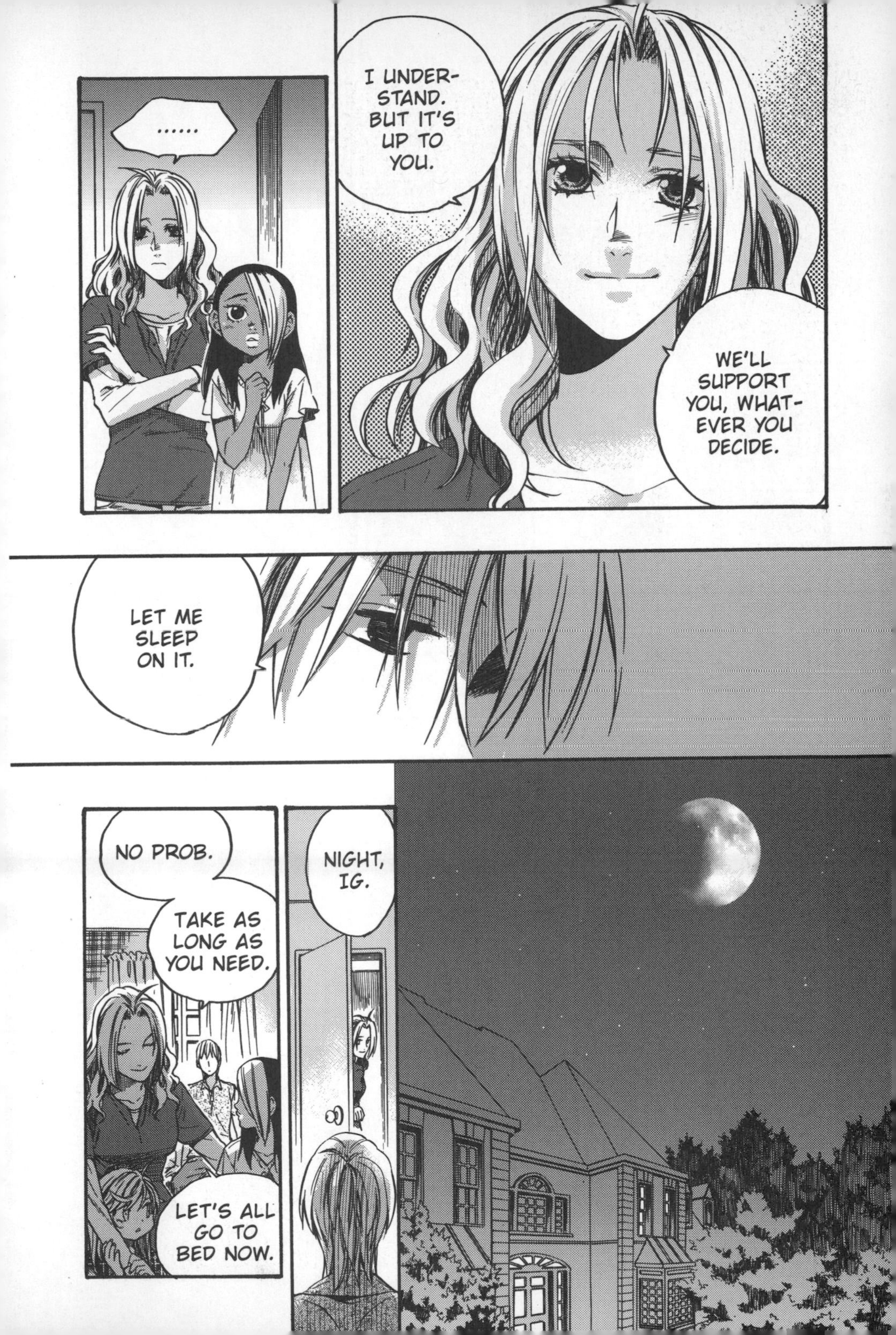
......
I UNDER-STAND. BUT IT'S UP TO YOU.
WE'LL SUPPORT YOU, WHAT-EVER YOU DECIDE.
LET ME SLEEP ON IT.
NO PROB.
TAKE AS LONG AS YOU NEED.
LET'S ALL GO TO BED NOW.
NIGHT, IG.

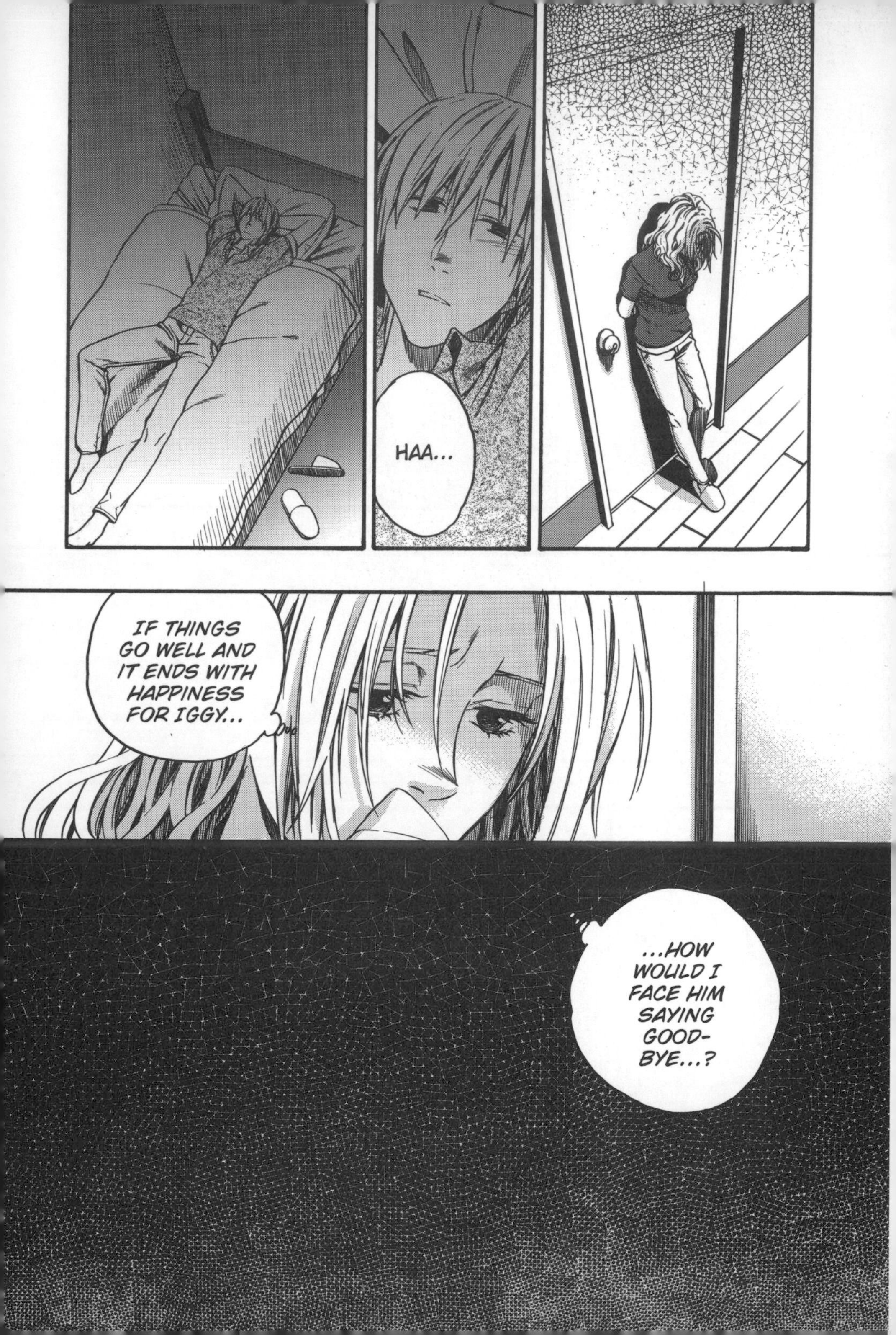
HAA...
IF THINGS GO WELL AND IT ENDS WITH HAPPINESS FOR IGGY...
...HOW WOULD I FACE HIM SAYING GOOD-BYE...?

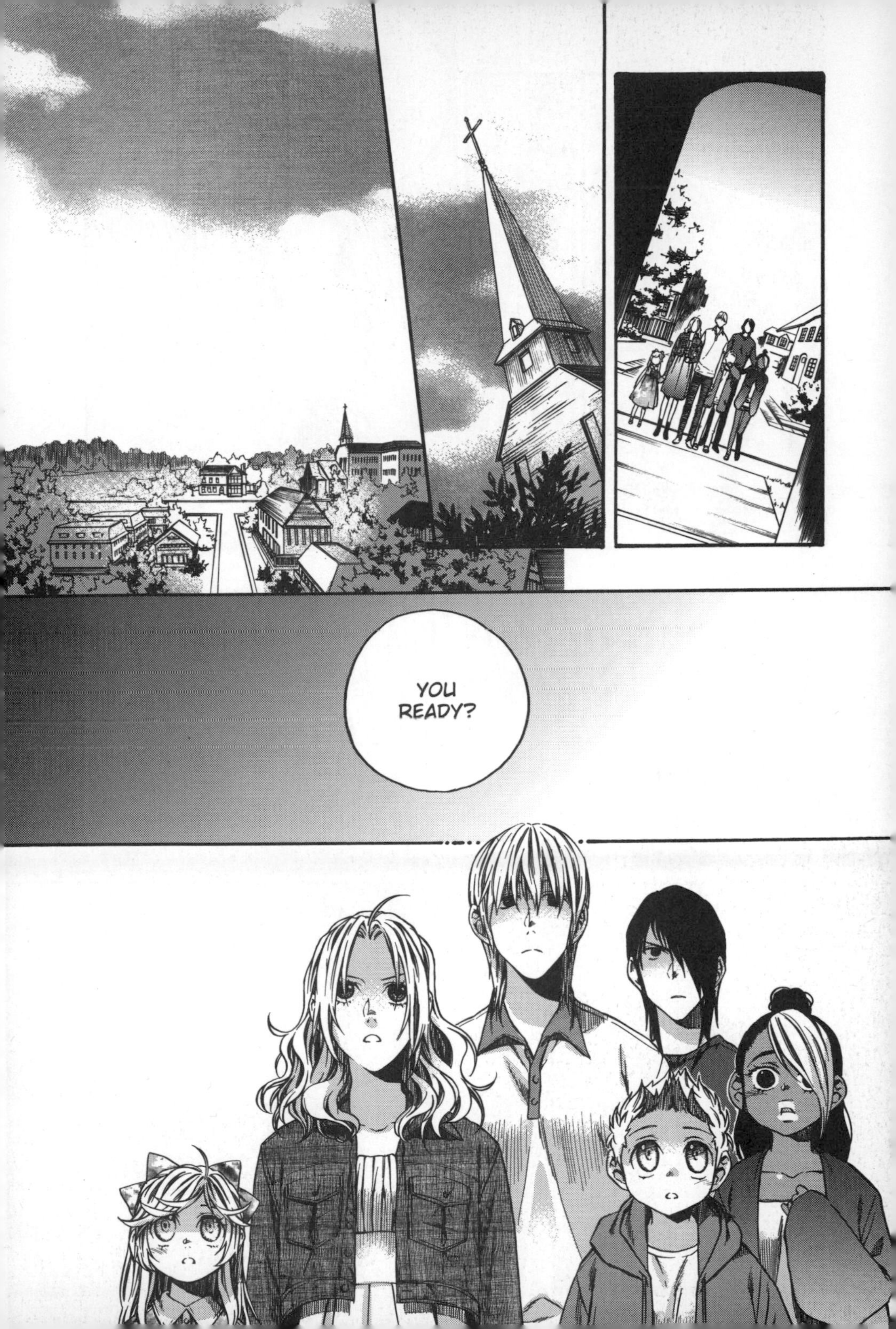
YOU READY?

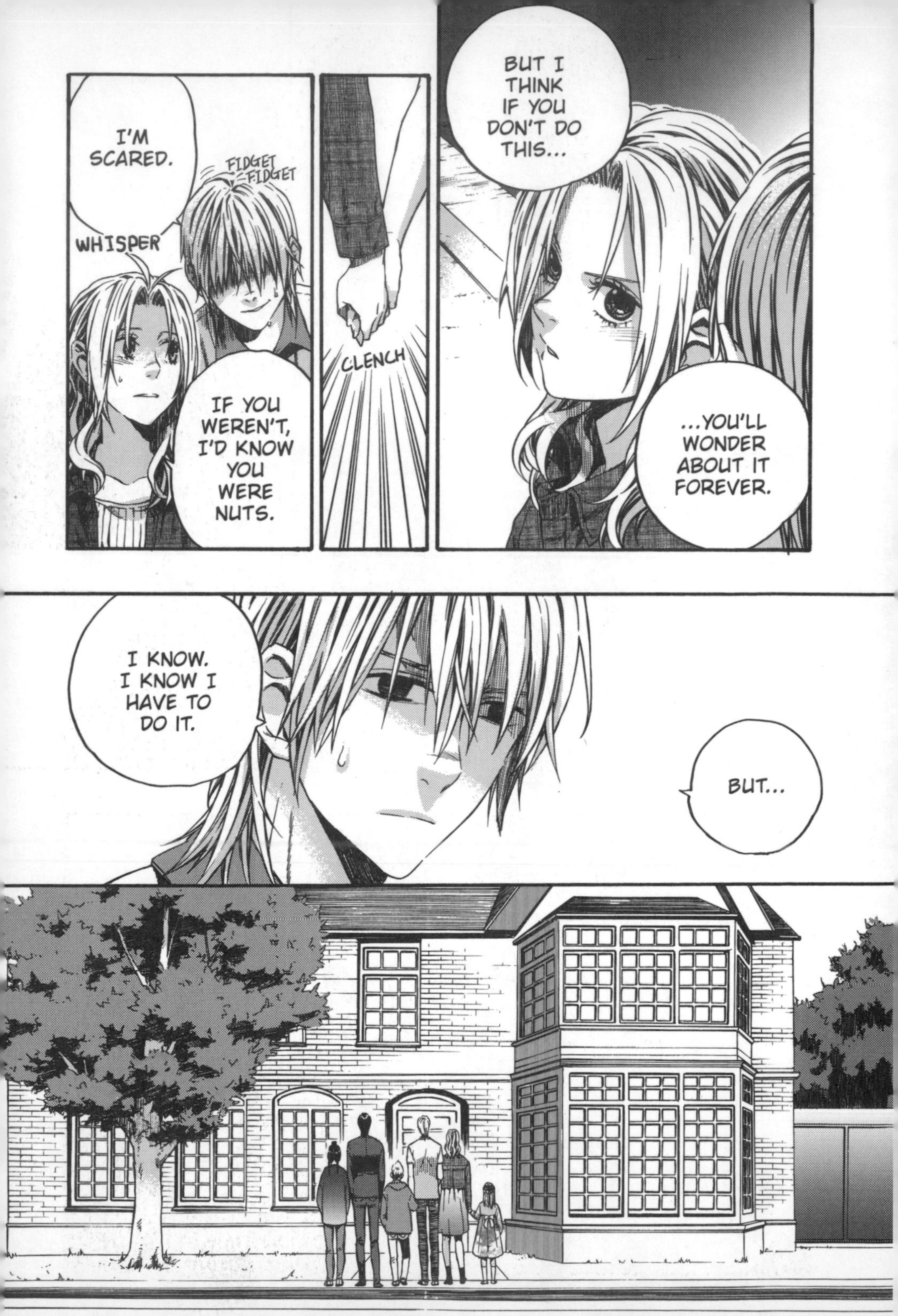
I'M SCARED.
WHISPER
FIDGET FIDGET
IF YOU WEREN'T, I'D KNOW YOU WERE NUTS.
CLENCH
BUT I THINK IF YOU DON'T DO THIS...
...YOU'LL WONDER ABOUT IT FOREVER.
I KNOW. I KNOW I HAVE TO DO IT.
BUT...

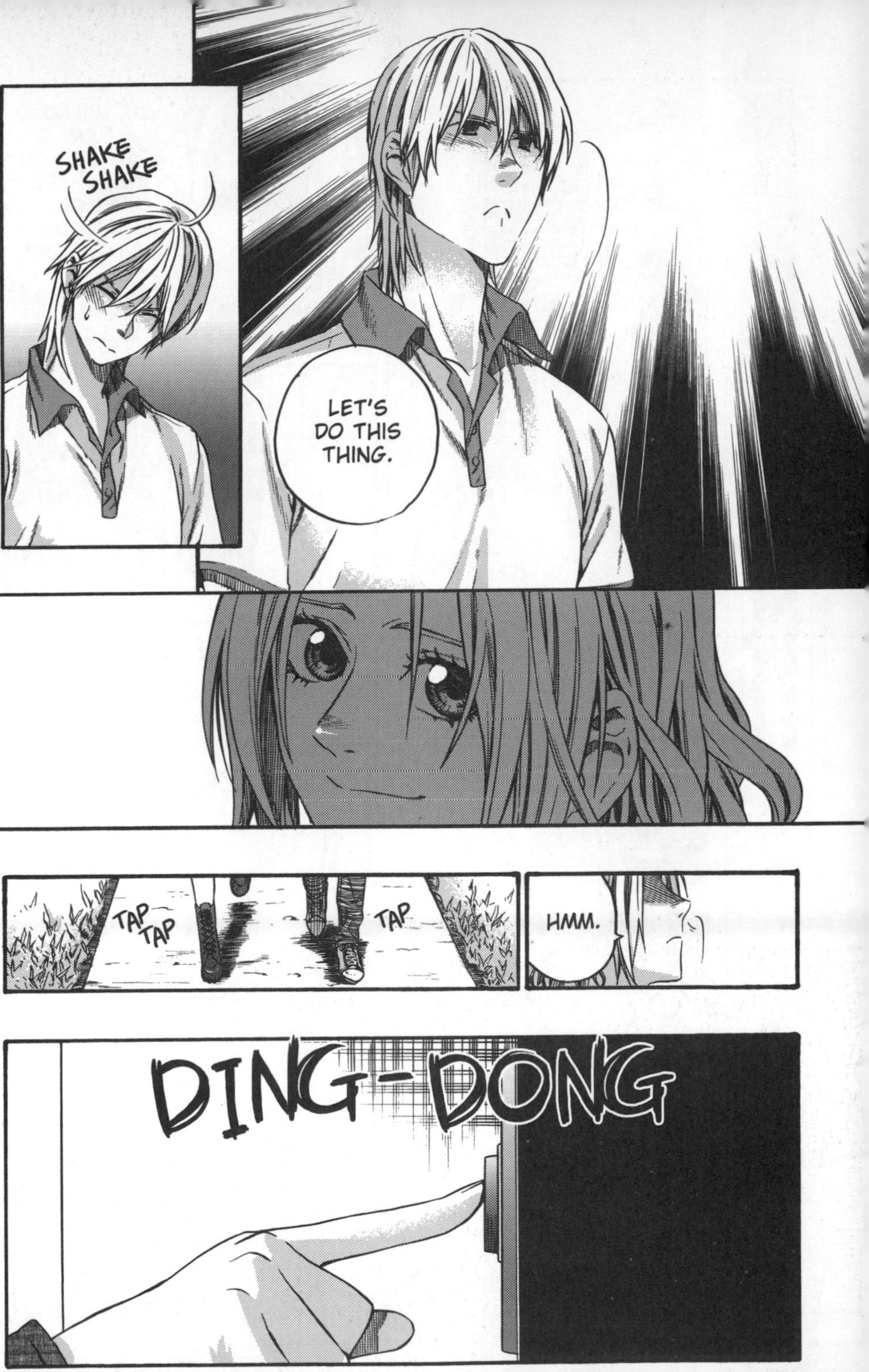
SHAKE SHAKE
LET'S DO THIS THING.
TAP TAP
TAP
HMM.
DING-DONG

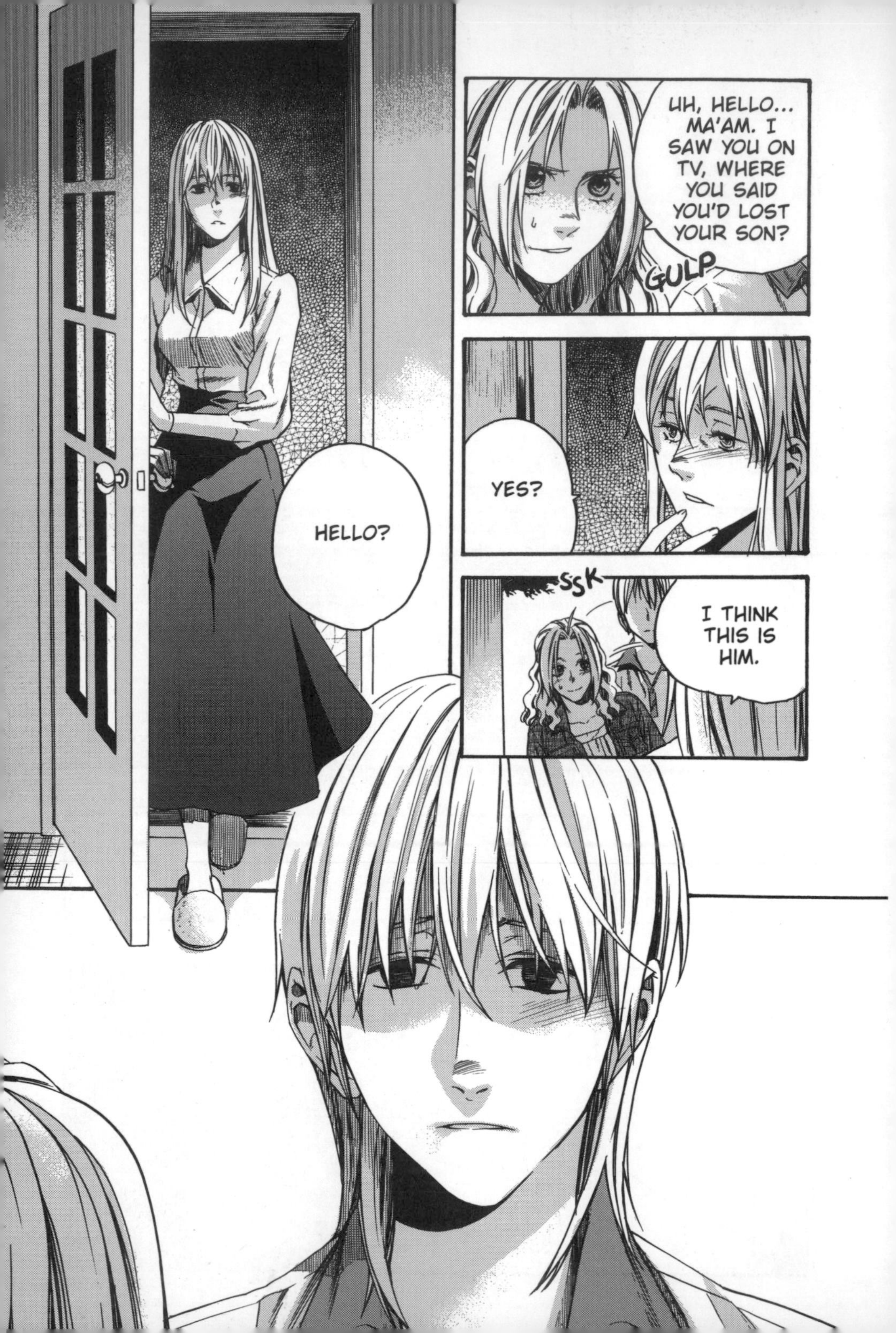
HELLO?
UH, HELLO... MA'AM. I SAW YOU ON TV, WHERE YOU SAID YOU'D LOST YOUR SON?
GULP
YES?
SSK
I THINK THIS IS HIM.

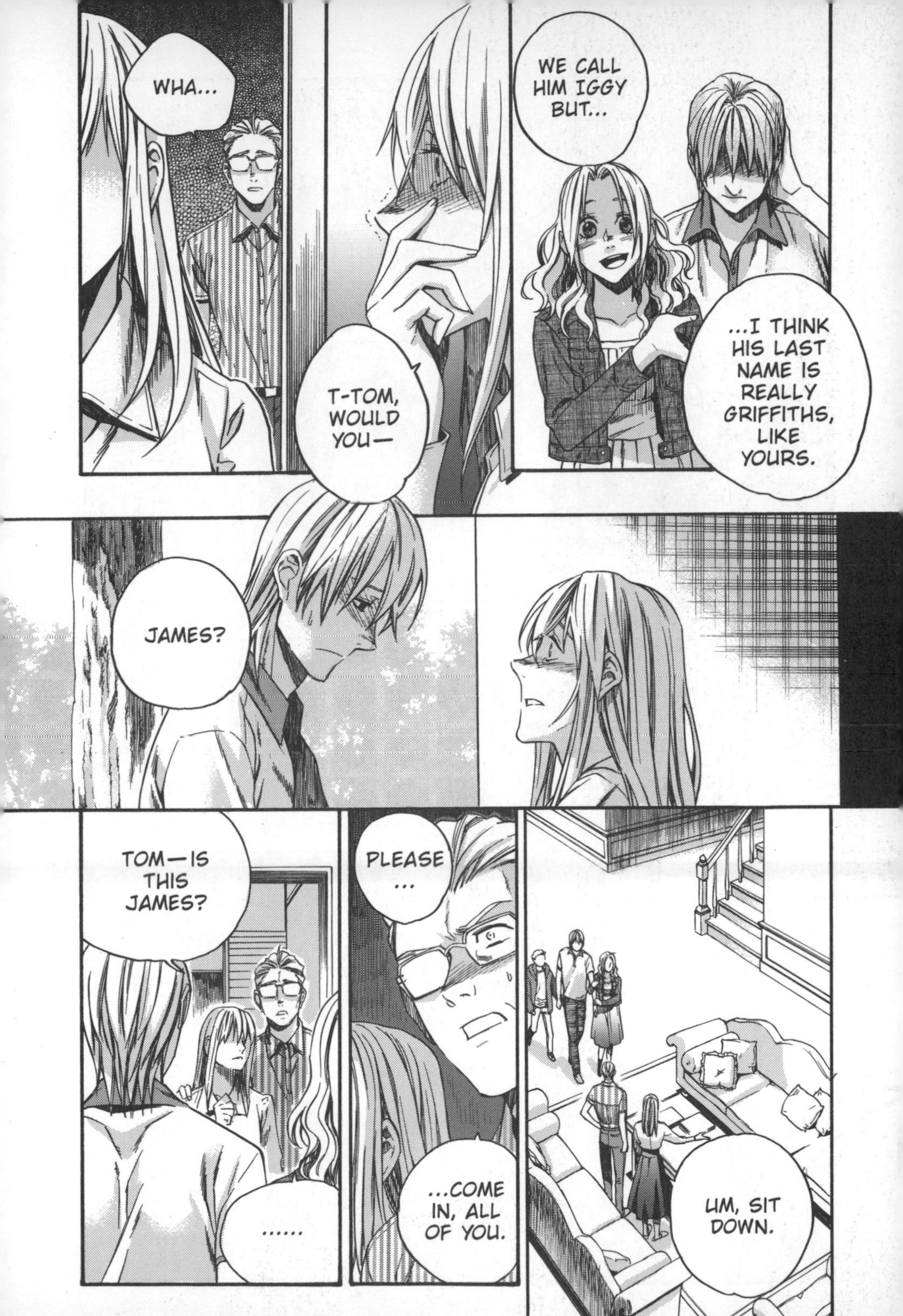
WHA...
T-TOM, WOULD YOU—
WE CALL HIM IGGY BUT...
...I THINK HIS LAST NAME IS REALLY GRIFFITHS, LIKE YOURS.
JAMES?
TOM—IS THIS JAMES?
......
PLEASE ...
...COME IN, ALL OF YOU.
UM, SIT DOWN.

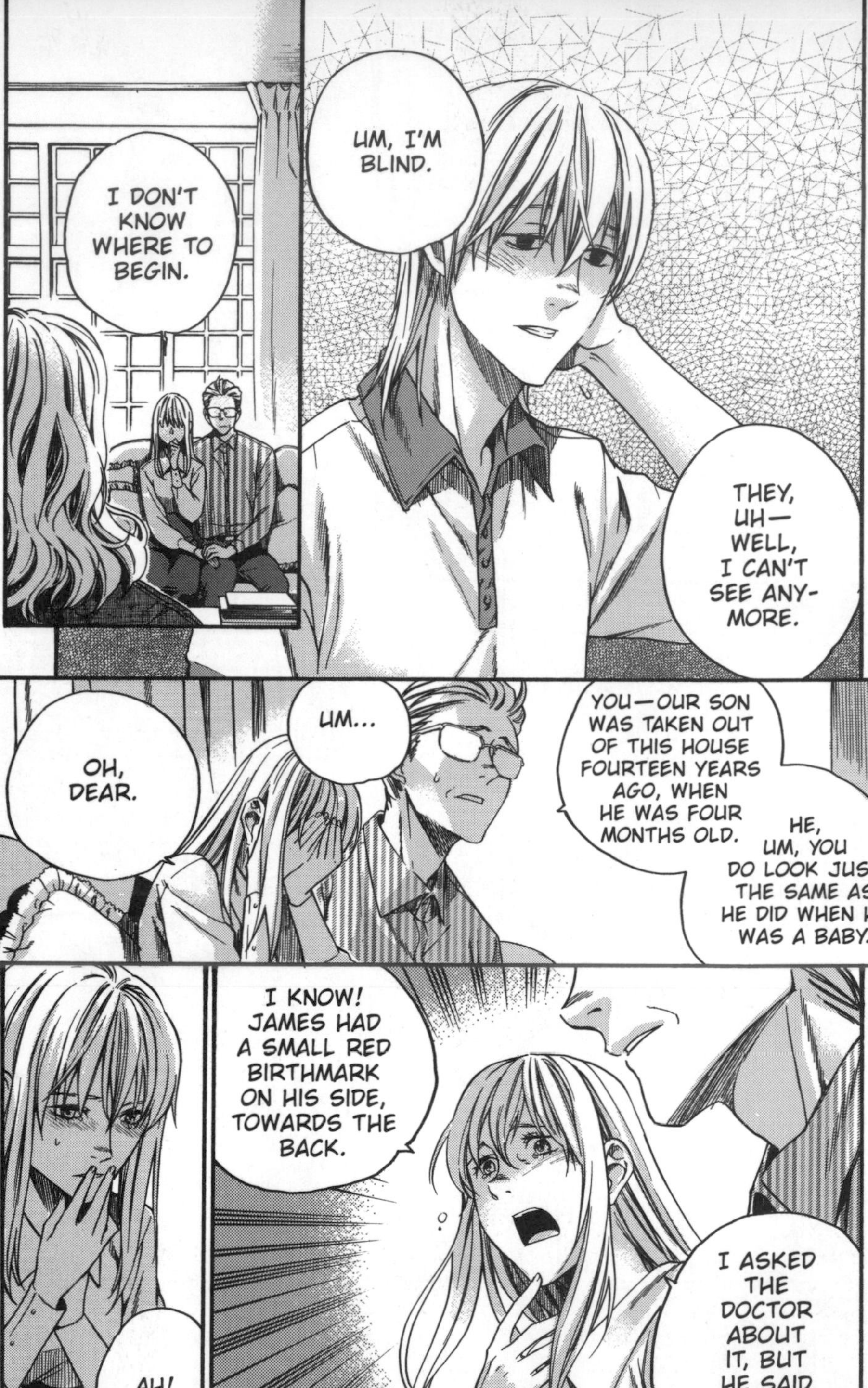
I DON'T KNOW WHERE TO BEGIN.
UM, I'M BLIND.
THEY, UH— WELL, I CAN'T SEE ANY-MORE.
OH, DEAR.
UM...
YOU—OUR SON WAS TAKEN OUT OF THIS HOUSE FOURTEEN YEARS AGO, WHEN HE WAS FOUR MONTHS OLD.
HE, UM, YOU DO LOOK JUST THE SAME AS HE DID WHEN HE WAS A BABY.
AH!
I KNOW! JAMES HAD A SMALL RED BIRTHMARK ON HIS SIDE, TOWARDS THE BACK.
I ASKED THE DOCTOR ABOUT IT, BUT HE SAID IT WAS FINE.

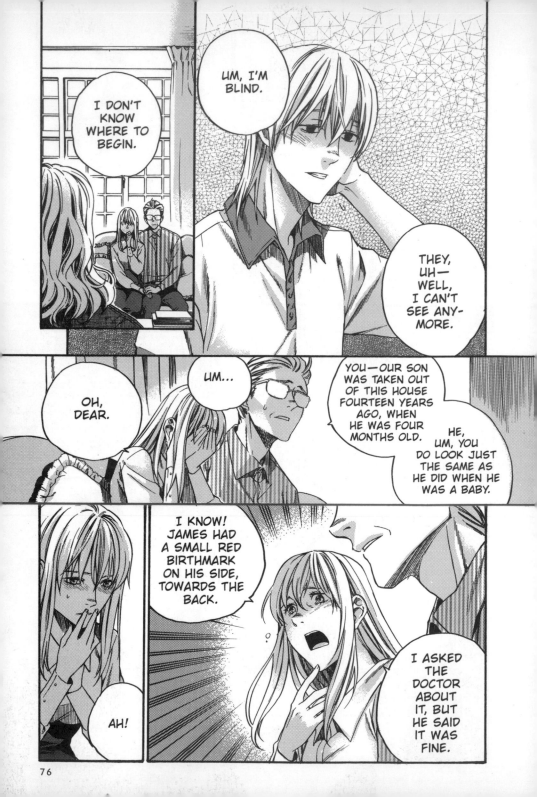

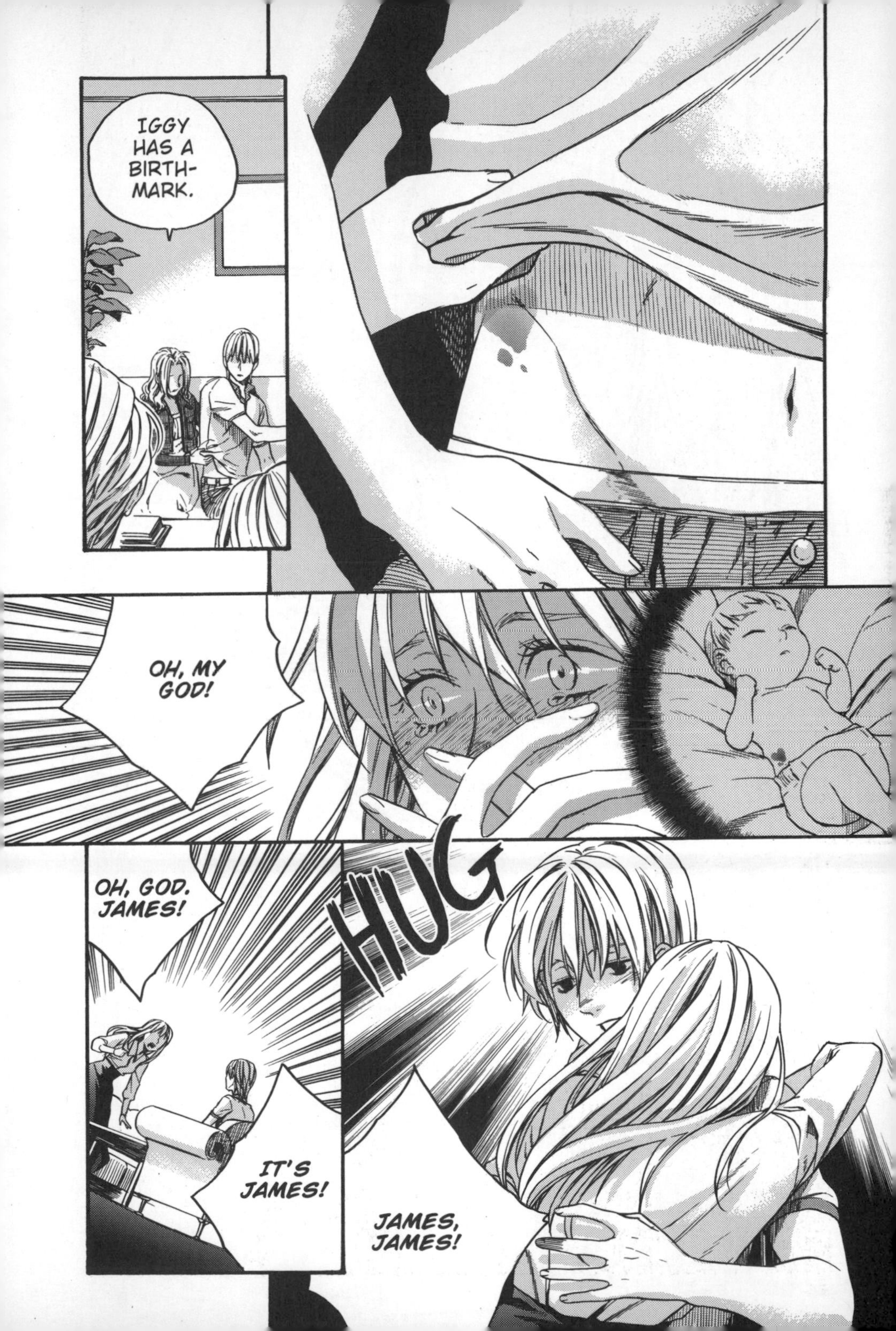
IGGY HAS A BIRTH-MARK.
OH, MY GOD!
OH, GOD. JAMES!
HUG
IT'S JAMES!
JAMES, JAMES!

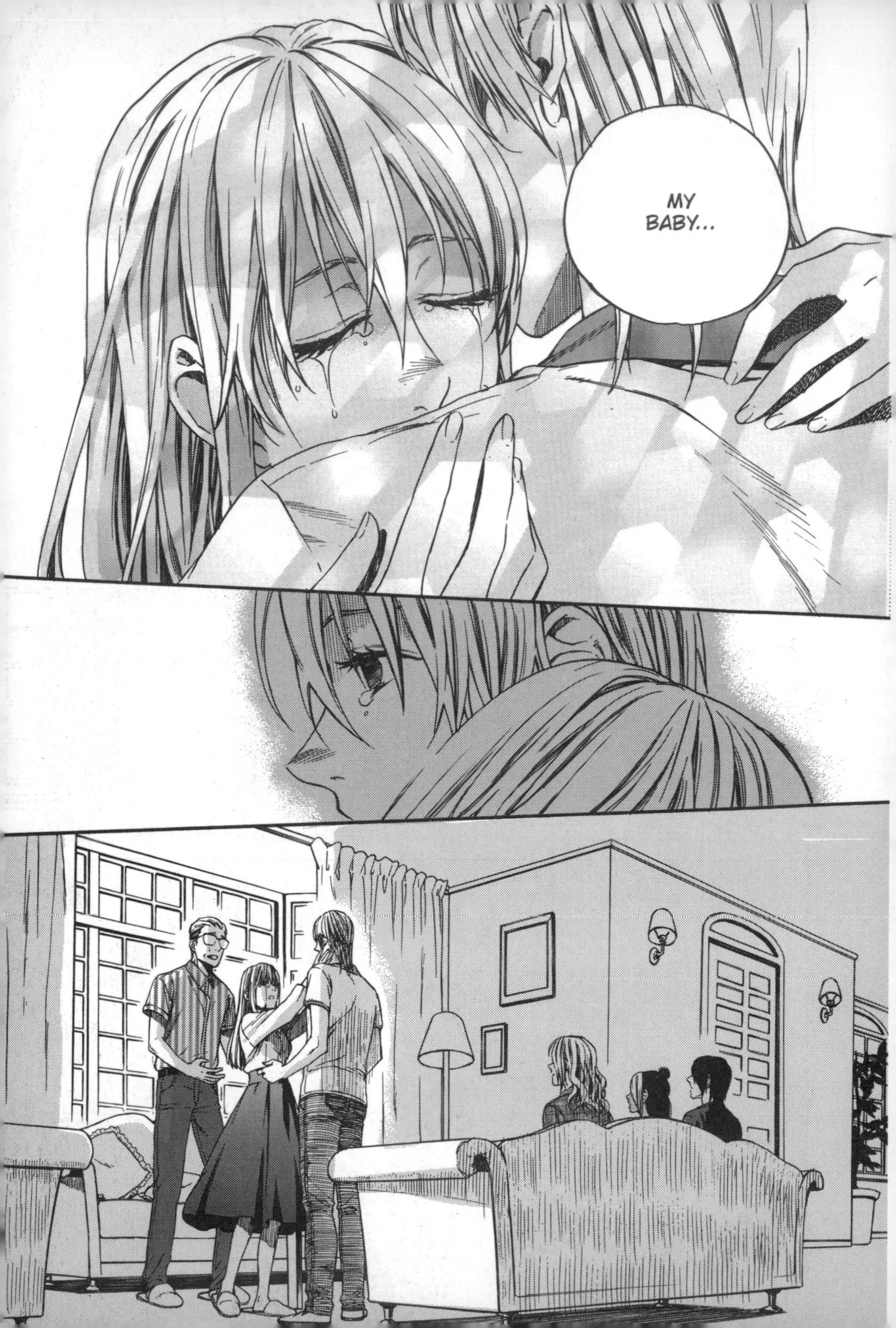
MY BABY...

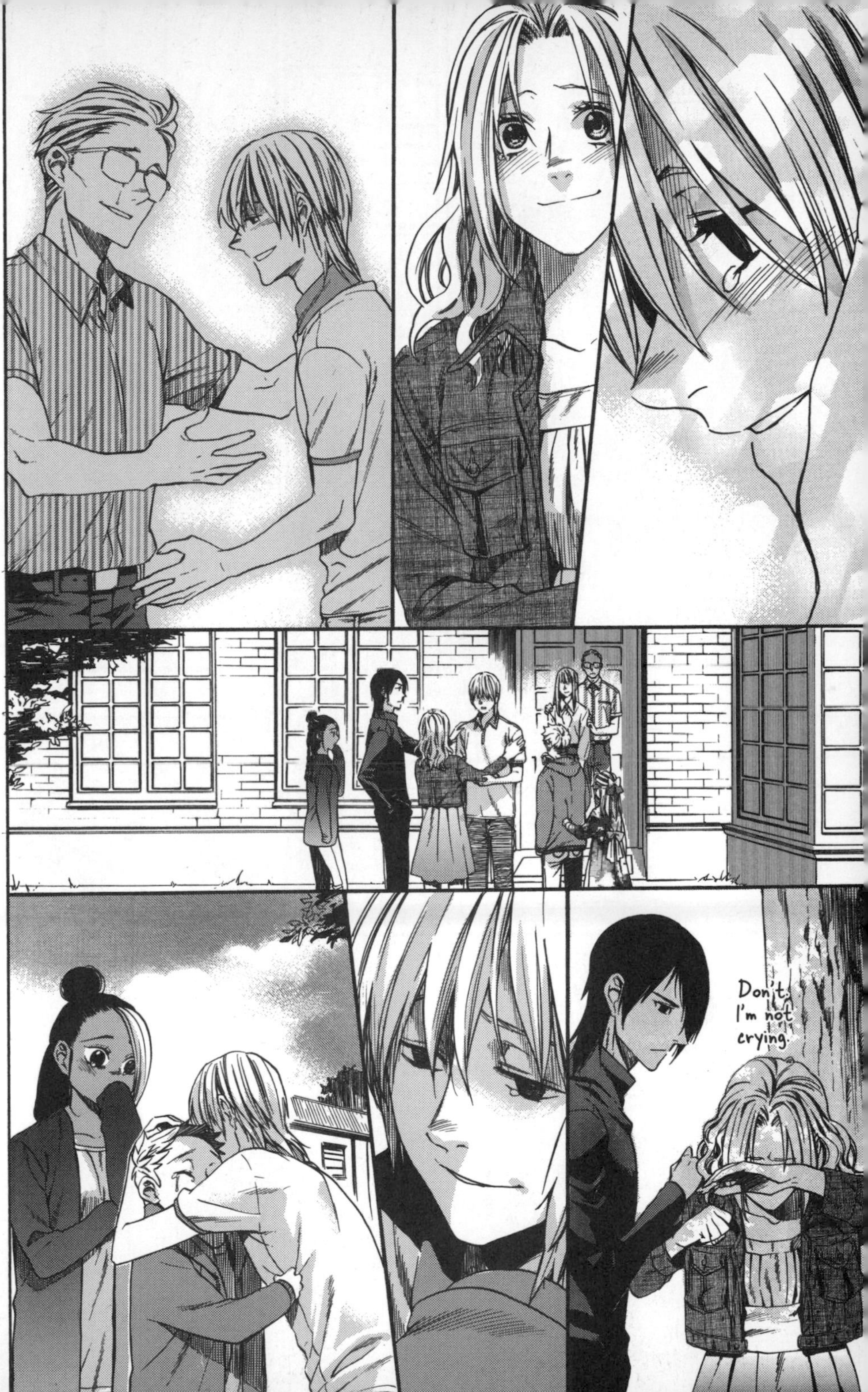
Don't. I'm not crying.

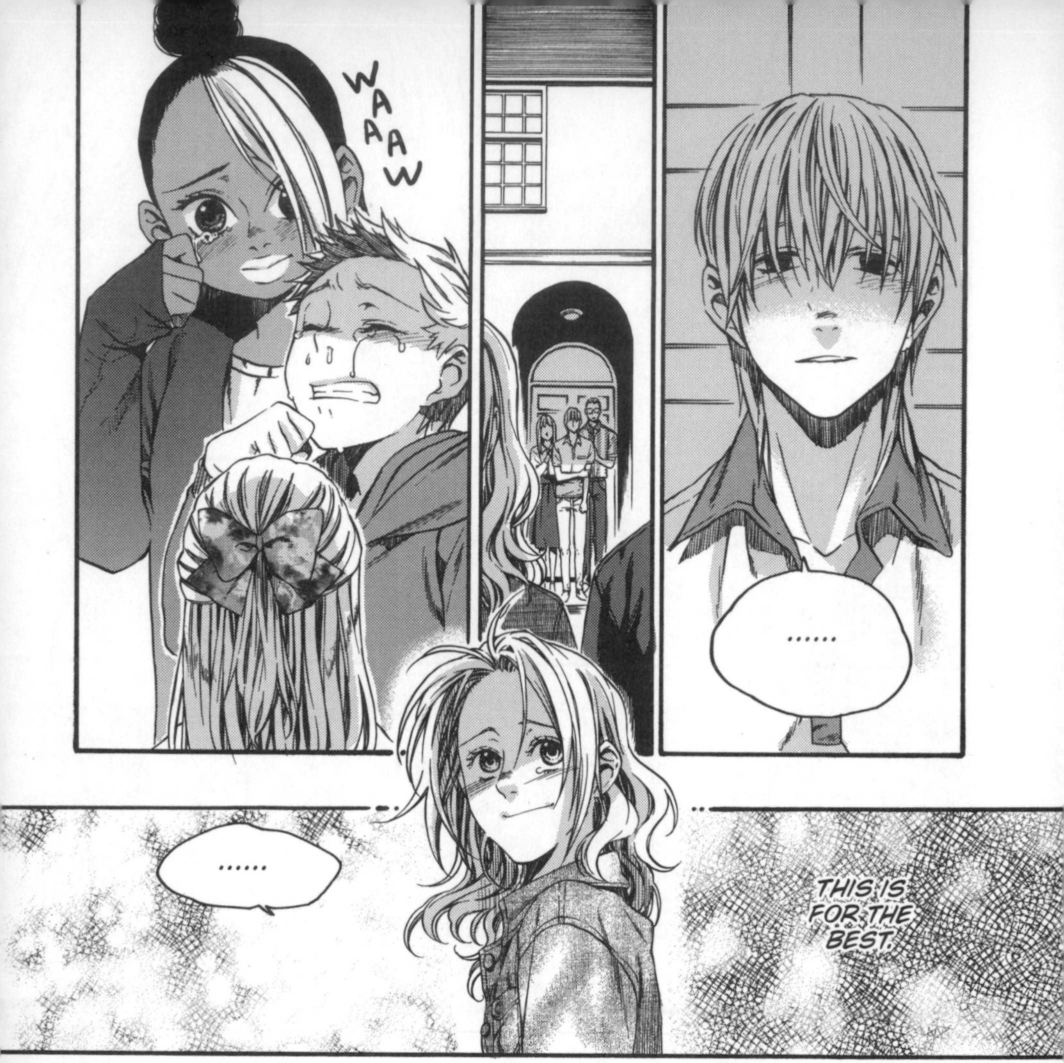
WAAAW
......
......
THIS IS FOR THE BEST.

GOOD-
BYE,
IGGY.

MAXIMUM
RIDE

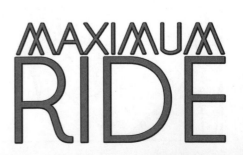

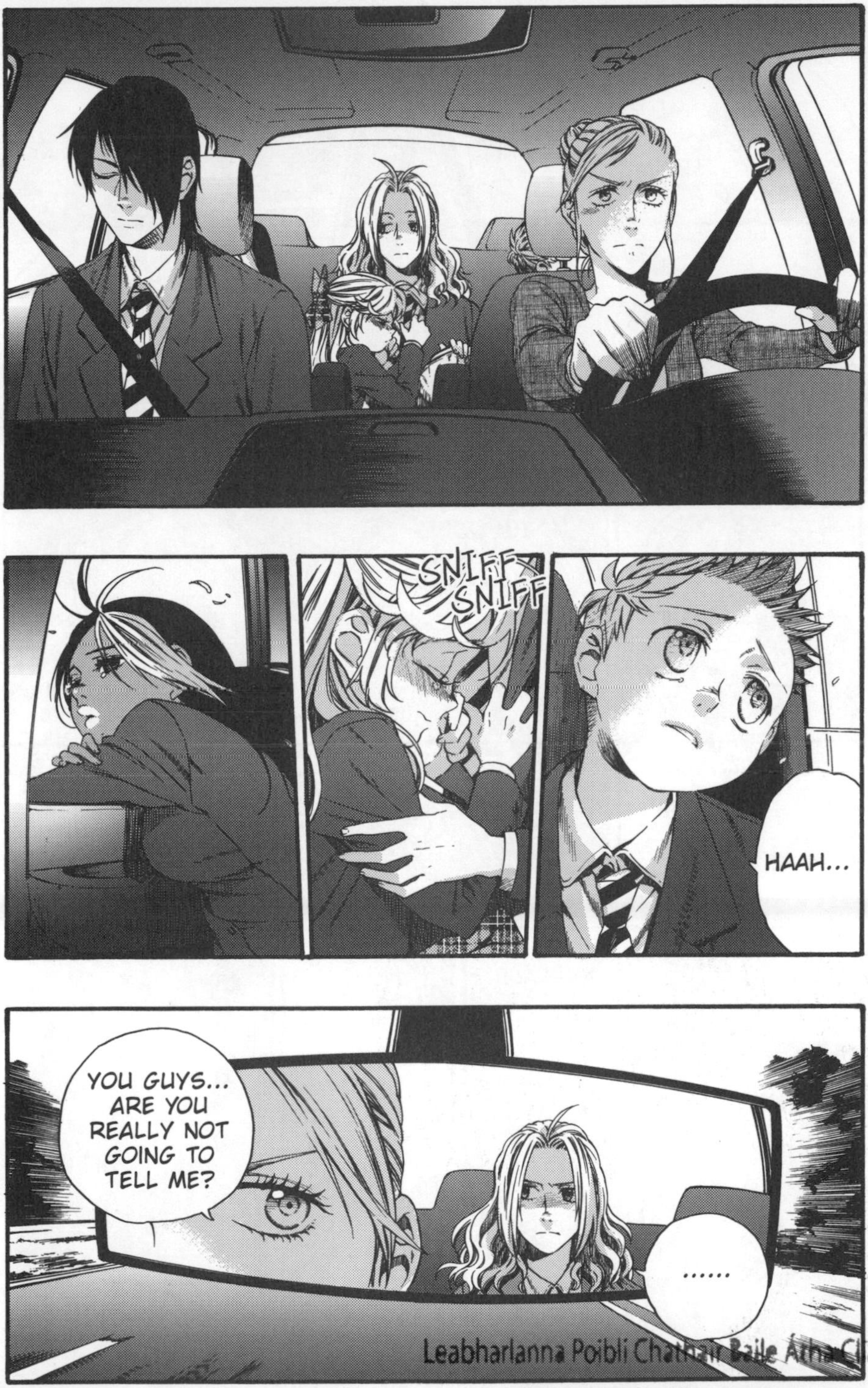
SNIFF SNIFF
HAAH...
YOU GUYS... ARE YOU REALLY NOT GOING TO TELL ME?
......

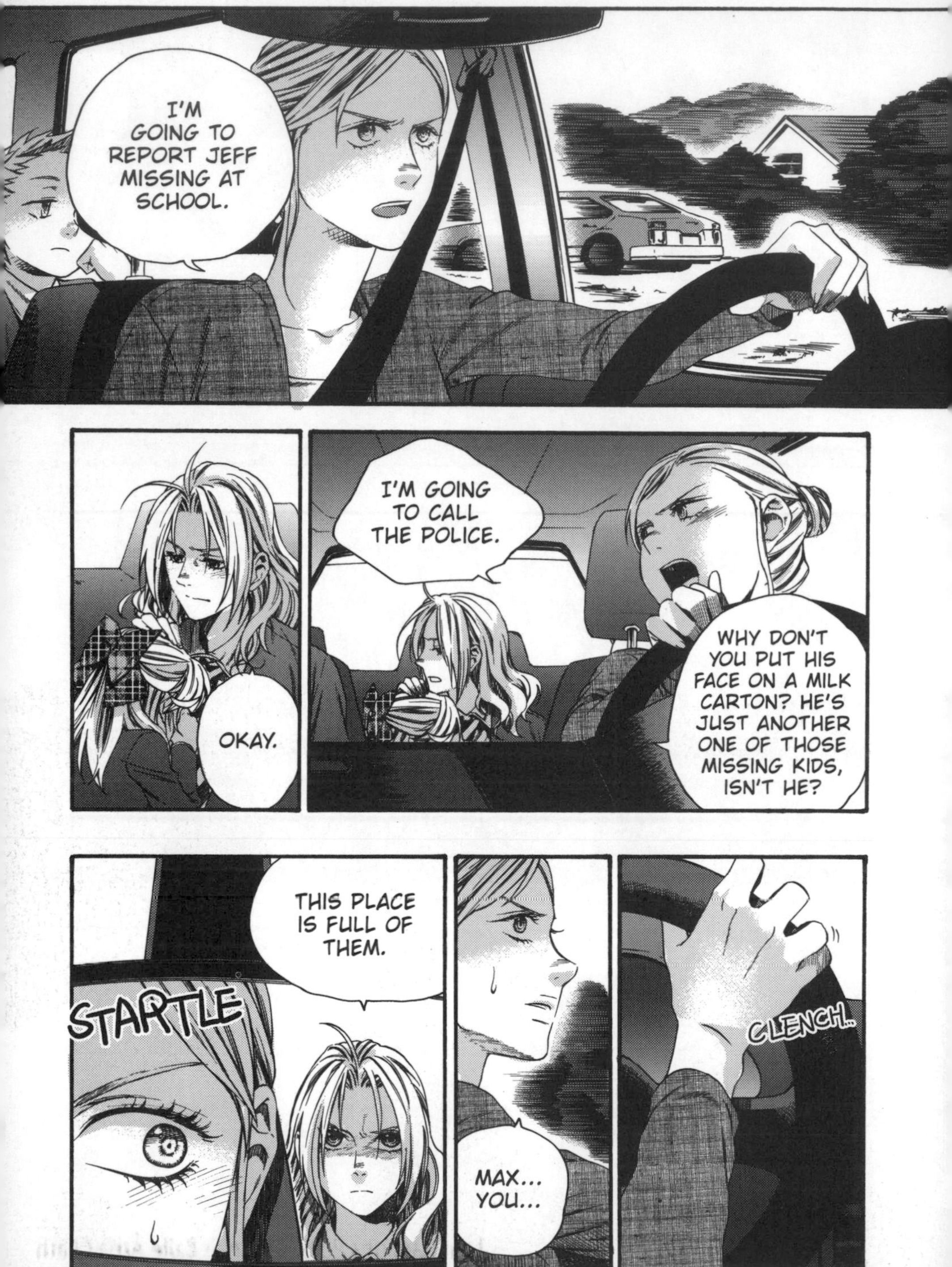
I'M GOING TO REPORT JEFF MISSING AT SCHOOL.
OKAY.
I'M GOING TO CALL THE POLICE.
WHY DON'T YOU PUT HIS FACE ON A MILK CARTON? HE'S JUST ANOTHER ONE OF THOSE MISSING KIDS, ISN'T HE?
STARTLE
THIS PLACE IS FULL OF THEM.
MAX... YOU...
CLENCH...

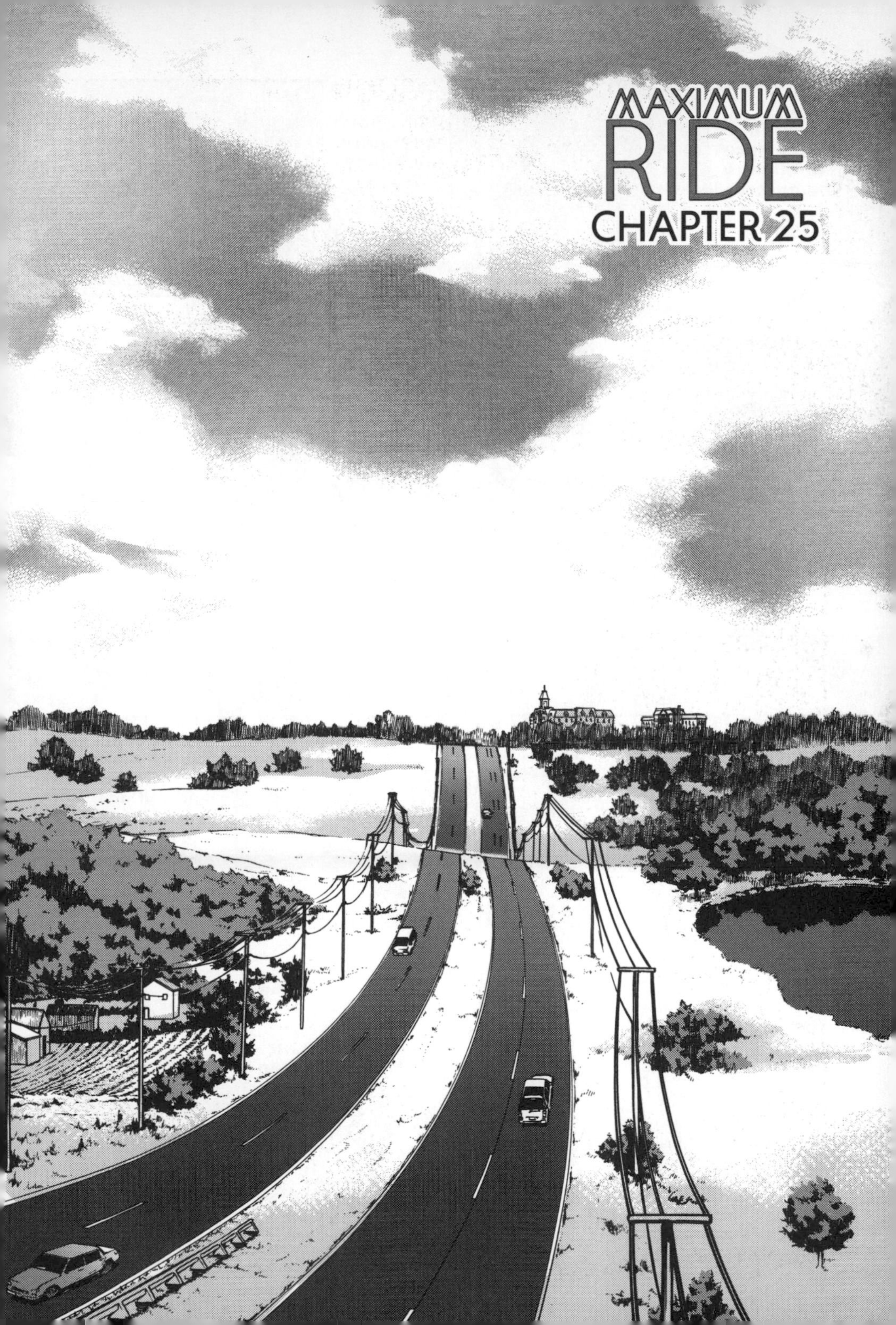
MAXIMUM RIDE
CHAPTER 25

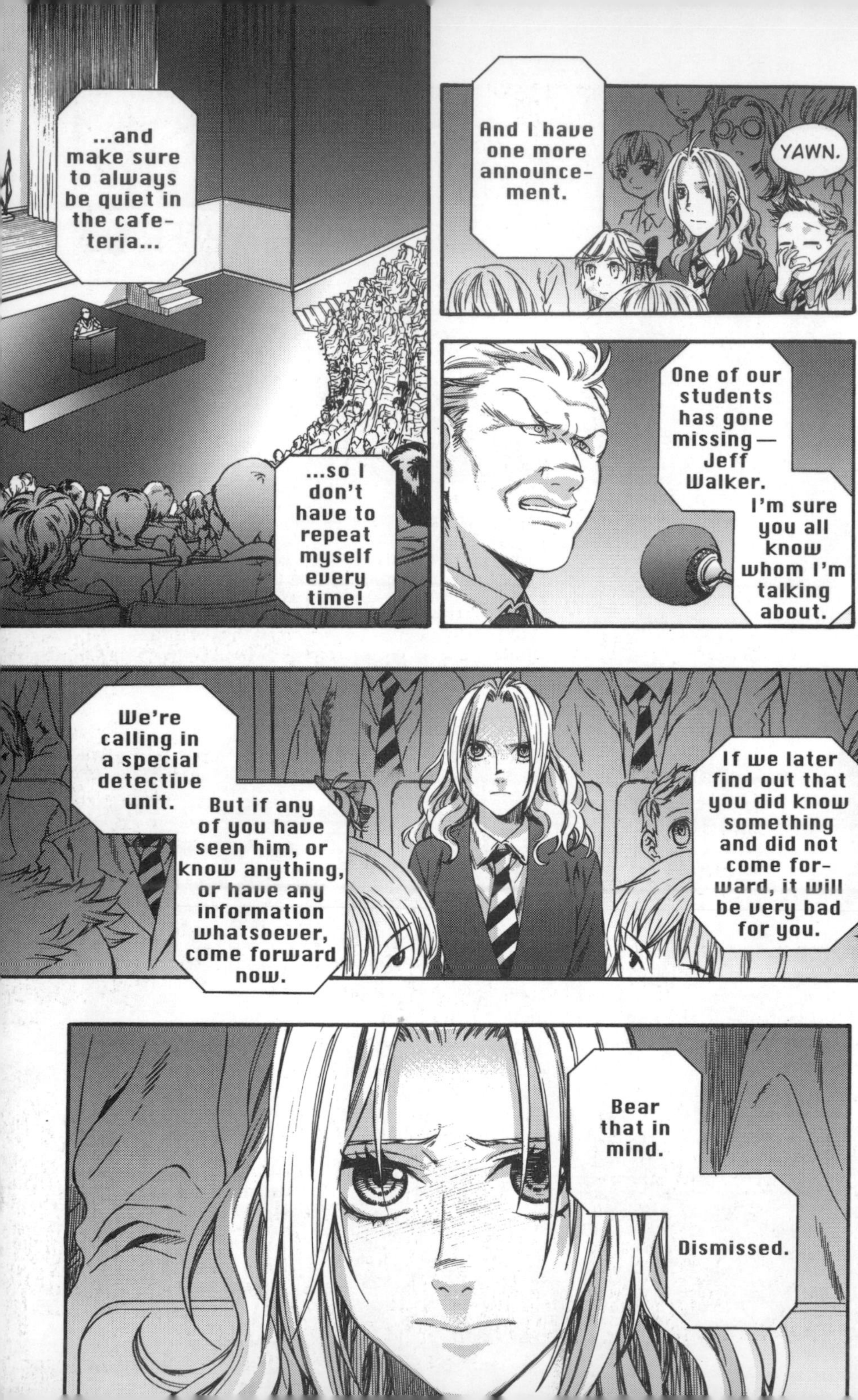
...and make sure to always be quiet in the cafe-teria...
...so I don't have to repeat myself every time!
And I have one more announce-ment.
YAWN.
One of our students has gone missing—Jeff Walker.
I'm sure you all know whom I'm talking about.
We're calling in a special detective unit.
But if any of you have seen him, or know anything, or have any information whatsoever, come forward now.
If we later find out that you did know something and did not come for-ward, it will be very bad for you.
Bear that in mind.
Dismissed.

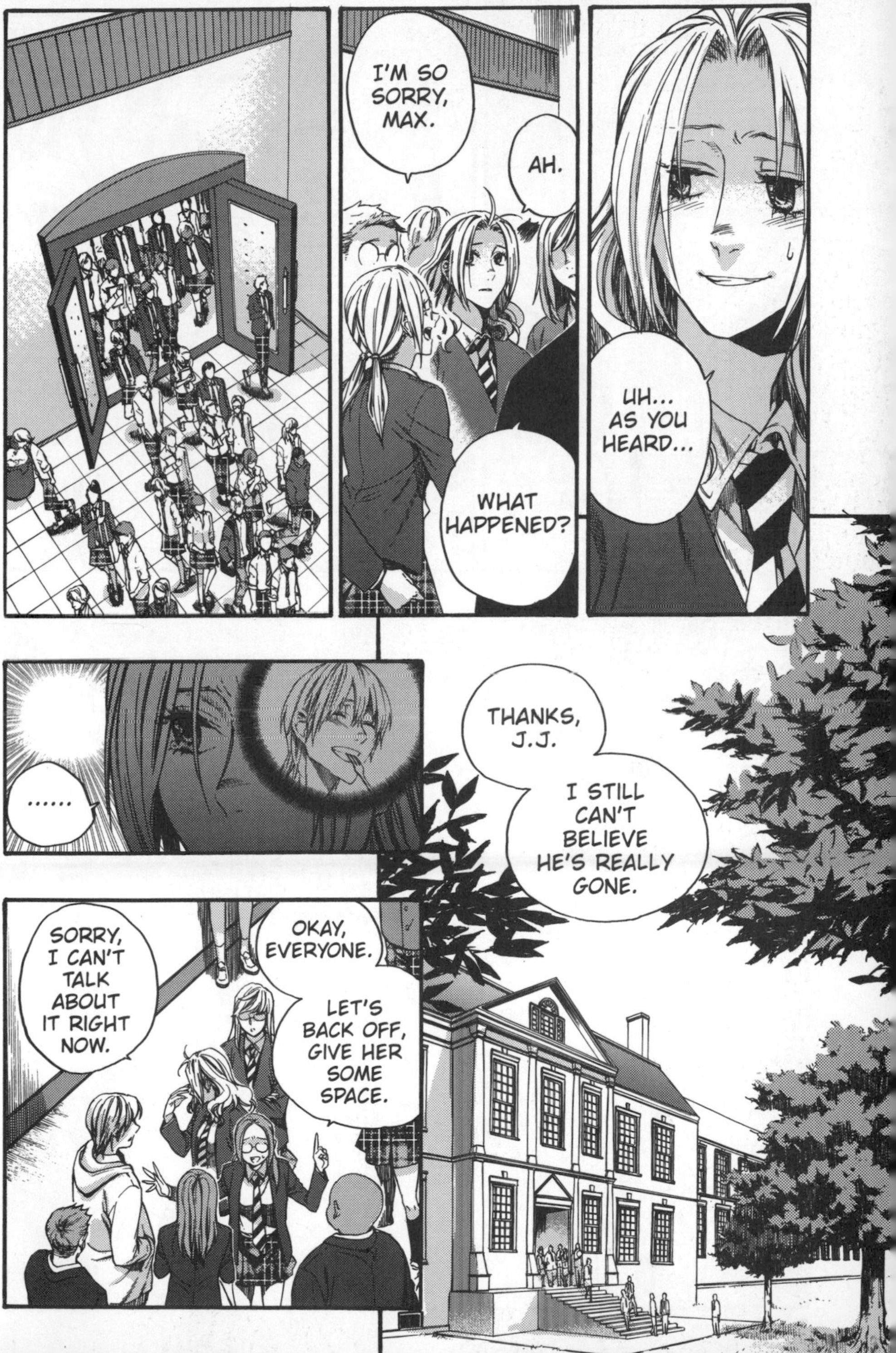
I'M SO SORRY, MAX.
AH.
WHAT HAPPENED?
UH... AS YOU HEARD...
......
SORRY, I CAN'T TALK ABOUT IT RIGHT NOW.
OKAY, EVERYONE.
LET'S BACK OFF, GIVE HER SOME SPACE.
THANKS, J.J.
I STILL CAN'T BELIEVE HE'S REALLY GONE.

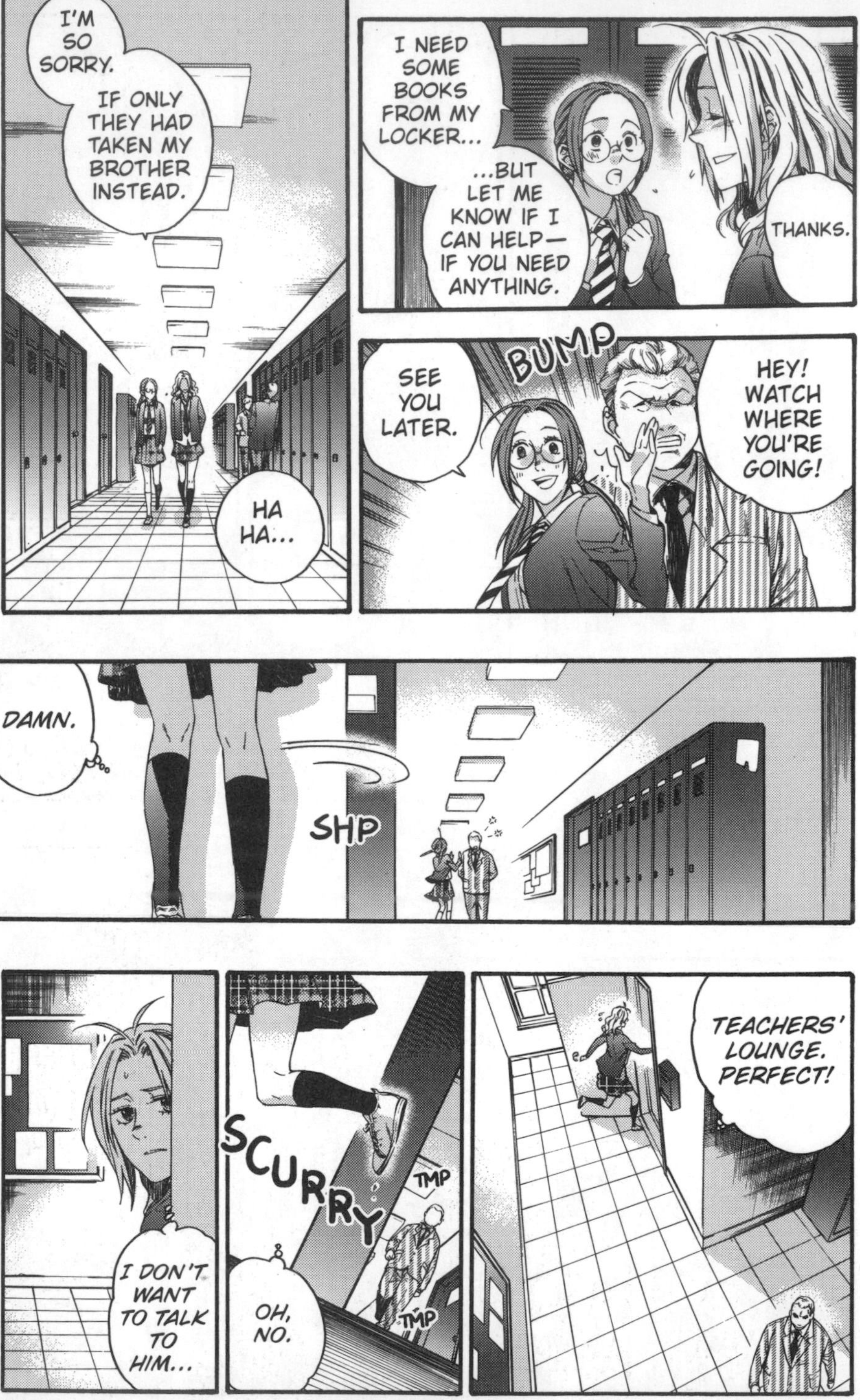
I'M SO SORRY.
IF ONLY THEY HAD TAKEN MY BROTHER INSTEAD.
HA HA...
I NEED SOME BOOKS FROM MY LOCKER...
...BUT LET ME KNOW IF I CAN HELP— IF YOU NEED ANYTHING.
THANKS.
SEE YOU LATER.
BUMP
HEY! WATCH WHERE YOU'RE GOING!
DAMN.
SHP
I DON'T WANT TO TALK TO HIM...
SCURRY
TMP
TMP
OH, NO.
TEACHERS' LOUNGE. PERFECT!

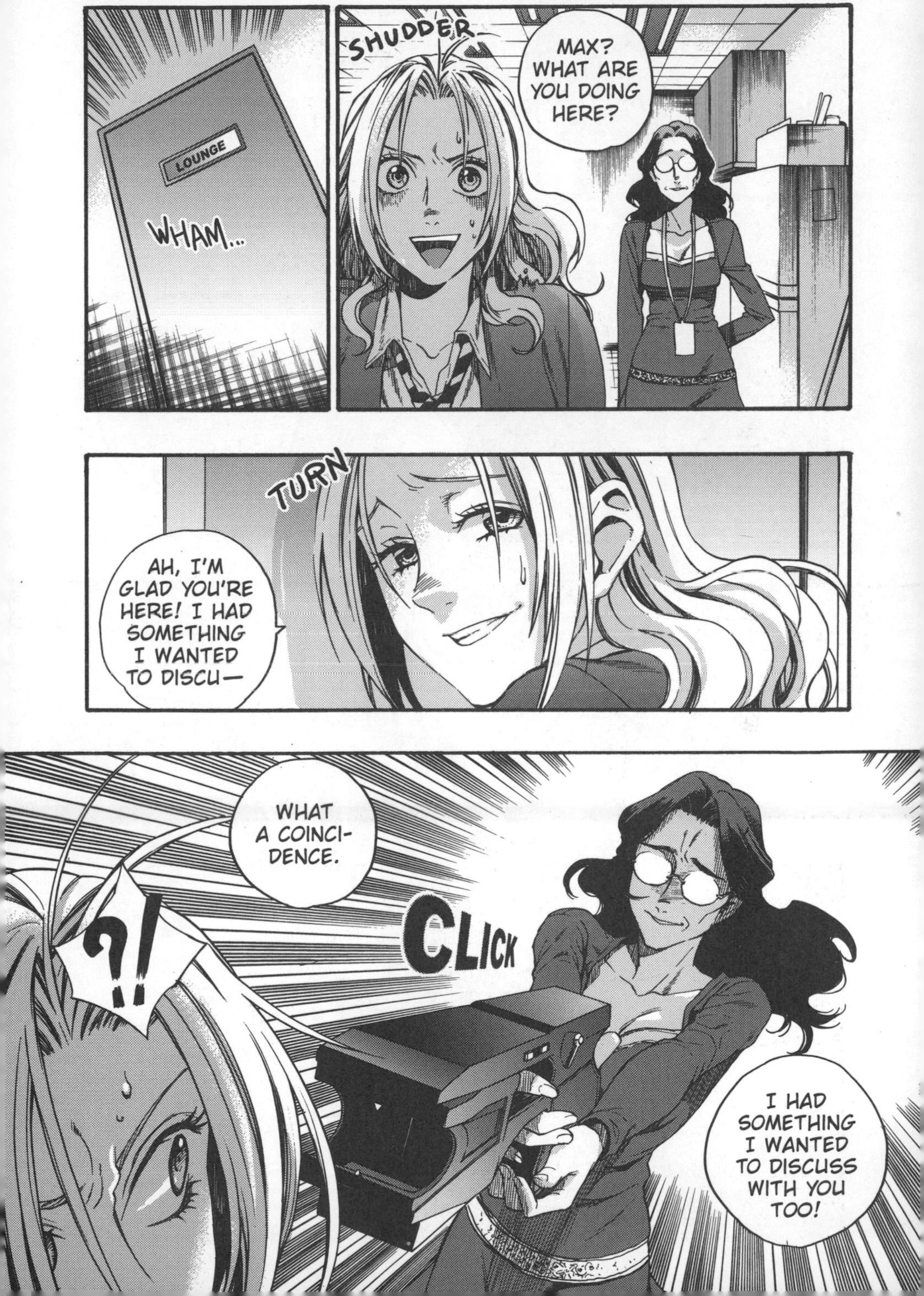
LOUNGE
WHAM...
SHUDDER
MAX? WHAT ARE YOU DOING HERE?
TURN
AH, I'M GLAD YOU'RE HERE! I HAD SOMETHING I WANTED TO DISCU—
WHAT A COINCI-DENCE.
?!
CLICK
I HAD SOMETHING I WANTED TO DISCUSS WITH YOU TOO!

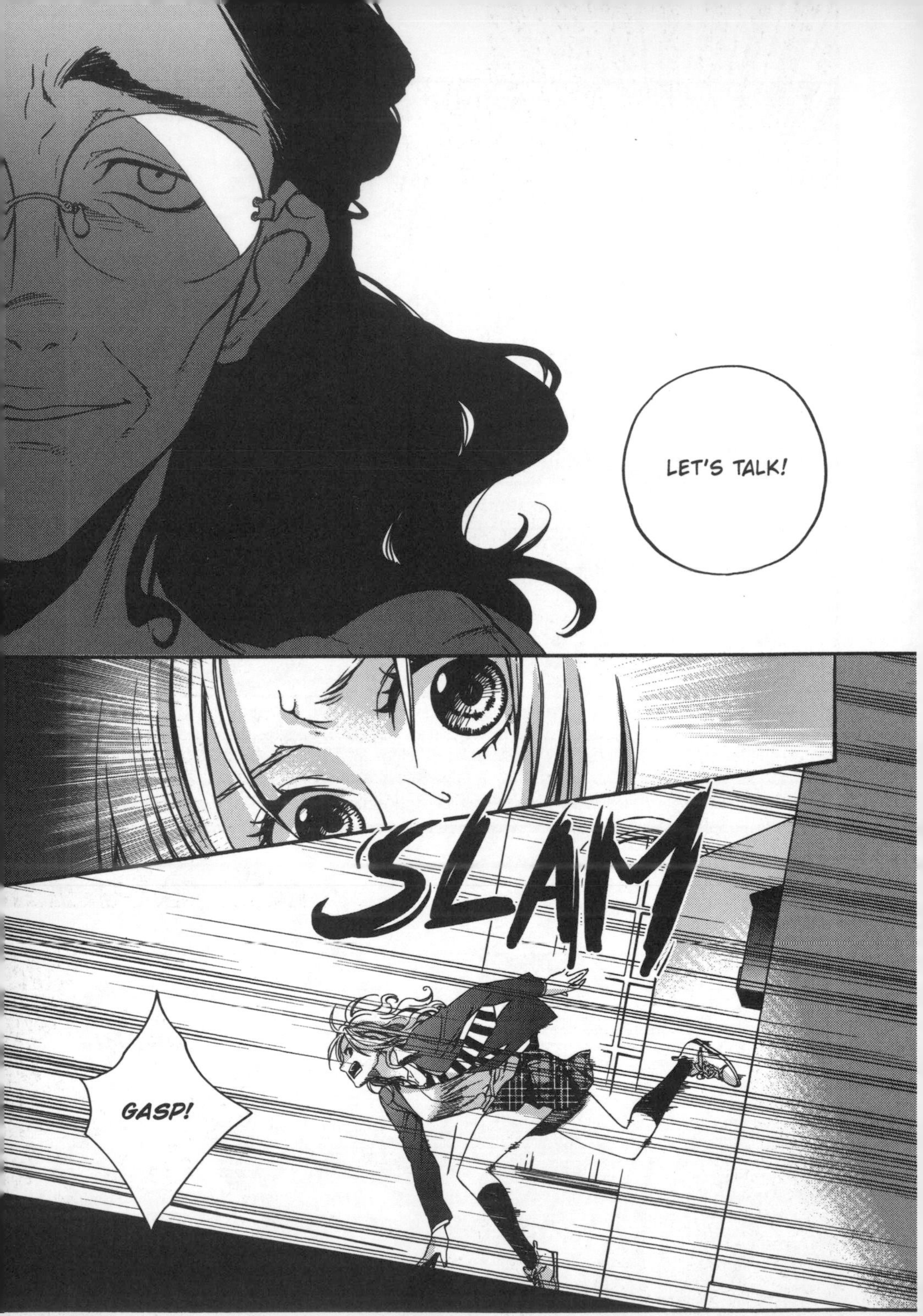
LET'S TALK!
SLAM
GASP!

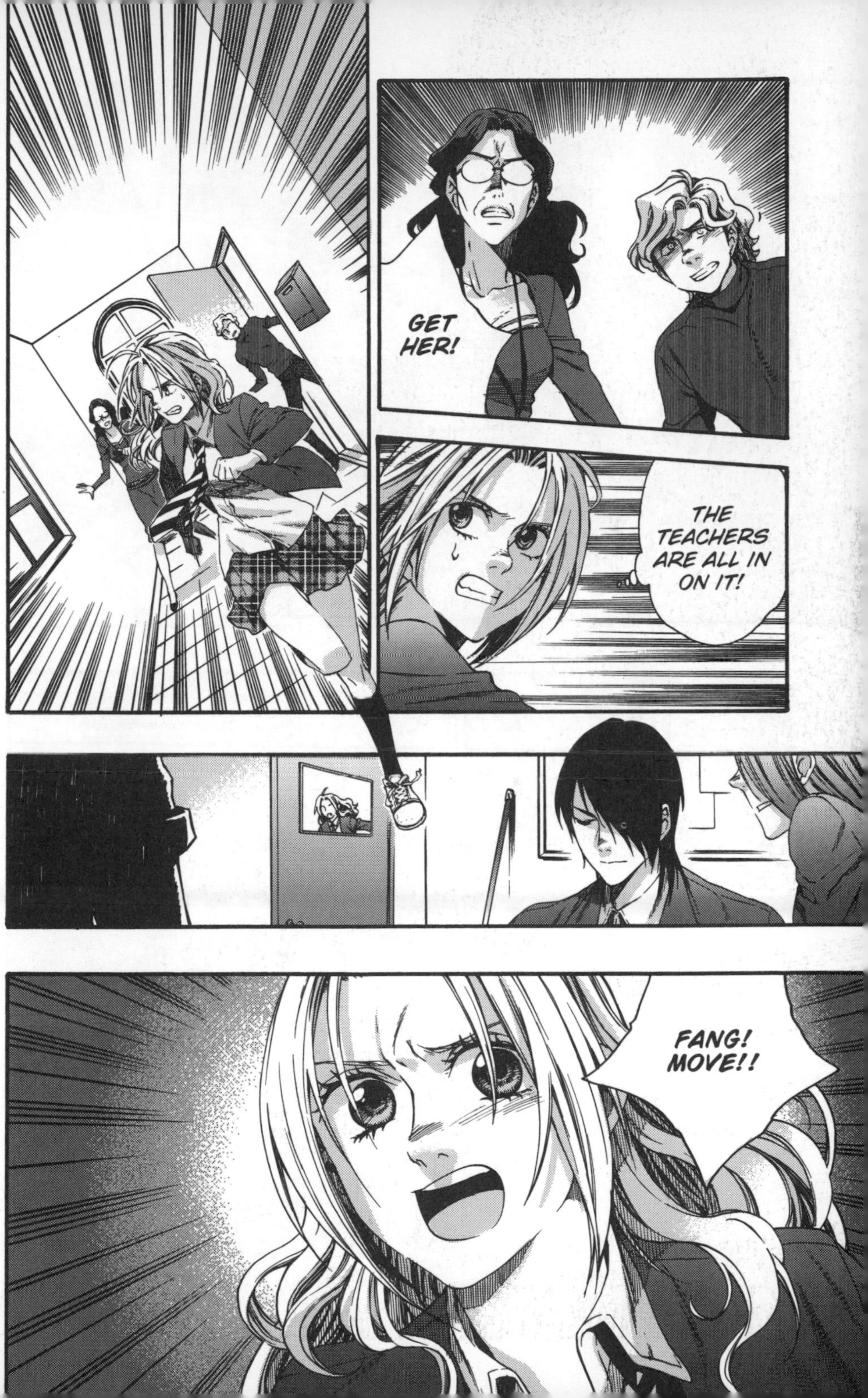
GET HER!
THE TEACHERS ARE ALL IN ON IT!
FANG! MOVE!!

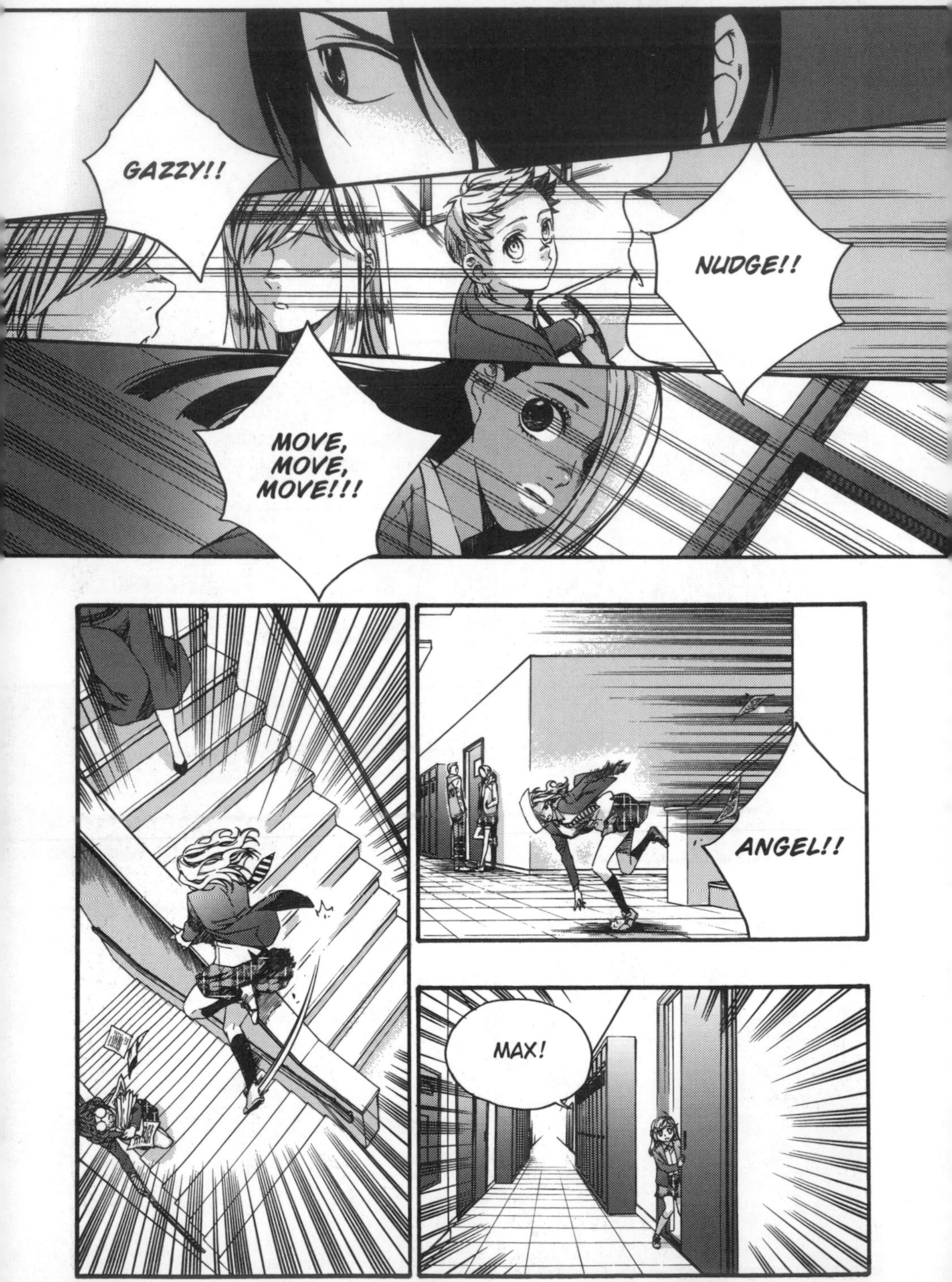
GAZZY!!
NUDGE!!
MOVE, MOVE, MOVE!!!
ANGEL!!
MAX!

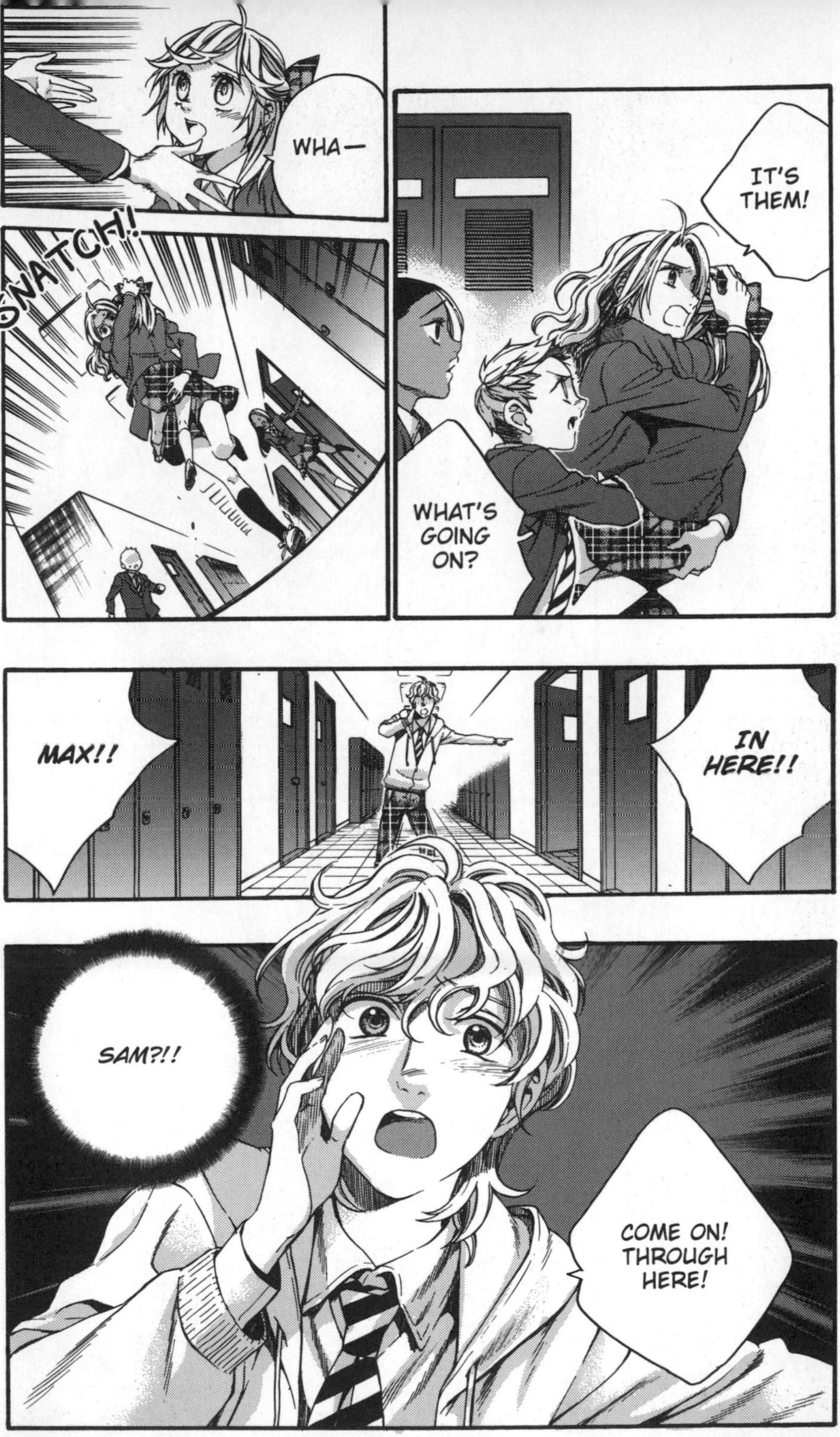
WHA—
SNATCH!
IT'S THEM!
WHAT'S GOING ON?
MAX!!
IN HERE!!
SAM?!!
COME ON! THROUGH HERE!

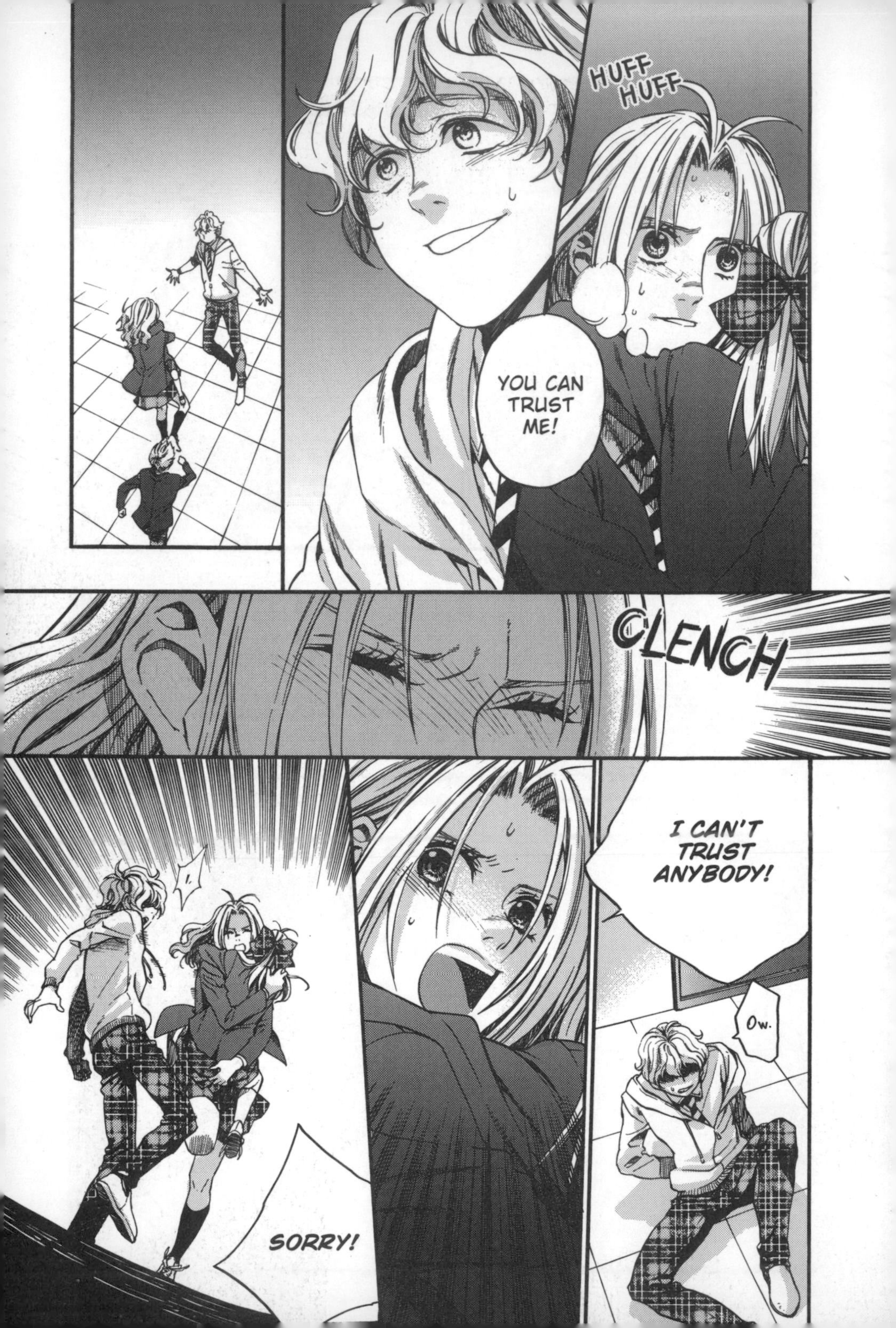
YOU CAN TRUST ME!
HUFF HUFF
CLENCH
!
SORRY!
I CAN'T TRUST ANYBODY!
Ow.

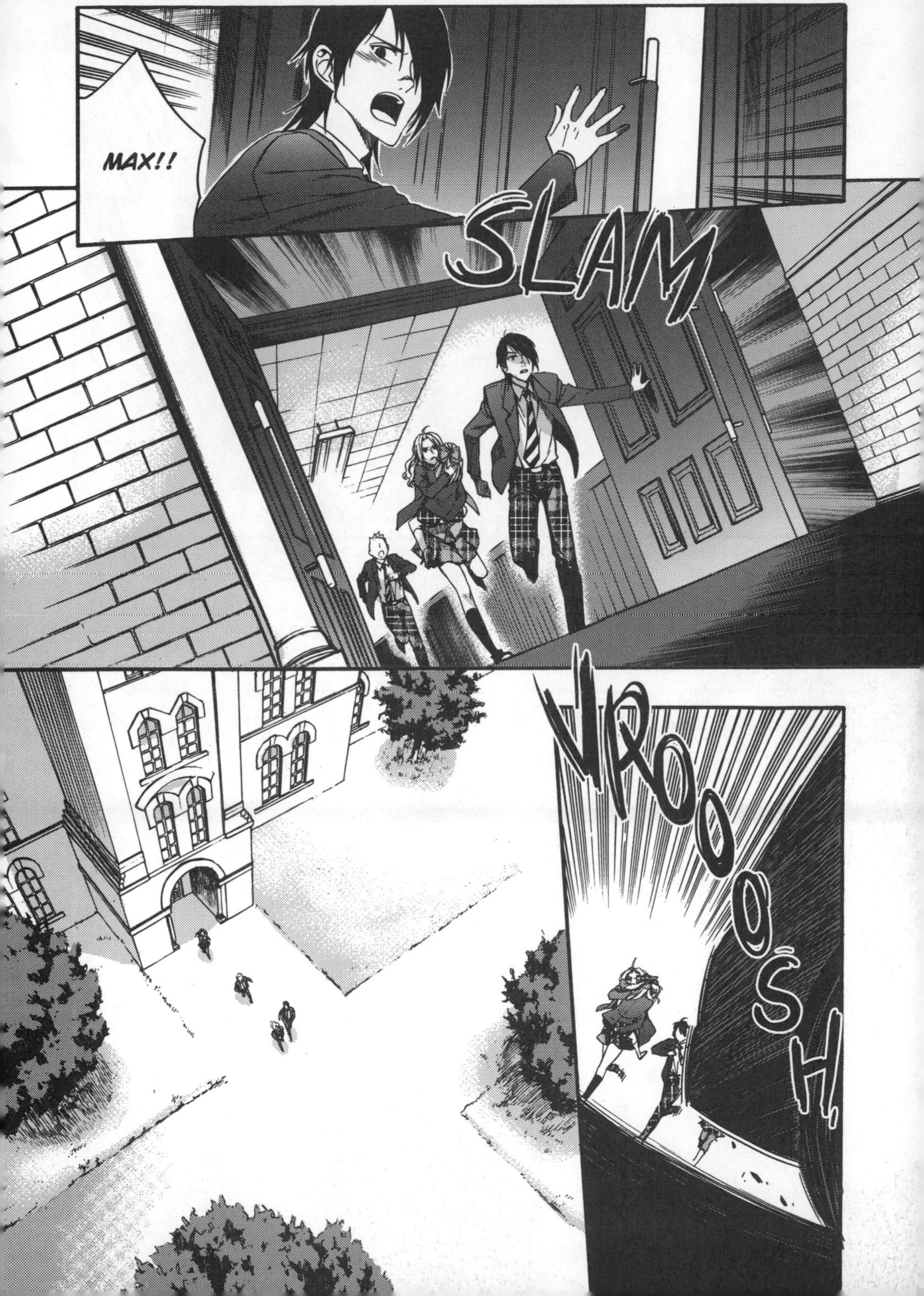
MAX!!
SLAM
VROOOOSH

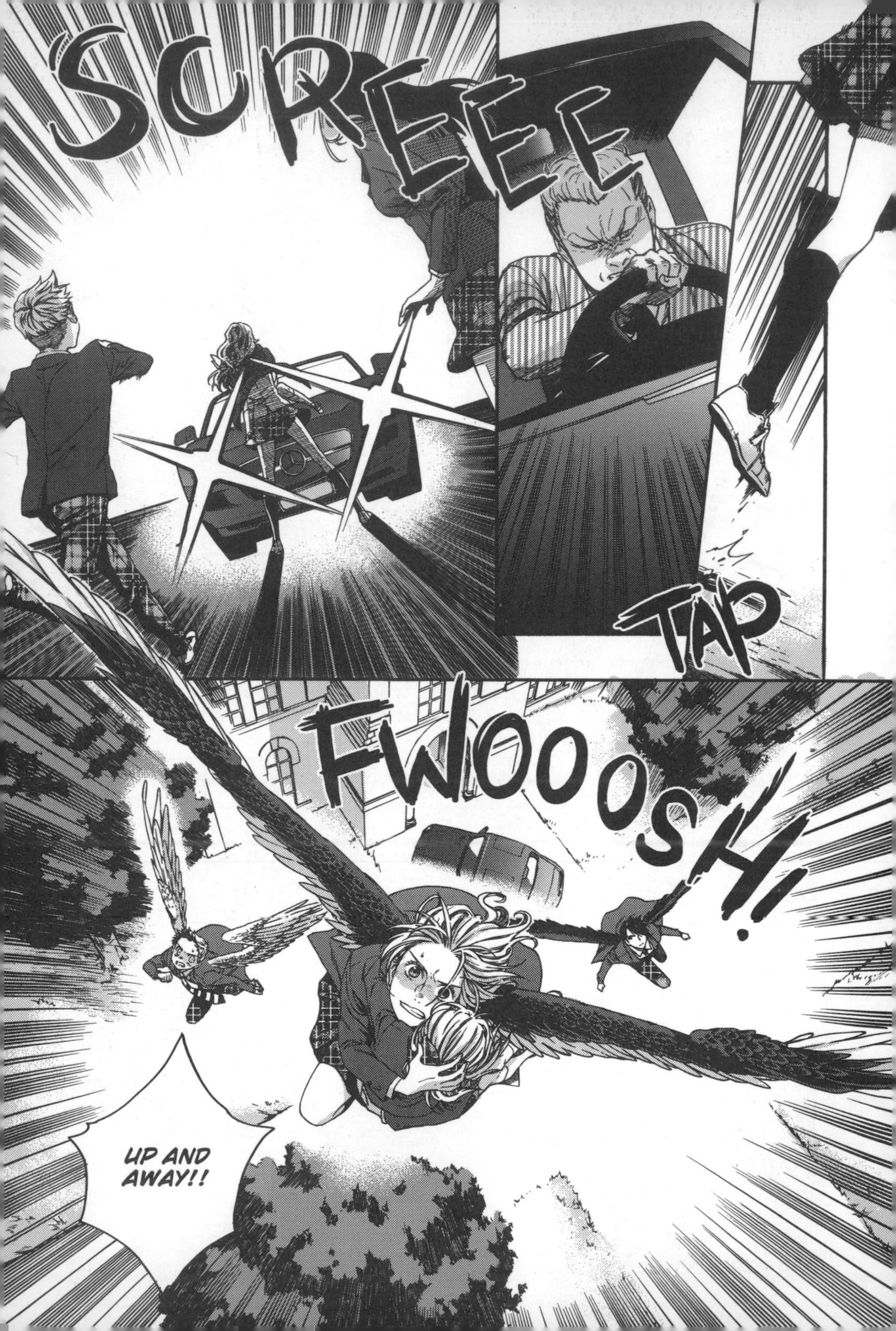
SCREEEE
TAP
FWOOOSH!!
UP AND AWAY!!

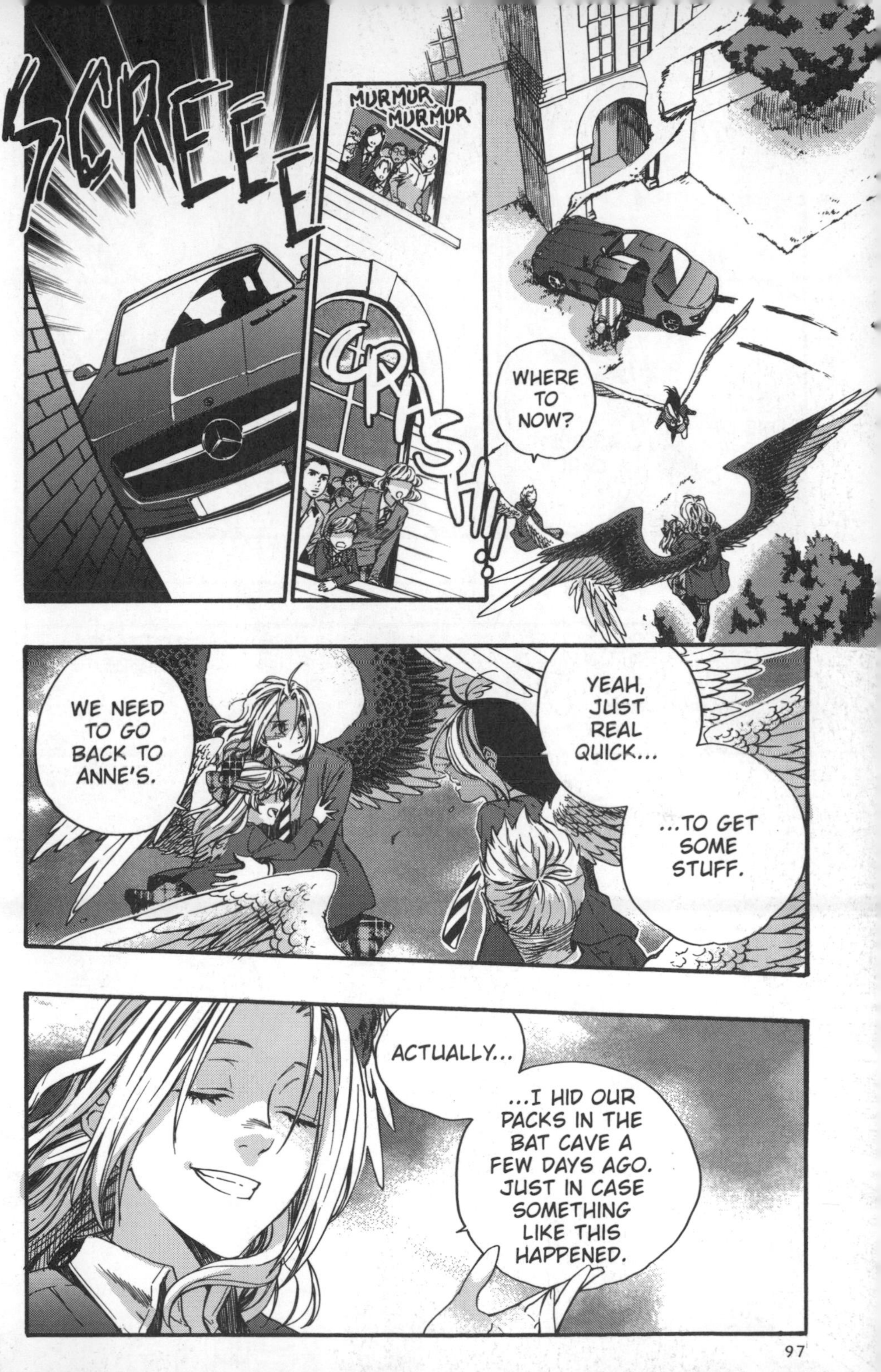
SCREEE
MURMUR MURMUR
CRASH!!
WHERE TO NOW?
WE NEED TO GO BACK TO ANNE'S.
YEAH, JUST REAL QUICK...
...TO GET SOME STUFF.
ACTUALLY...
...I HID OUR PACKS IN THE BAT CAVE A FEW DAYS AGO. JUST IN CASE SOMETHING LIKE THIS HAPPENED.

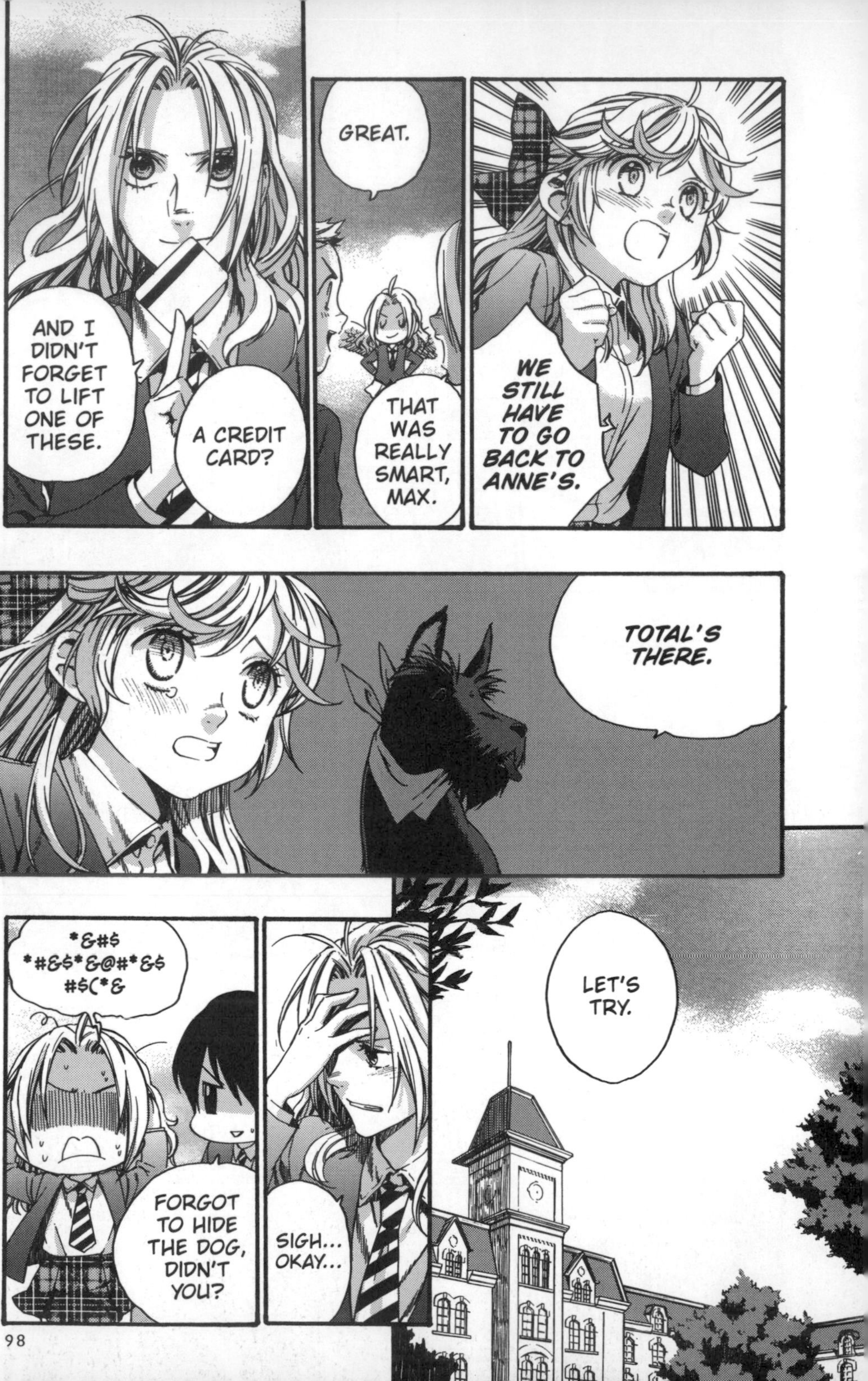
AND I DIDN'T FORGET TO LIFT ONE OF THESE.
A CREDIT CARD?
GREAT.
THAT WAS REALLY SMART, MAX.
WE STILL HAVE TO GO BACK TO ANNE'S.
TOTAL'S THERE.
*&#$ *#&$*&@#*&$ #$(*&
FORGOT TO HIDE THE DOG, DIDN'T YOU?
SIGH... OKAY...
LET'S TRY.

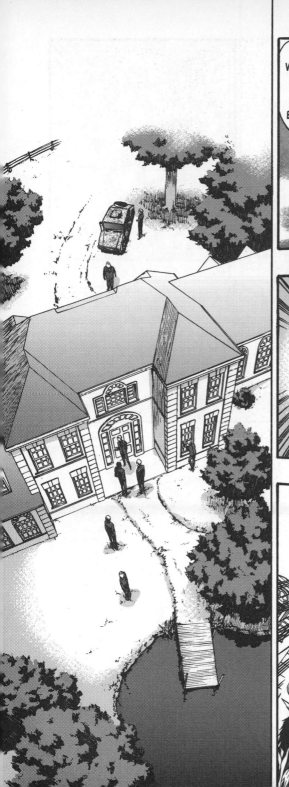

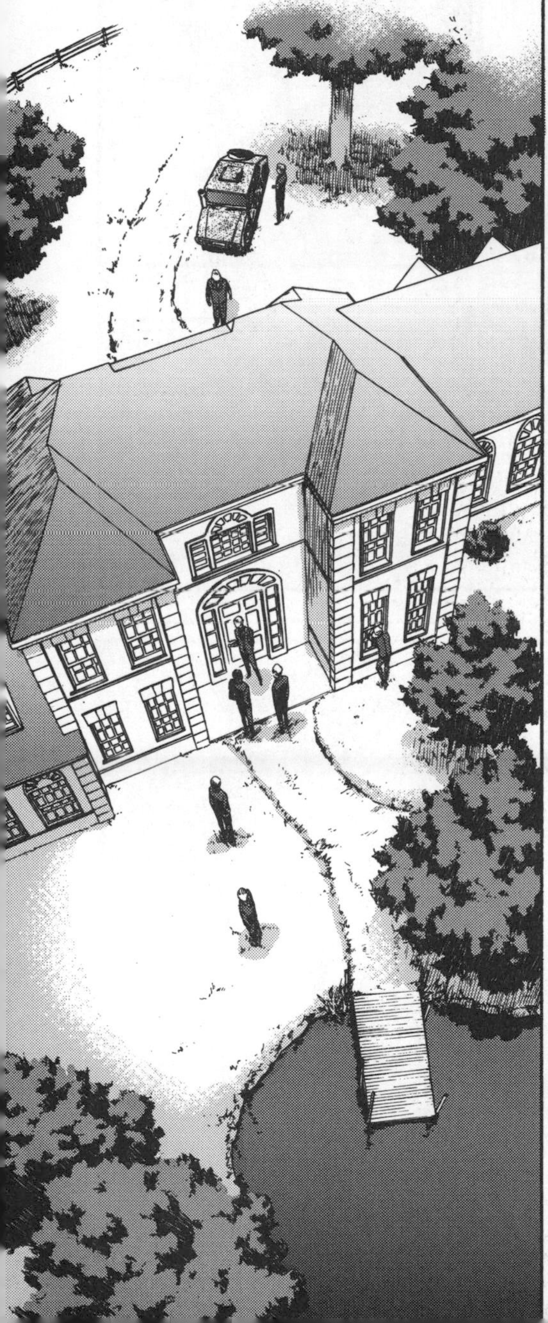
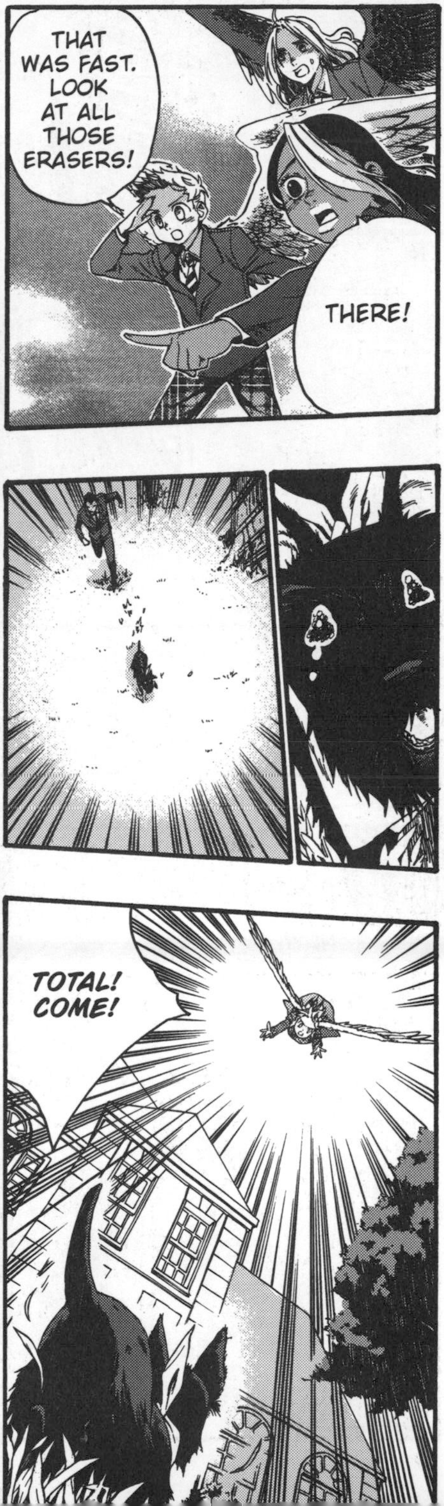
THAT WAS FAST. LOOK AT ALL THOSE ERASERS!
THERE!
TOTAL! COME!

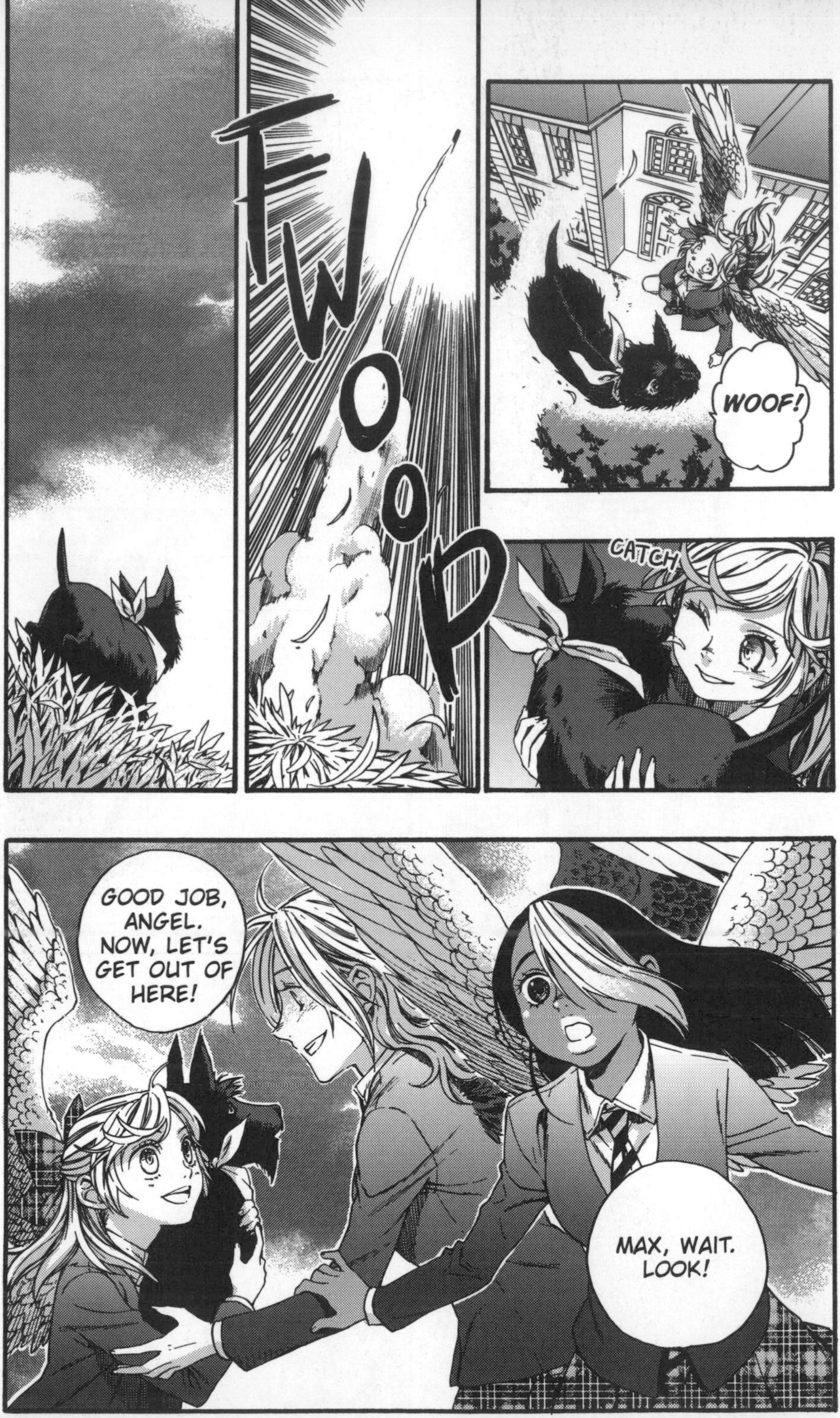
FWOOP
WOOF!
CATCH
GOOD JOB, ANGEL. NOW, LET'S GET OUT OF HERE!
MAX, WAIT. LOOK!

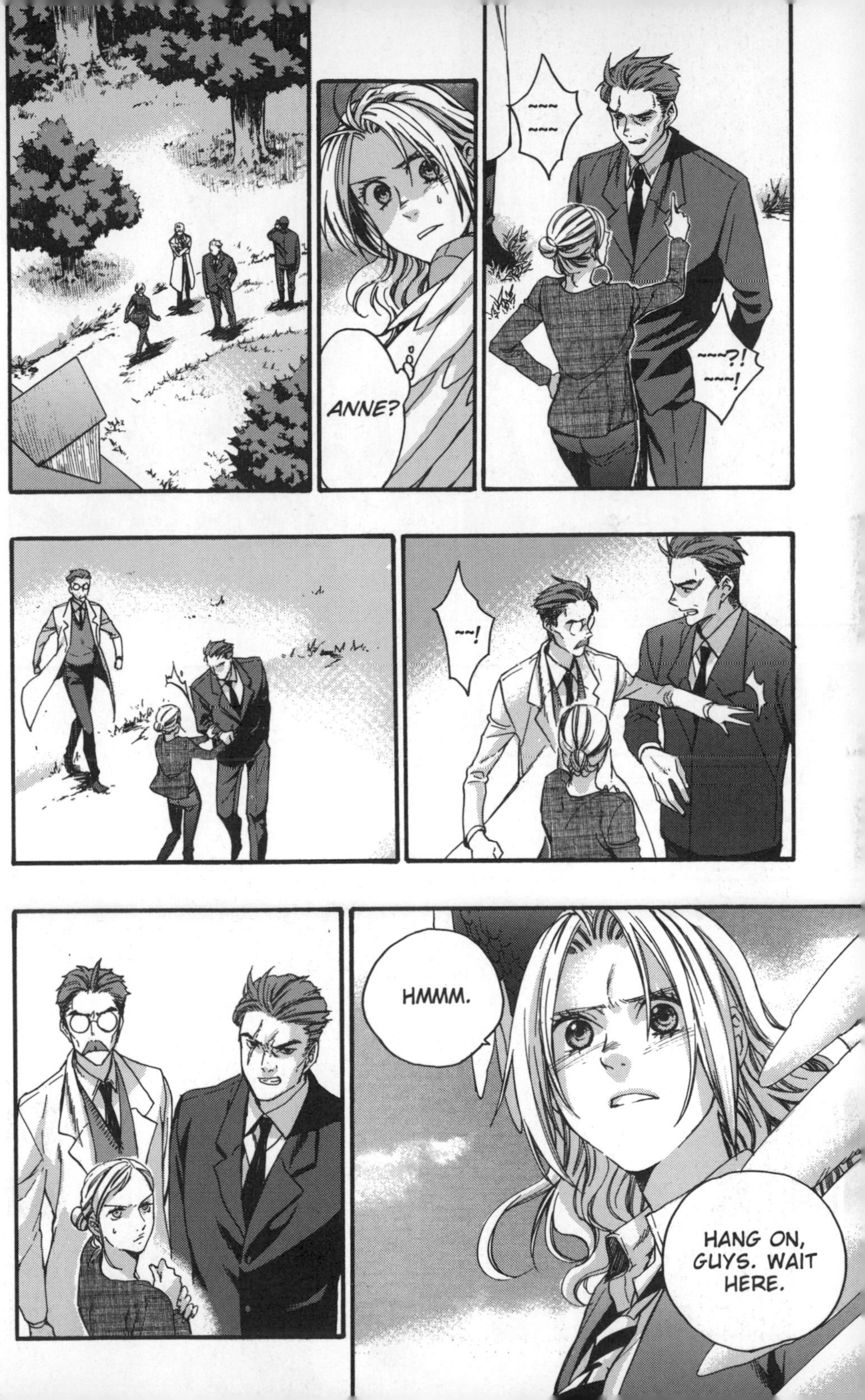
ANNE?
~~~
~~~
~~~?!
~~~!
~~!
HMMM.
HANG ON, GUYS. WAIT HERE.

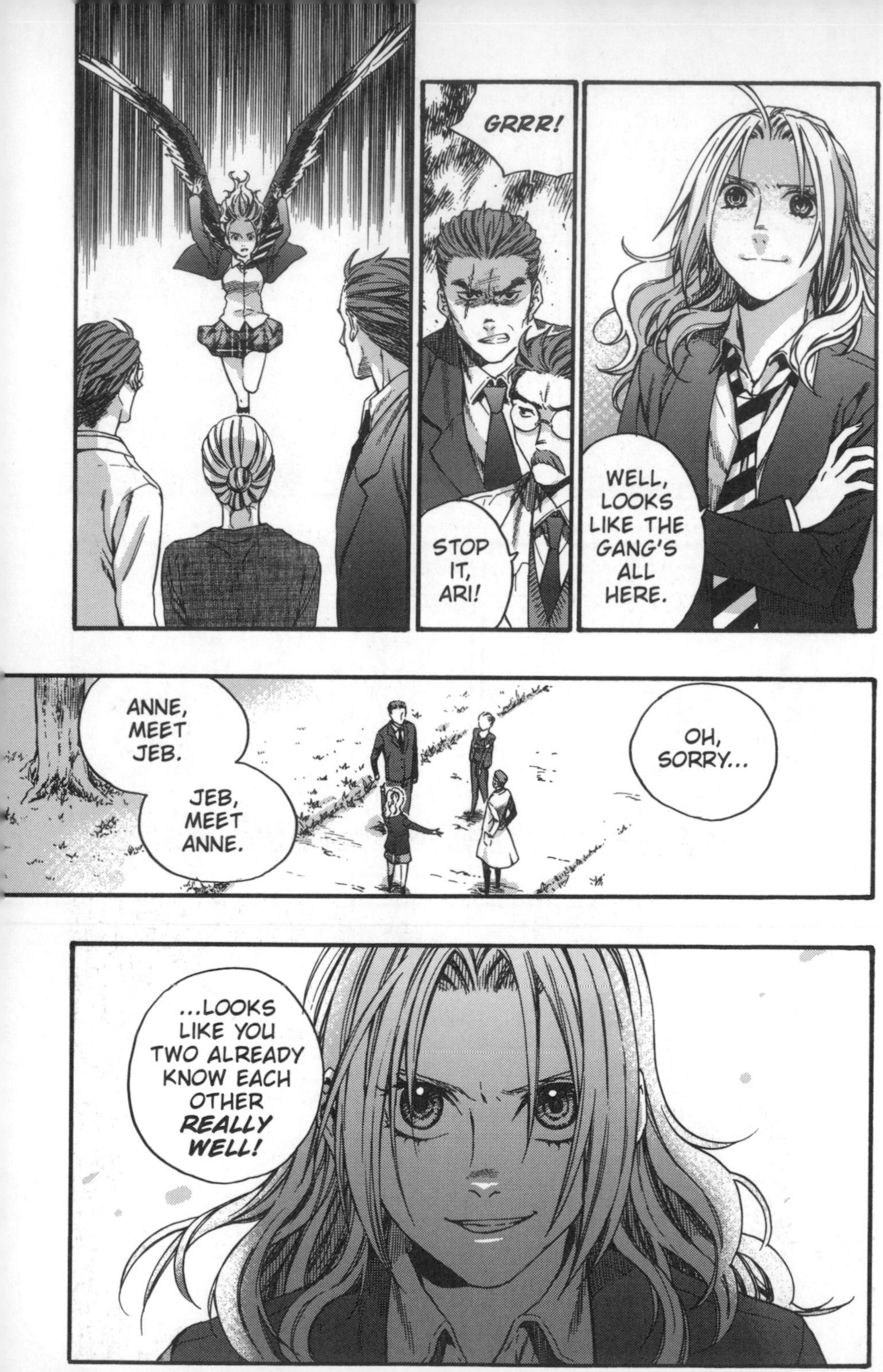
GRRR!
STOP IT, ARI!
WELL, LOOKS LIKE THE GANG'S ALL HERE.
ANNE, MEET JEB.
JEB, MEET ANNE.
OH, SORRY...
...LOOKS LIKE YOU TWO ALREADY KNOW EACH OTHER ***REALLY WELL!***

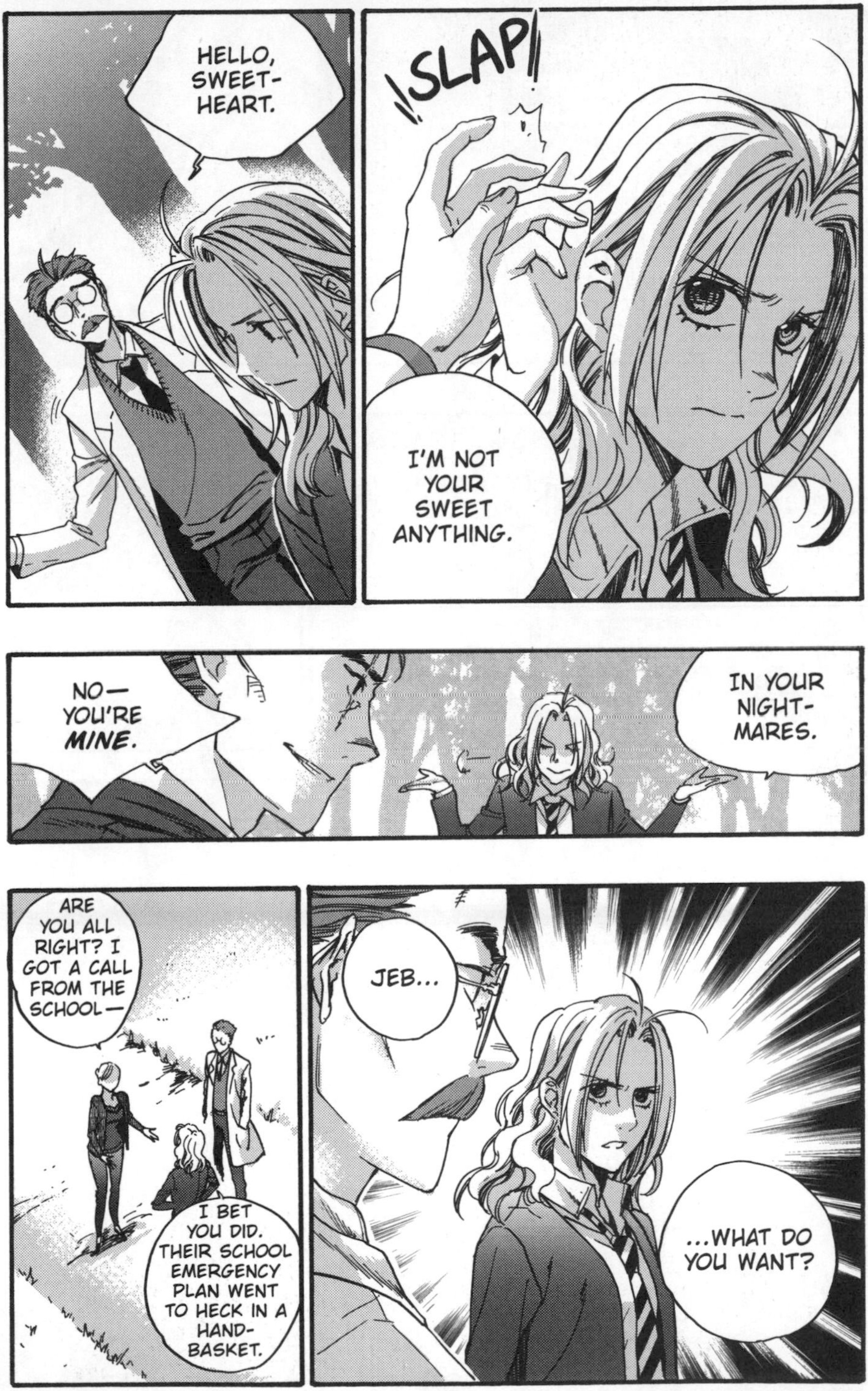
HELLO, SWEET-HEART.
SLAP
I'M NOT YOUR SWEET ANYTHING.
NO— YOU'RE *MINE*.
IN YOUR NIGHT-MARES.
ARE YOU ALL RIGHT? I GOT A CALL FROM THE SCHOOL—
I BET YOU DID. THEIR SCHOOL EMERGENCY PLAN WENT TO HECK IN A HAND-BASKET.
JEB...
...WHAT DO YOU WANT?

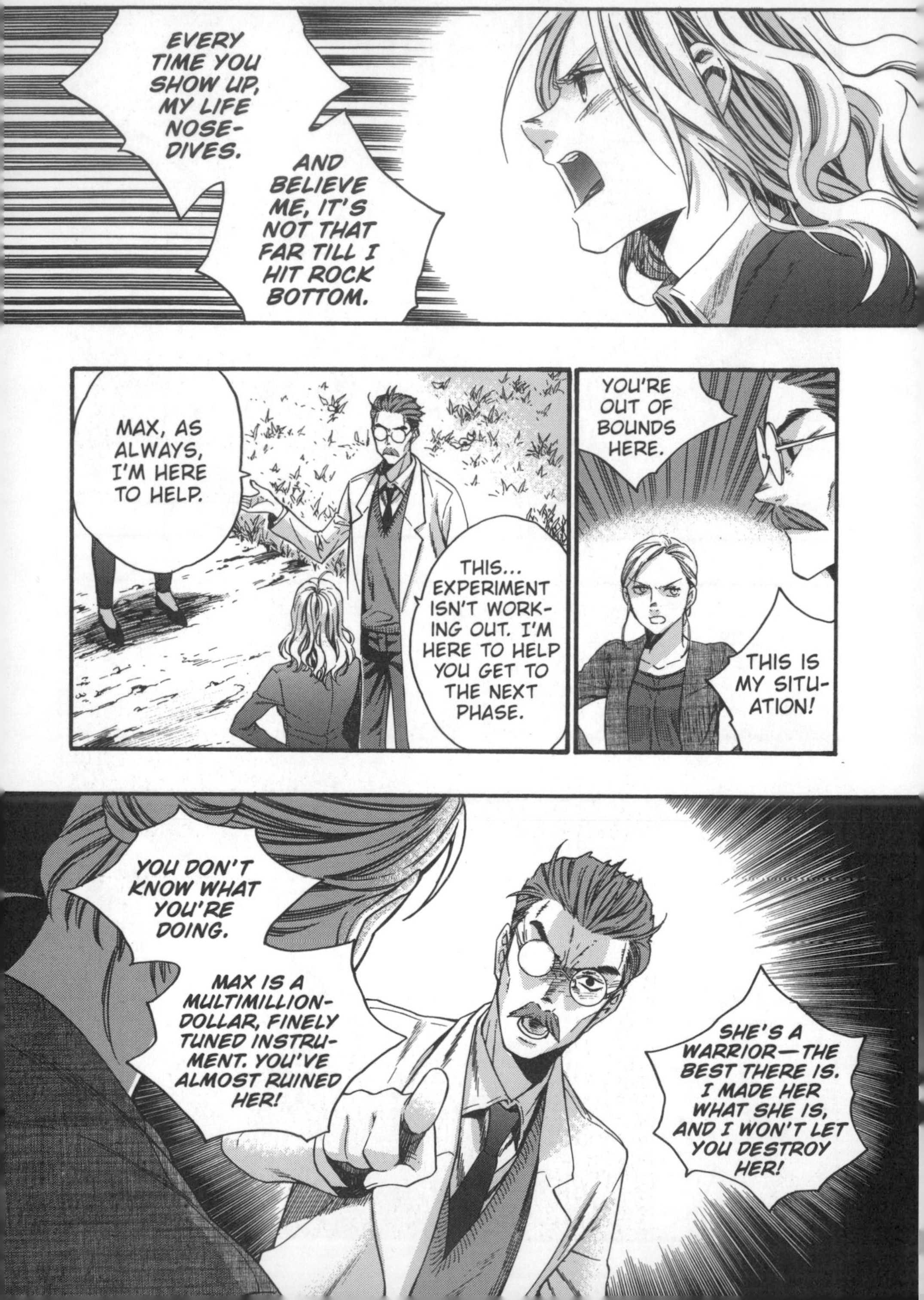
EVERY TIME YOU SHOW UP, MY LIFE NOSE-DIVES.
AND BELIEVE ME, IT'S NOT THAT FAR TILL I HIT ROCK BOTTOM.
MAX, AS ALWAYS, I'M HERE TO HELP.
THIS... EXPERIMENT ISN'T WORKING OUT. I'M HERE TO HELP YOU GET TO THE NEXT PHASE.
YOU'RE OUT OF BOUNDS HERE.
THIS IS MY SITU-ATION!
YOU DON'T KNOW WHAT YOU'RE DOING.
MAX IS A MULTIMILLION-DOLLAR, FINELY TUNED INSTRU-MENT. YOU'VE ALMOST RUINED HER!
SHE'S A WARRIOR—THE BEST THERE IS. I MADE HER WHAT SHE IS, AND I WON'T LET YOU DESTROY HER!

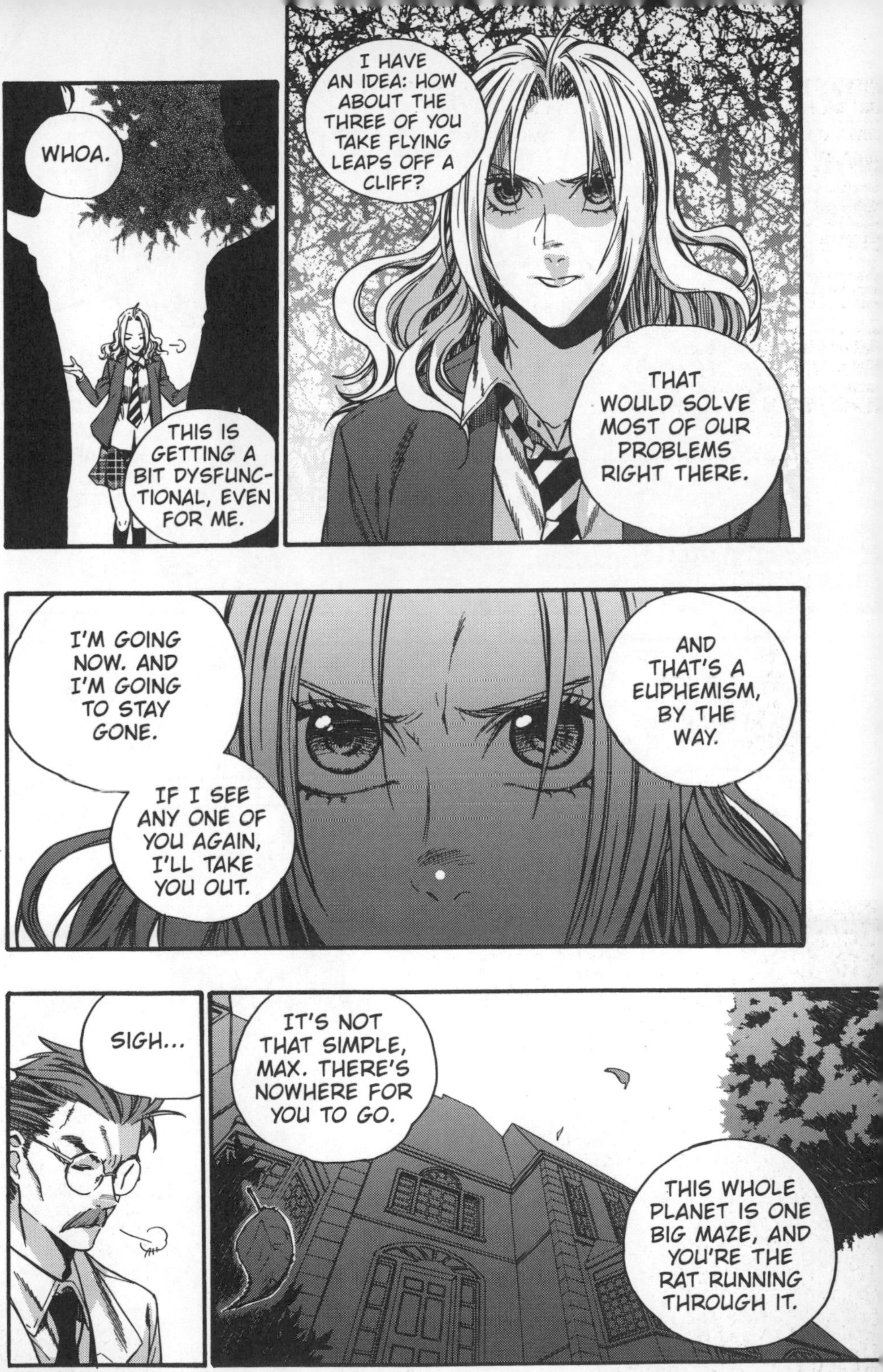
WHOA.
THIS IS GETTING A BIT DYSFUNCTIONAL, EVEN FOR ME.
I HAVE AN IDEA: HOW ABOUT THE THREE OF YOU TAKE FLYING LEAPS OFF A CLIFF?
THAT WOULD SOLVE MOST OF OUR PROBLEMS RIGHT THERE.
I'M GOING NOW. AND I'M GOING TO STAY GONE.
IF I SEE ANY ONE OF YOU AGAIN, I'LL TAKE YOU OUT.
AND THAT'S A EUPHEMISM, BY THE WAY.
SIGH...
IT'S NOT THAT SIMPLE, MAX. THERE'S NOWHERE FOR YOU TO GO.
THIS WHOLE PLANET IS ONE BIG MAZE, AND YOU'RE THE RAT RUNNING THROUGH IT.

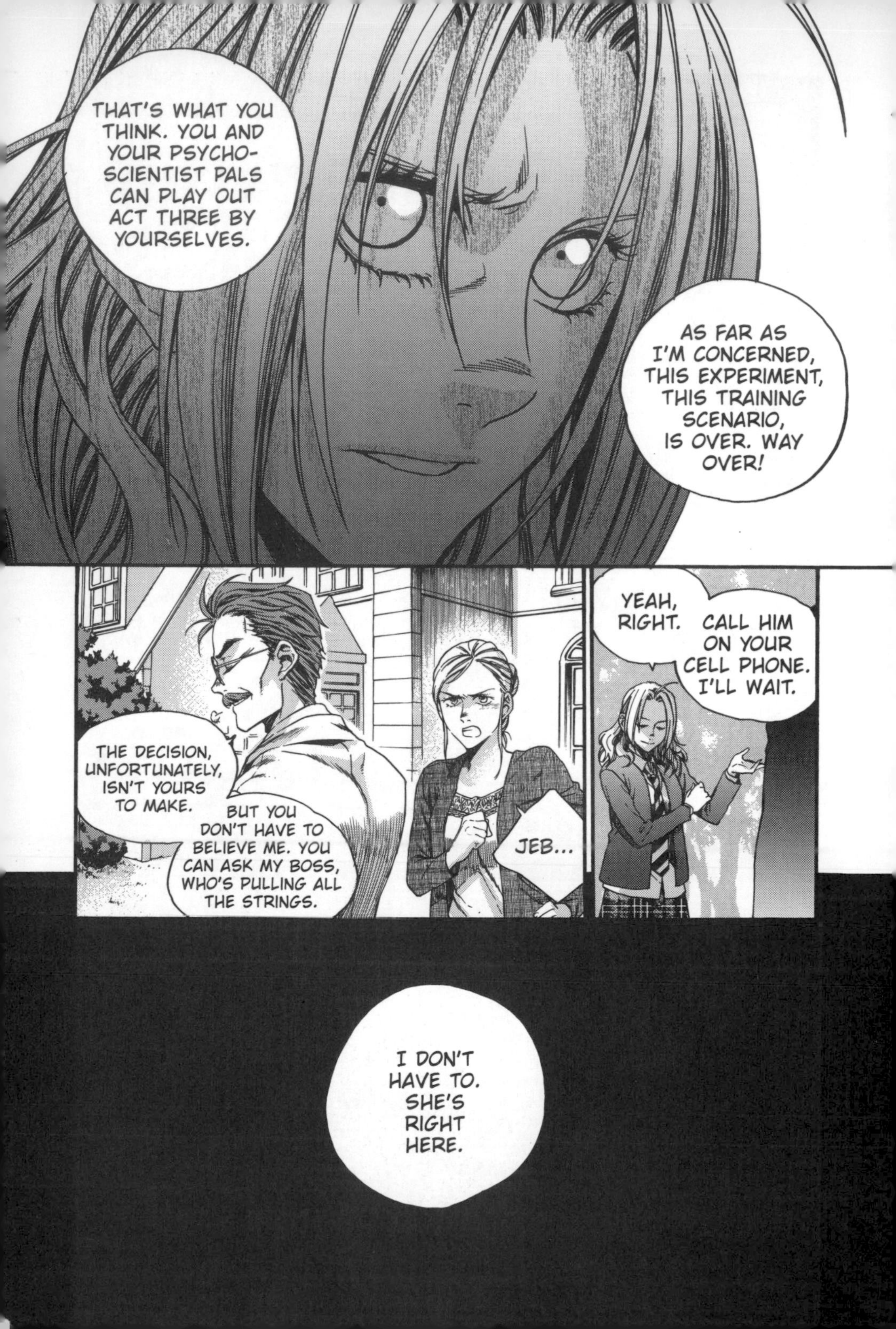
THAT'S WHAT YOU THINK. YOU AND YOUR PSYCHO-SCIENTIST PALS CAN PLAY OUT ACT THREE BY YOURSELVES.
AS FAR AS I'M CONCERNED, THIS EXPERIMENT, THIS TRAINING SCENARIO, IS OVER. WAY OVER!
THE DECISION, UNFORTUNATELY, ISN'T YOURS TO MAKE.
BUT YOU DON'T HAVE TO BELIEVE ME. YOU CAN ASK MY BOSS, WHO'S PULLING ALL THE STRINGS.
JEB...
YEAH, RIGHT.
CALL HIM ON YOUR CELL PHONE. I'LL WAIT.
I DON'T HAVE TO. SHE'S RIGHT HERE.

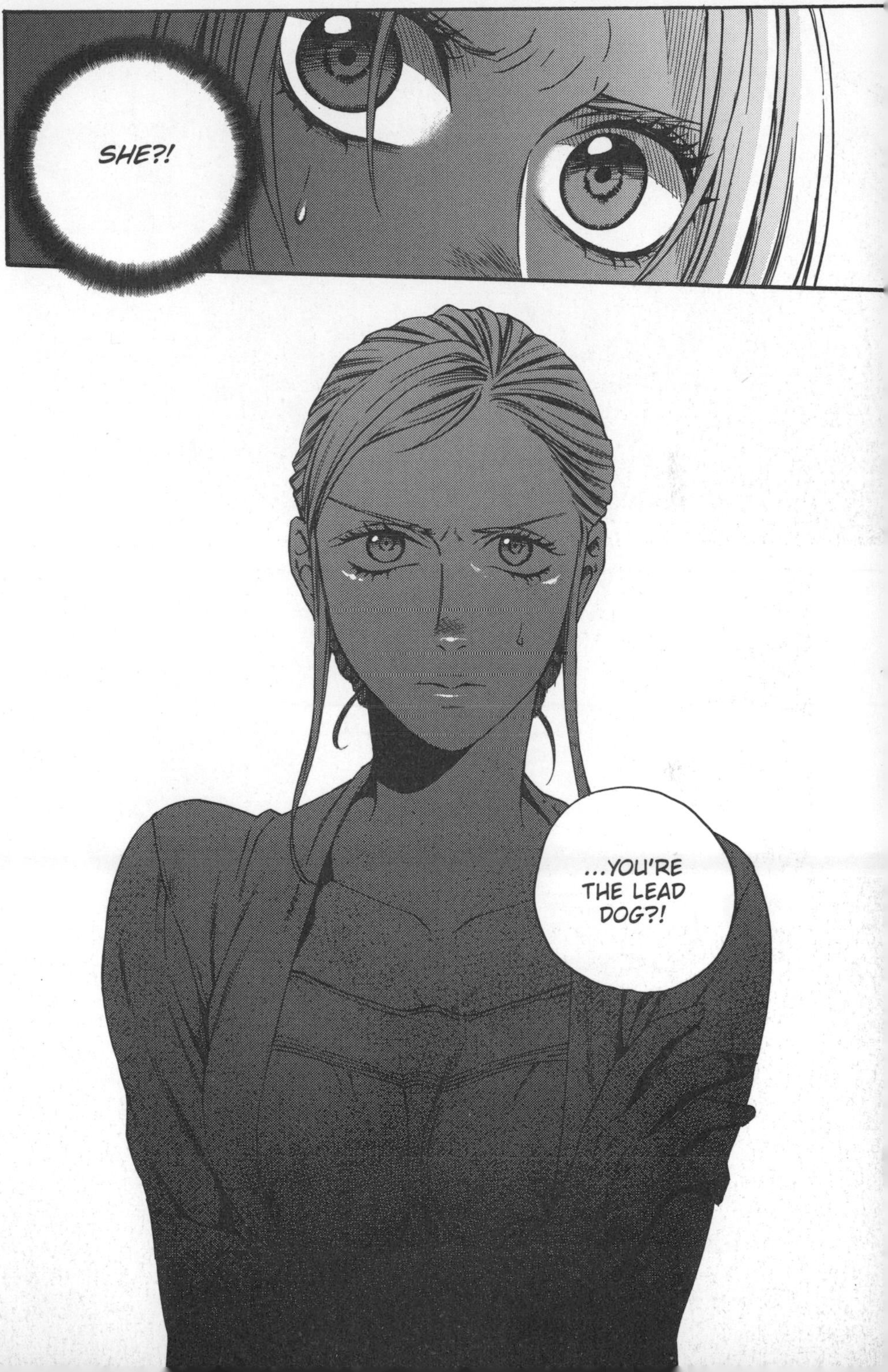
SHE?!
...YOU'RE THE LEAD DOG?!

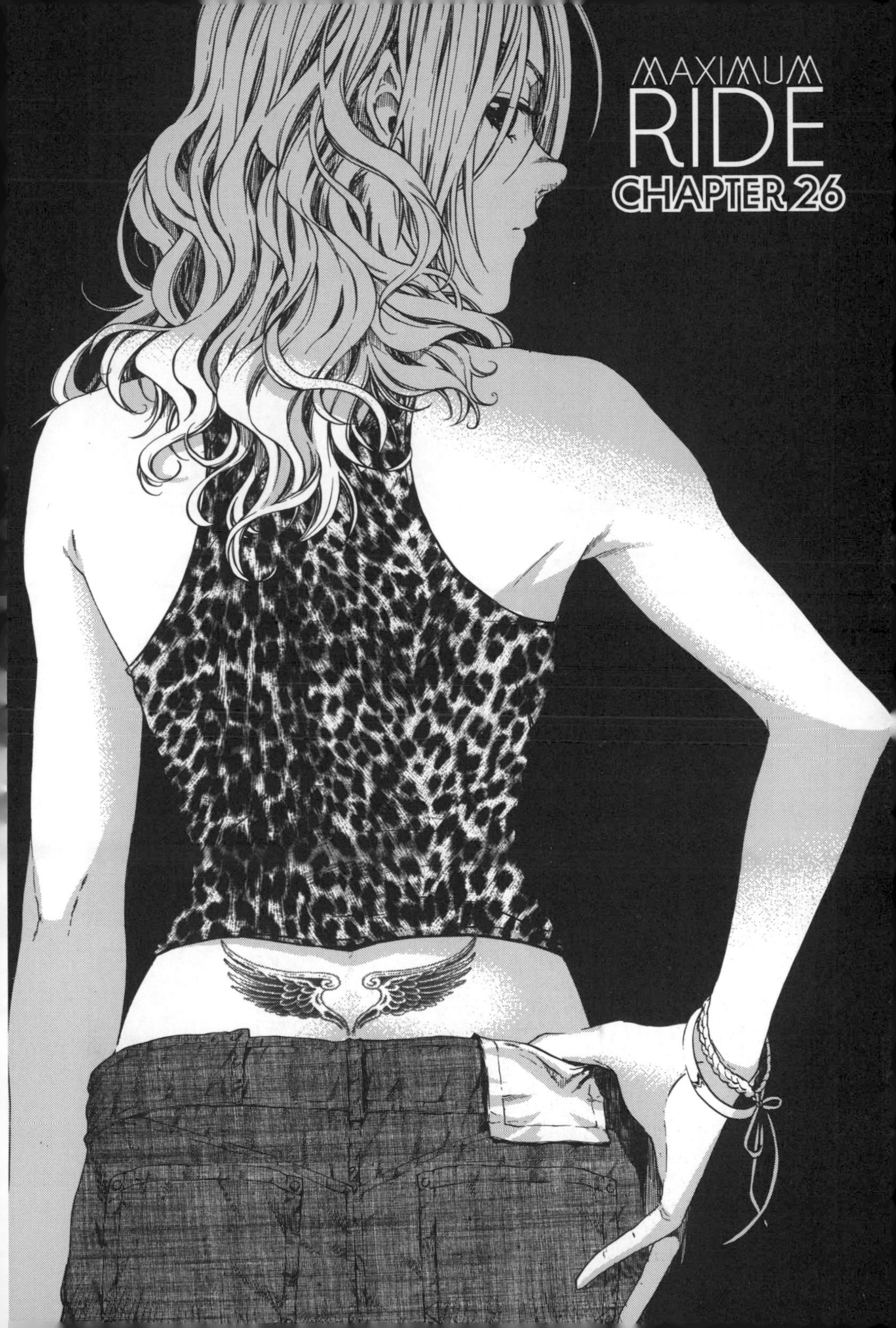
MAXIMUM
RIDE
CHAPTER 26

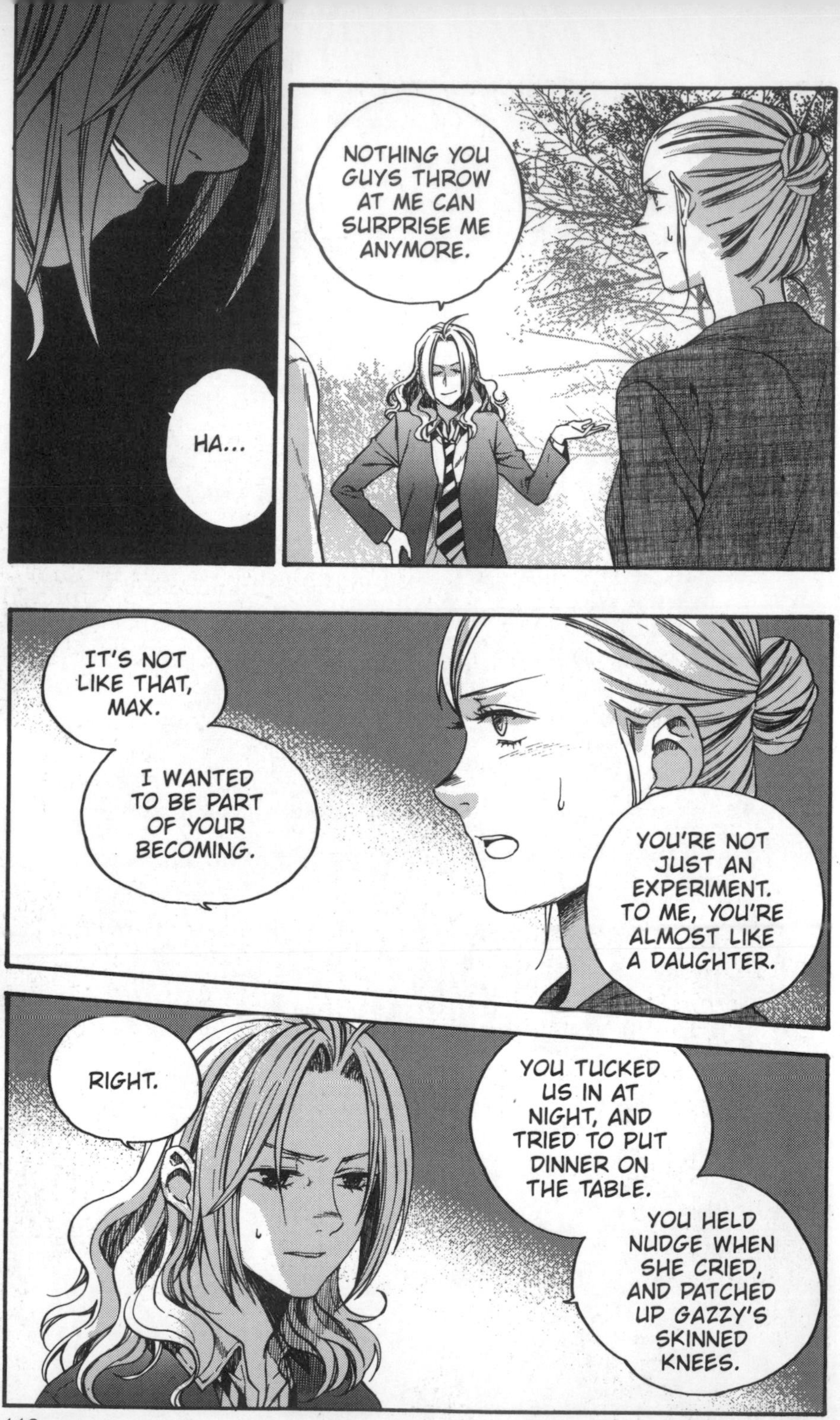

HA...
NOTHING YOU GUYS THROW AT ME CAN SURPRISE ME ANYMORE.
IT'S NOT LIKE THAT, MAX.
I WANTED TO BE PART OF YOUR BECOMING.
YOU'RE NOT JUST AN EXPERIMENT. TO ME, YOU'RE ALMOST LIKE A DAUGHTER.
RIGHT.
YOU TUCKED US IN AT NIGHT, AND TRIED TO PUT DINNER ON THE TABLE.
YOU HELD NUDGE WHEN SHE CRIED, AND PATCHED UP GAZZY'S SKINNED KNEES.

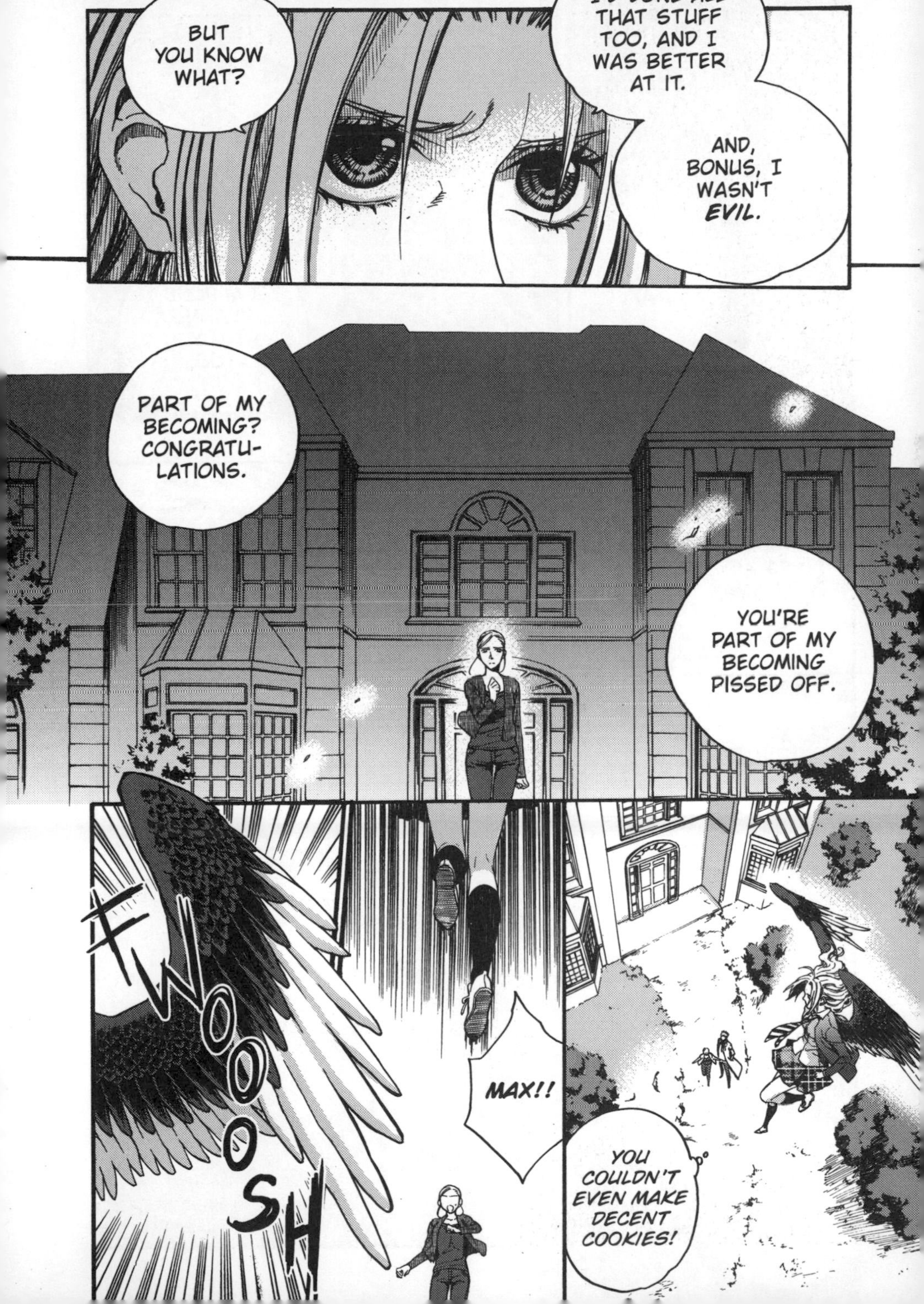
BUT YOU KNOW WHAT?
I'D DONE ALL THAT STUFF TOO, AND I WAS BETTER AT IT.
AND, BONUS, I WASN'T *EVIL*.
PART OF MY BECOMING? CONGRATU-LATIONS.
YOU'RE PART OF MY BECOMING PISSED OFF.
FWOOOSH
MAX!!
YOU COULDN'T EVEN MAKE DECENT COOKIES!

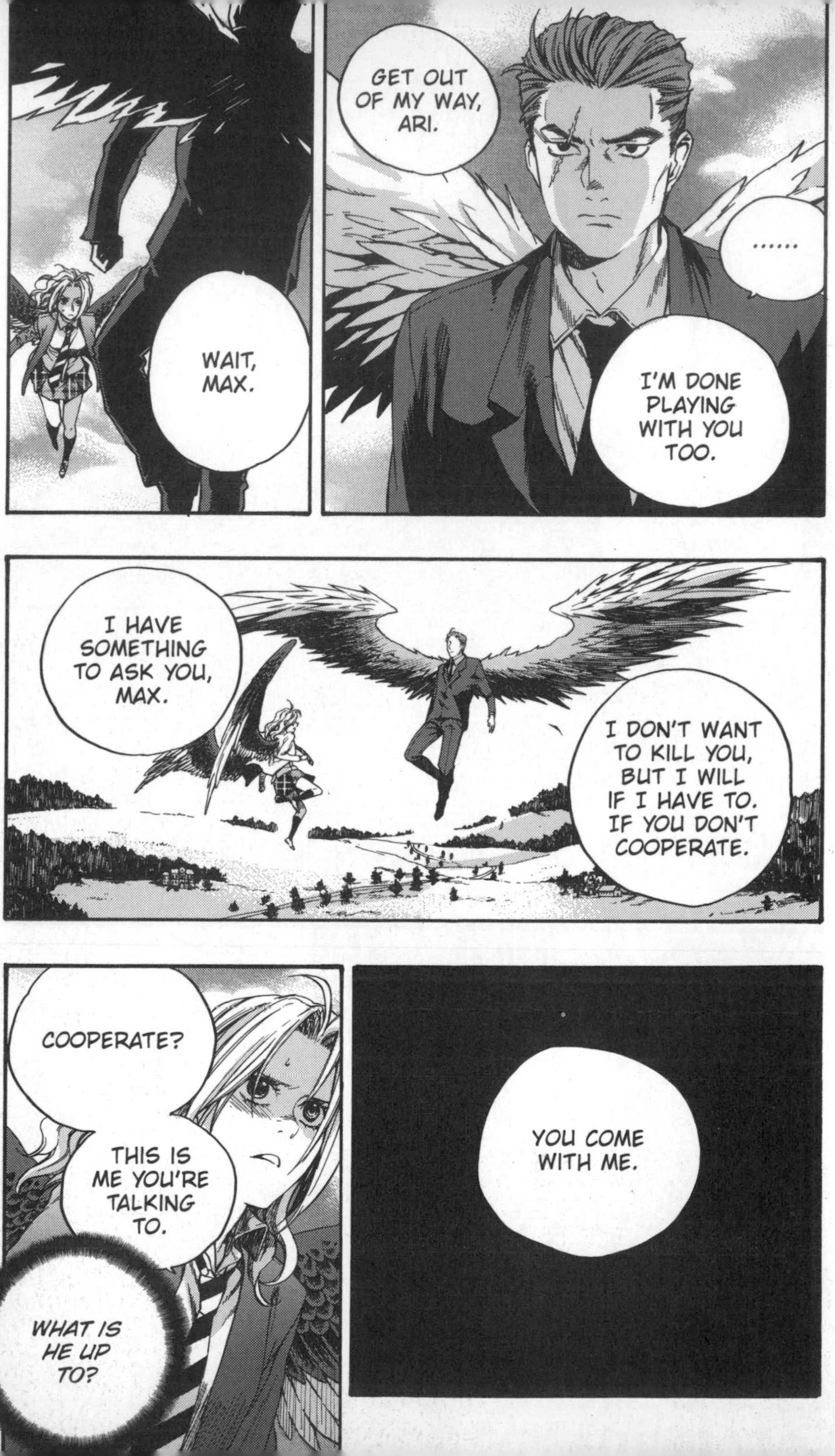
WAIT, MAX.
GET OUT OF MY WAY, ARI.
......
I'M DONE PLAYING WITH YOU TOO.
I HAVE SOMETHING TO ASK YOU, MAX.
I DON'T WANT TO KILL YOU, BUT I WILL IF I HAVE TO. IF YOU DON'T COOPERATE.
COOPERATE?
THIS IS ME YOU'RE TALKING TO.
WHAT IS HE UP TO?
YOU COME WITH ME.

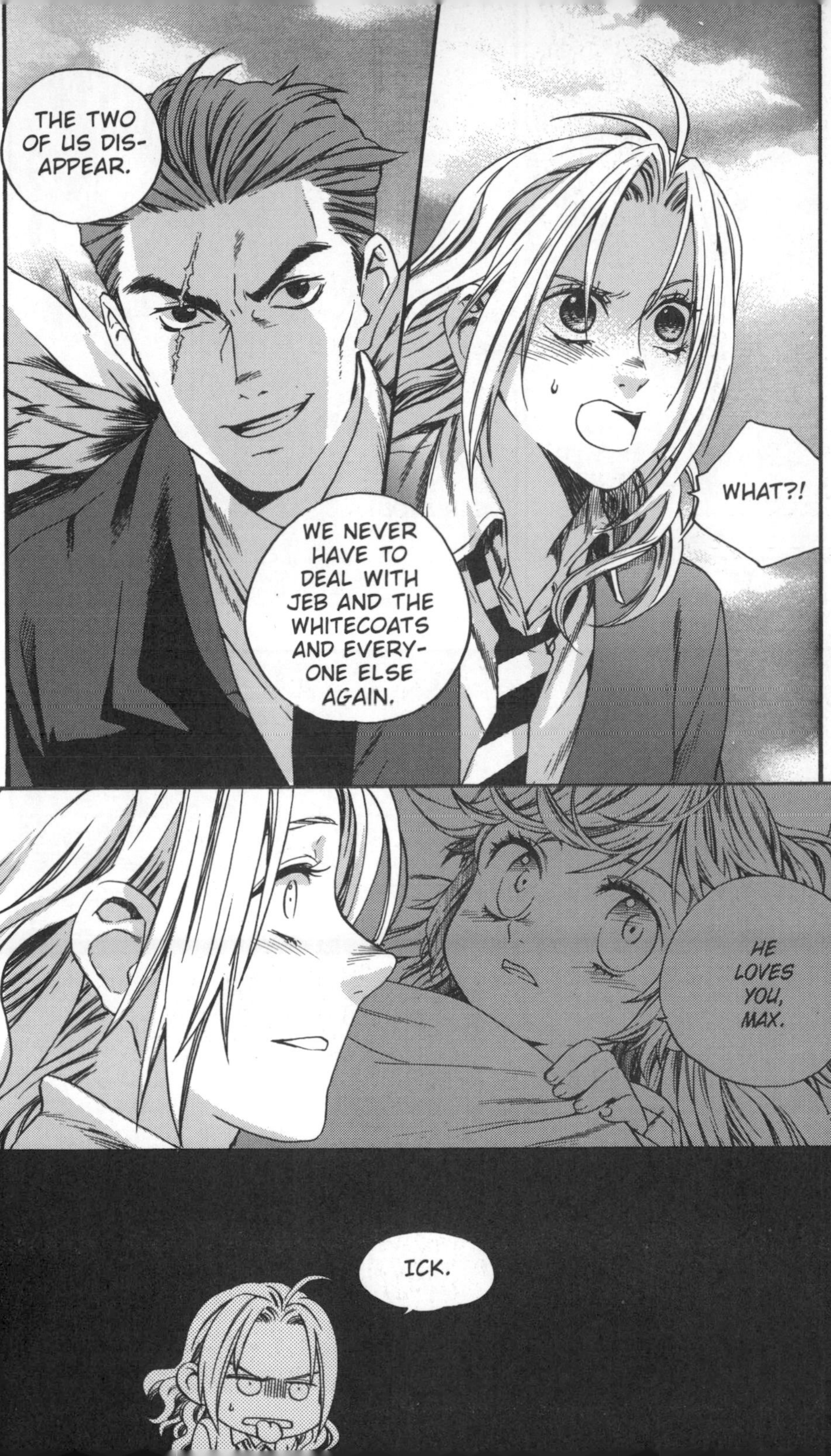
THE TWO OF US DIS-APPEAR.
WHAT?!
WE NEVER HAVE TO DEAL WITH JEB AND THE WHITECOATS AND EVERY-ONE ELSE AGAIN.
HE LOVES YOU, MAX.
ICK.

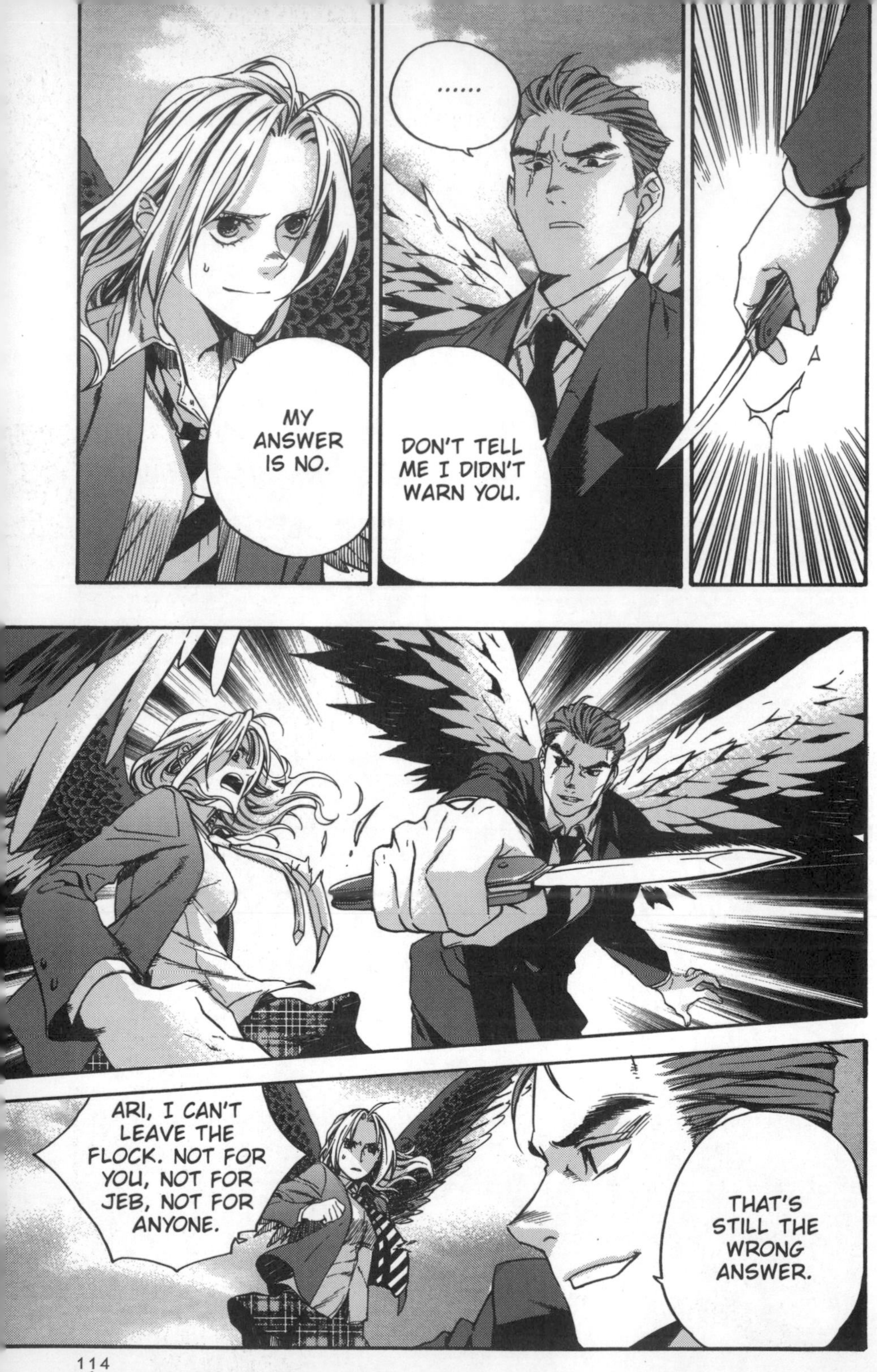
......
MY ANSWER IS NO.
DON'T TELL ME I DIDN'T WARN YOU.
ARI, I CAN'T LEAVE THE FLOCK. NOT FOR YOU, NOT FOR JEB, NOT FOR ANYONE.
THAT'S STILL THE WRONG ANSWER.

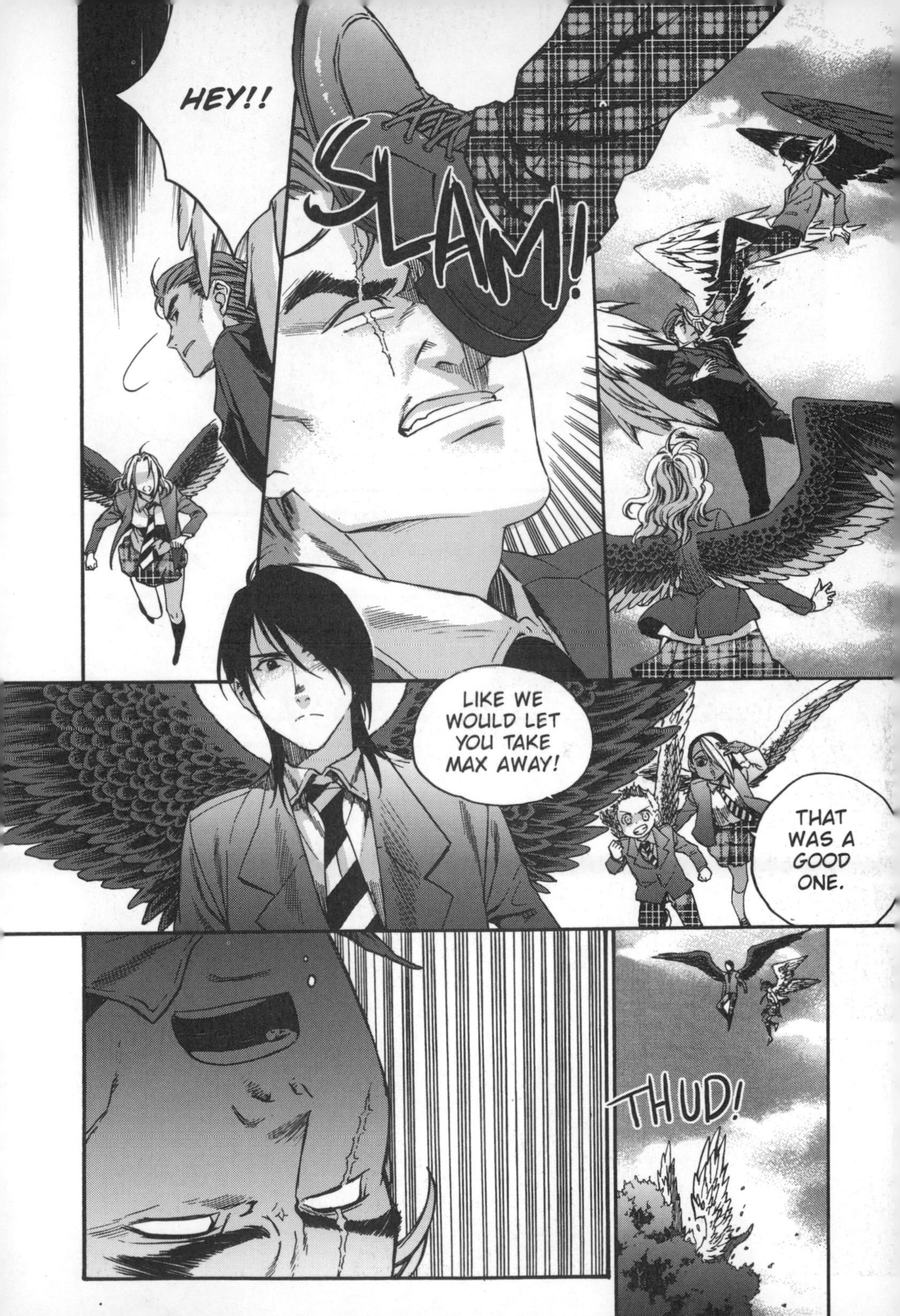
HEY!!
SLAM!
LIKE WE WOULD LET YOU TAKE MAX AWAY!
THAT WAS A GOOD ONE.
THUD!

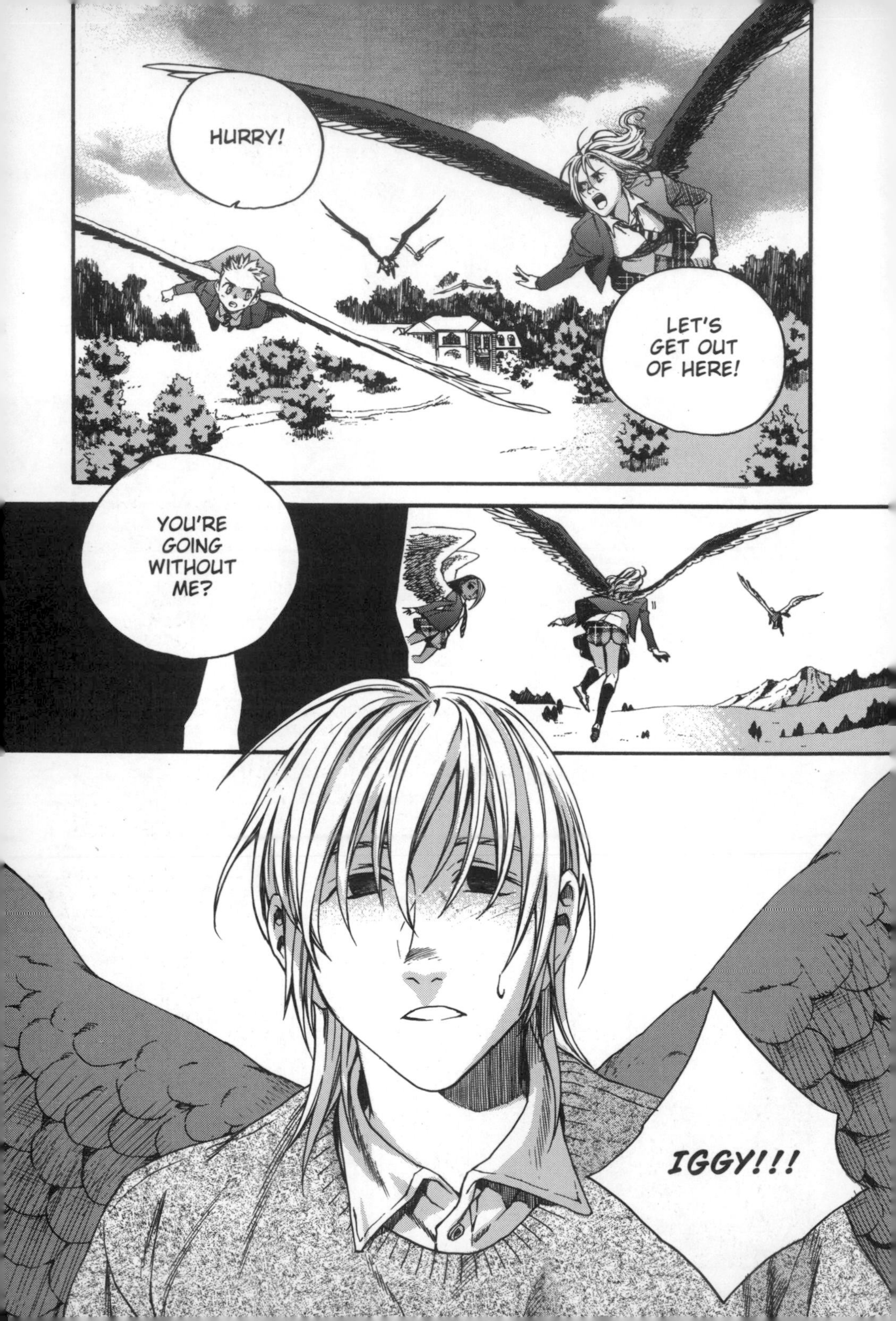
HURRY!
LET'S GET OUT OF HERE!
YOU'RE GOING WITHOUT ME?
IGGY!!!

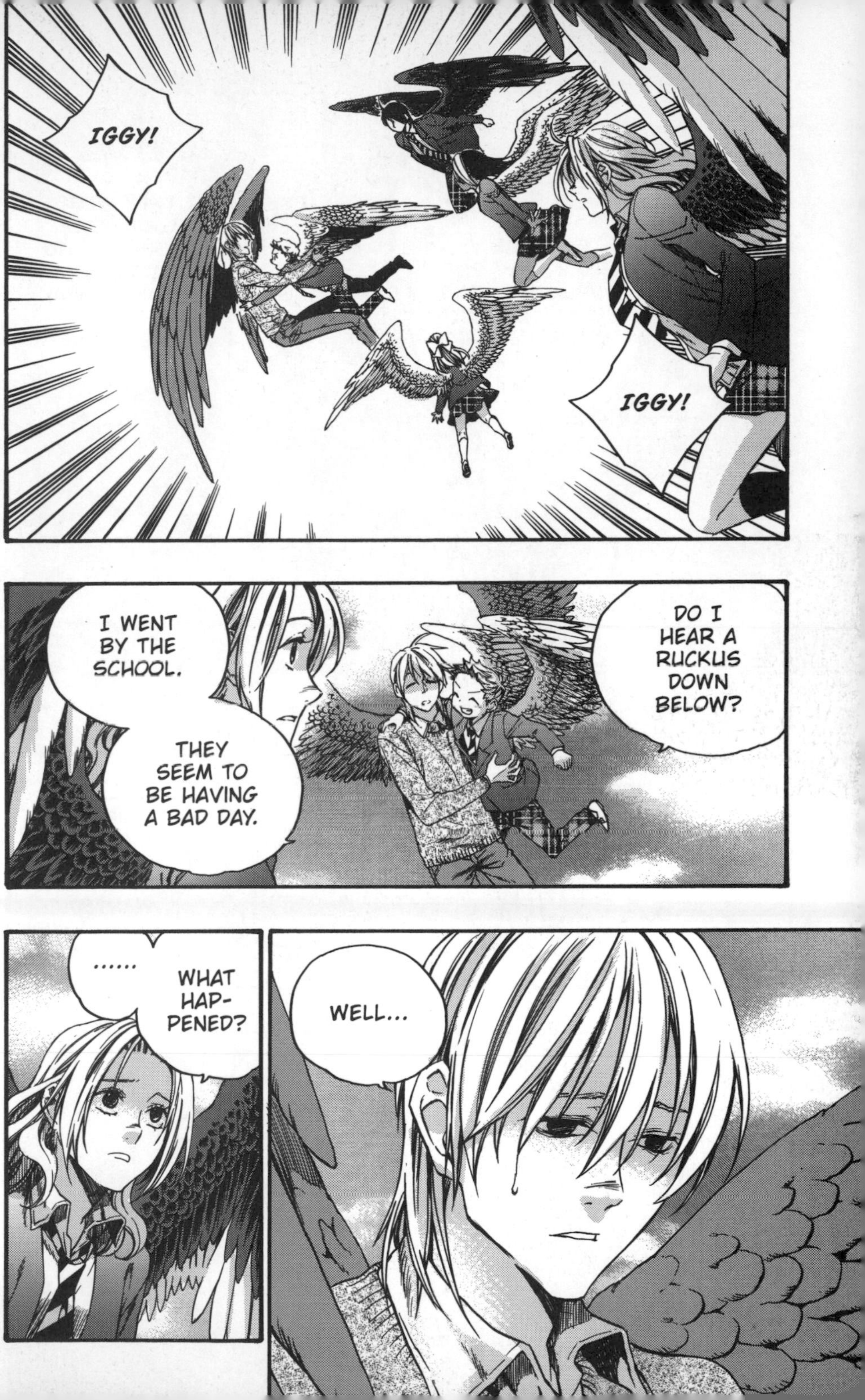
IGGY!
IGGY!
I WENT BY THE SCHOOL.
THEY SEEM TO BE HAVING A BAD DAY.
DO I HEAR A RUCKUS DOWN BELOW?
......
WHAT HAP-PENED?
WELL...

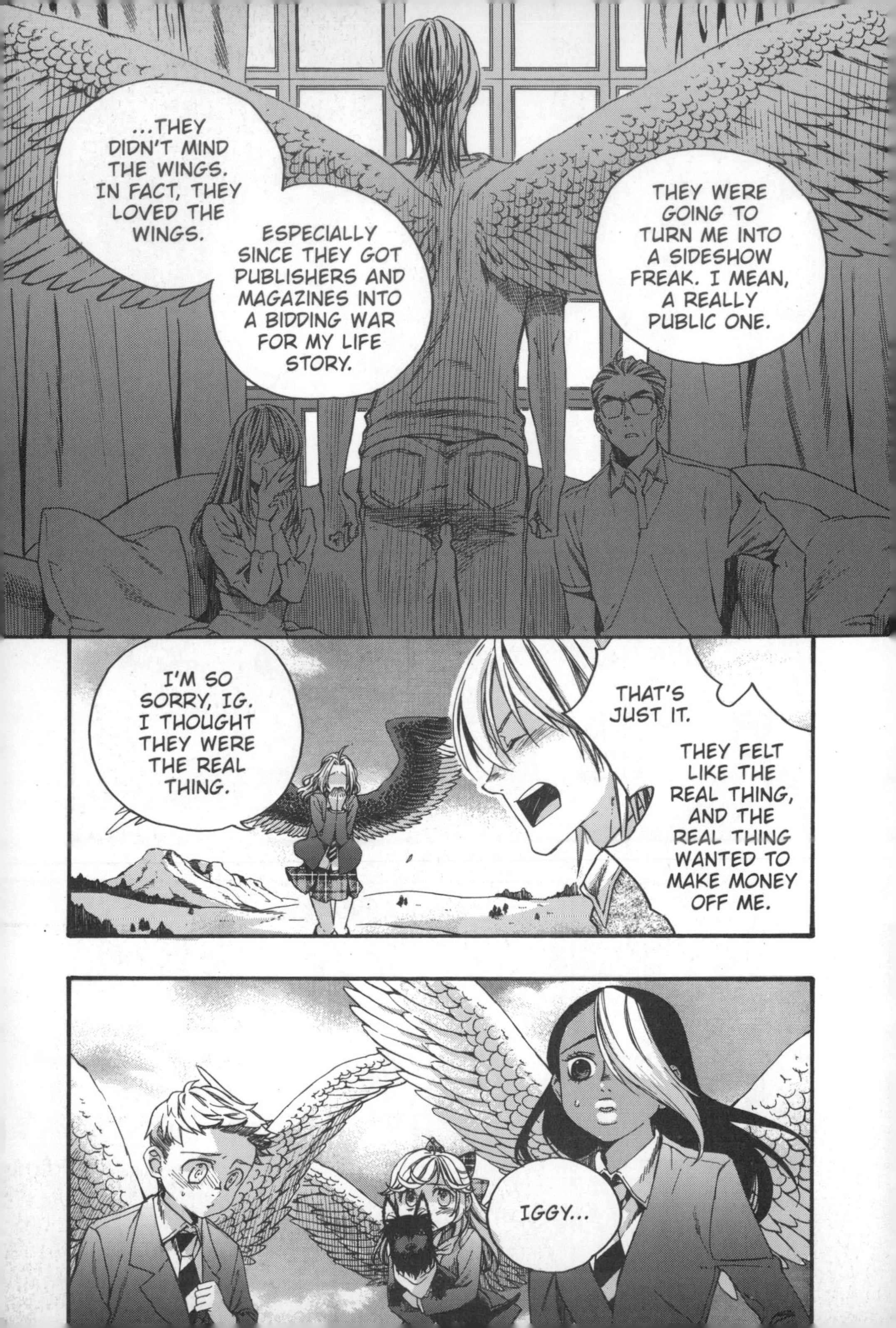
...THEY DIDN'T MIND THE WINGS. IN FACT, THEY LOVED THE WINGS.
ESPECIALLY SINCE THEY GOT PUBLISHERS AND MAGAZINES INTO A BIDDING WAR FOR MY LIFE STORY.
THEY WERE GOING TO TURN ME INTO A SIDESHOW FREAK. I MEAN, A REALLY PUBLIC ONE.
I'M SO SORRY, IG. I THOUGHT THEY WERE THE REAL THING.
THAT'S JUST IT.
THEY FELT LIKE THE REAL THING, AND THE REAL THING WANTED TO MAKE MONEY OFF ME.
IGGY...

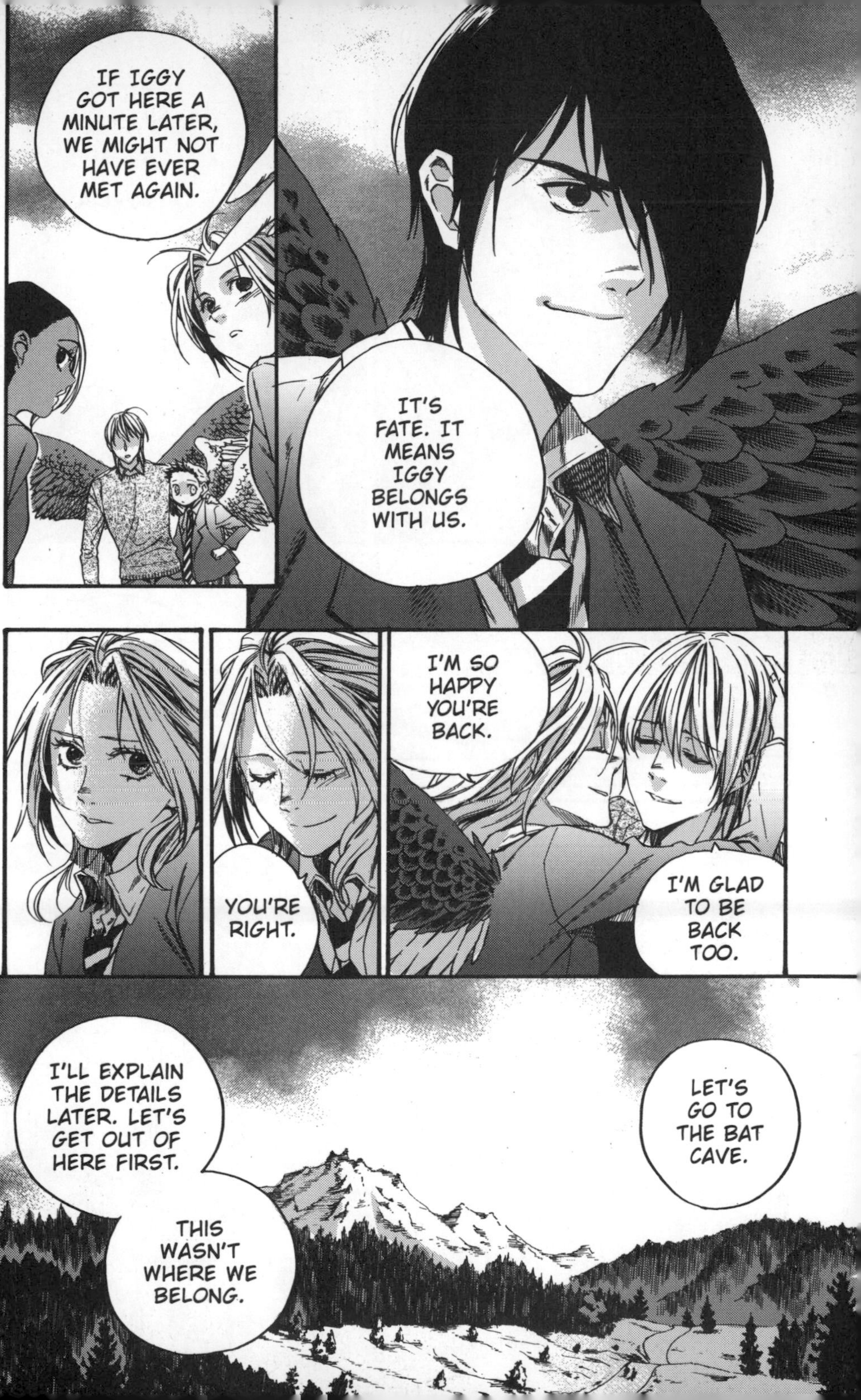
IF IGGY GOT HERE A MINUTE LATER, WE MIGHT NOT HAVE EVER MET AGAIN.
IT'S FATE. IT MEANS IGGY BELONGS WITH US.
YOU'RE RIGHT.
I'M SO HAPPY YOU'RE BACK.
I'M GLAD TO BE BACK TOO.
I'LL EXPLAIN THE DETAILS LATER. LET'S GET OUT OF HERE FIRST.
THIS WASN'T WHERE WE BELONG.
LET'S GO TO THE BAT CAVE.

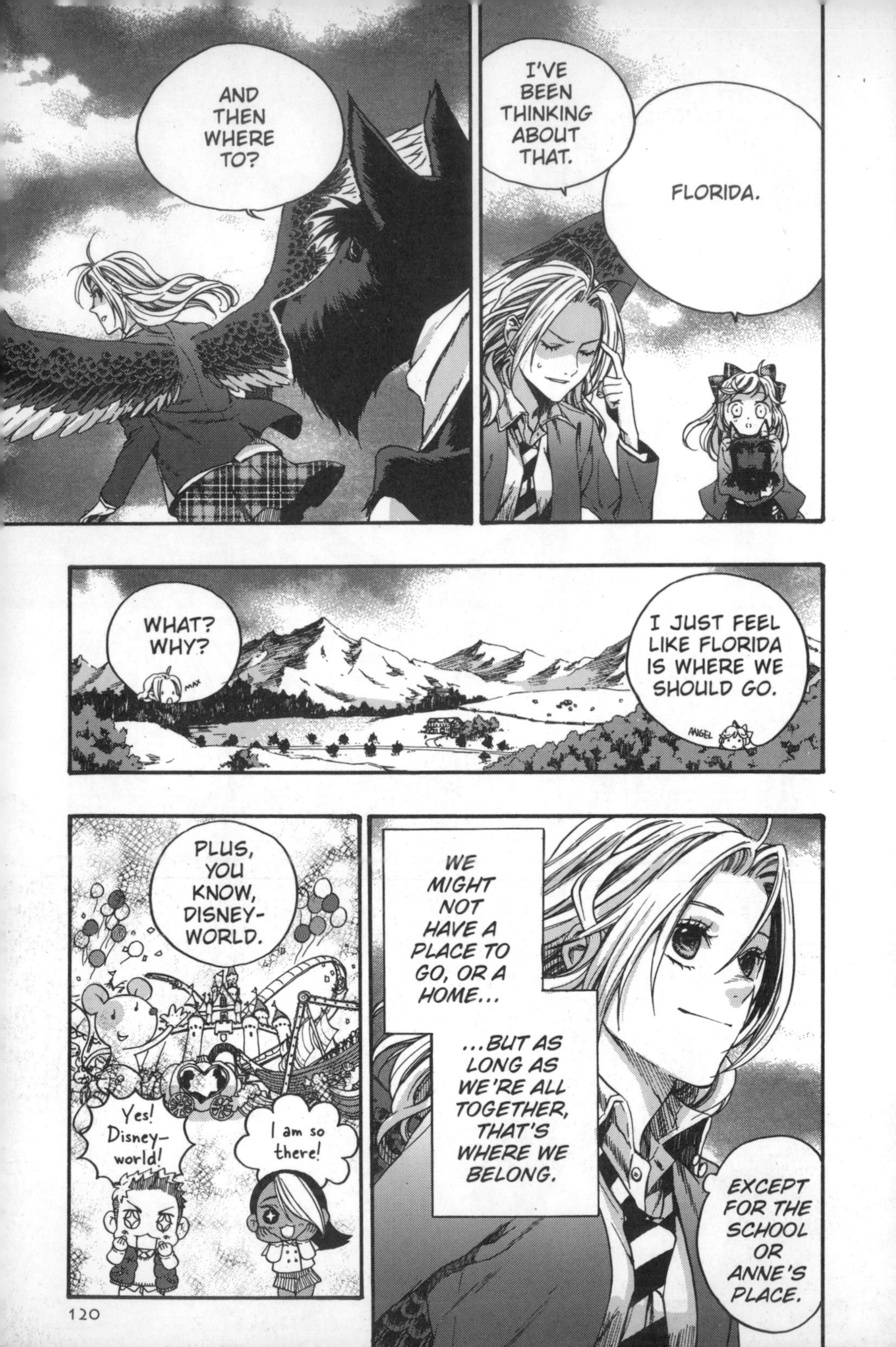
AND THEN WHERE TO?
I'VE BEEN THINKING ABOUT THAT.
FLORIDA.
WHAT? WHY?
MAX
I JUST FEEL LIKE FLORIDA IS WHERE WE SHOULD GO.
ANGEL
PLUS, YOU KNOW, DISNEY-WORLD.
Yes! Disney-world!
I am so there!
WE MIGHT NOT HAVE A PLACE TO GO, OR A HOME...
...BUT AS LONG AS WE'RE ALL TOGETHER, THAT'S WHERE WE BELONG.
EXCEPT FOR THE SCHOOL OR ANNE'S PLACE.

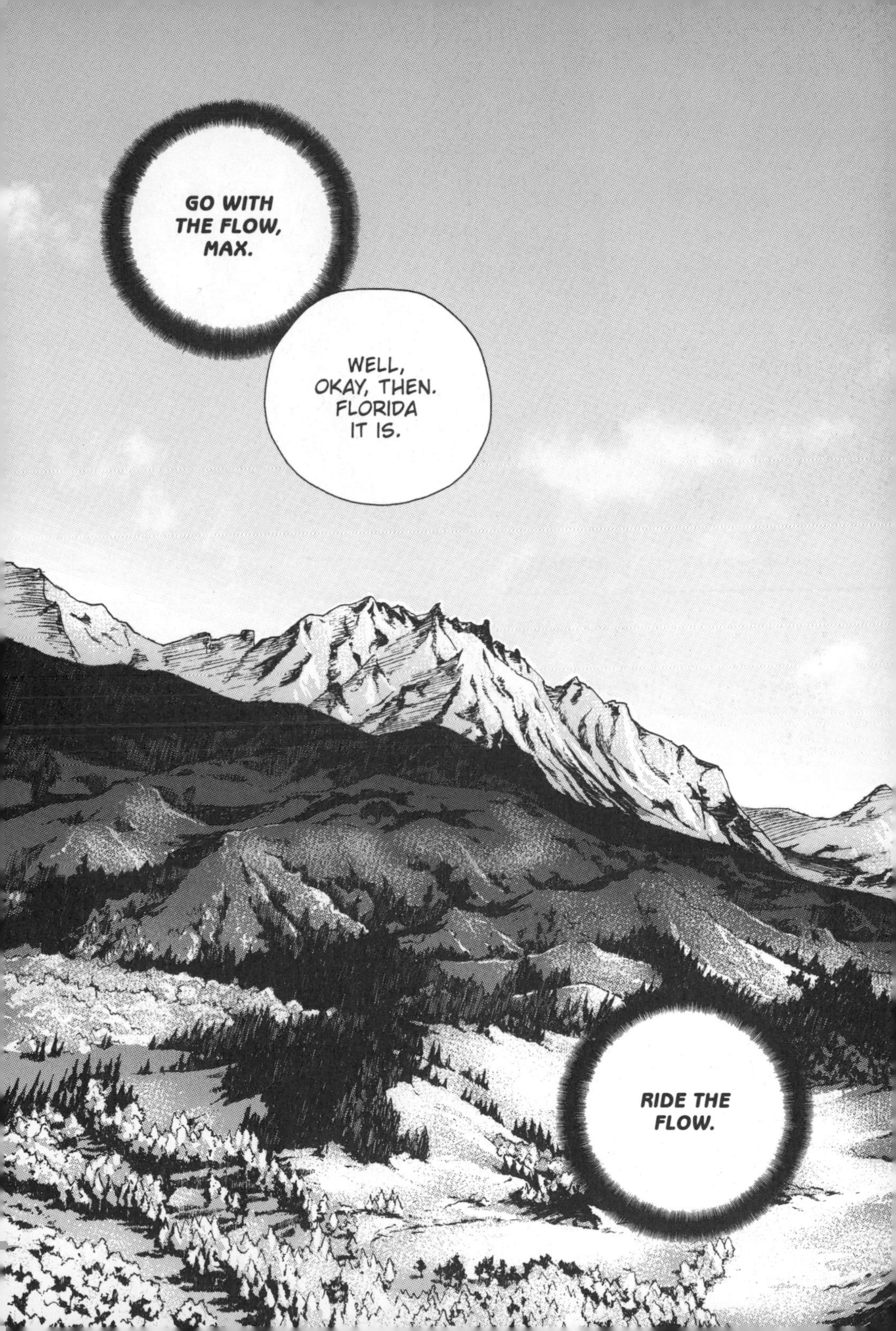
GO WITH THE FLOW, MAX.
WELL, OKAY, THEN. FLORIDA IT IS.
RIDE THE FLOW.

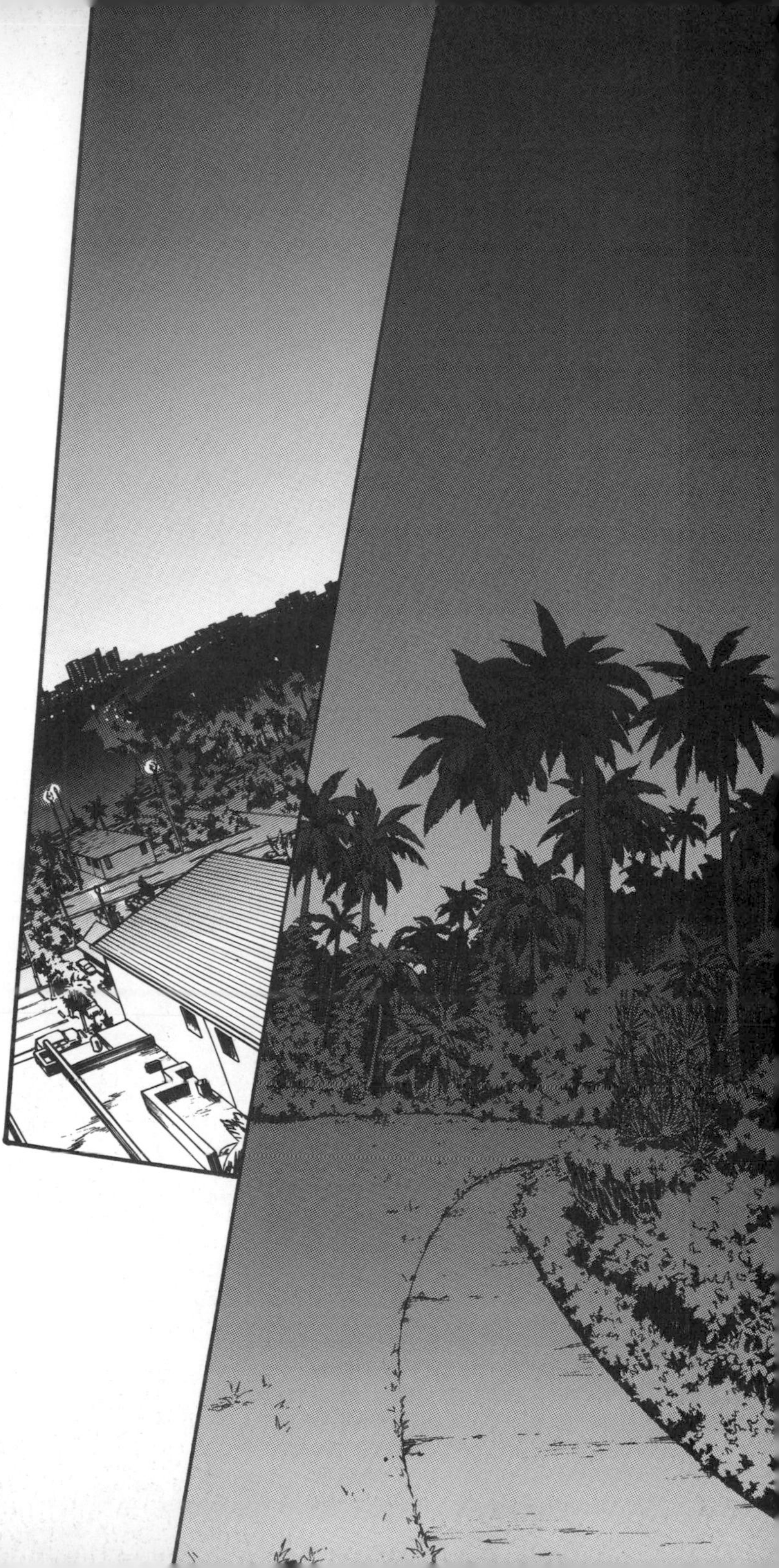

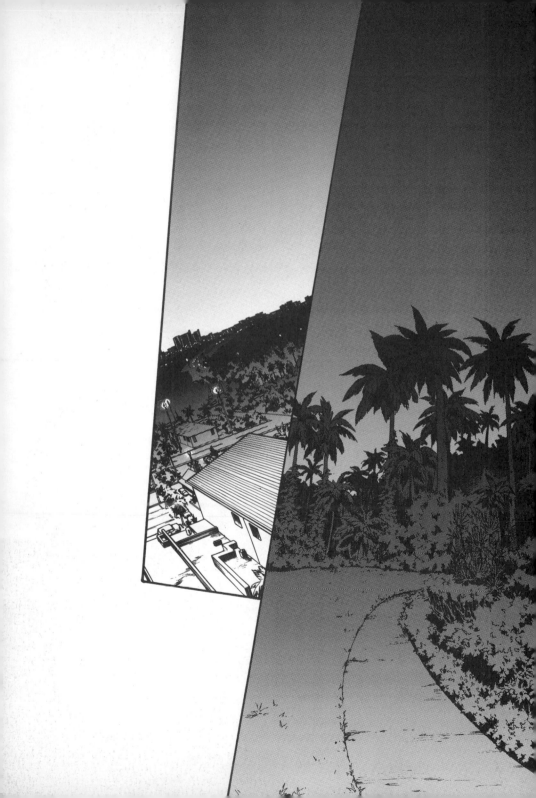

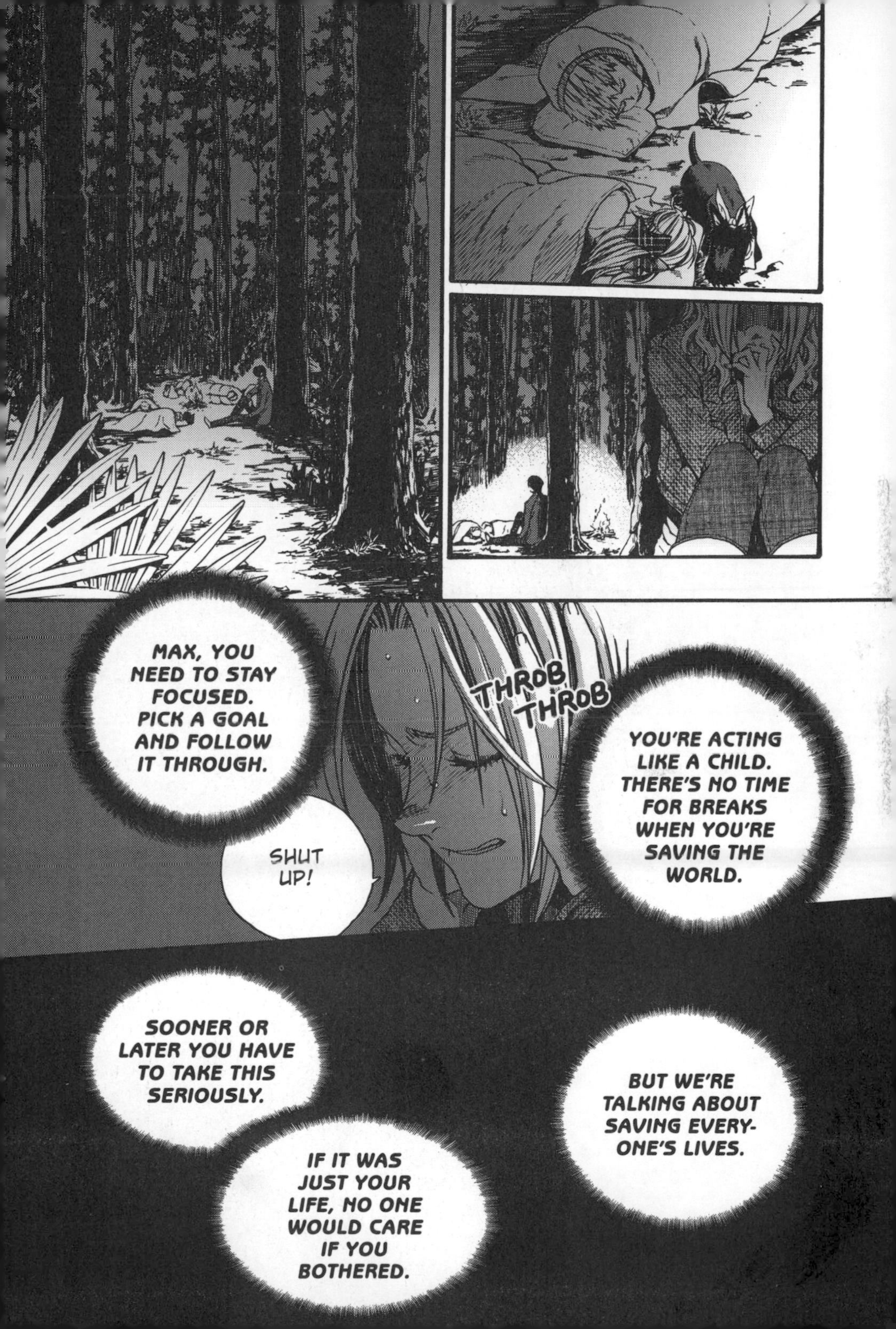
MAX, YOU NEED TO STAY FOCUSED. PICK A GOAL AND FOLLOW IT THROUGH.
THROB THROB
SHUT UP!
YOU'RE ACTING LIKE A CHILD. THERE'S NO TIME FOR BREAKS WHEN YOU'RE SAVING THE WORLD.
SOONER OR LATER YOU HAVE TO TAKE THIS SERIOUSLY.
IF IT WAS JUST YOUR LIFE, NO ONE WOULD CARE IF YOU BOTHERED.
BUT WE'RE TALKING ABOUT SAVING EVERY-ONE'S LIVES.

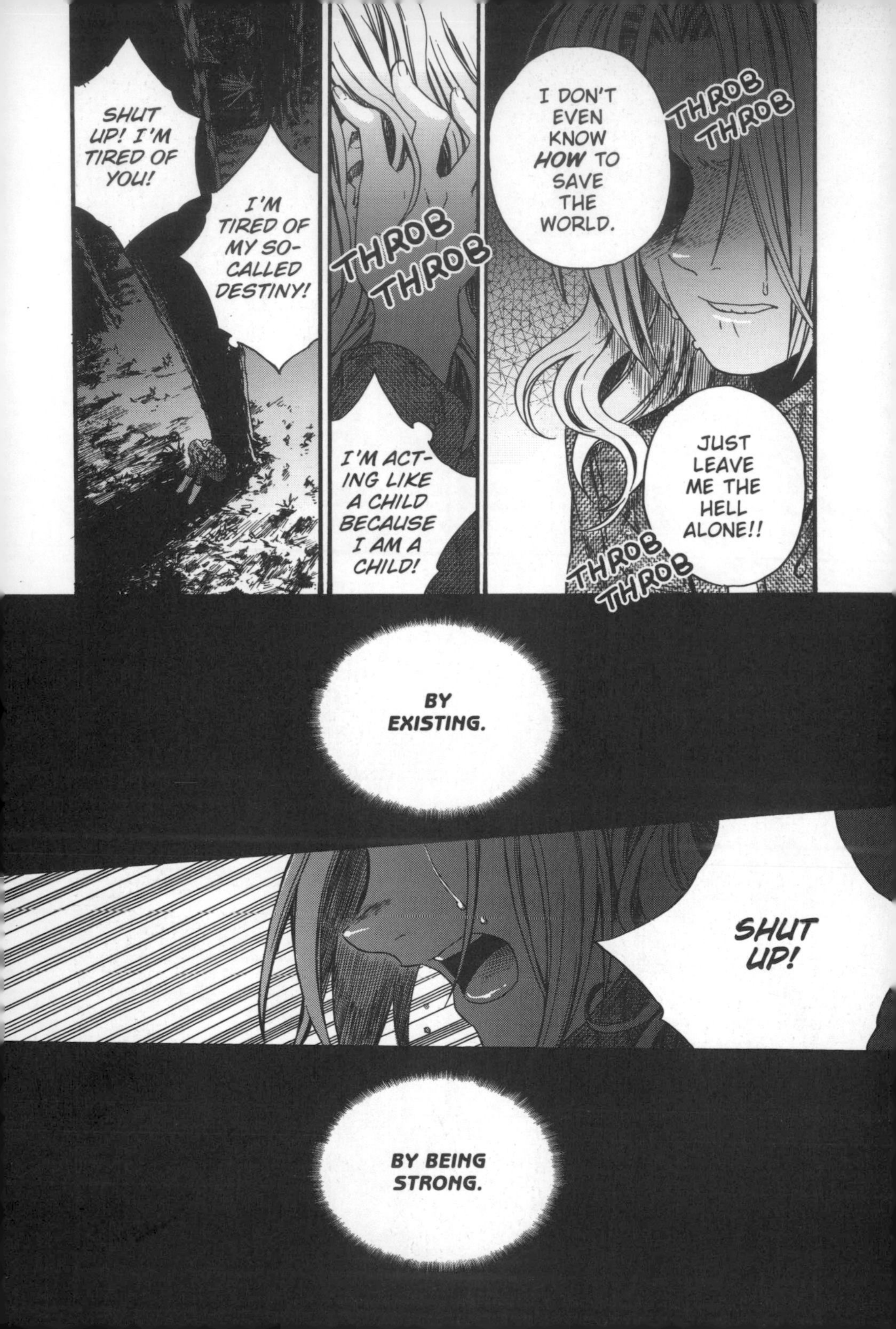
SHUT UP! I'M TIRED OF YOU!
I'M TIRED OF MY SO-CALLED DESTINY!
THROB THROB
I'M ACT-ING LIKE A CHILD BECAUSE I AM A CHILD!
I DON'T EVEN KNOW HOW TO SAVE THE WORLD.
THROB THROB
JUST LEAVE ME THE HELL ALONE!!
THROB THROB
BY EXISTING.
SHUT UP!
BY BEING STRONG.

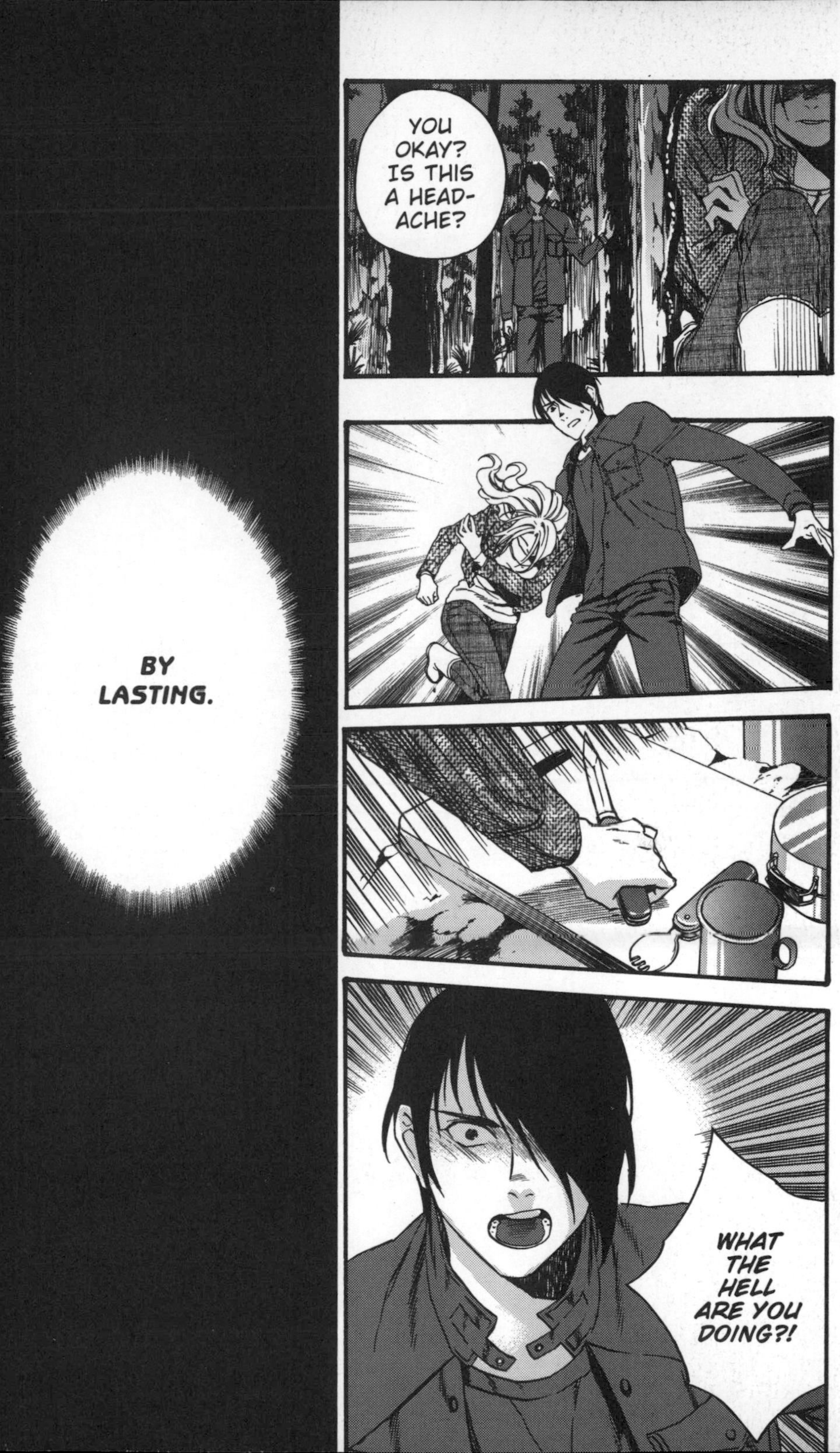
BY LASTING.
YOU OKAY? IS THIS A HEAD-ACHE?
WHAT THE HELL ARE YOU DOING?!

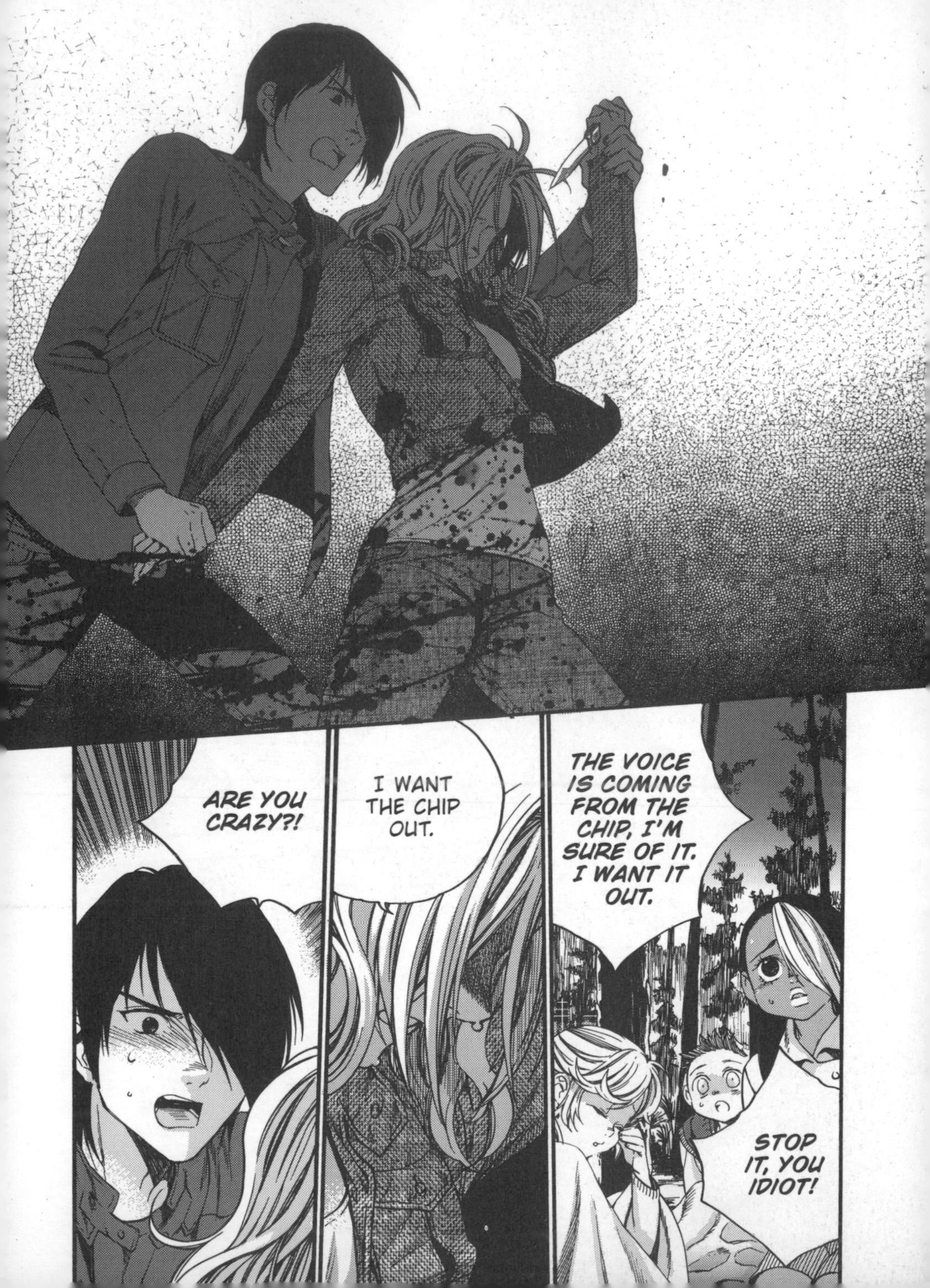
ARE YOU CRAZY?!
I WANT THE CHIP OUT.
THE VOICE IS COMING FROM THE CHIP, I'M SURE OF IT. I WANT IT OUT.
STOP IT, YOU IDIOT!

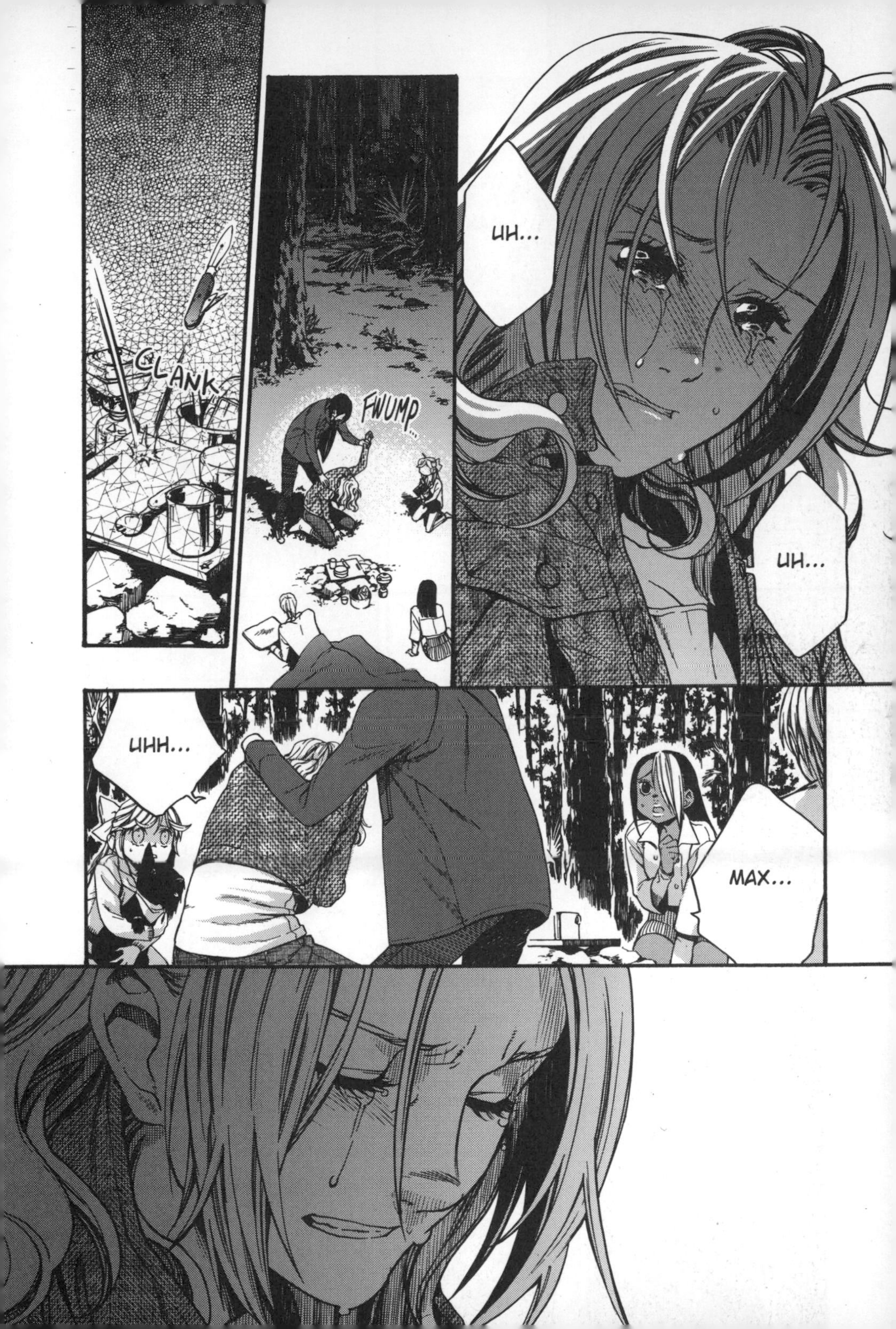
CLANK
FWUMP...
UH...
UH...
UHH...
MAX...

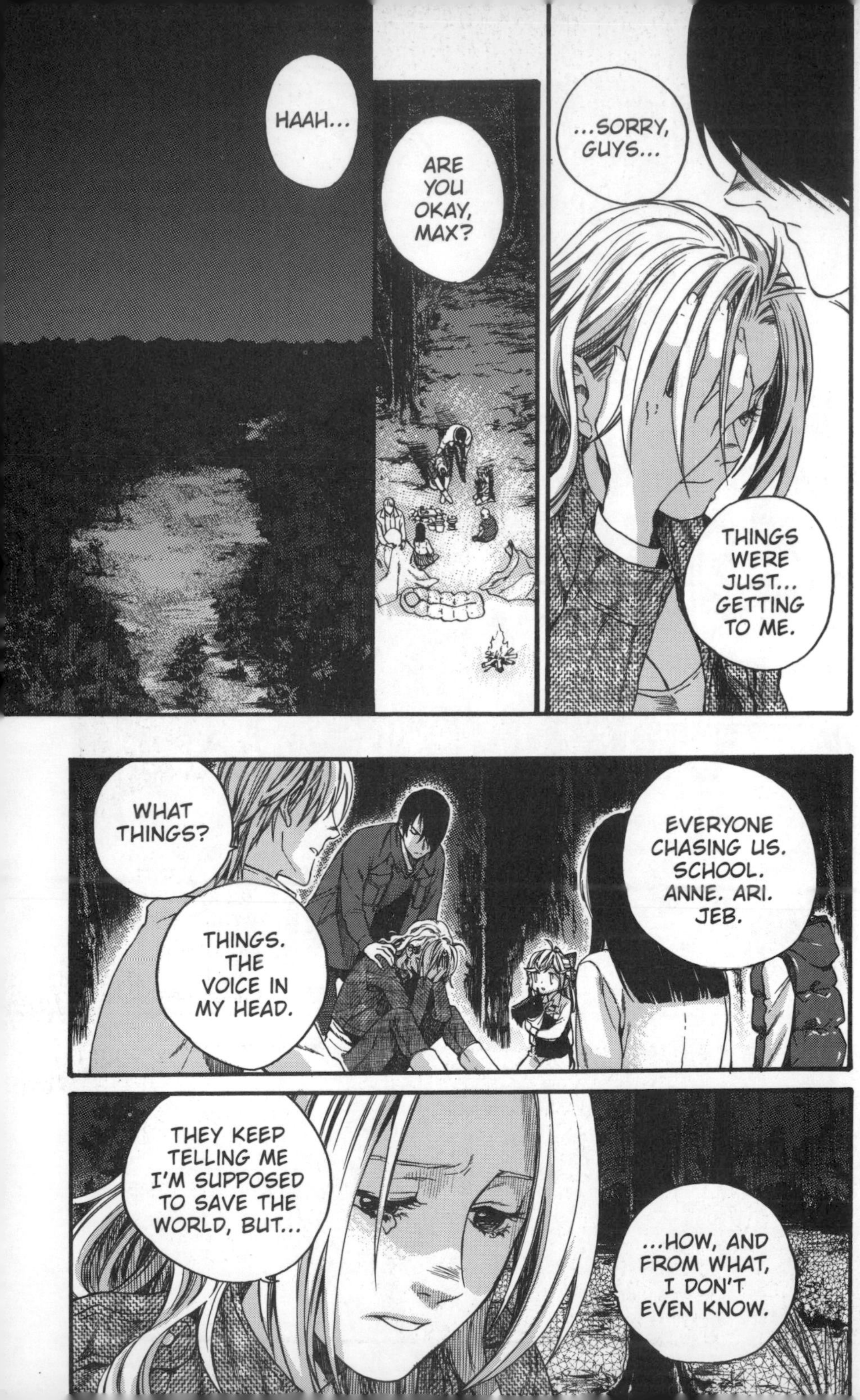
HAAH...
ARE YOU OKAY, MAX?
...SORRY, GUYS...
THINGS WERE JUST... GETTING TO ME.
WHAT THINGS?
THINGS. THE VOICE IN MY HEAD.
EVERYONE CHASING US. SCHOOL. ANNE. ARI. JEB.
THEY KEEP TELLING ME I'M SUPPOSED TO SAVE THE WORLD, BUT...
...HOW, AND FROM WHAT, I DON'T EVEN KNOW.

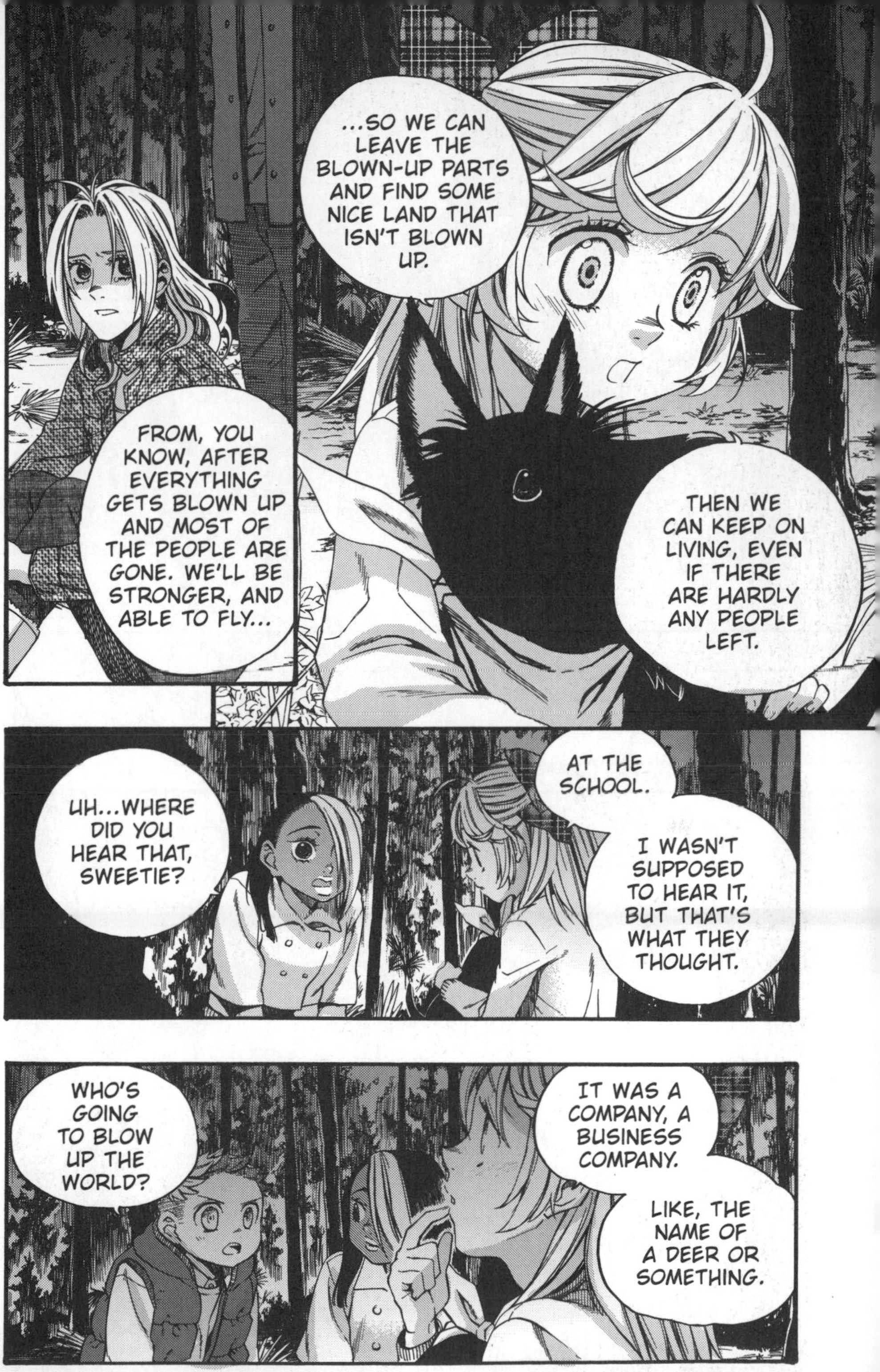
FROM, YOU KNOW, AFTER EVERYTHING GETS BLOWN UP AND MOST OF THE PEOPLE ARE GONE. WE'LL BE STRONGER, AND ABLE TO FLY...
...SO WE CAN LEAVE THE BLOWN-UP PARTS AND FIND SOME NICE LAND THAT ISN'T BLOWN UP.
THEN WE CAN KEEP ON LIVING, EVEN IF THERE ARE HARDLY ANY PEOPLE LEFT.
UH...WHERE DID YOU HEAR THAT, SWEETIE?
AT THE SCHOOL.
I WASN'T SUPPOSED TO HEAR IT, BUT THAT'S WHAT THEY THOUGHT.
WHO'S GOING TO BLOW UP THE WORLD?
IT WAS A COMPANY, A BUSINESS COMPANY.
LIKE, THE NAME OF A DEER OR SOMETHING.

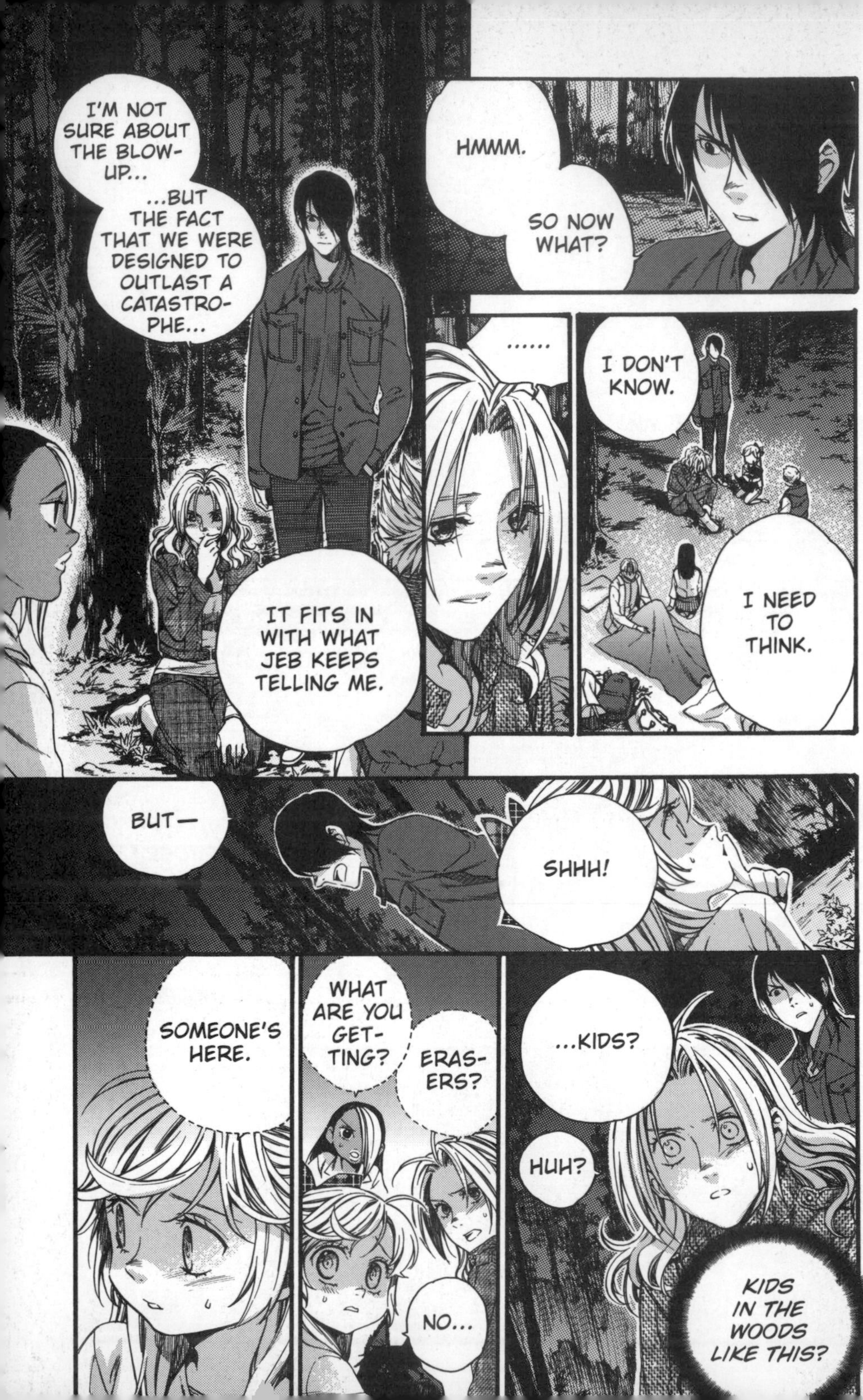
I'M NOT SURE ABOUT THE BLOW-UP...
...BUT THE FACT THAT WE WERE DESIGNED TO OUTLAST A CATASTRO-PHE...
IT FITS IN WITH WHAT JEB KEEPS TELLING ME.
HMMM.
SO NOW WHAT?
......
I DON'T KNOW.
I NEED TO THINK.
BUT—
SHHH!
SOMEONE'S HERE.
WHAT ARE YOU GET-TING?
ERAS-ERS?
NO...
...KIDS?
HUH?
KIDS IN THE WOODS LIKE THIS?

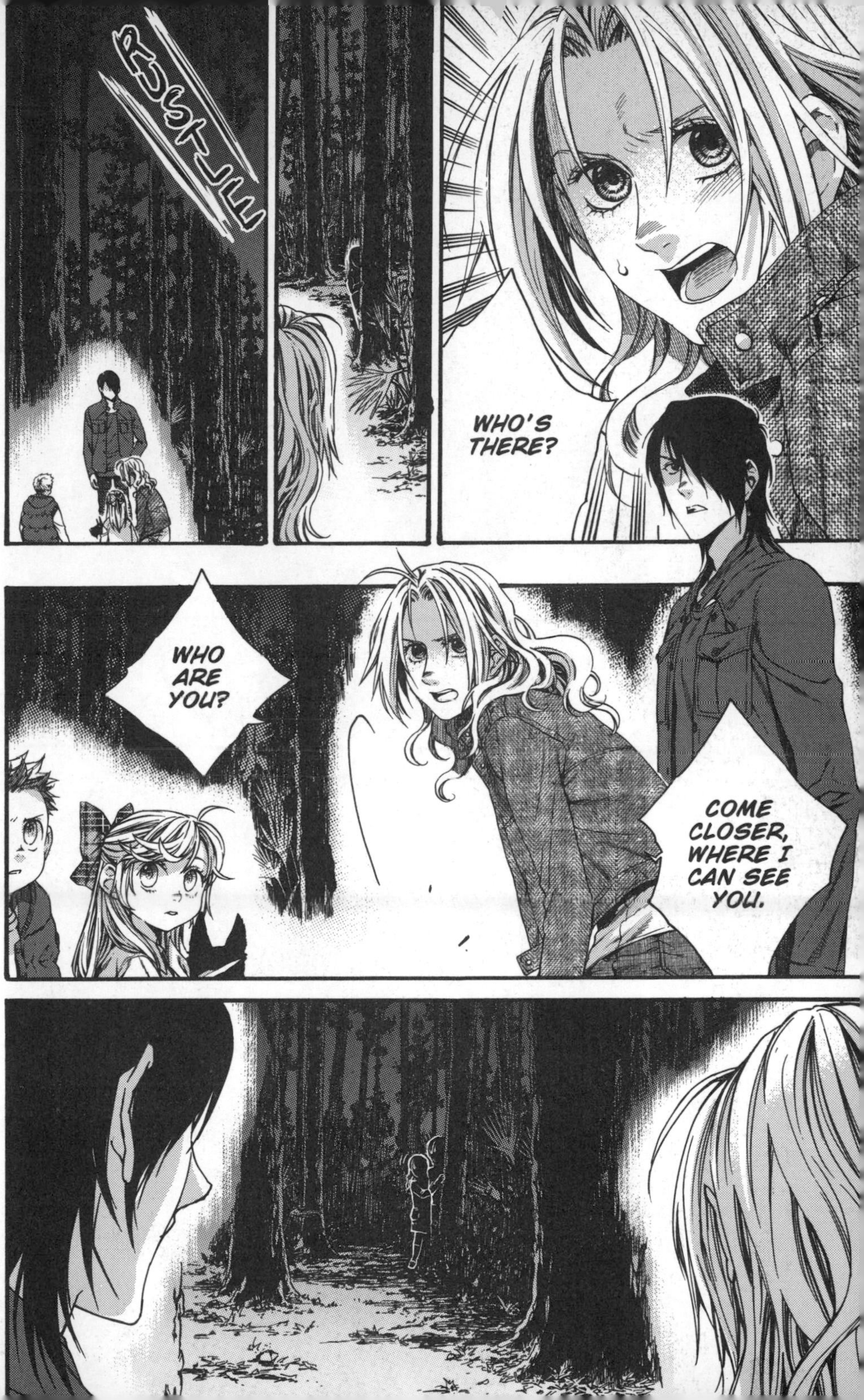
RUSTLE
WHO'S THERE?
WHO ARE YOU?
COME CLOSER, WHERE I CAN SEE YOU.

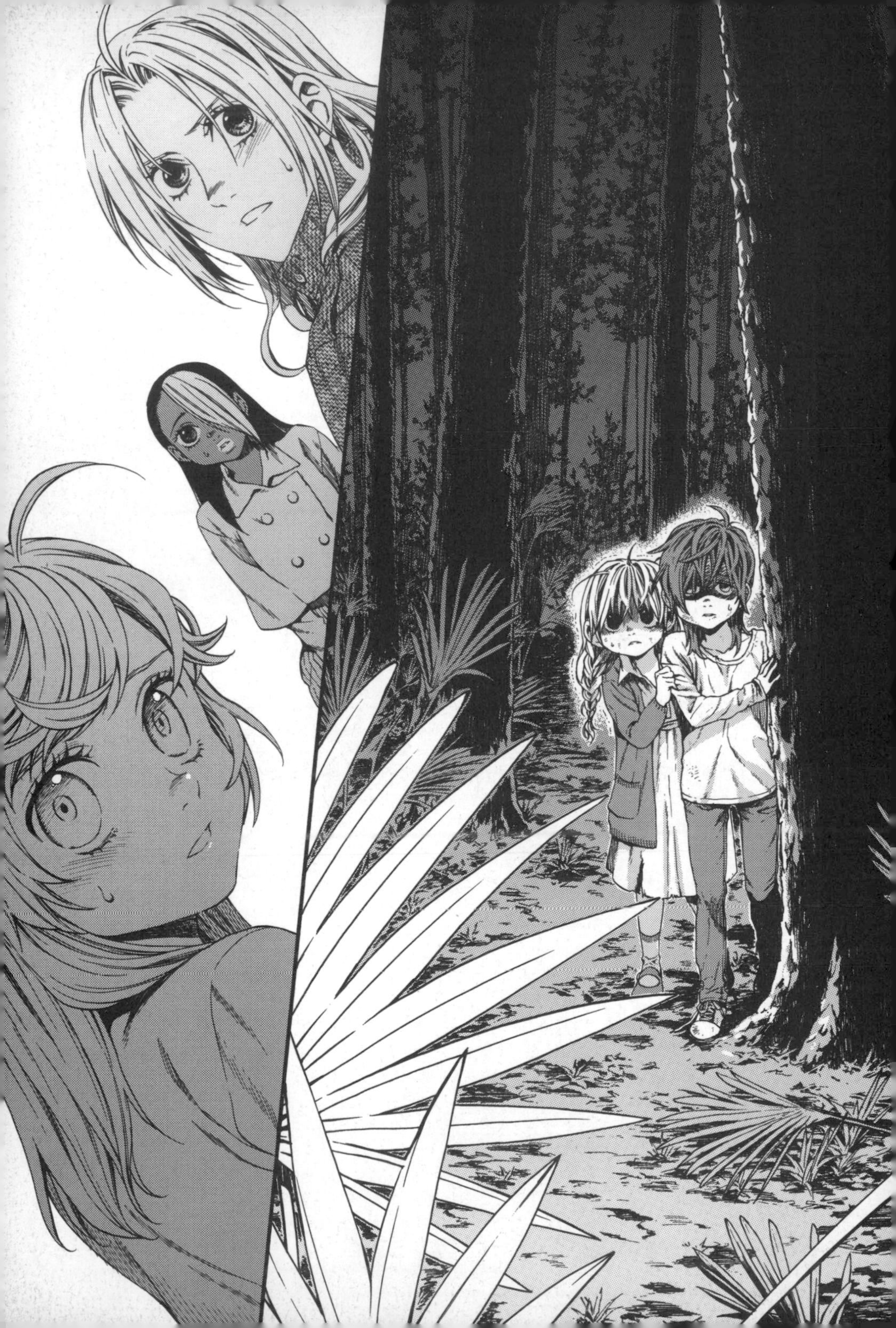

MAXIMUM
RIDE

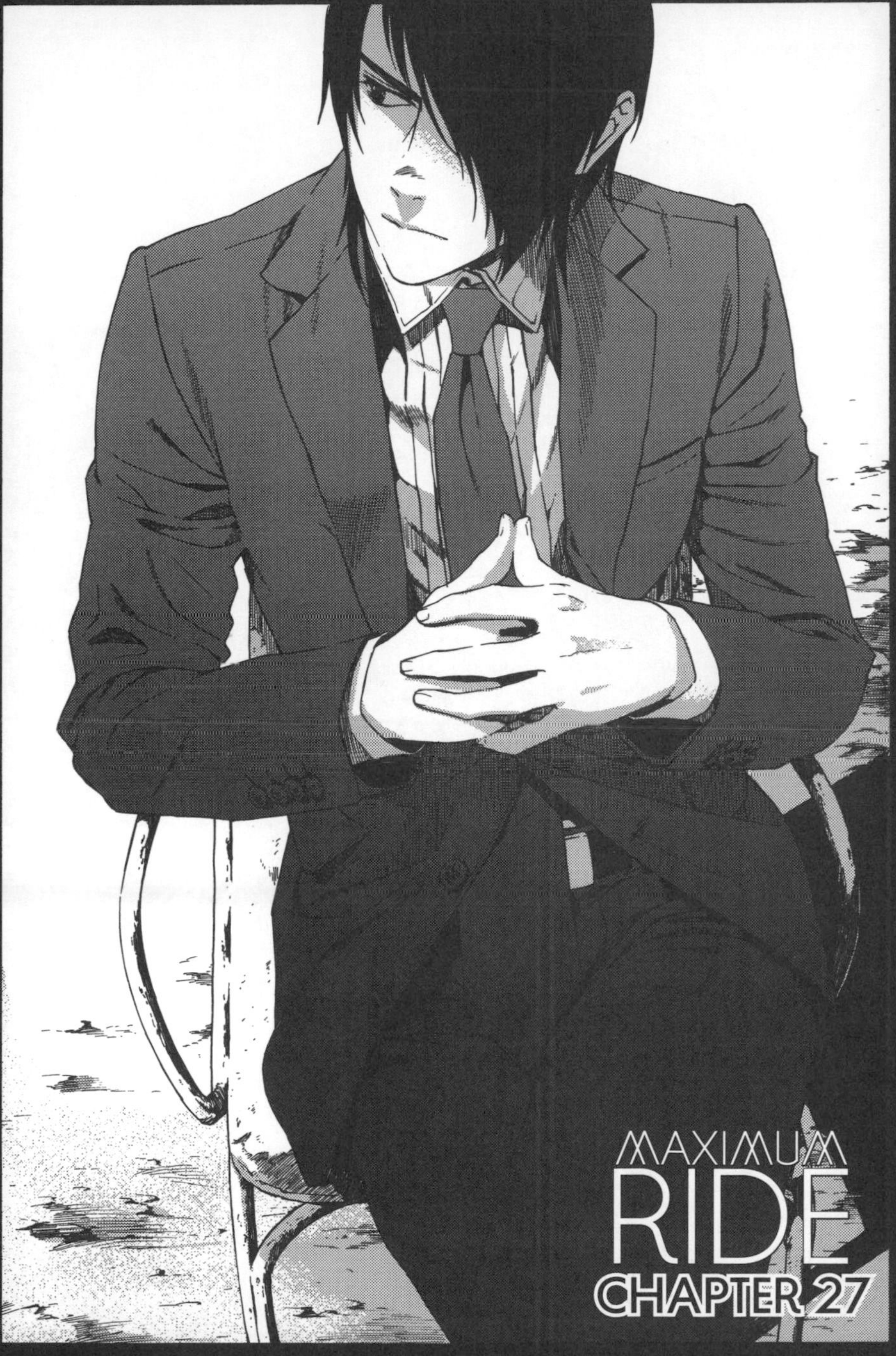
MAXIMUM
RIDE
CHAPTER 27

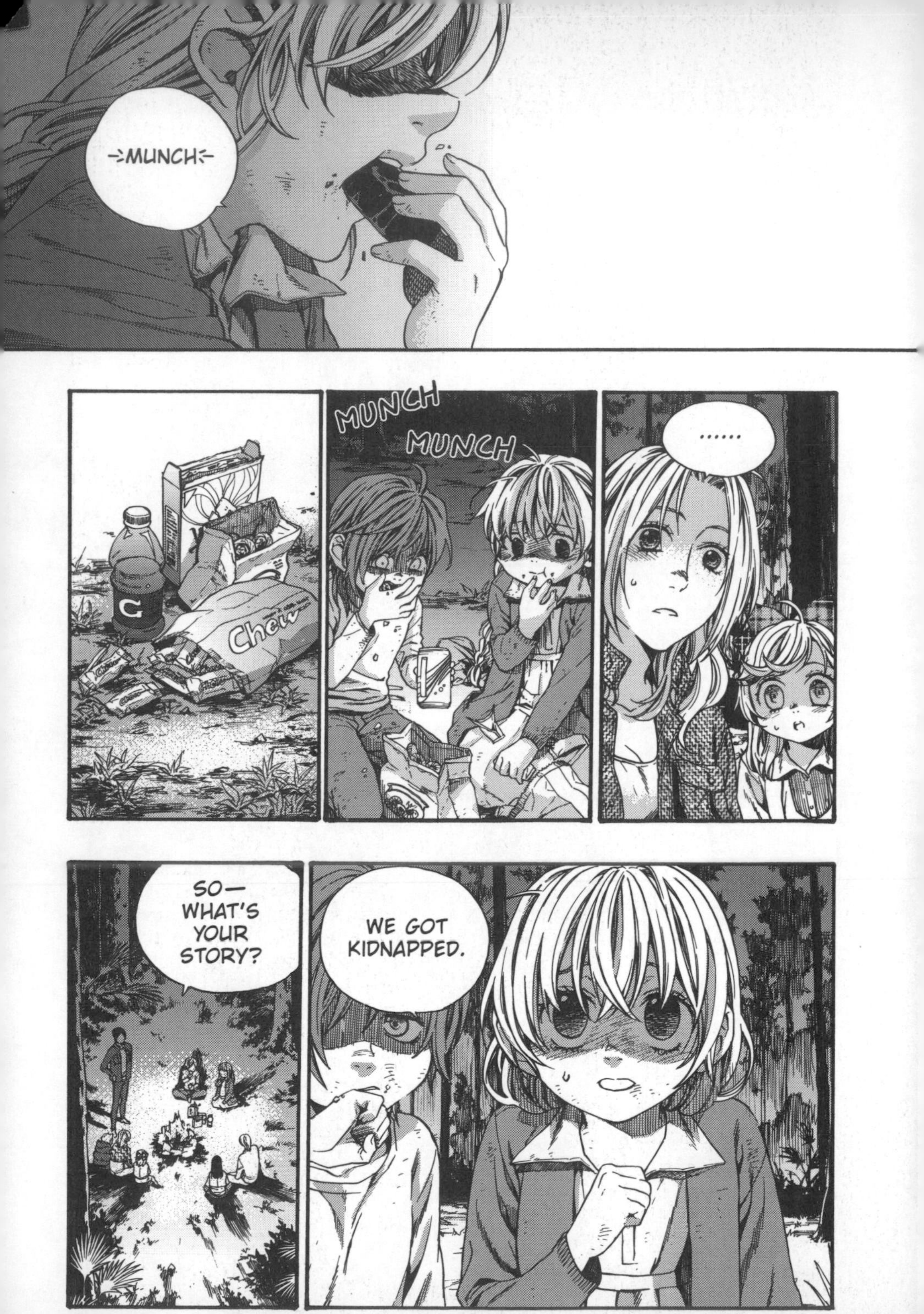
MUNCH
Chew
MUNCH
MUNCH
......
SO— WHAT'S YOUR STORY?
WE GOT KIDNAPPED.

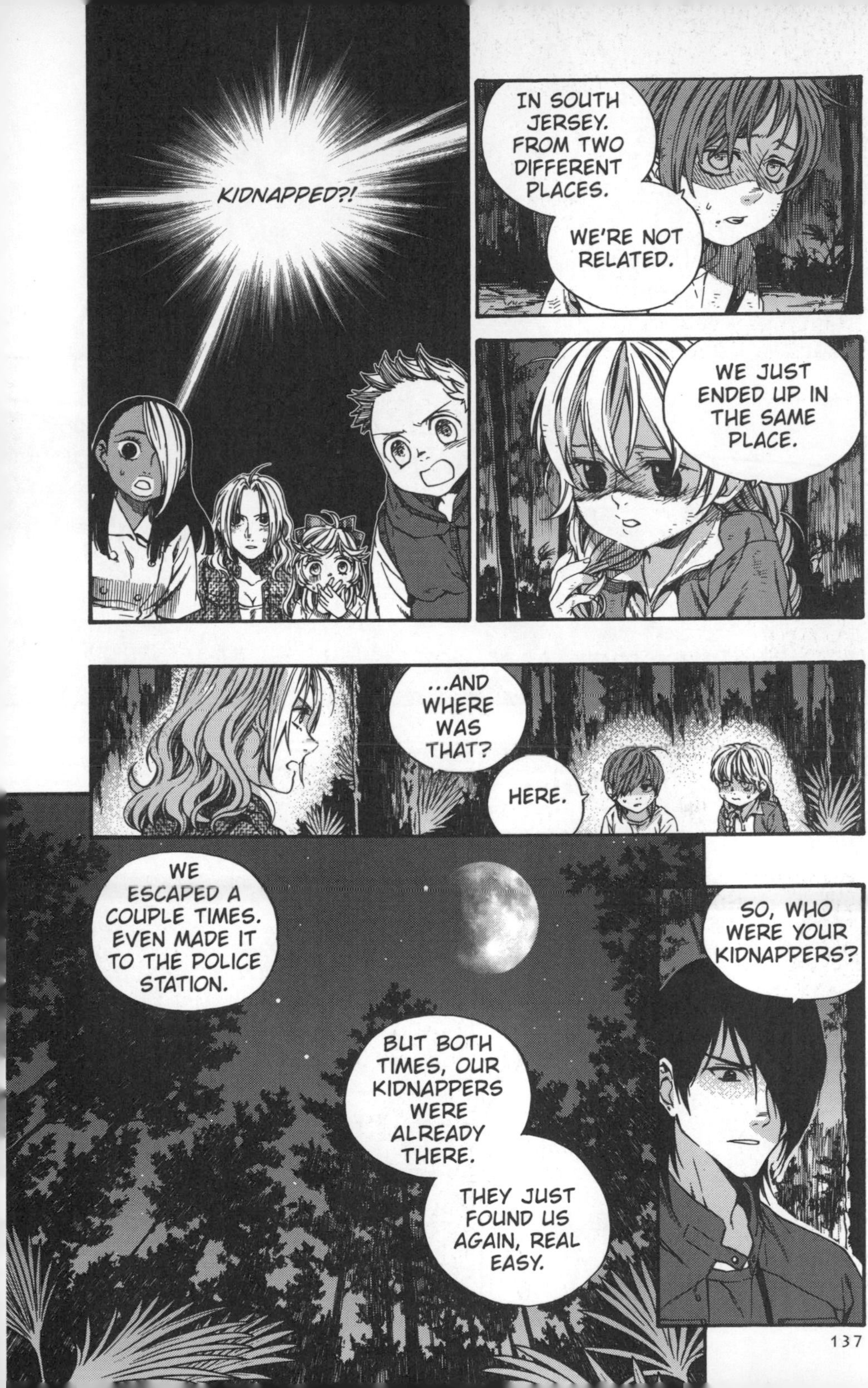
KIDNAPPED?!
IN SOUTH JERSEY. FROM TWO DIFFERENT PLACES.
WE'RE NOT RELATED.
WE JUST ENDED UP IN THE SAME PLACE.
...AND WHERE WAS THAT?
HERE.
WE ESCAPED A COUPLE TIMES. EVEN MADE IT TO THE POLICE STATION.
BUT BOTH TIMES, OUR KIDNAPPERS WERE ALREADY THERE.
THEY JUST FOUND US AGAIN, REAL EASY.
SO, WHO WERE YOUR KIDNAPPERS?

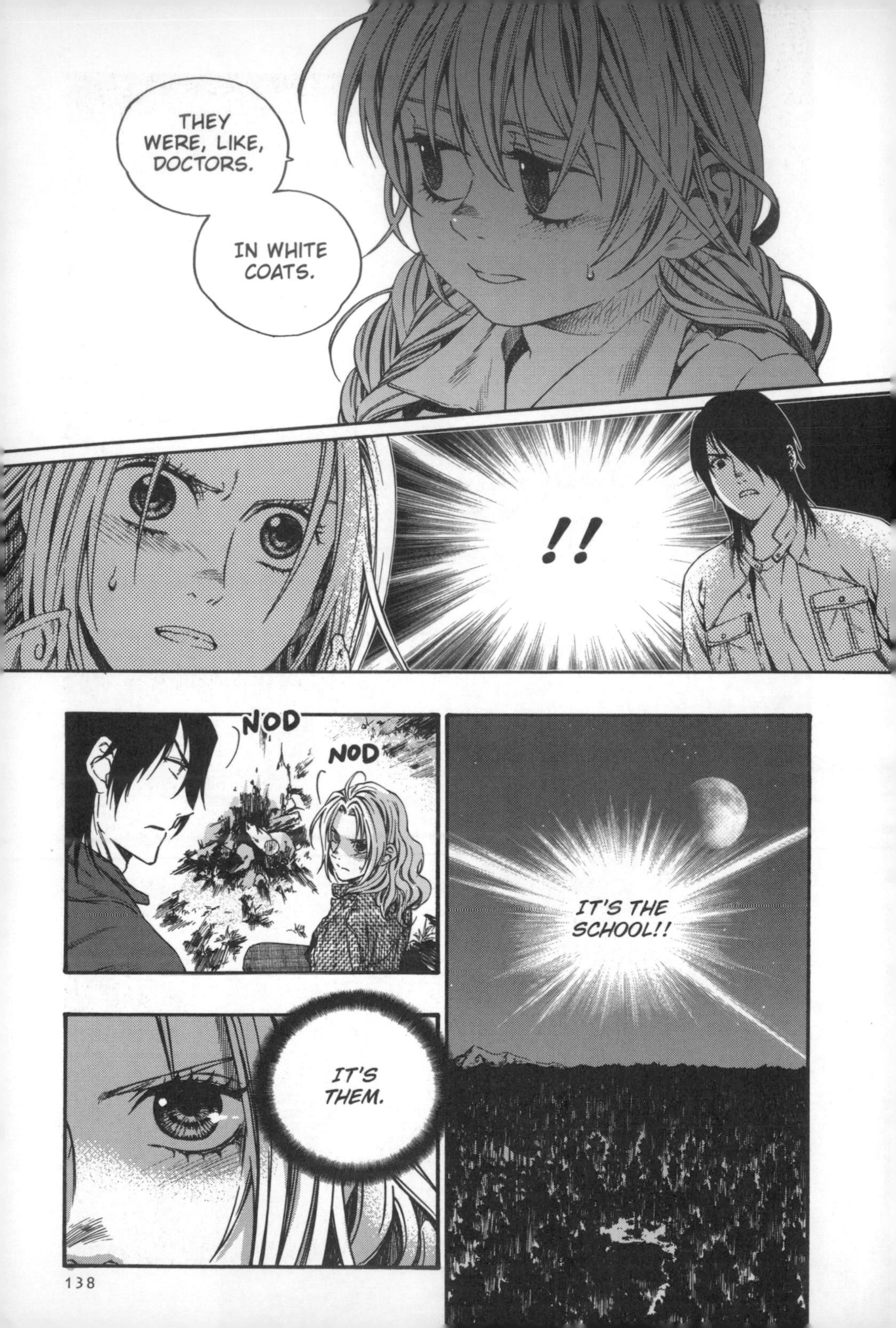
THEY WERE, LIKE, DOCTORS.
IN WHITE COATS.
!!
NOD
NOD
IT'S THEM.
IT'S THE SCHOOL!!

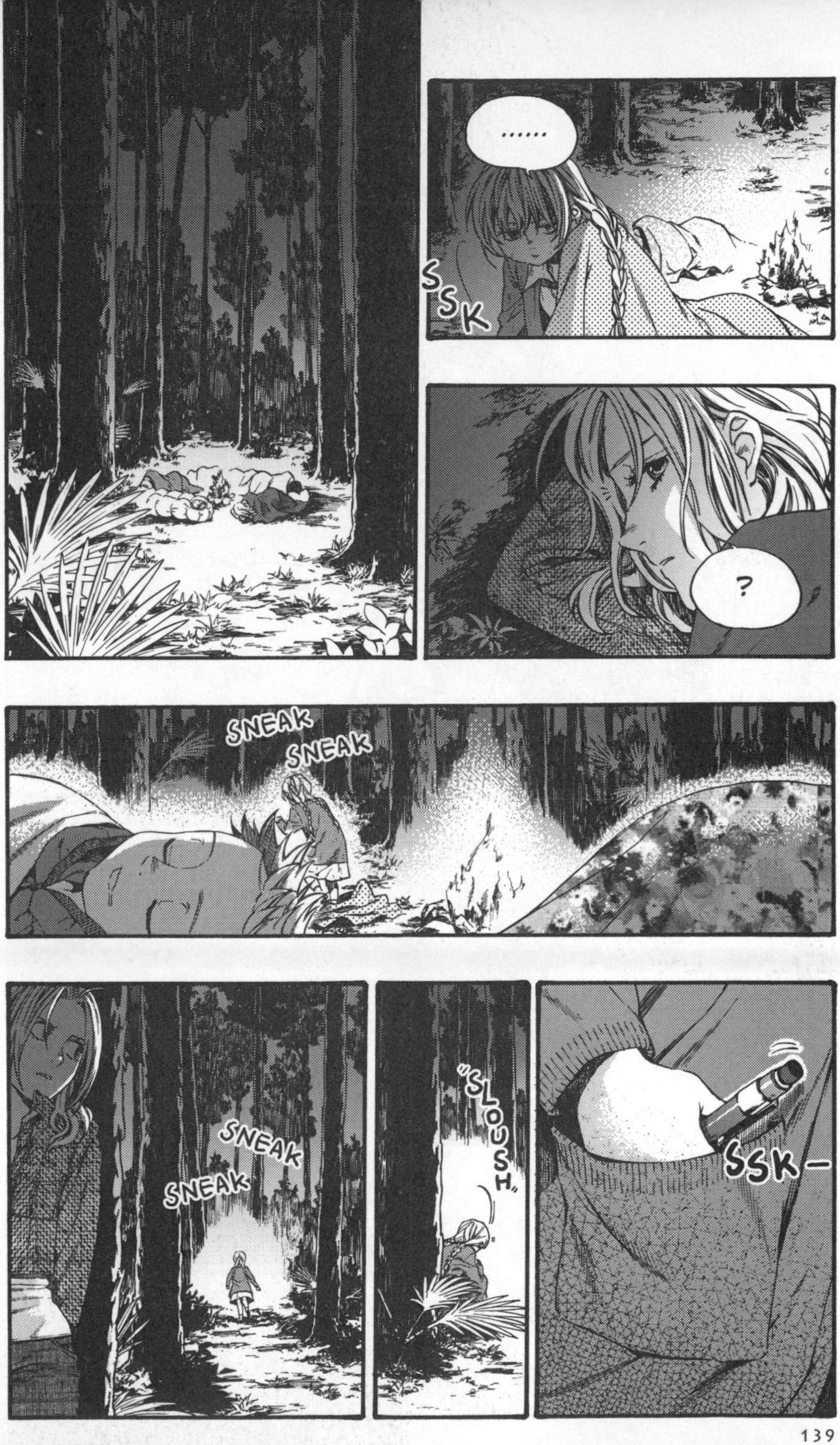
....
SSK
?
SNEAK
SNEAK
SNEAK
SNEAK
"SLOUSH"
SSK–

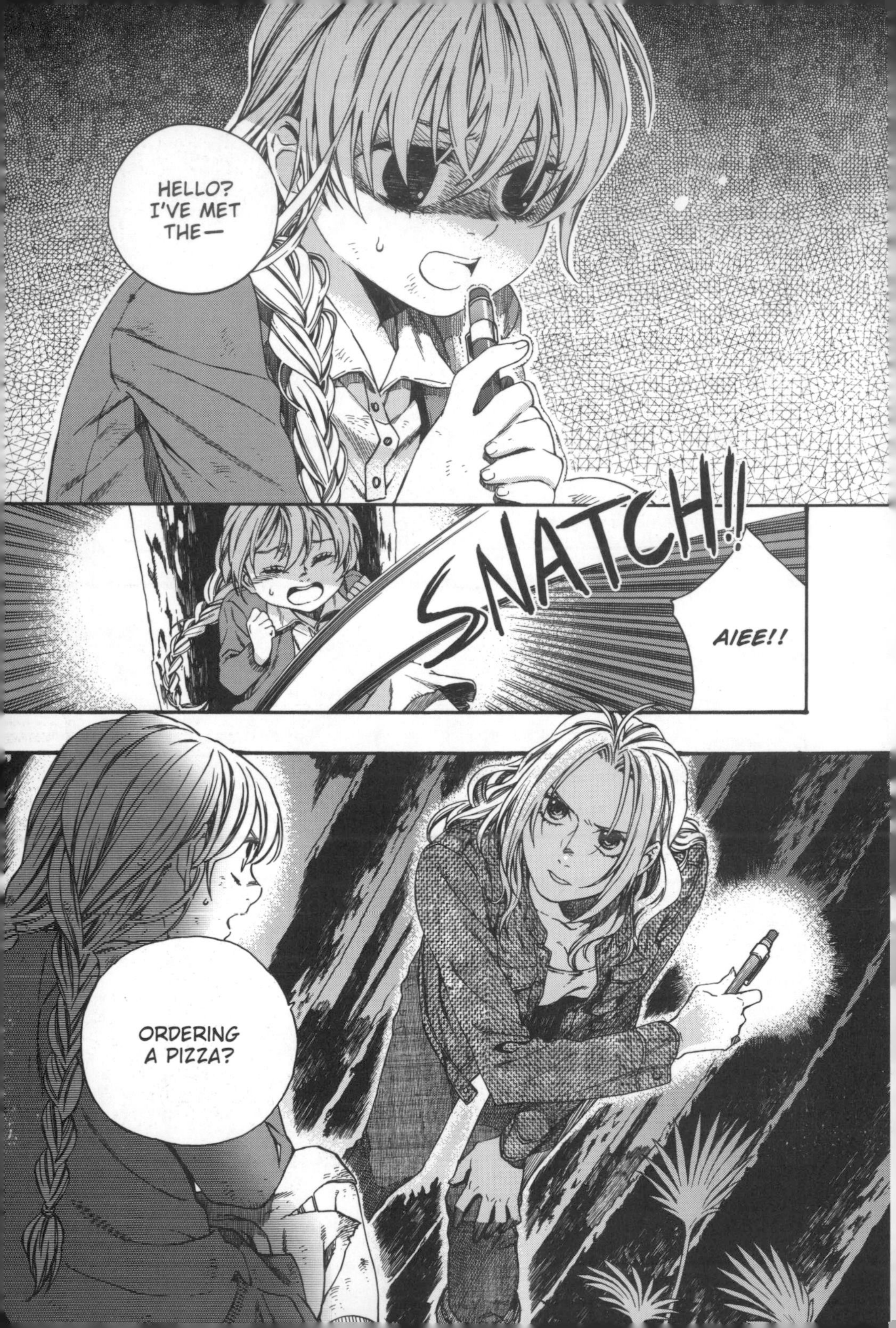
HELLO? I'VE MET THE—
SNATCH!!
AIEE!!
ORDERING A PIZZA?

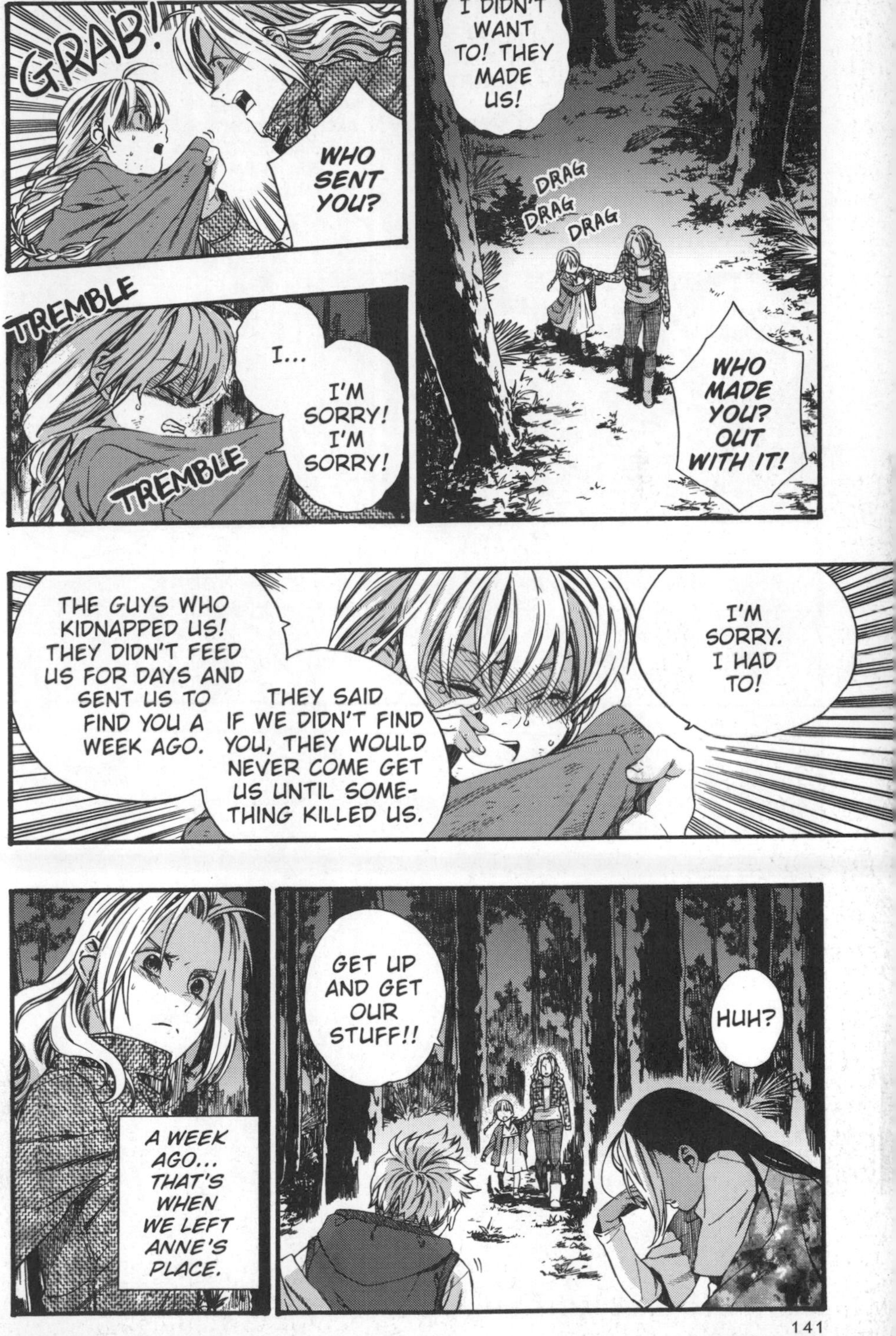
GRAB!
WHO SENT YOU?
TREMBLE
I...
I'M SORRY! I'M SORRY!
TREMBLE
I DIDN'T WANT TO! THEY MADE US!
DRAG DRAG DRAG
WHO MADE YOU? OUT WITH IT!
THE GUYS WHO KIDNAPPED US! THEY DIDN'T FEED US FOR DAYS AND SENT US TO FIND YOU A WEEK AGO.
THEY SAID IF WE DIDN'T FIND YOU, THEY WOULD NEVER COME GET US UNTIL SOME-THING KILLED US.
I'M SORRY. I HAD TO!
A WEEK AGO... THAT'S WHEN WE LEFT ANNE'S PLACE.
GET UP AND GET OUR STUFF!!
HUH?

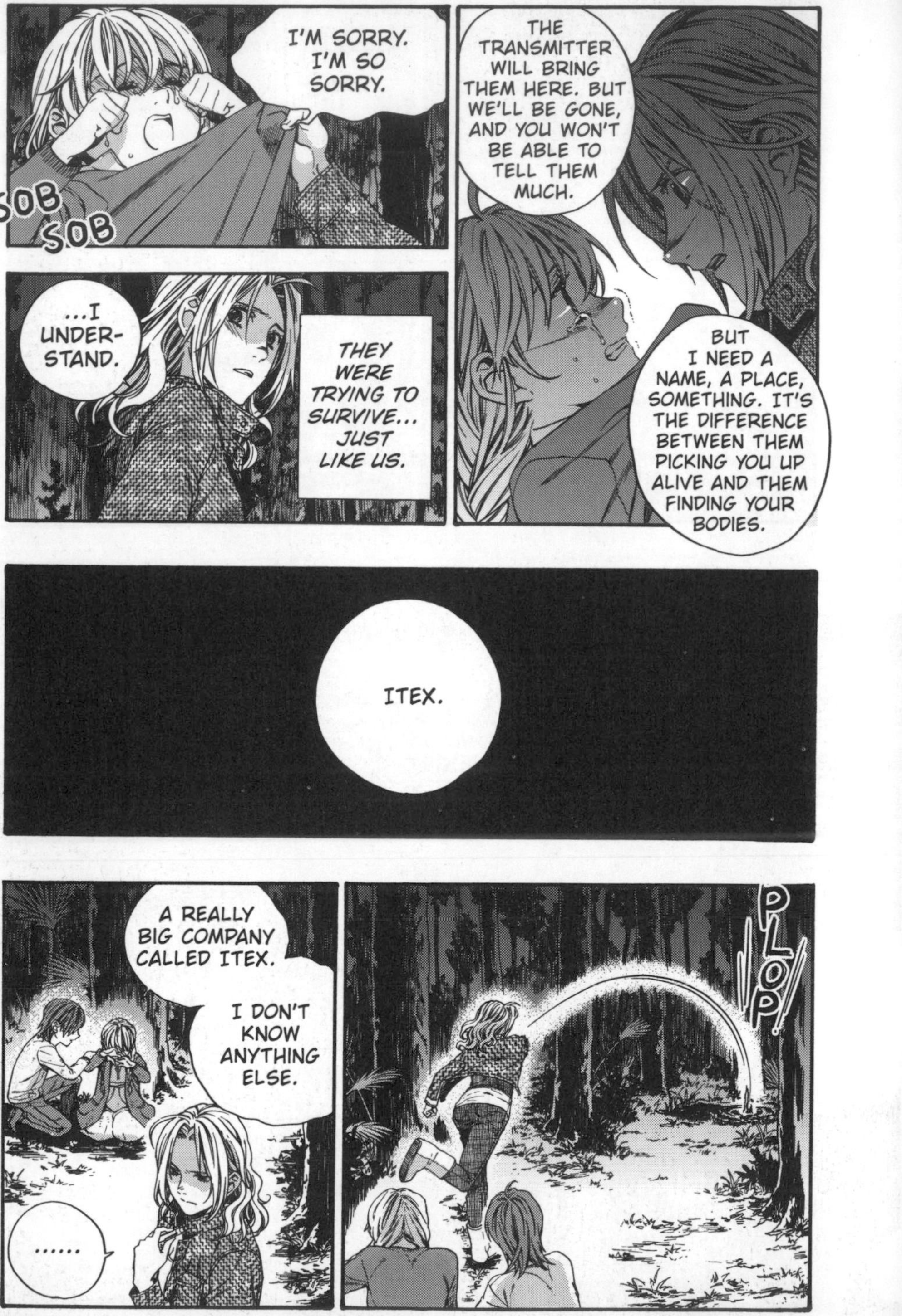
I'M SORRY. I'M SO SORRY.
SOB SOB
...I UNDER-STAND.
THEY WERE TRYING TO SURVIVE... JUST LIKE US.
THE TRANSMITTER WILL BRING THEM HERE. BUT WE'LL BE GONE, AND YOU WON'T BE ABLE TO TELL THEM MUCH.
BUT I NEED A NAME, A PLACE, SOMETHING. IT'S THE DIFFERENCE BETWEEN THEM PICKING YOU UP ALIVE AND THEM FINDING YOUR BODIES.
ITEX.
A REALLY BIG COMPANY CALLED ITEX.
I DON'T KNOW ANYTHING ELSE.
......
PLOP!

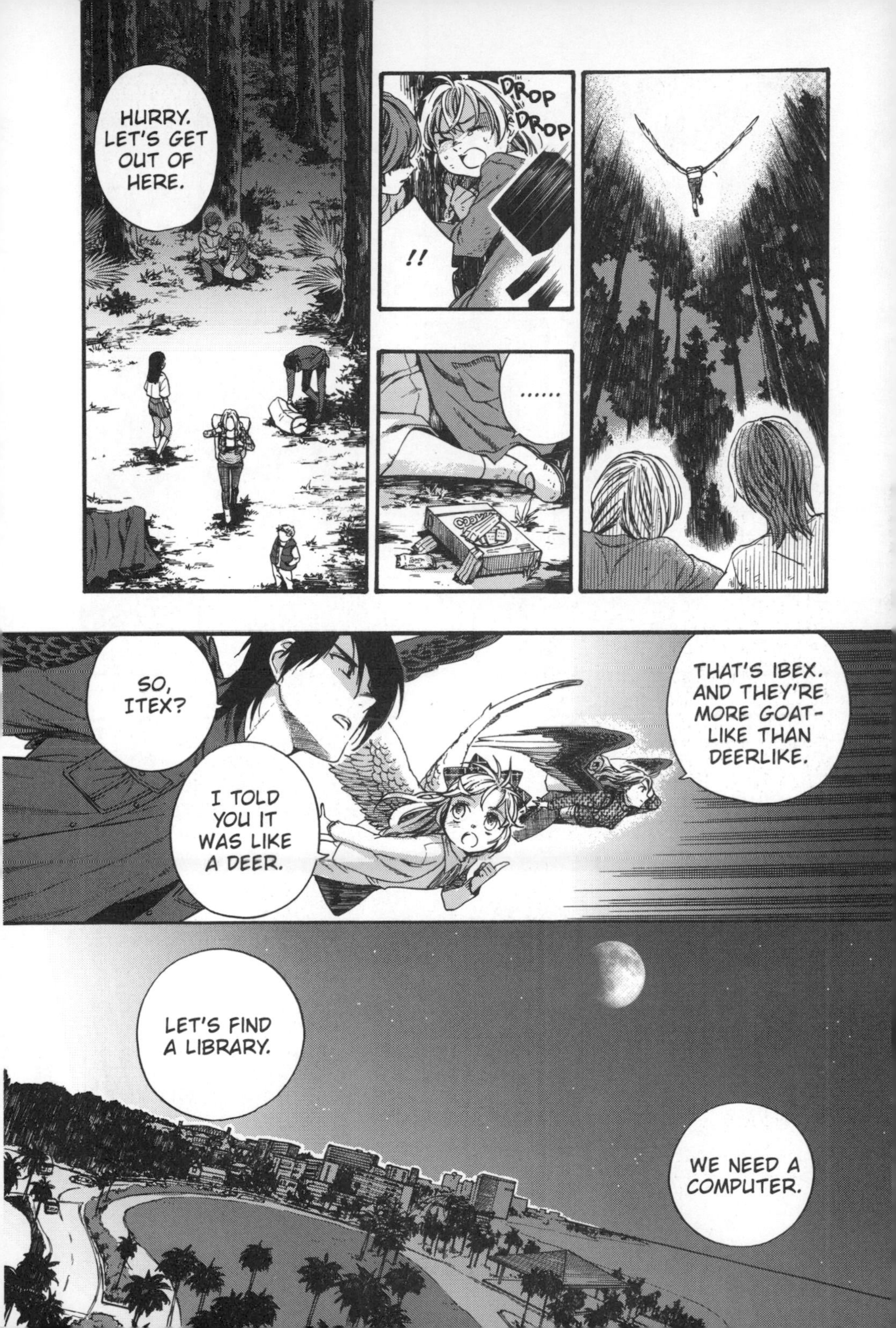
HURRY. LET'S GET OUT OF HERE.
DROP
DROP
!!
......
SO, ITEX?
I TOLD YOU IT WAS LIKE A DEER.
THAT'S IBEX. AND THEY'RE MORE GOAT-LIKE THAN DEERLIKE.
LET'S FIND A LIBRARY.
WE NEED A COMPUTER.

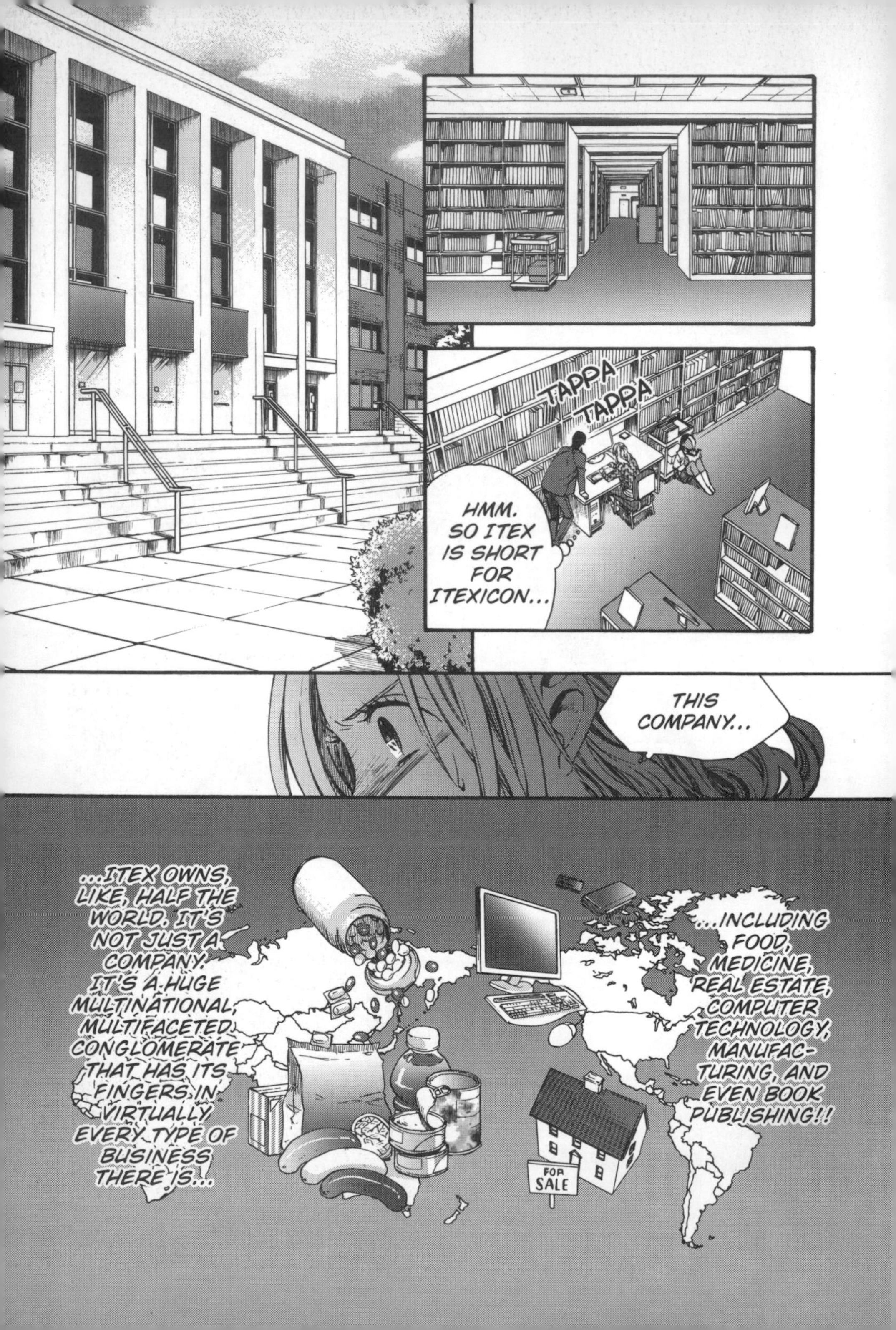
TAPPA
TAPPA
HMM. SO ITEX IS SHORT FOR ITEXICON...
THIS COMPANY...
...ITEX OWNS, LIKE, HALF THE WORLD. IT'S NOT JUST A COMPANY. IT'S A HUGE MULTINATIONAL, MULTIFACETED CONGLOMERATE THAT HAS ITS FINGERS IN VIRTUALLY EVERY TYPE OF BUSINESS THERE IS...
FOR SALE
...INCLUDING FOOD, MEDICINE, REAL ESTATE, COMPUTER TECHNOLOGY, MANUFAC-TURING, AND EVEN BOOK PUBLISHING!!

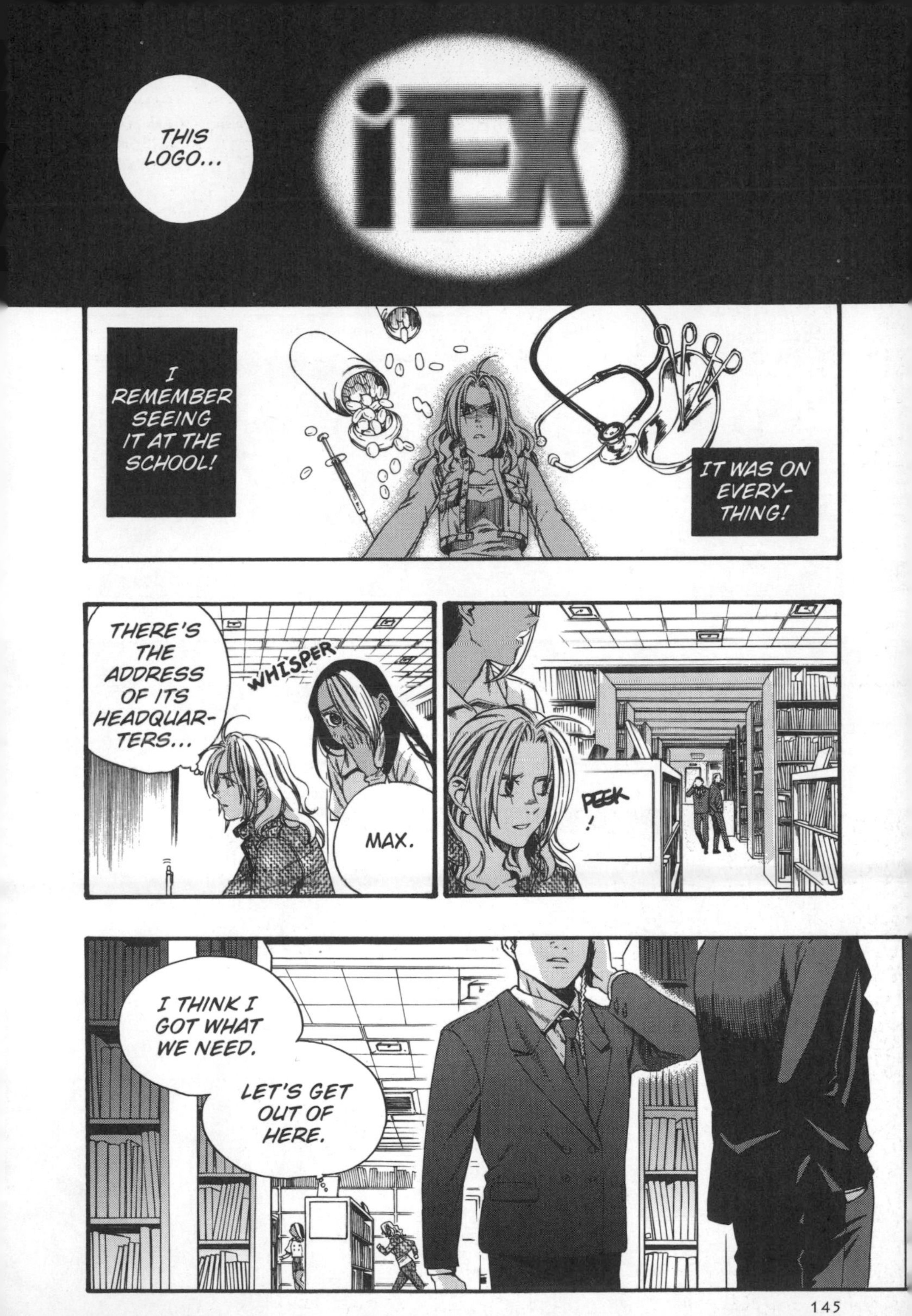
THIS LOGO...
iTEX
I REMEMBER SEEING IT AT THE SCHOOL!
IT WAS ON EVERY-THING!
THERE'S THE ADDRESS OF ITS HEADQUAR-TERS...
WHISPER
MAX.
PEEK!
I THINK I GOT WHAT WE NEED.
LET'S GET OUT OF HERE.

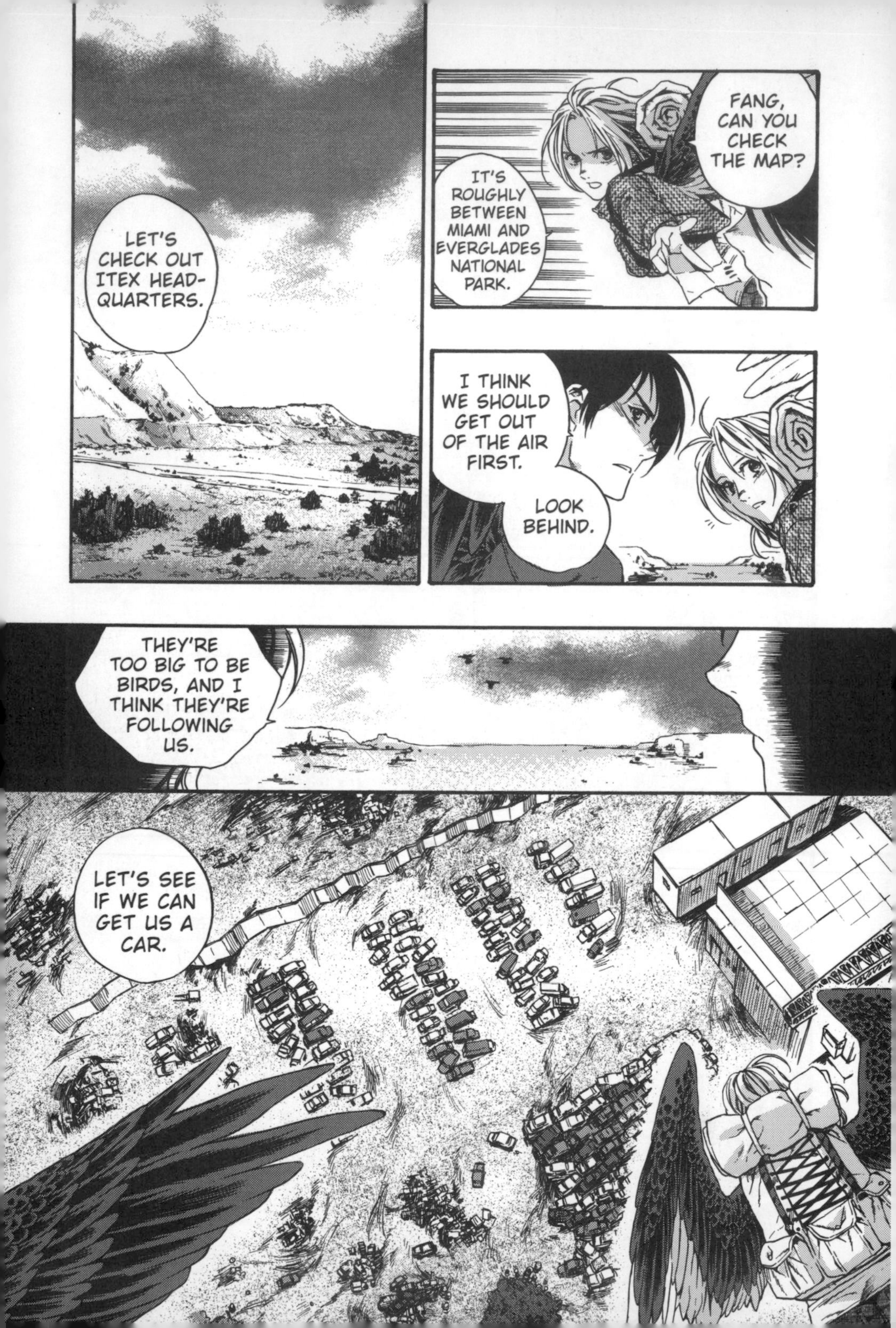
LET'S CHECK OUT ITEX HEAD-QUARTERS.
FANG, CAN YOU CHECK THE MAP?
IT'S ROUGHLY BETWEEN MIAMI AND EVERGLADES NATIONAL PARK.
I THINK WE SHOULD GET OUT OF THE AIR FIRST.
LOOK BEHIND.
THEY'RE TOO BIG TO BE BIRDS, AND I THINK THEY'RE FOLLOWING US.
LET'S SEE IF WE CAN GET US A CAR.

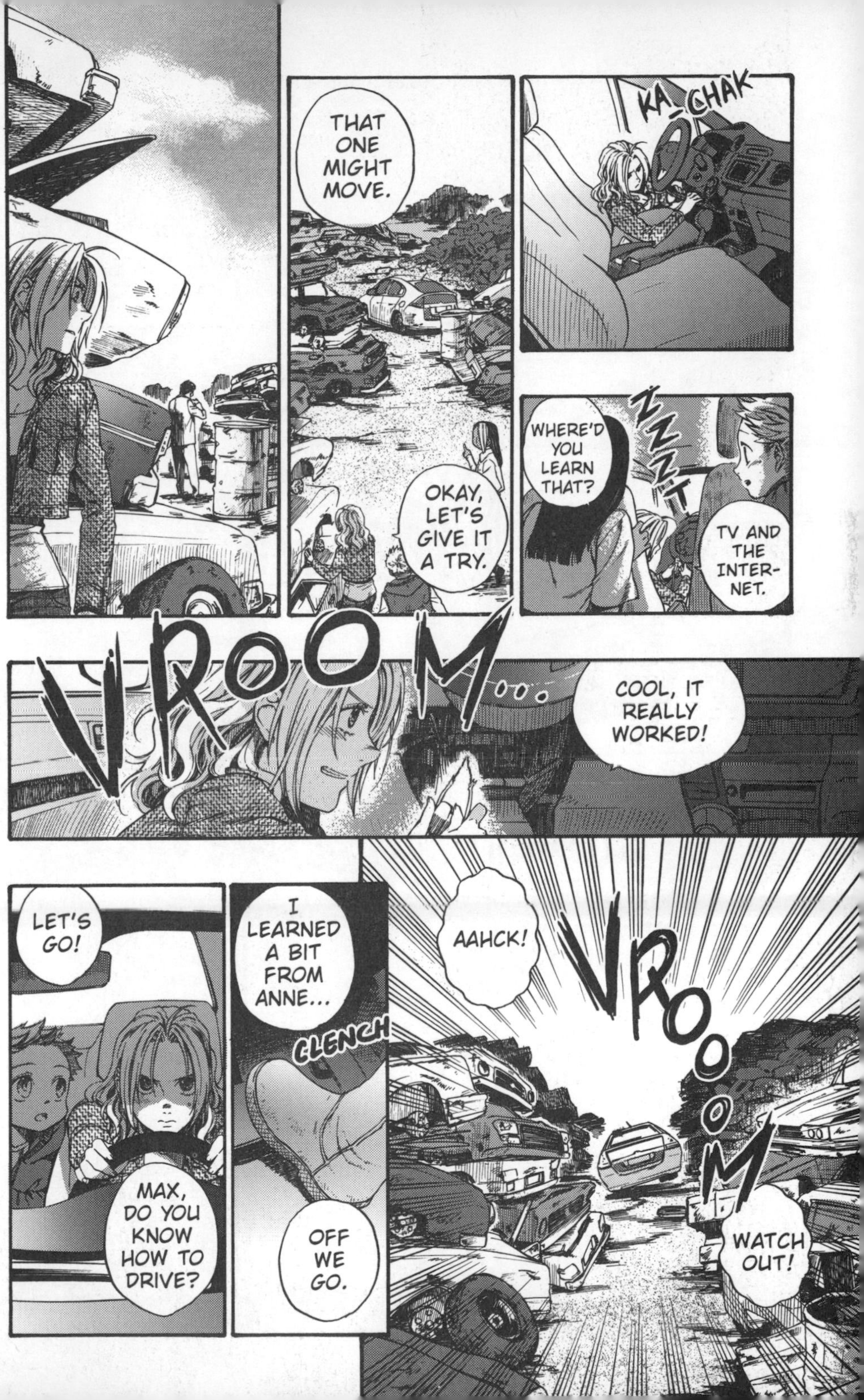
THAT ONE MIGHT MOVE.
OKAY, LET'S GIVE IT A TRY.
KA-CHAK
WHERE'D YOU LEARN THAT?
ZZZT
TV AND THE INTER-NET.
VROOM...
COOL, IT REALLY WORKED!
LET'S GO!
MAX, DO YOU KNOW HOW TO DRIVE?
I LEARNED A BIT FROM ANNE...
CLENCH
OFF WE GO.
AAHCK!
VROOOOM
WATCH OUT!

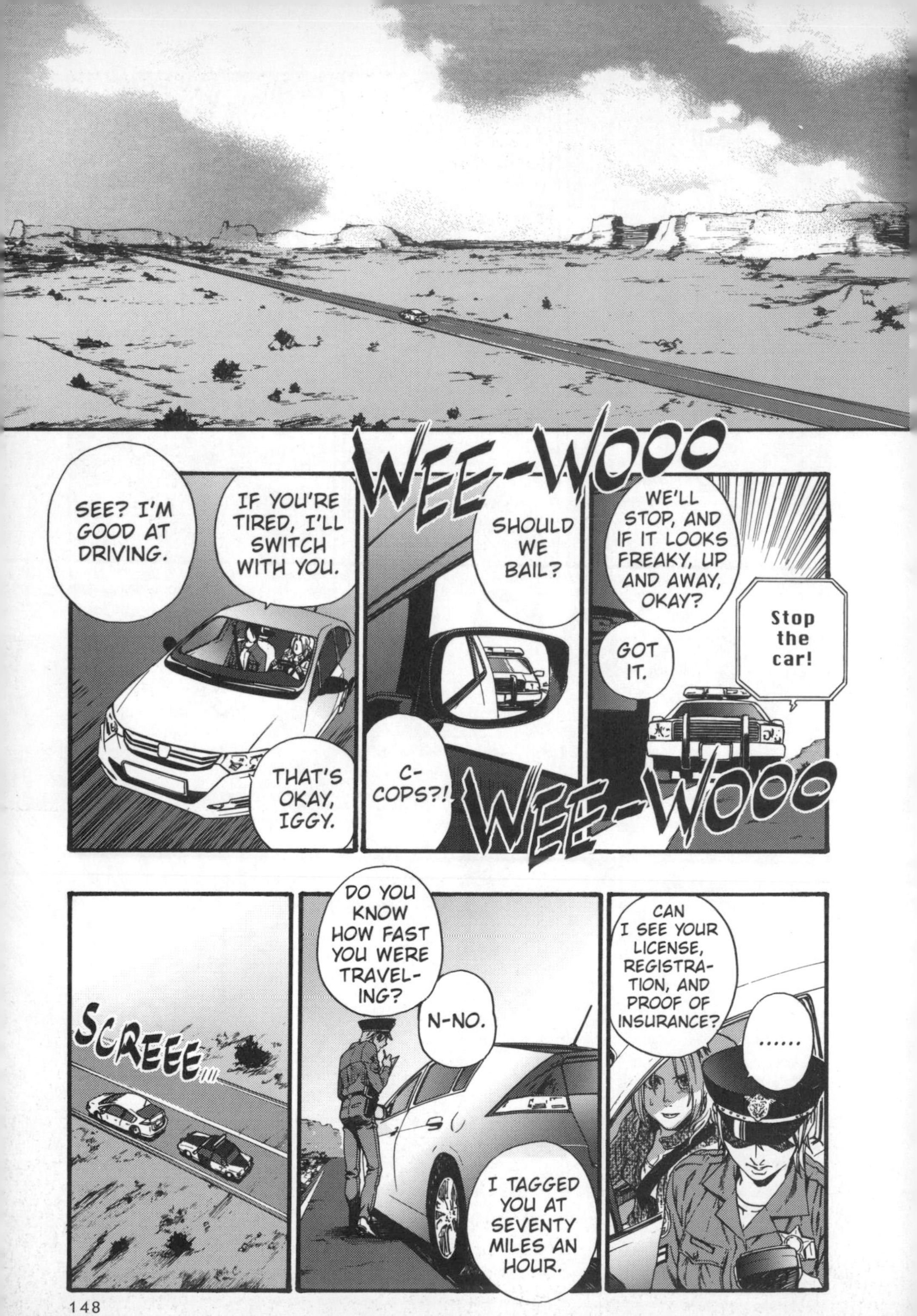
WEE-WOOO
SEE? I'M GOOD AT DRIVING.
IF YOU'RE TIRED, I'LL SWITCH WITH YOU.
THAT'S OKAY, IGGY.
SHOULD WE BAIL?
C-COPS?!
WE'LL STOP, AND IF IT LOOKS FREAKY, UP AND AWAY, OKAY?
GOT IT.
Stop the car!
WEE-WOOO
SCREEE...
DO YOU KNOW HOW FAST YOU WERE TRAVEL-ING?
N-NO.
I TAGGED YOU AT SEVENTY MILES AN HOUR.
CAN I SEE YOUR LICENSE, REGISTRA-TION, AND PROOF OF INSURANCE?
......

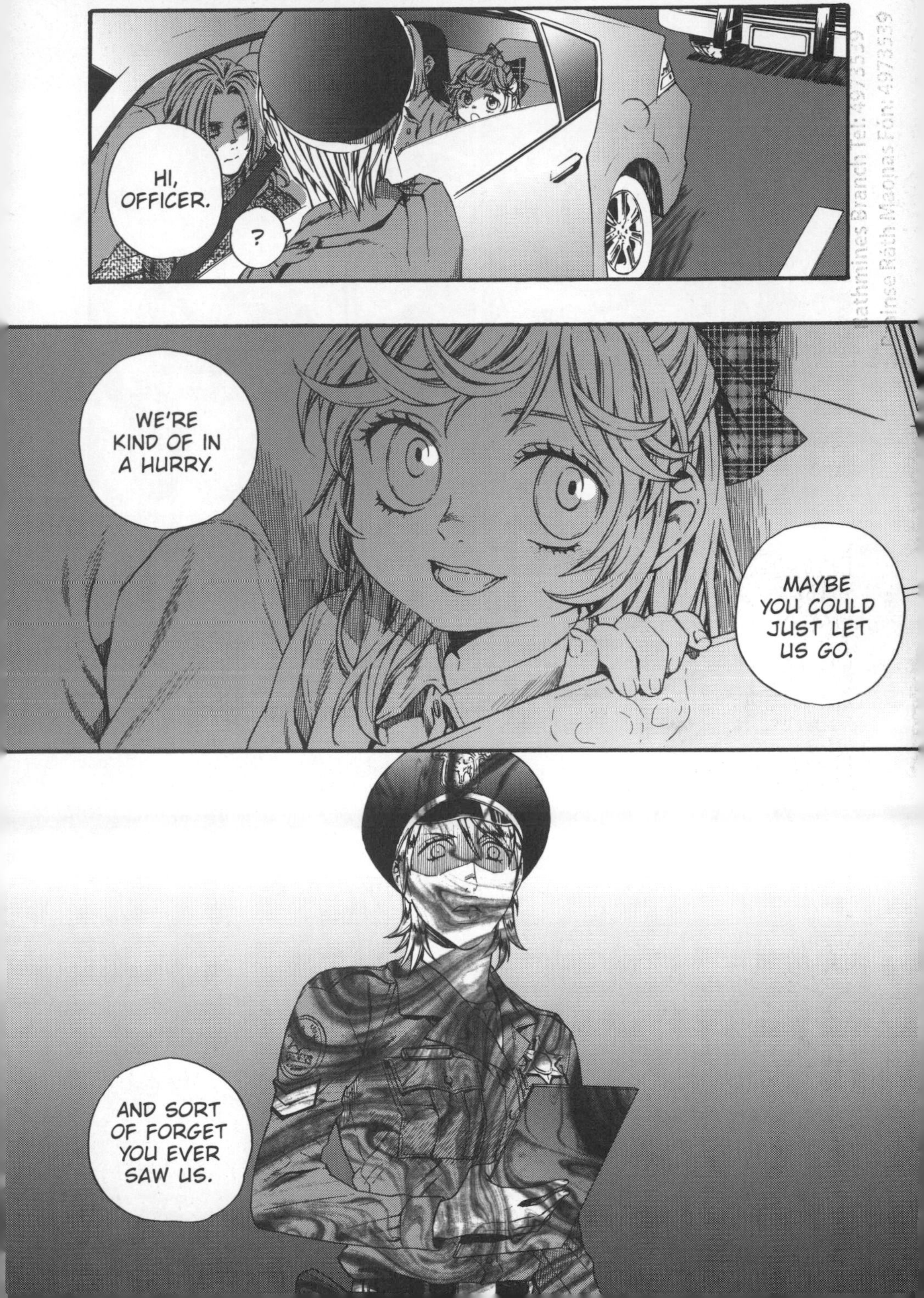
HI, OFFICER.
?
WE'RE KIND OF IN A HURRY.
MAYBE YOU COULD JUST LET US GO.
AND SORT OF FORGET YOU EVER SAW US.

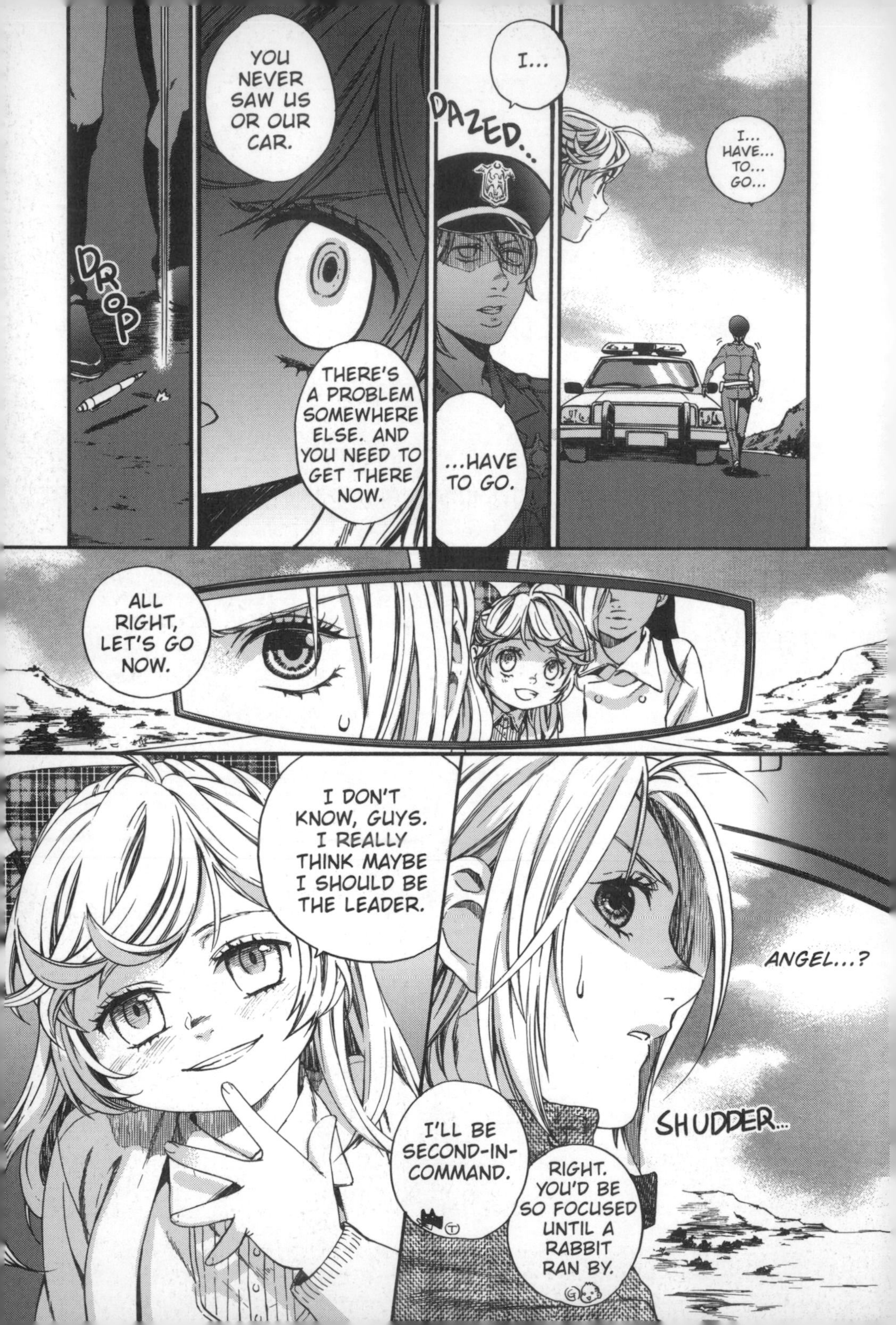
DROP
YOU NEVER SAW US OR OUR CAR.
THERE'S A PROBLEM SOMEWHERE ELSE. AND YOU NEED TO GET THERE NOW.
I...
DAZED...
...HAVE TO GO.
I... HAVE... TO... GO...
ALL RIGHT, LET'S GO NOW.
I DON'T KNOW, GUYS. I REALLY THINK MAYBE I SHOULD BE THE LEADER.
I'LL BE SECOND-IN-COMMAND.
RIGHT. YOU'D BE SO FOCUSED UNTIL A RABBIT RAN BY.
ANGEL...?
SHUDDER...

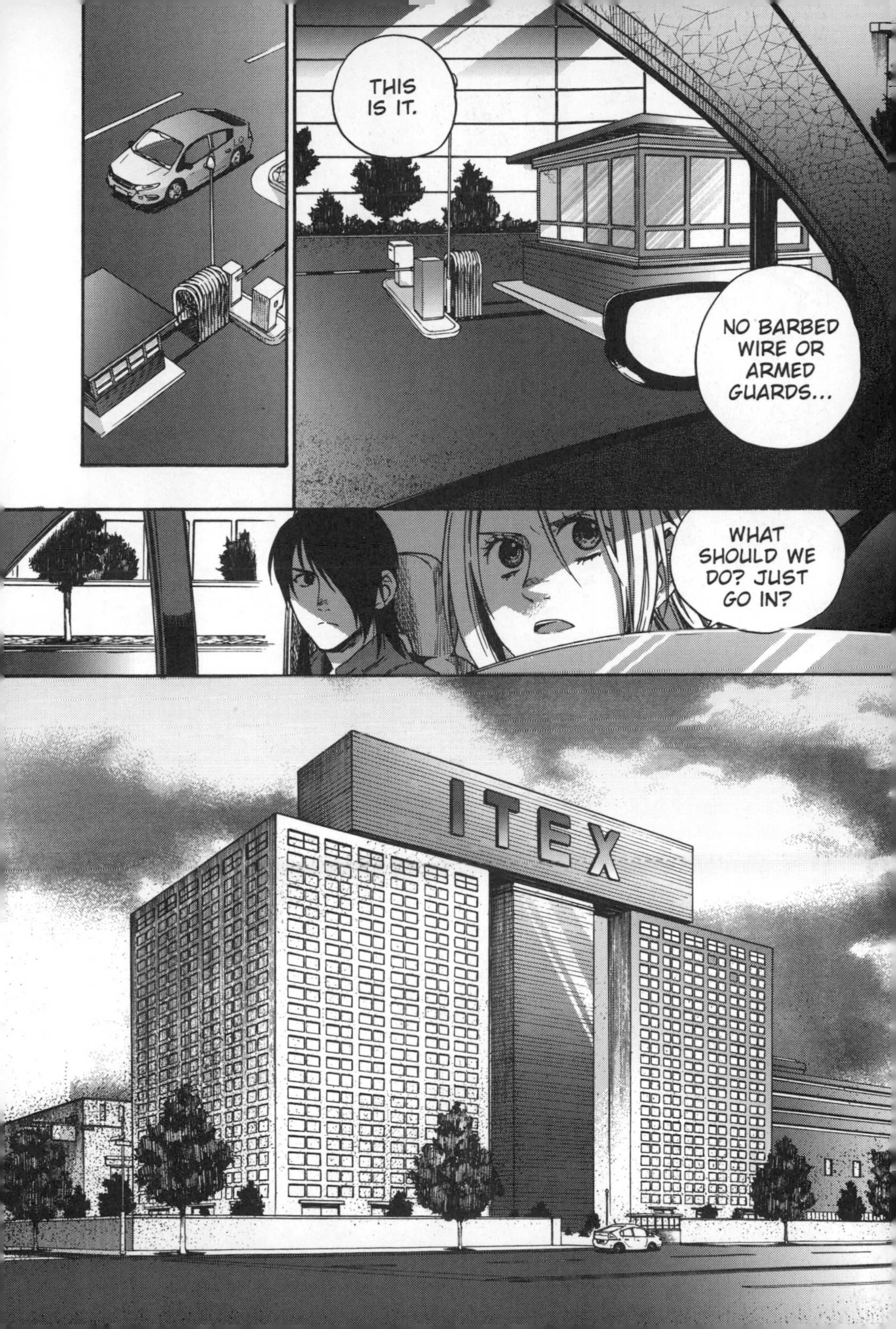
THIS IS IT.
NO BARBED WIRE OR ARMED GUARDS...
WHAT SHOULD WE DO? JUST GO IN?
ITEX

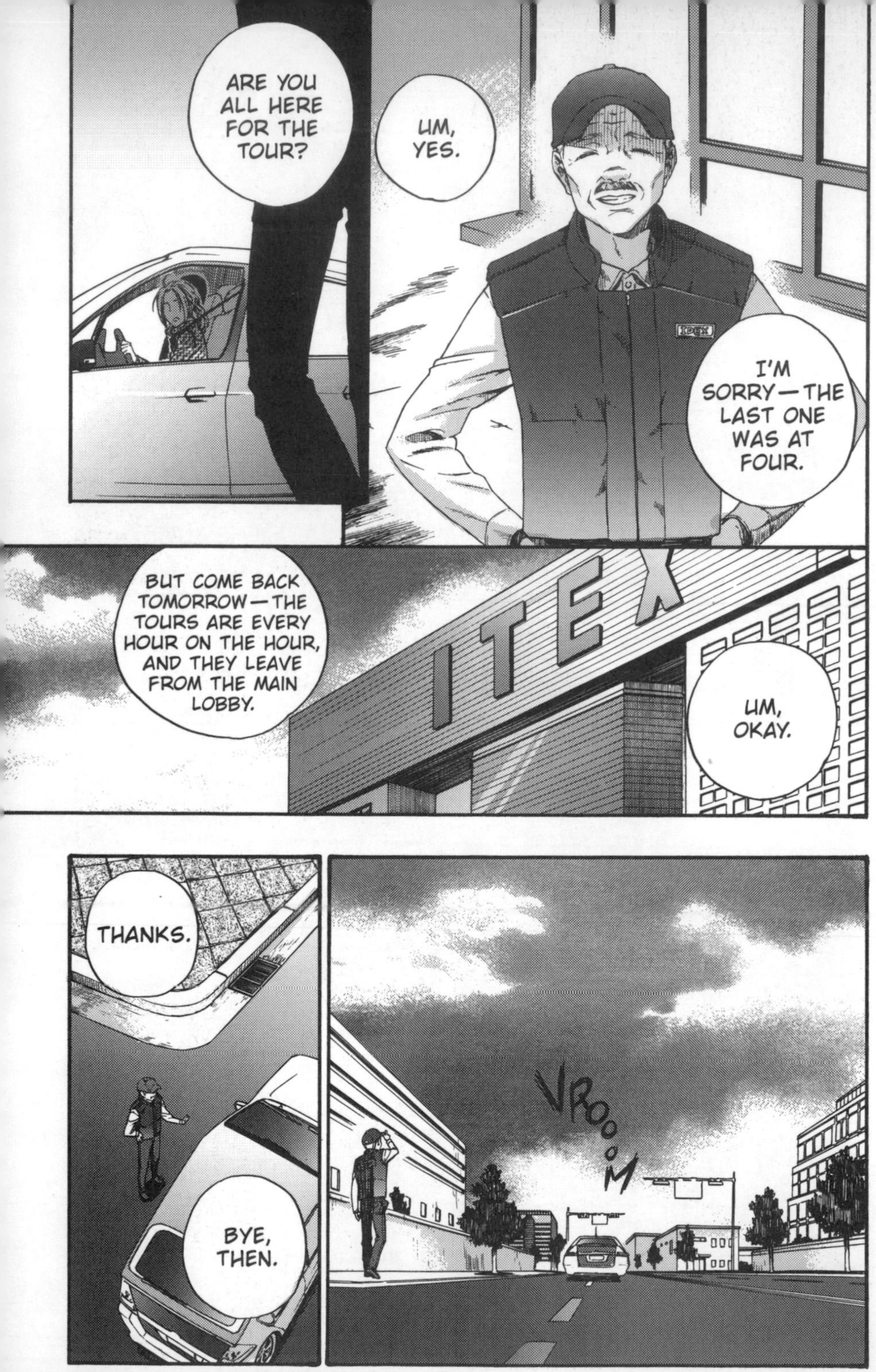
ARE YOU ALL HERE FOR THE TOUR?
UM, YES.
I'M SORRY—THE LAST ONE WAS AT FOUR.
BUT COME BACK TOMORROW—THE TOURS ARE EVERY HOUR ON THE HOUR, AND THEY LEAVE FROM THE MAIN LOBBY.
ITEX
UM, OKAY.
THANKS.
BYE, THEN.
VROOOM

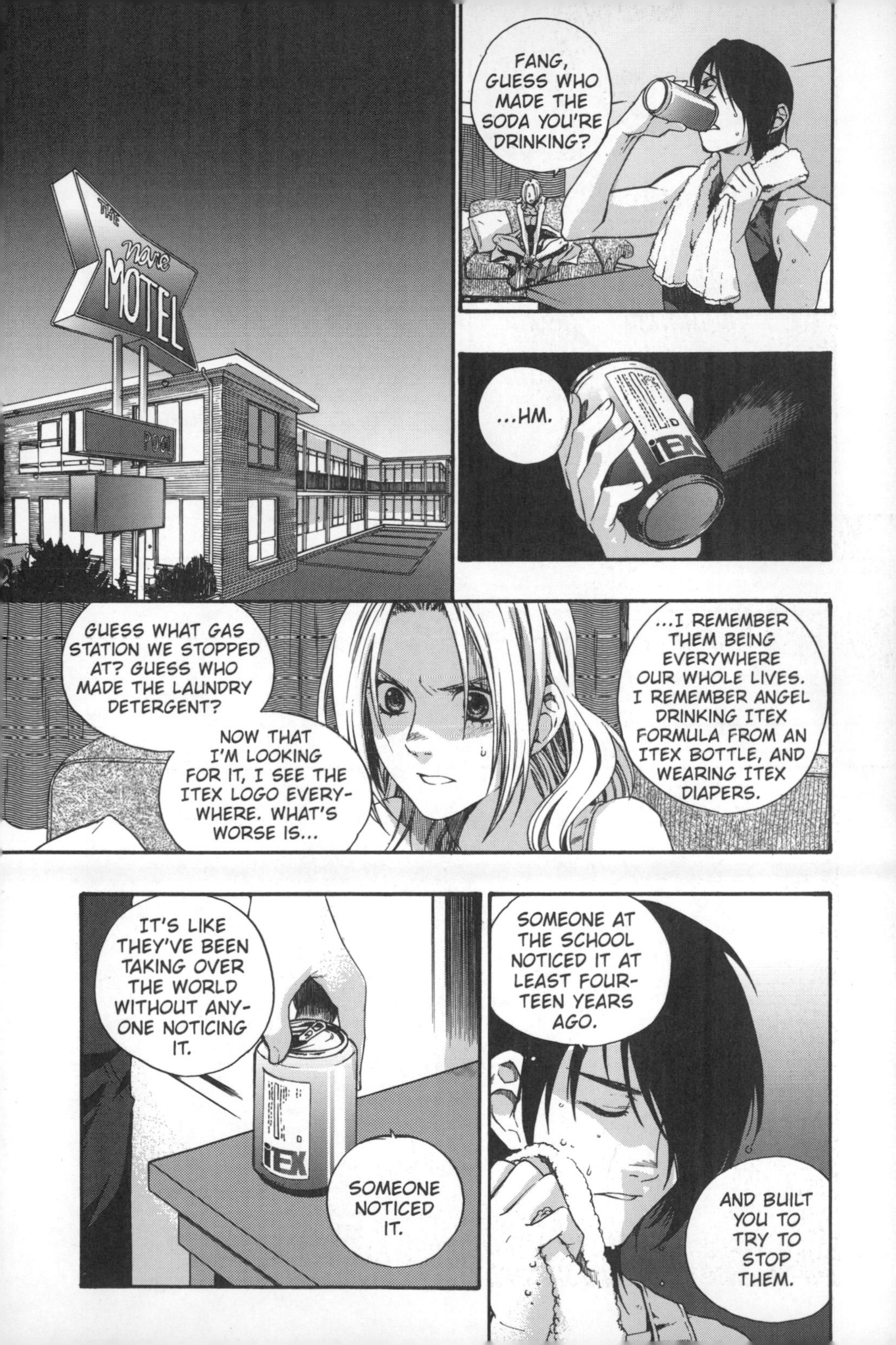
MOTEL
FANG, GUESS WHO MADE THE SODA YOU'RE DRINKING?
...HM.
iTEX
GUESS WHAT GAS STATION WE STOPPED AT? GUESS WHO MADE THE LAUNDRY DETERGENT?
NOW THAT I'M LOOKING FOR IT, I SEE THE ITEX LOGO EVERY-WHERE. WHAT'S WORSE IS...
...I REMEMBER THEM BEING EVERYWHERE OUR WHOLE LIVES. I REMEMBER ANGEL DRINKING ITEX FORMULA FROM AN ITEX BOTTLE, AND WEARING ITEX DIAPERS.
IT'S LIKE THEY'VE BEEN TAKING OVER THE WORLD WITHOUT ANY-ONE NOTICING IT.
iTEX
SOMEONE NOTICED IT.
SOMEONE AT THE SCHOOL NOTICED IT AT LEAST FOUR-TEEN YEARS AGO.
AND BUILT YOU TO TRY TO STOP THEM.

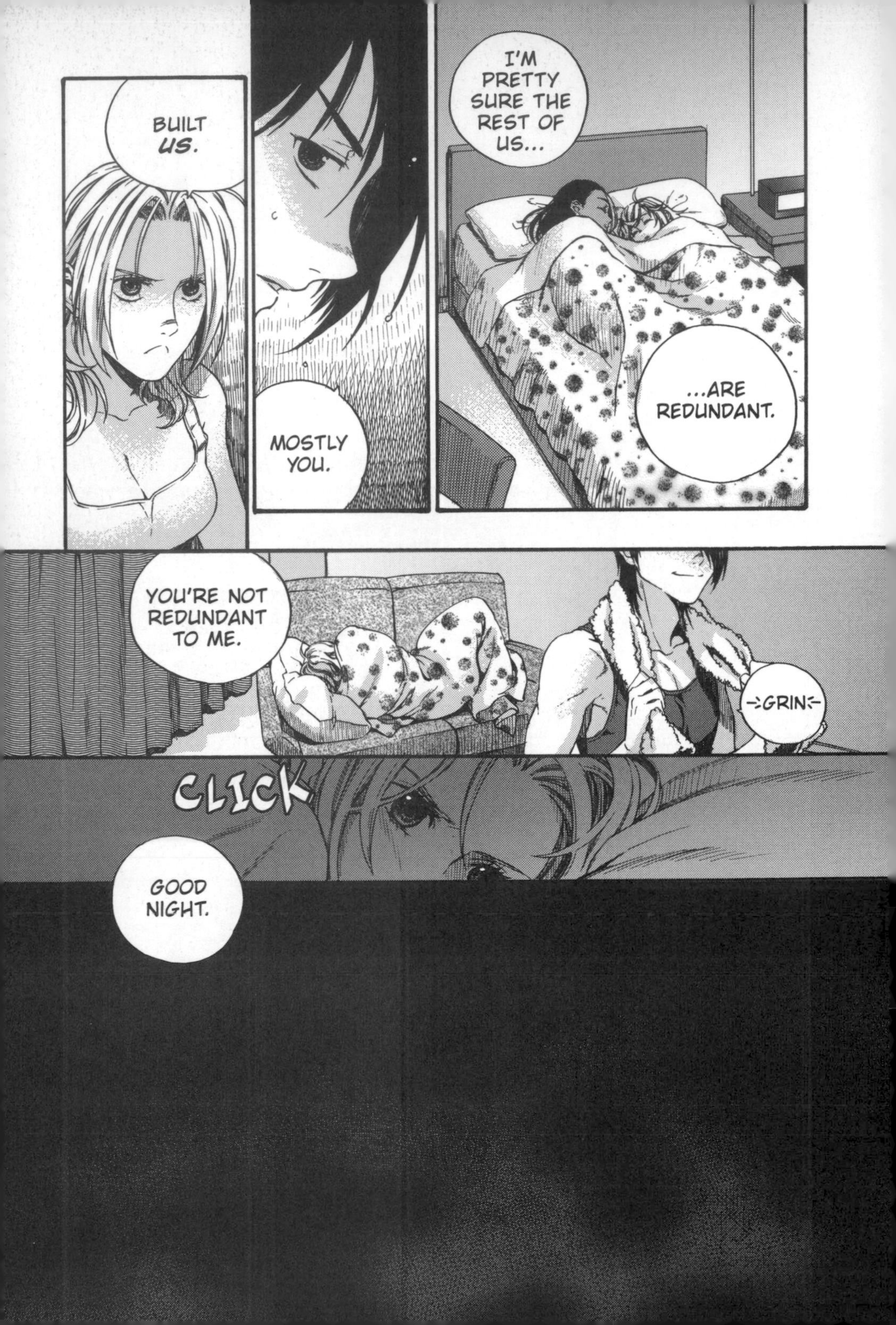
BUILT US.
MOSTLY YOU.
I'M PRETTY SURE THE REST OF US...
...ARE REDUNDANT.
YOU'RE NOT REDUNDANT TO ME.
GRIN
CLICK
GOOD NIGHT.

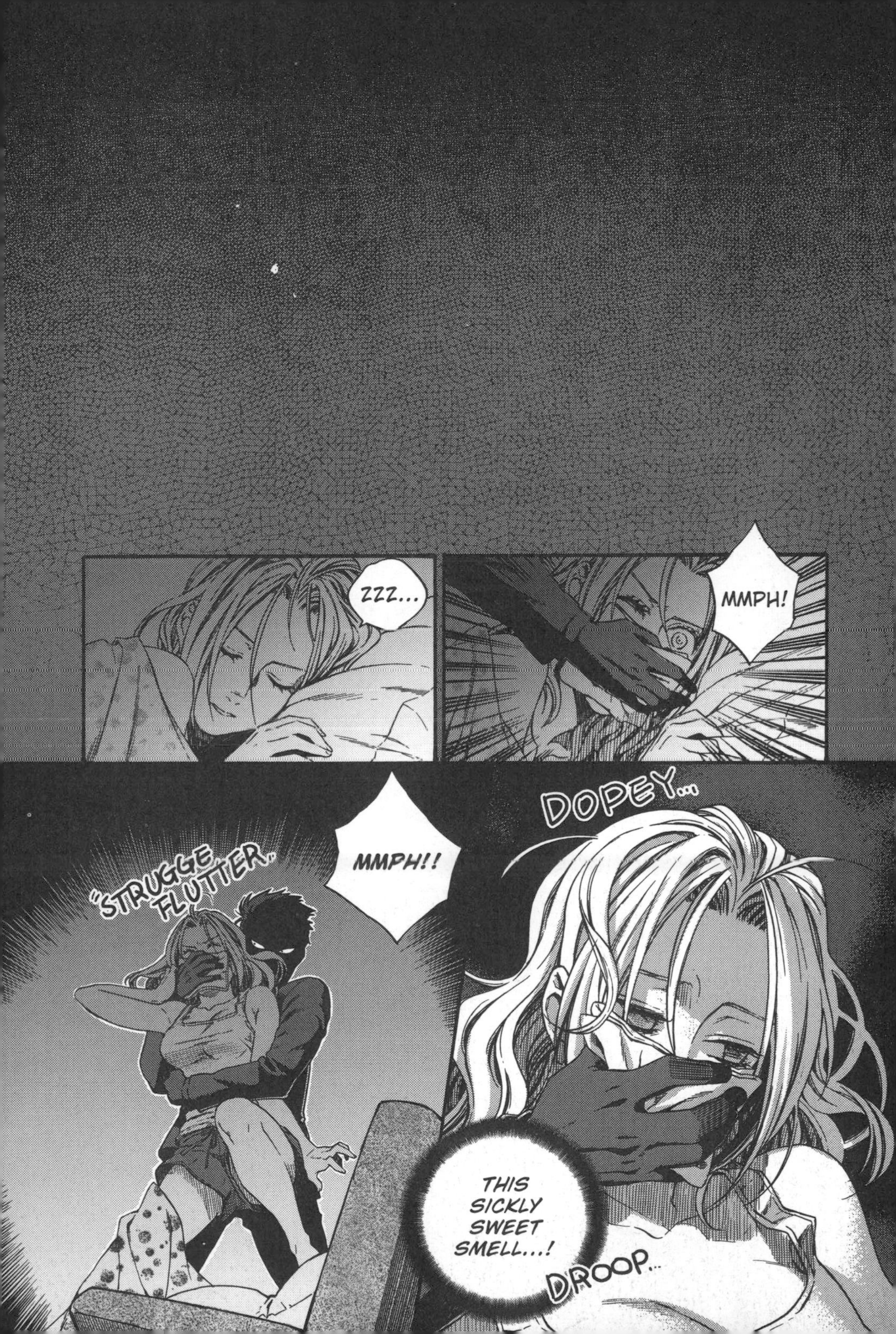
ZZZ...
MMPH!
"STRUGGE FLUTTER"
MMPH!!
DOPEY...
THIS SICKLY SWEET SMELL...!
DROOP...

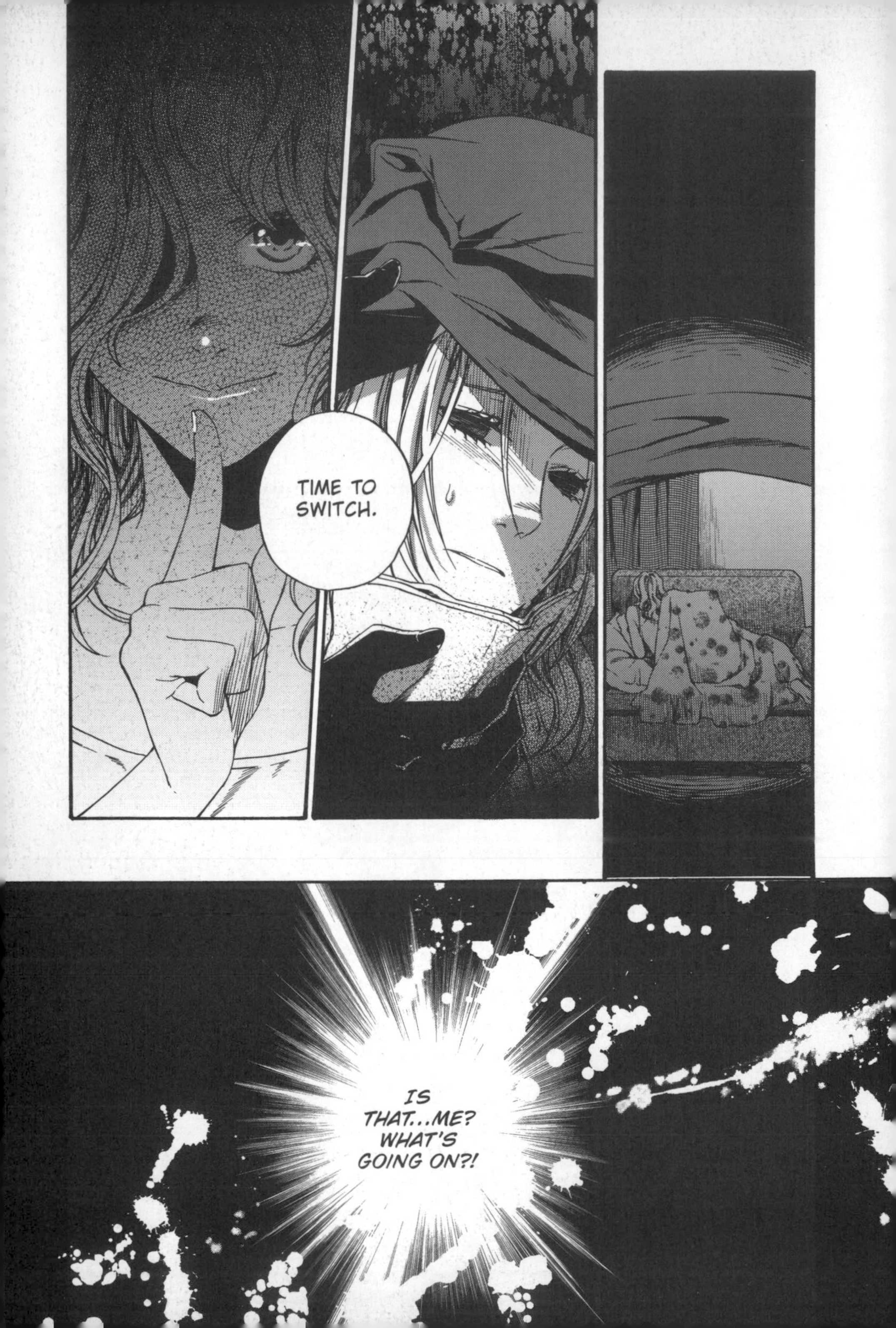
TIME TO SWITCH.
IS THAT...ME? WHAT'S GOING ON?!

MAXIMUM
RIDE

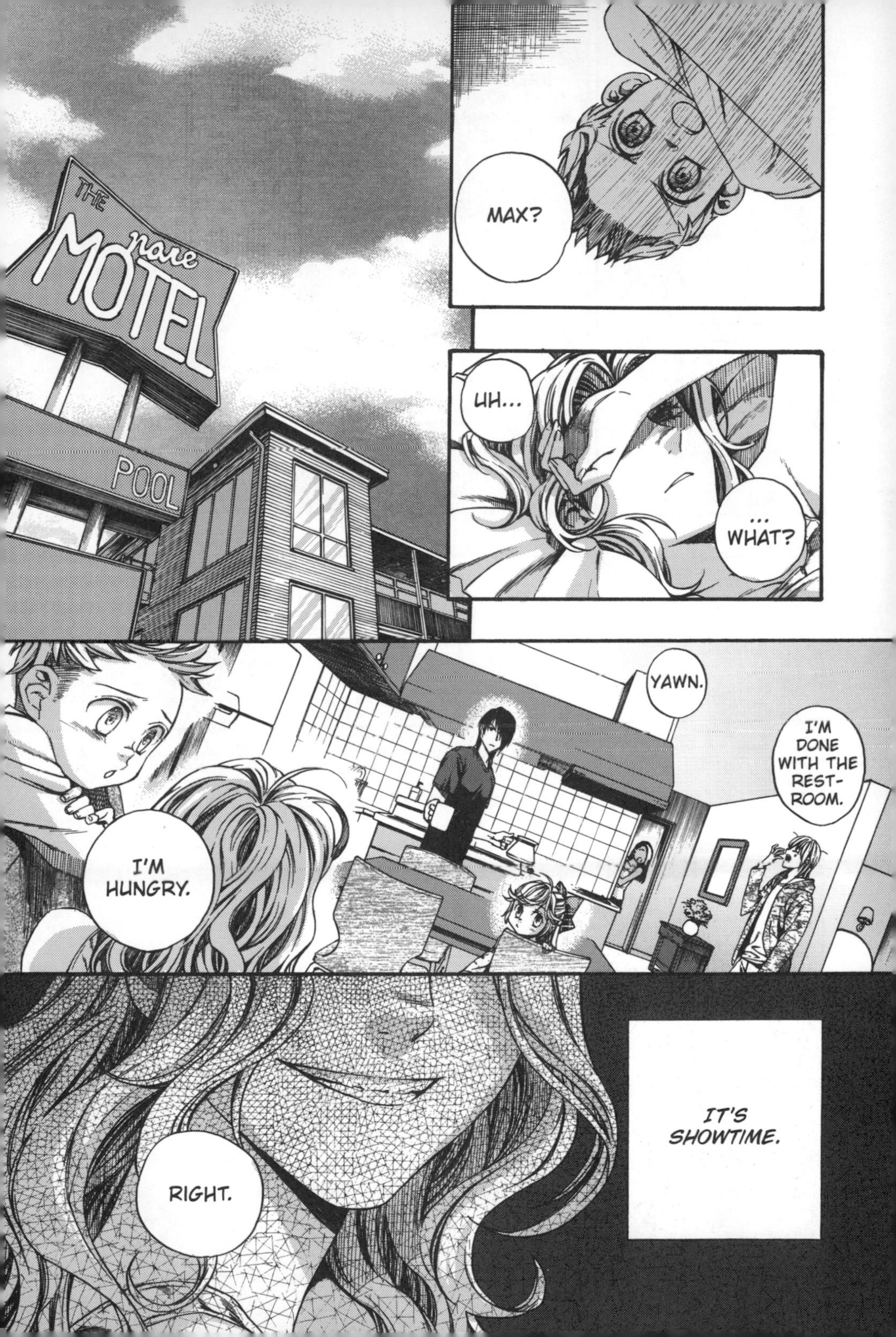
THE
MOTEL
POOL
MAX?
UH...
... WHAT?
I'M HUNGRY.
YAWN.
I'M DONE WITH THE REST-ROOM.
RIGHT.
IT'S SHOWTIME.

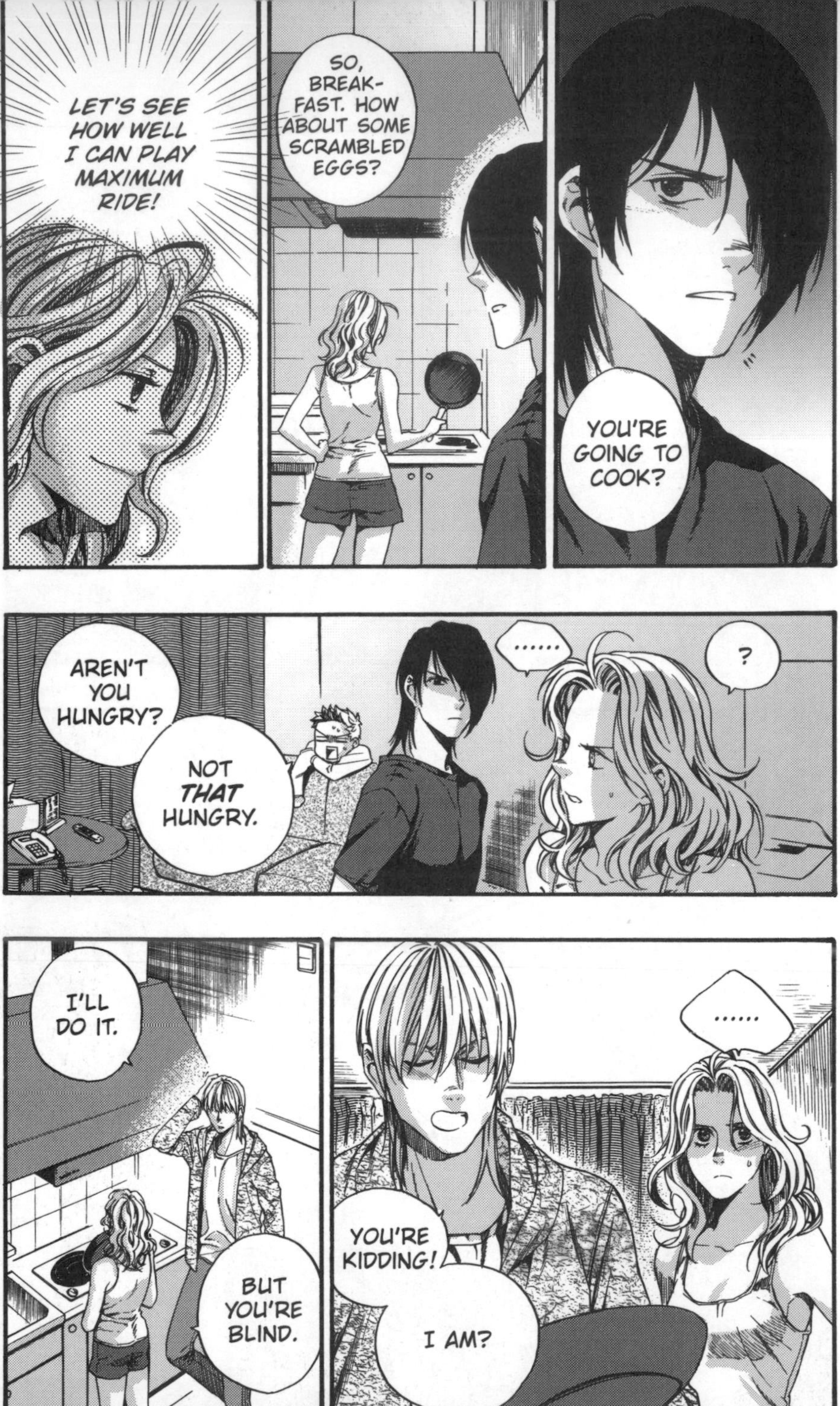
LET'S SEE HOW WELL I CAN PLAY MAXIMUM RIDE!
SO, BREAK-FAST. HOW ABOUT SOME SCRAMBLED EGGS?
YOU'RE GOING TO COOK?
AREN'T YOU HUNGRY?
NOT *THAT* HUNGRY.
......
?
I'LL DO IT.
BUT YOU'RE BLIND.
......
YOU'RE KIDDING!
I AM?

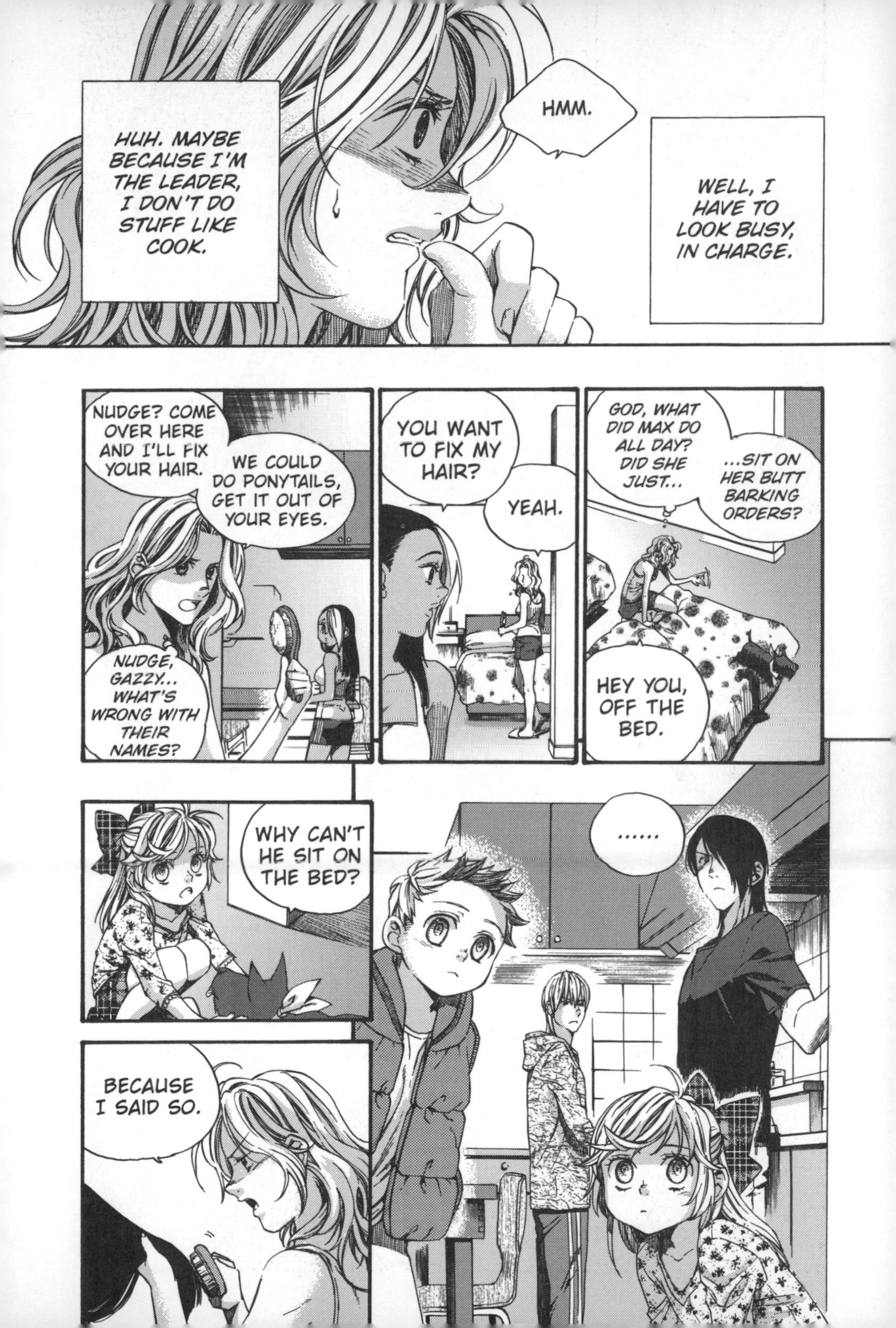
HUH. MAYBE BECAUSE I'M THE LEADER, I DON'T DO STUFF LIKE COOK.
HMM.
WELL, I HAVE TO LOOK BUSY, IN CHARGE.
NUDGE? COME OVER HERE AND I'LL FIX YOUR HAIR.
WE COULD DO PONYTAILS, GET IT OUT OF YOUR EYES.
NUDGE, GAZZY... WHAT'S WRONG WITH THEIR NAMES?
YOU WANT TO FIX MY HAIR?
YEAH.
GOD, WHAT DID MAX DO ALL DAY? DID SHE JUST...
...SIT ON HER BUTT BARKING ORDERS?
HEY YOU, OFF THE BED.
WHY CAN'T HE SIT ON THE BED?
......
BECAUSE I SAID SO.

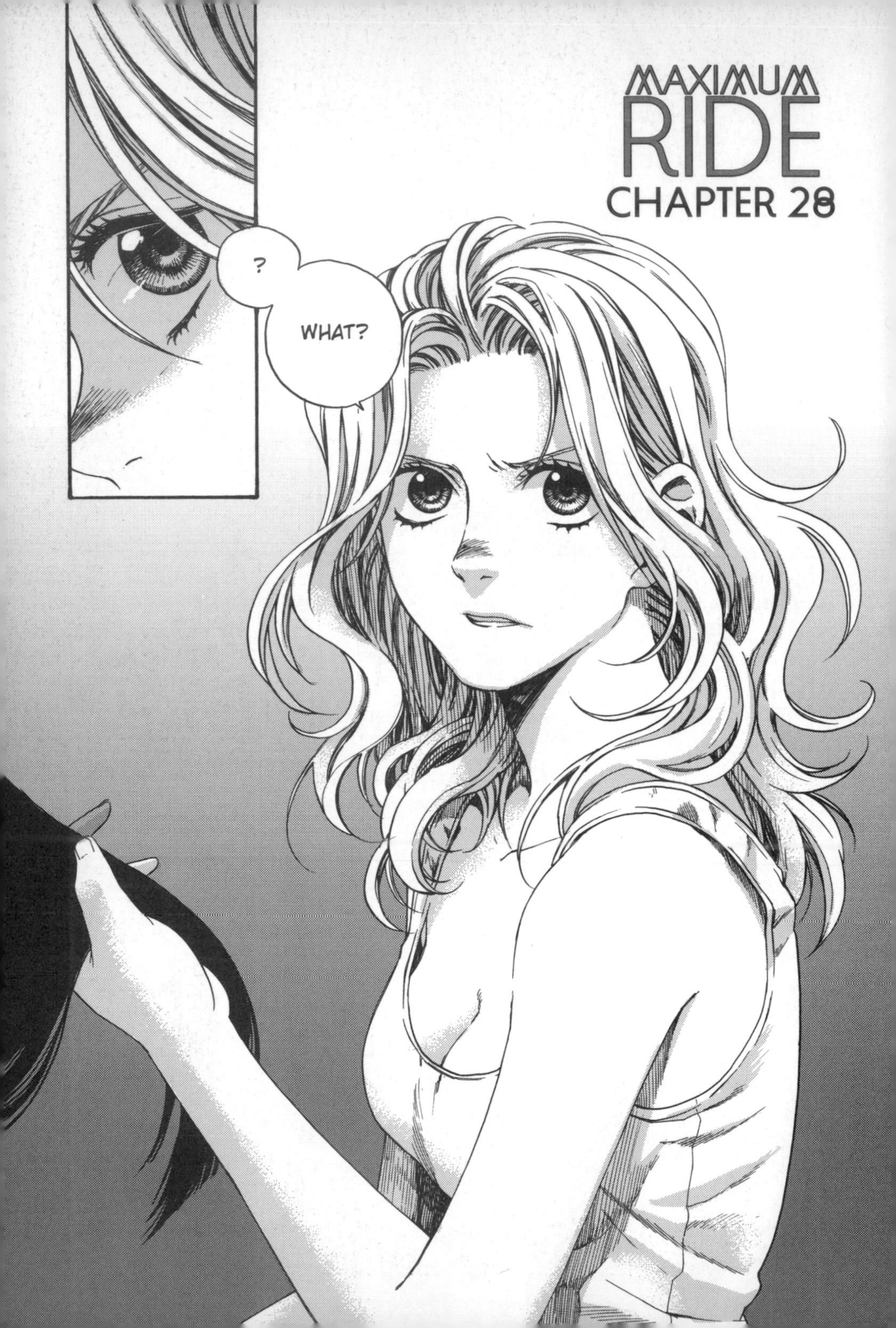
MAXIMUM
RIDE
CHAPTER 28
?
WHAT?

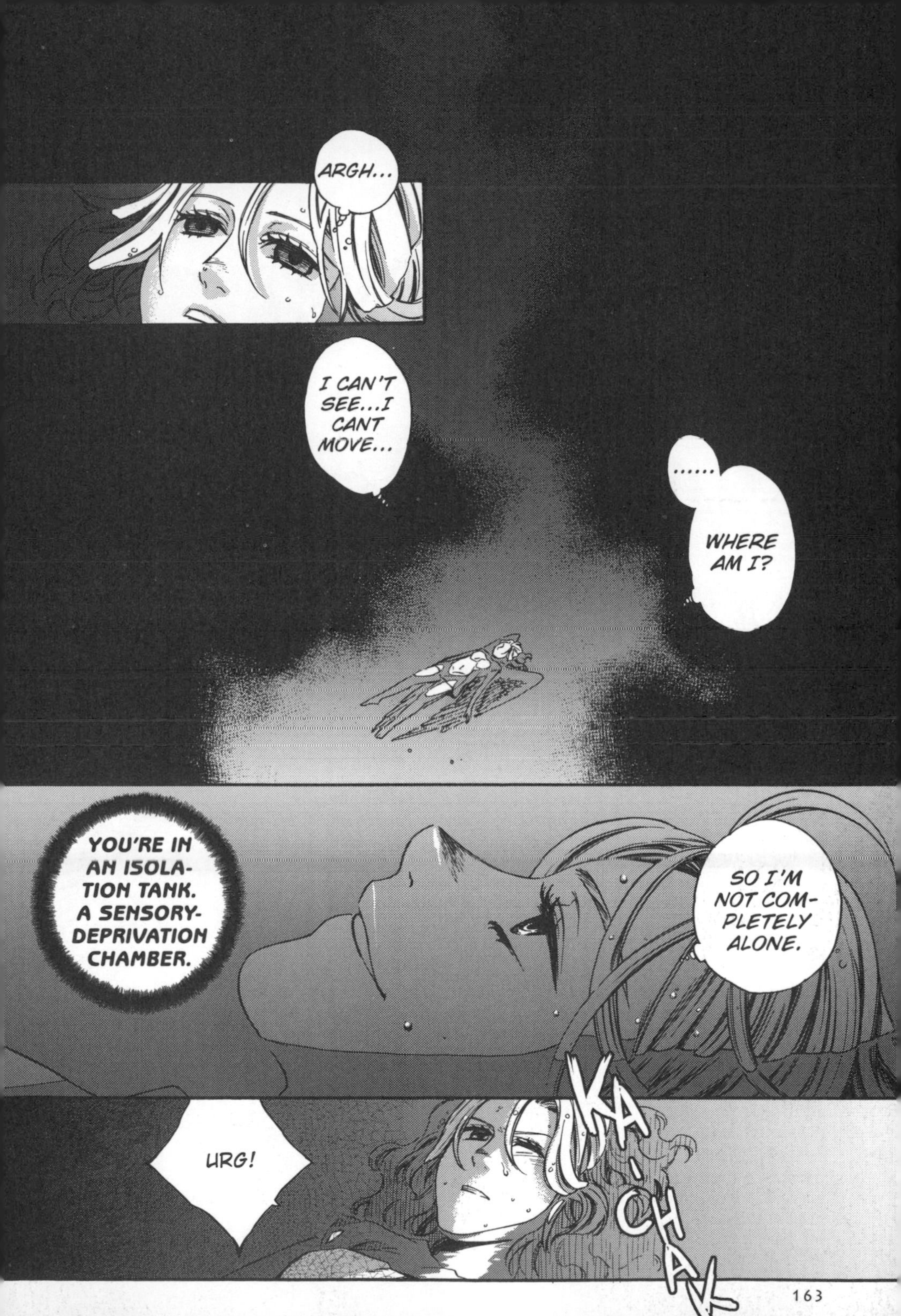
ARGH...
I CAN'T SEE...I CANT MOVE...
......
WHERE AM I?
YOU'RE IN AN ISOLATION TANK. A SENSORY-DEPRIVATION CHAMBER.
SO I'M NOT COMPLETELY ALONE.
URG!
KA-CHACK

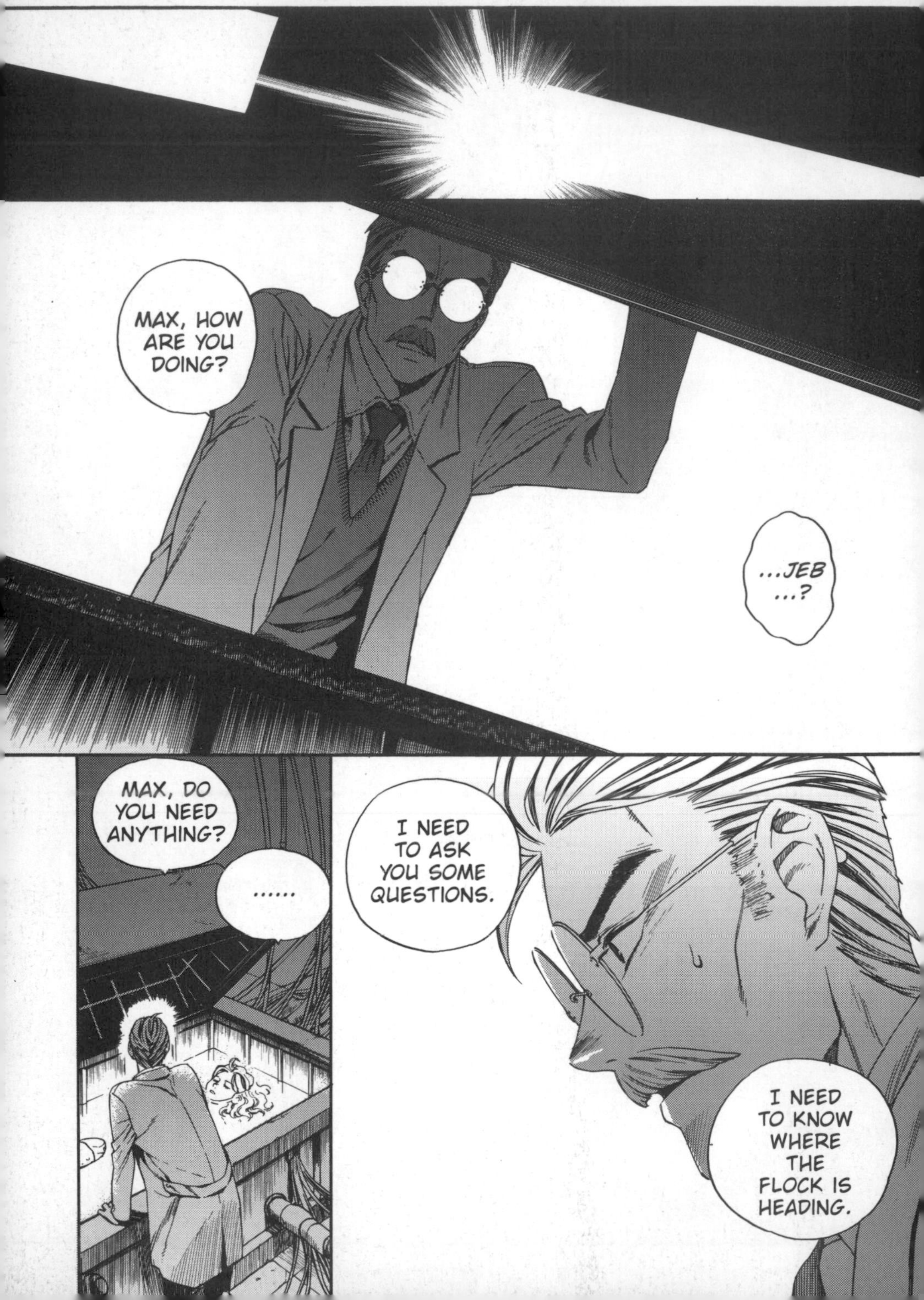
MAX, HOW ARE YOU DOING?
...JEB ...?
MAX, DO YOU NEED ANYTHING?
......
I NEED TO ASK YOU SOME QUESTIONS.
I NEED TO KNOW WHERE THE FLOCK IS HEADING.

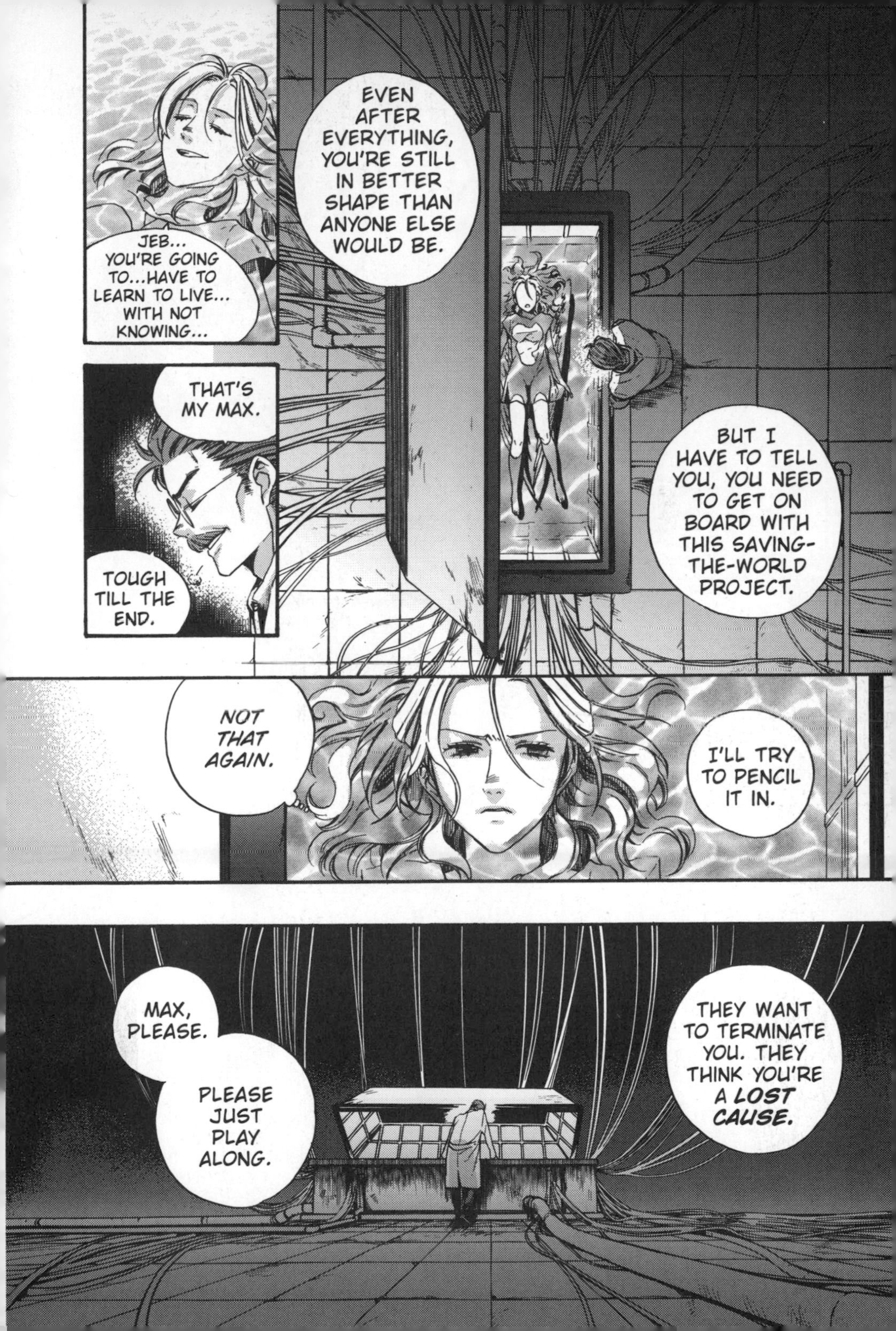
JEB... YOU'RE GOING TO...HAVE TO LEARN TO LIVE... WITH NOT KNOWING...
EVEN AFTER EVERYTHING, YOU'RE STILL IN BETTER SHAPE THAN ANYONE ELSE WOULD BE.
THAT'S MY MAX.
TOUGH TILL THE END.
BUT I HAVE TO TELL YOU, YOU NEED TO GET ON BOARD WITH THIS SAVING-THE-WORLD PROJECT.
NOT THAT AGAIN.
I'LL TRY TO PENCIL IT IN.
MAX, PLEASE.
PLEASE JUST PLAY ALONG.
THEY WANT TO TERMINATE YOU. THEY THINK YOU'RE A LOST CAUSE.

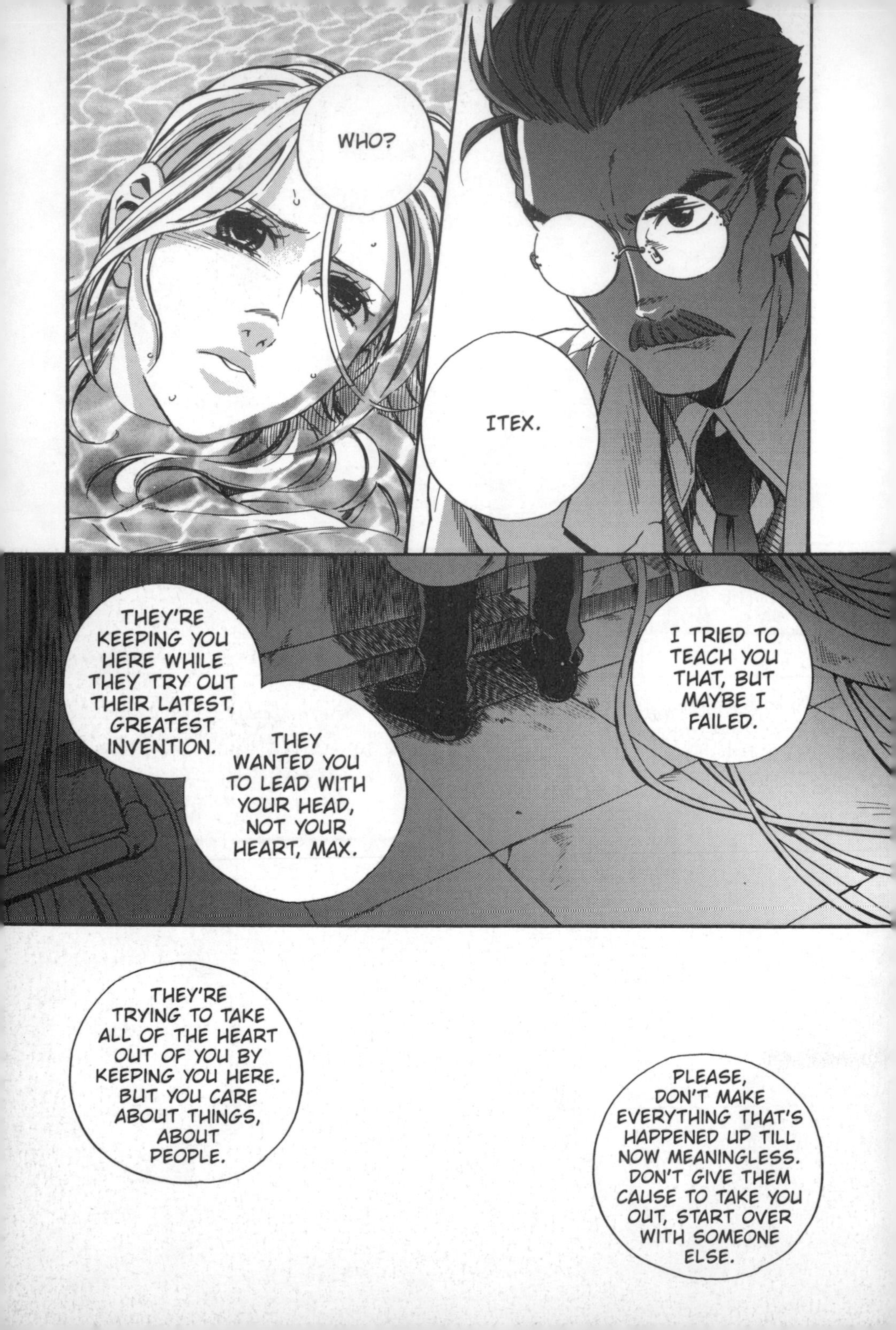
WHO?
ITEX.
THEY'RE KEEPING YOU HERE WHILE THEY TRY OUT THEIR LATEST, GREATEST INVENTION.
THEY WANTED YOU TO LEAD WITH YOUR HEAD, NOT YOUR HEART, MAX.
I TRIED TO TEACH YOU THAT, BUT MAYBE I FAILED.
THEY'RE TRYING TO TAKE ALL OF THE HEART OUT OF YOU BY KEEPING YOU HERE. BUT YOU CARE ABOUT THINGS, ABOUT PEOPLE.
PLEASE, DON'T MAKE EVERYTHING THAT'S HAPPENED UP TILL NOW MEANINGLESS. DON'T GIVE THEM CAUSE TO TAKE YOU OUT, START OVER WITH SOMEONE ELSE.

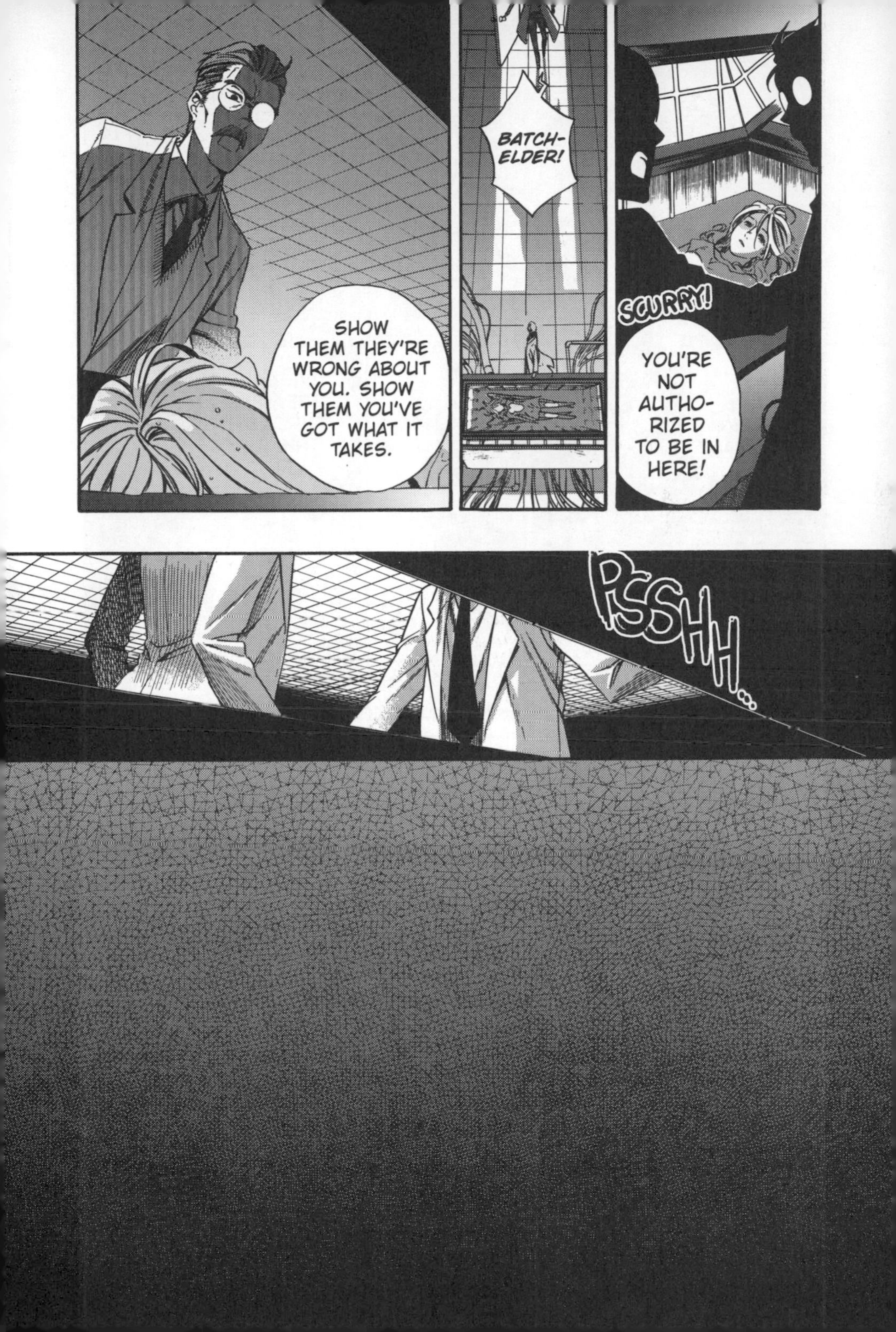
SHOW THEM THEY'RE WRONG ABOUT YOU. SHOW THEM YOU'VE GOT WHAT IT TAKES.
BATCH-ELDER!
SCURRY!
YOU'RE NOT AUTHO-RIZED TO BE IN HERE!
PSSHH...

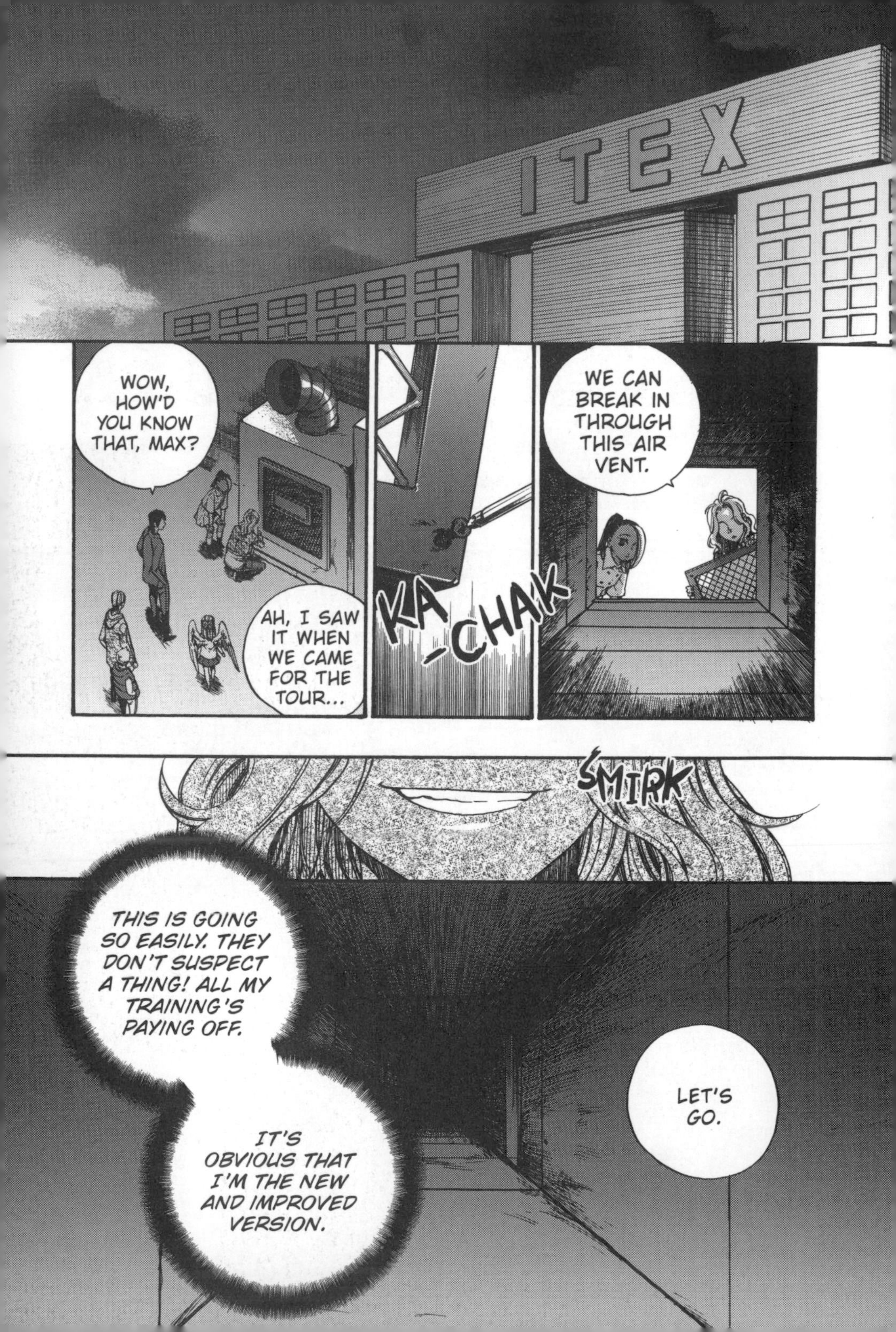
ITEX
WOW, HOW'D YOU KNOW THAT, MAX?
AH, I SAW IT WHEN WE CAME FOR THE TOUR...
KA-CHAK
WE CAN BREAK IN THROUGH THIS AIR VENT.
SMIRK
THIS IS GOING SO EASILY. THEY DON'T SUSPECT A THING! ALL MY TRAINING'S PAYING OFF.
IT'S OBVIOUS THAT I'M THE NEW AND IMPROVED VERSION.
LET'S GO.

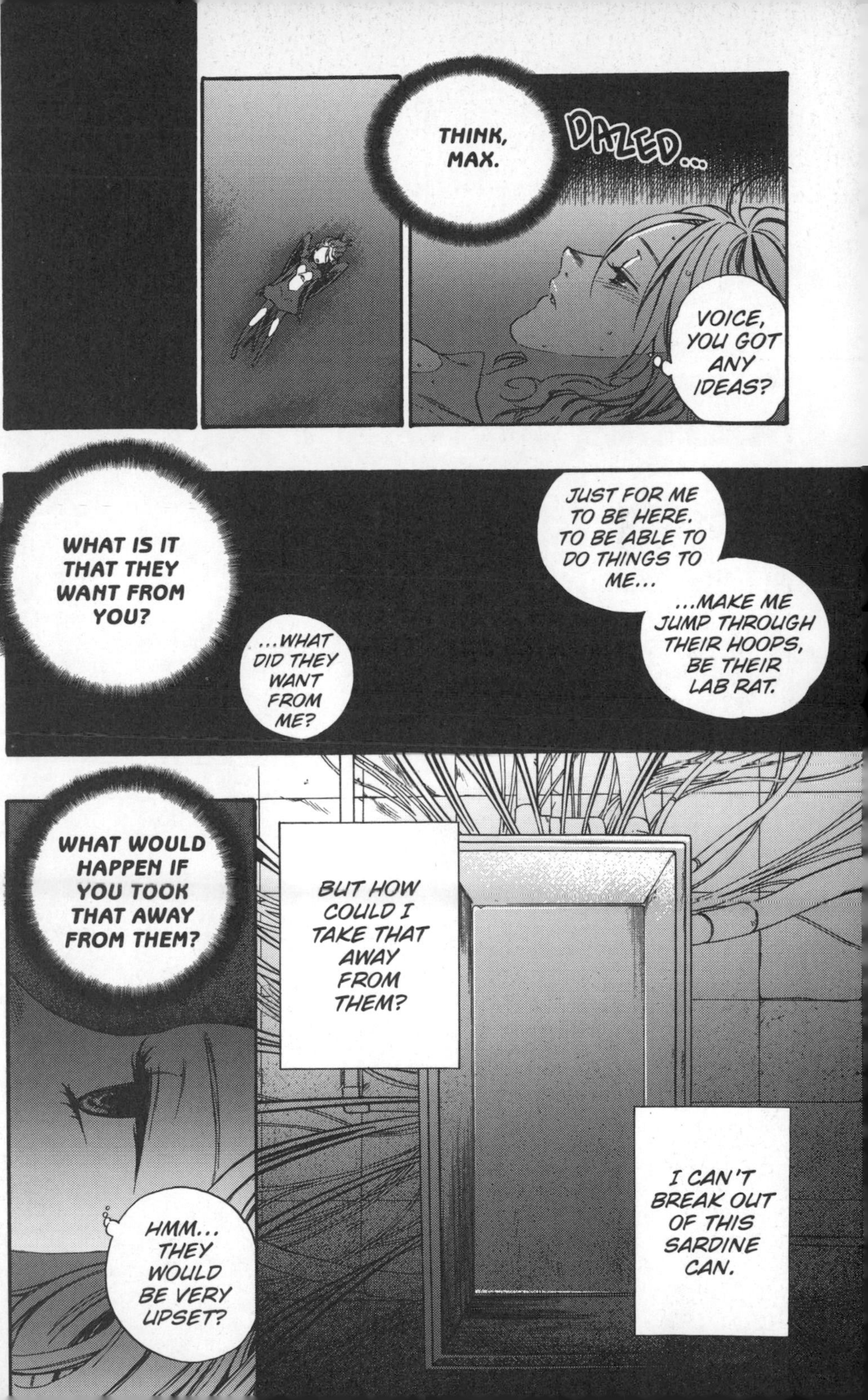
THINK, MAX.
DAZED...
VOICE, YOU GOT ANY IDEAS?
WHAT IS IT THAT THEY WANT FROM YOU?
...WHAT DID THEY WANT FROM ME?
JUST FOR ME TO BE HERE. TO BE ABLE TO DO THINGS TO ME...
...MAKE ME JUMP THROUGH THEIR HOOPS, BE THEIR LAB RAT.
WHAT WOULD HAPPEN IF YOU TOOK THAT AWAY FROM THEM?
HMM... THEY WOULD BE VERY UPSET?
BUT HOW COULD I TAKE THAT AWAY FROM THEM?
I CAN'T BREAK OUT OF THIS SARDINE CAN.

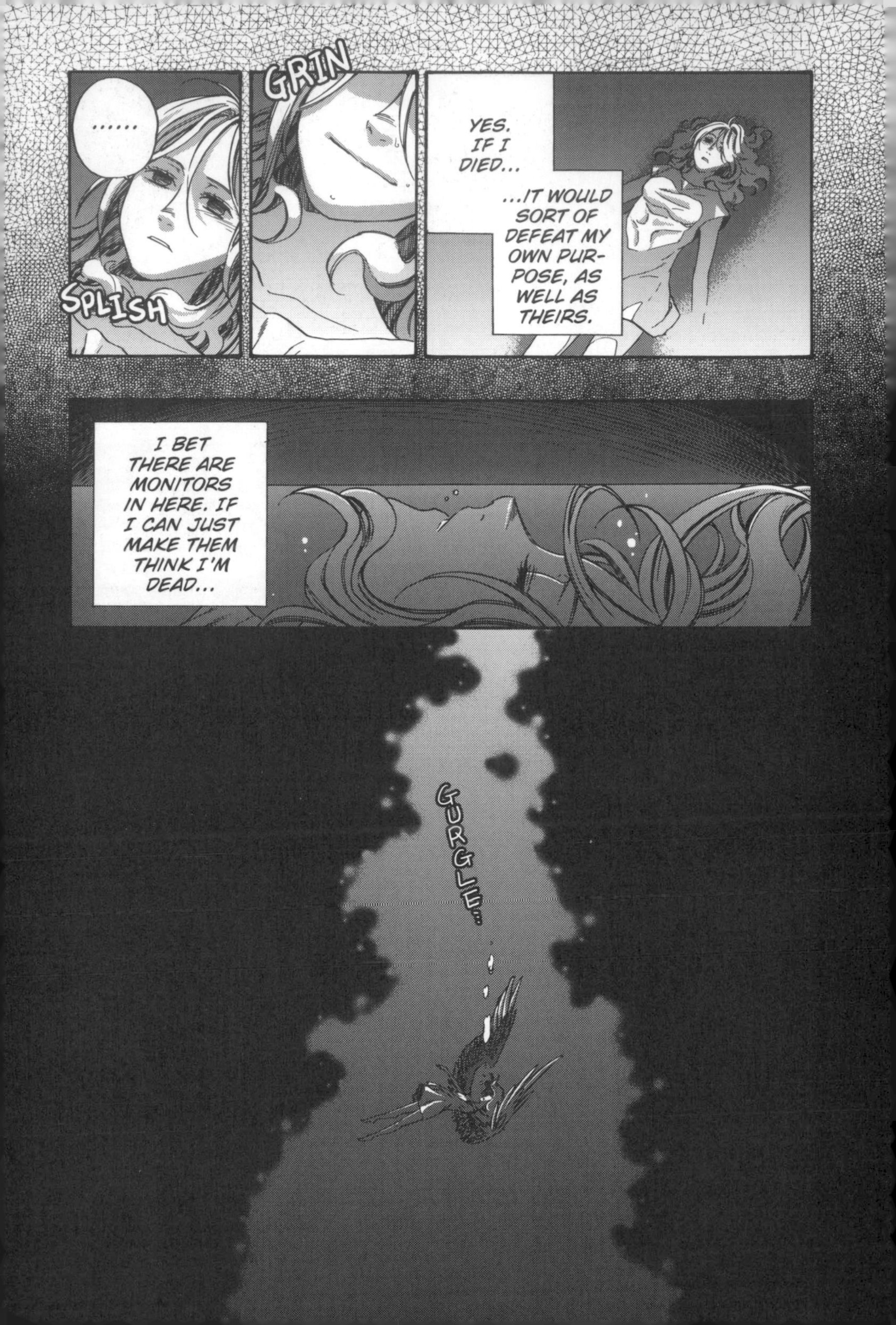
......
SPLISH
GRIN
YES. IF I DIED...
...IT WOULD SORT OF DEFEAT MY OWN PUR-POSE, AS WELL AS THEIRS.
I BET THERE ARE MONITORS IN HERE. IF I CAN JUST MAKE THEM THINK I'M DEAD...
GURGLE...

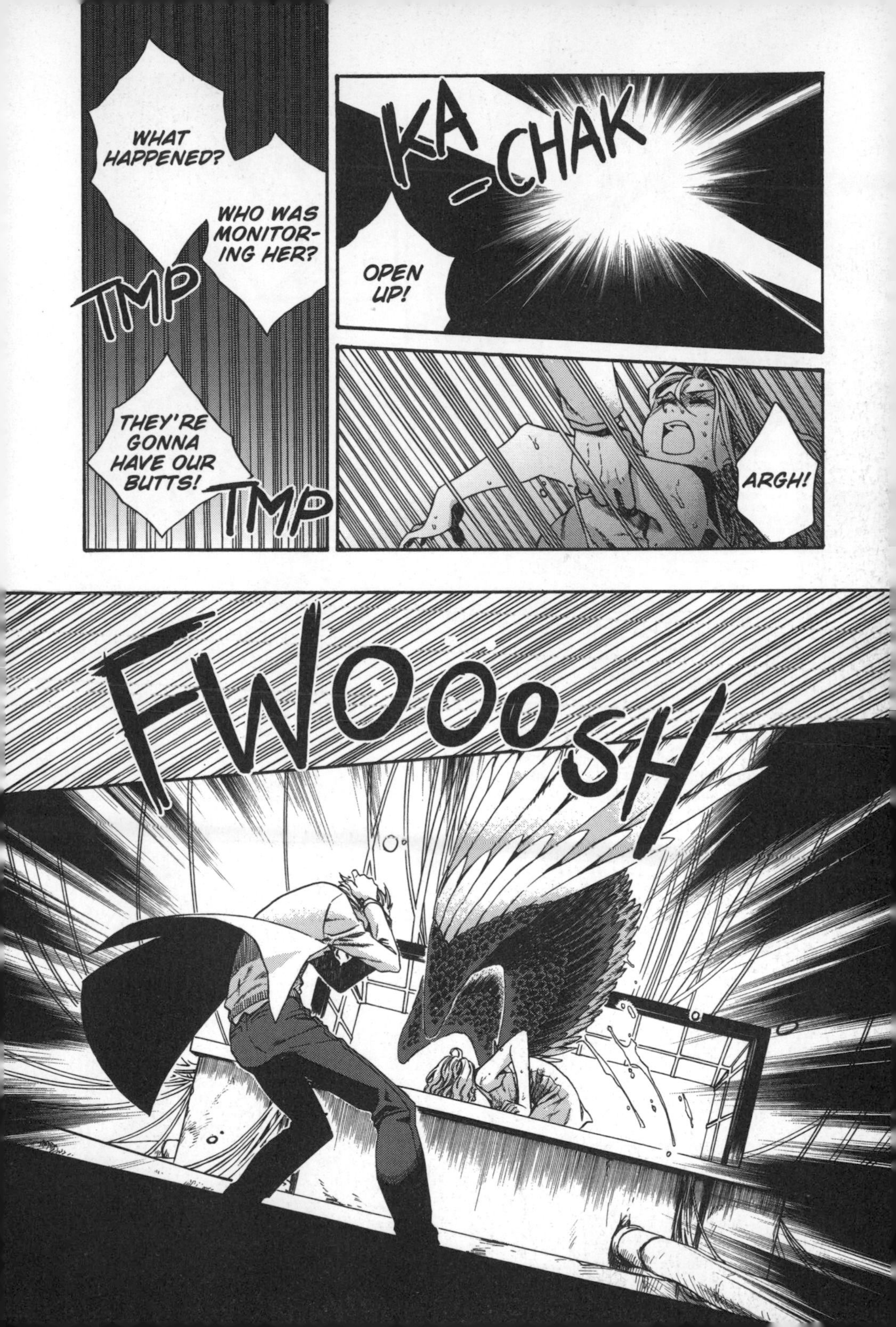
WHAT HAPPENED?
WHO WAS MONITORING HER?
TMP
THEY'RE GONNA HAVE OUR BUTTS!
TMP
KA-CHAK
OPEN UP!
ARGH!
FWOOOSH

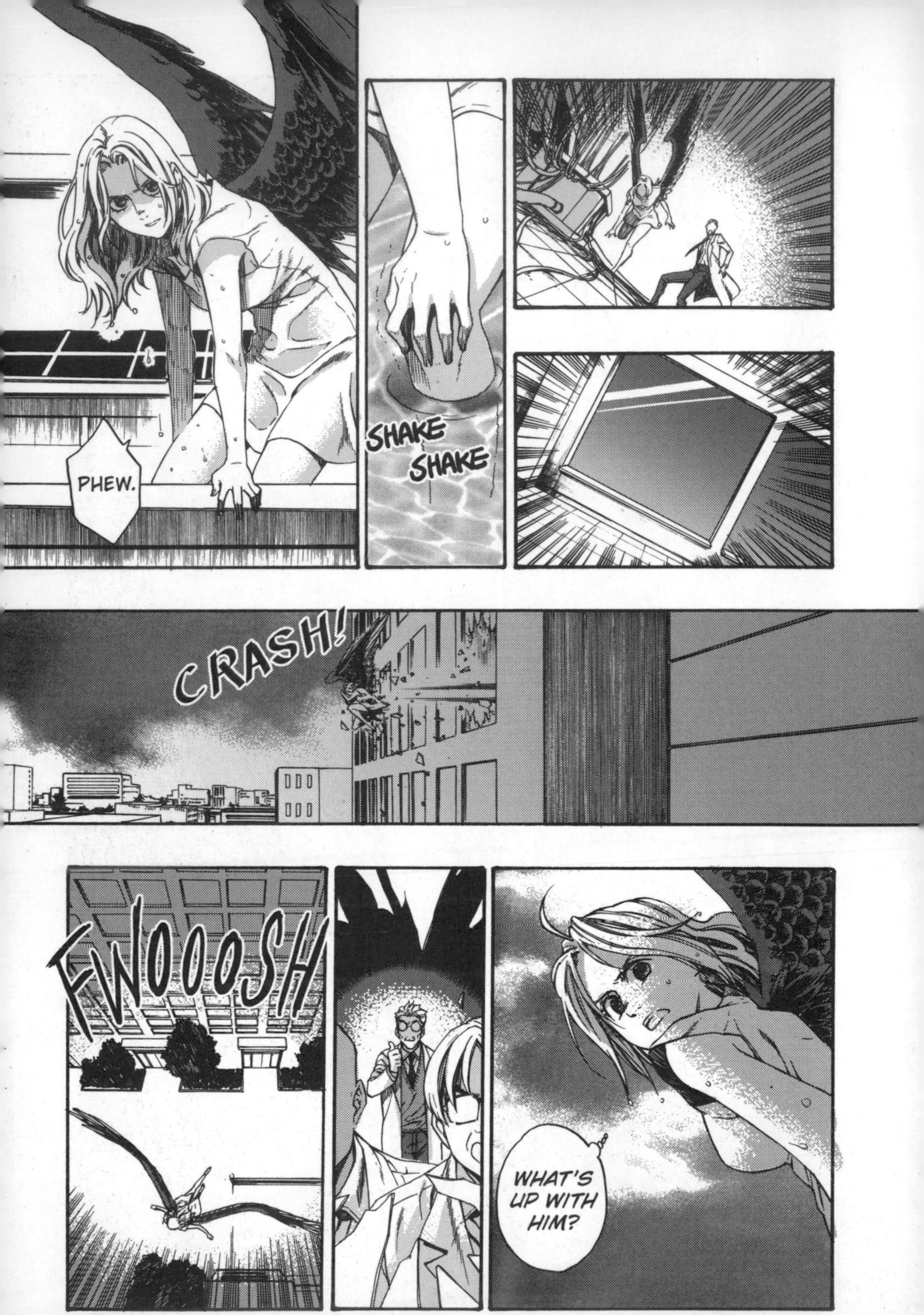
PHEW.
SHAKE
SHAKE
CRASH!
FWOOOSH
WHAT'S UP WITH HIM?

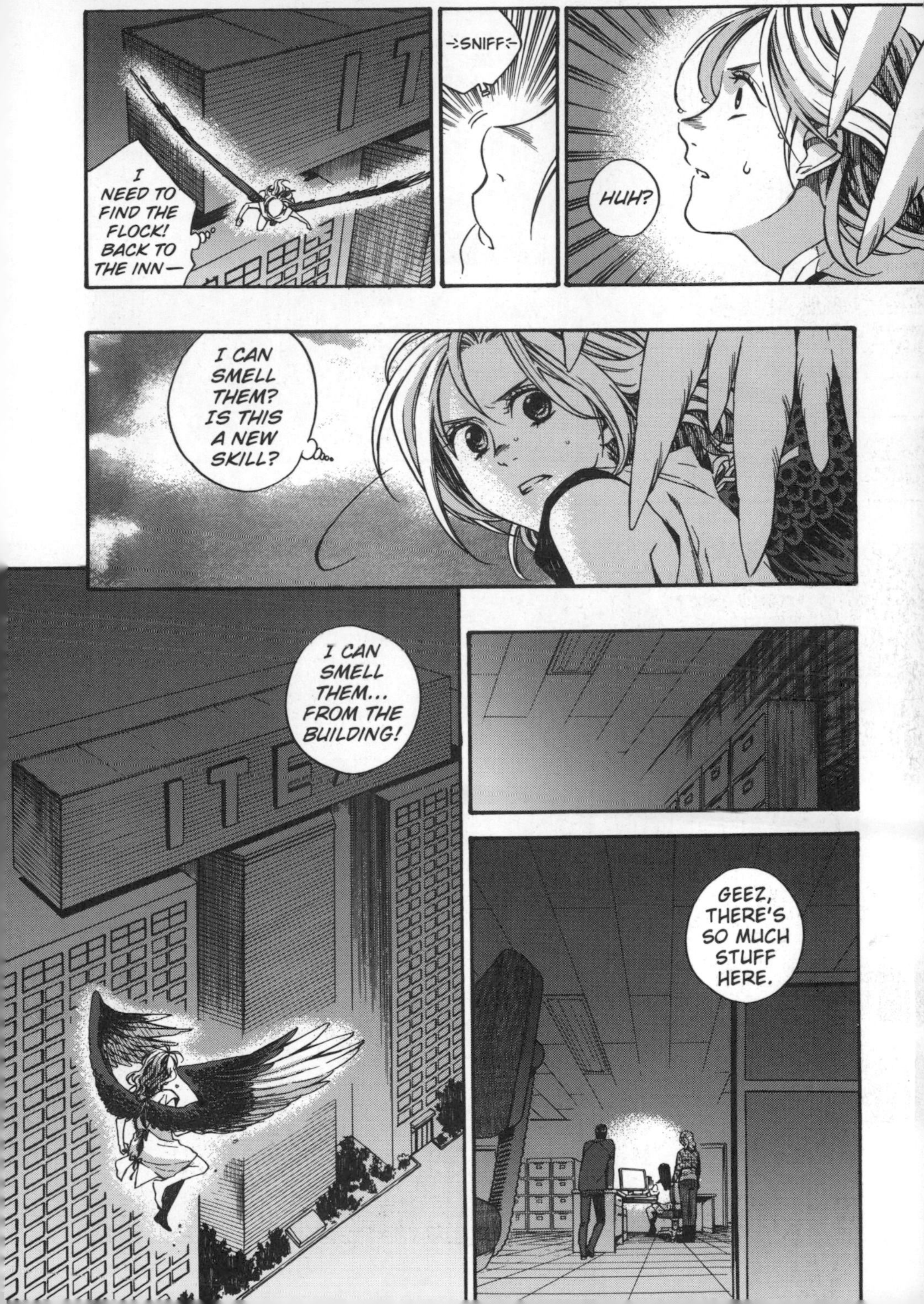
I NEED TO FIND THE FLOCK! BACK TO THE INN—
-SNIFF-
HUH?
I CAN SMELL THEM? IS THIS A NEW SKILL?
I CAN SMELL THEM... FROM THE BUILDING!
GEEZ, THERE'S SO MUCH STUFF HERE.

I WONDER...

...I WONDER IF JEB'S BEEN HERE.

I FEEL SOMETHING.

WHY WOULD JEB HAVE BEEN HERE?

HE HAS NOTHING TO DO WITH ITEX.

MAX, I CAN FEEL HIS VIBE. HE WAS HERE.

MAYBE THERE'S SOMETHING ON HIM, ON US, IN THE ITEX FILES.

WE CAME HERE TO LOOK FOR FILES ABOUT HOW ITEX IS POLLUTING THE PLANET, DESTROYING NATURAL RESOURCES.

NO AD-LIBBING—STICK TO THE PROGRAM.

I'M STARTING TO PUT MY FINGER ON WHY YOU GUYS ARE SLATED FOR TERMINATION.

MAX, MAX, LOOK AT THIS!

THIS IS JEB'S SIGNATURE!

WHERE?

SEE?

OH GOSH! THIS IS—!

174

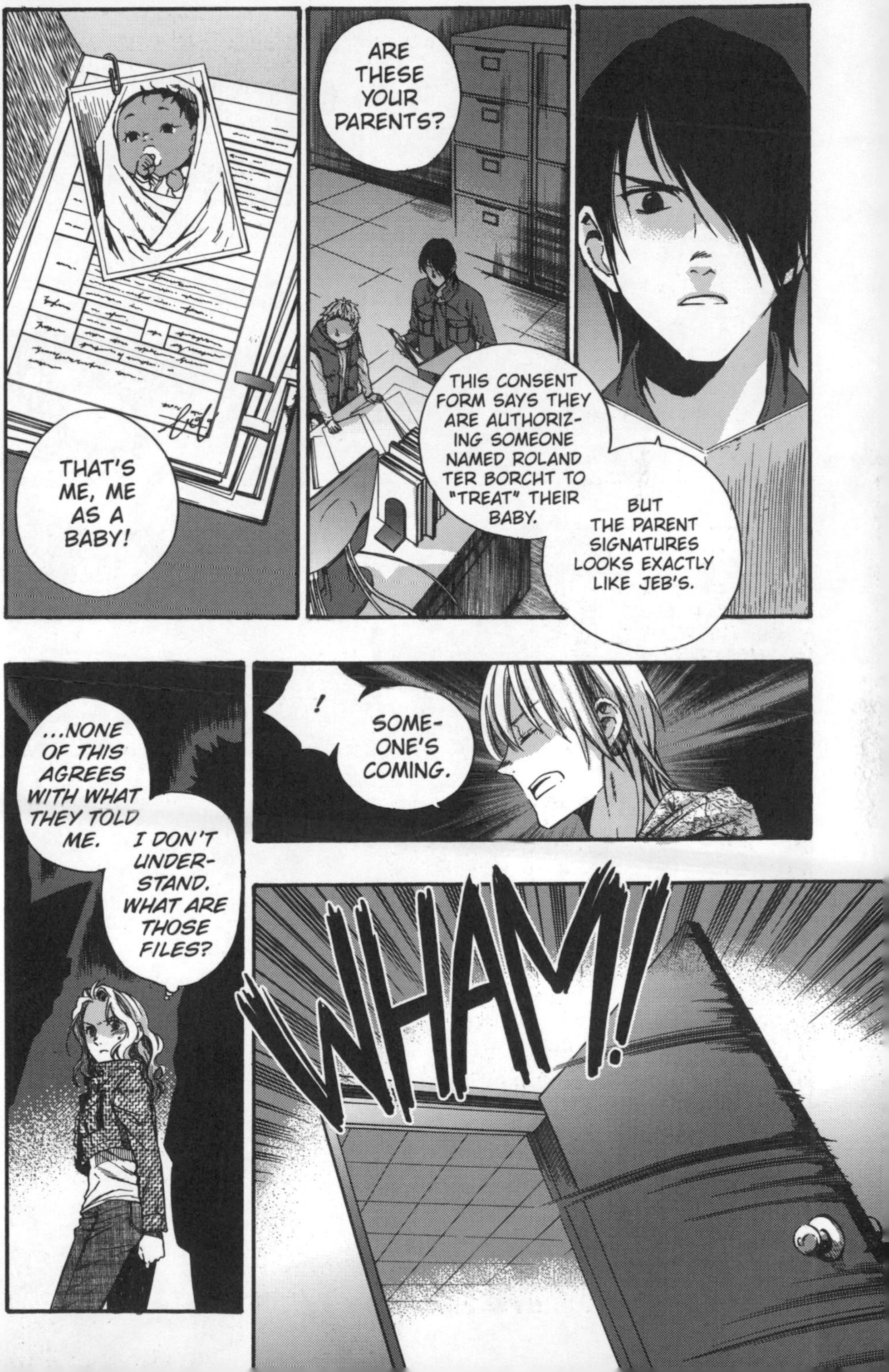
THAT'S ME, ME AS A BABY!
ARE THESE YOUR PARENTS?
THIS CONSENT FORM SAYS THEY ARE AUTHORIZ-ING SOMEONE NAMED ROLAND TER BORCHT TO "TREAT" THEIR BABY.
BUT THE PARENT SIGNATURES LOOKS EXACTLY LIKE JEB'S.
...NONE OF THIS AGREES WITH WHAT THEY TOLD ME.
I DON'T UNDER-STAND. WHAT ARE THOSE FILES?
!
SOME-ONE'S COMING.
WHAM!

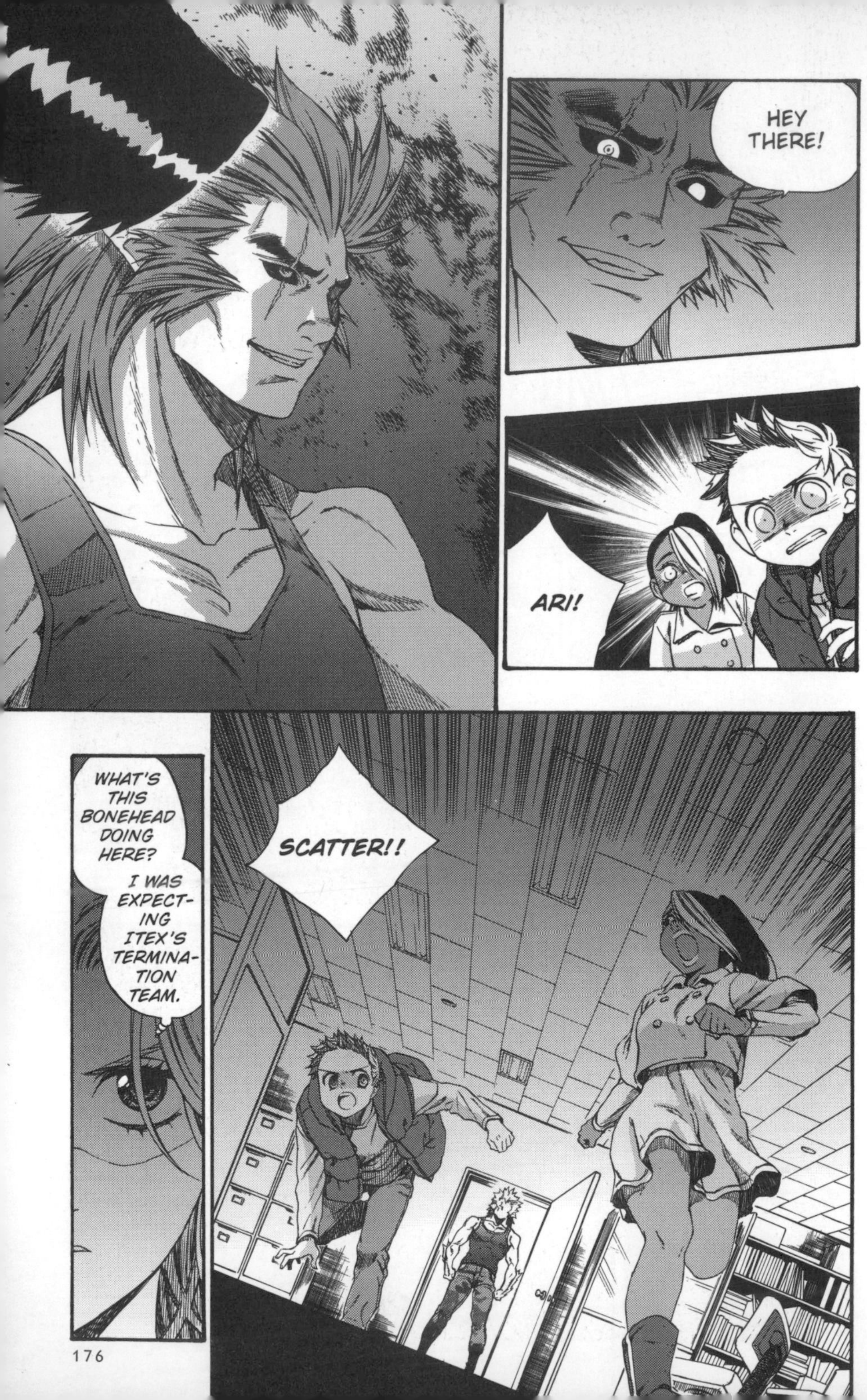
HEY THERE!
ARI!
WHAT'S THIS BONEHEAD DOING HERE?
I WAS EXPECTING ITEX'S TERMINATION TEAM.
SCATTER!!

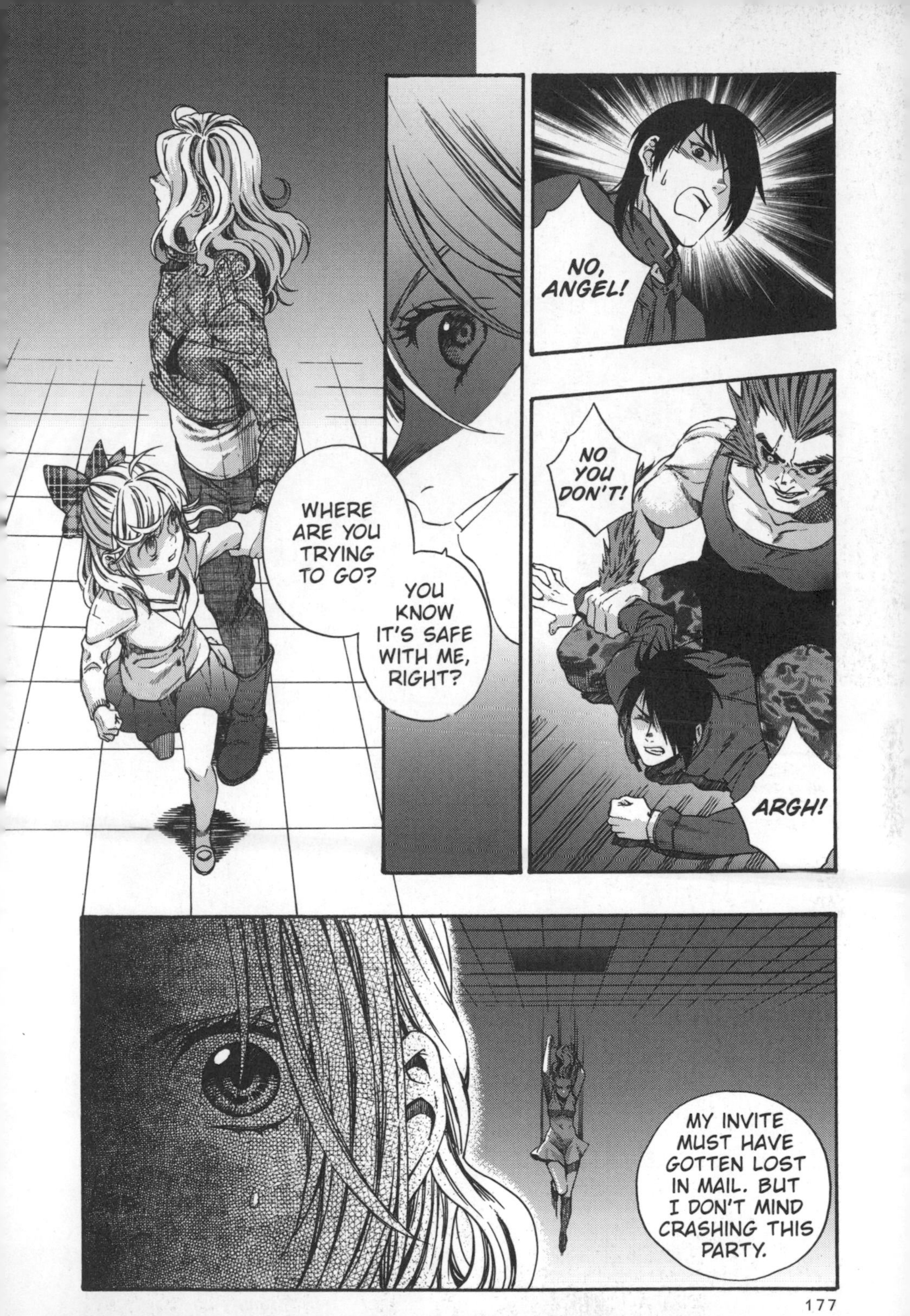
WHERE ARE YOU TRYING TO GO?
YOU KNOW IT'S SAFE WITH ME, RIGHT?
NO, ANGEL!
NO YOU DON'T!
ARGH!
MY INVITE MUST HAVE GOTTEN LOST IN MAIL. BUT I DON'T MIND CRASHING THIS PARTY.

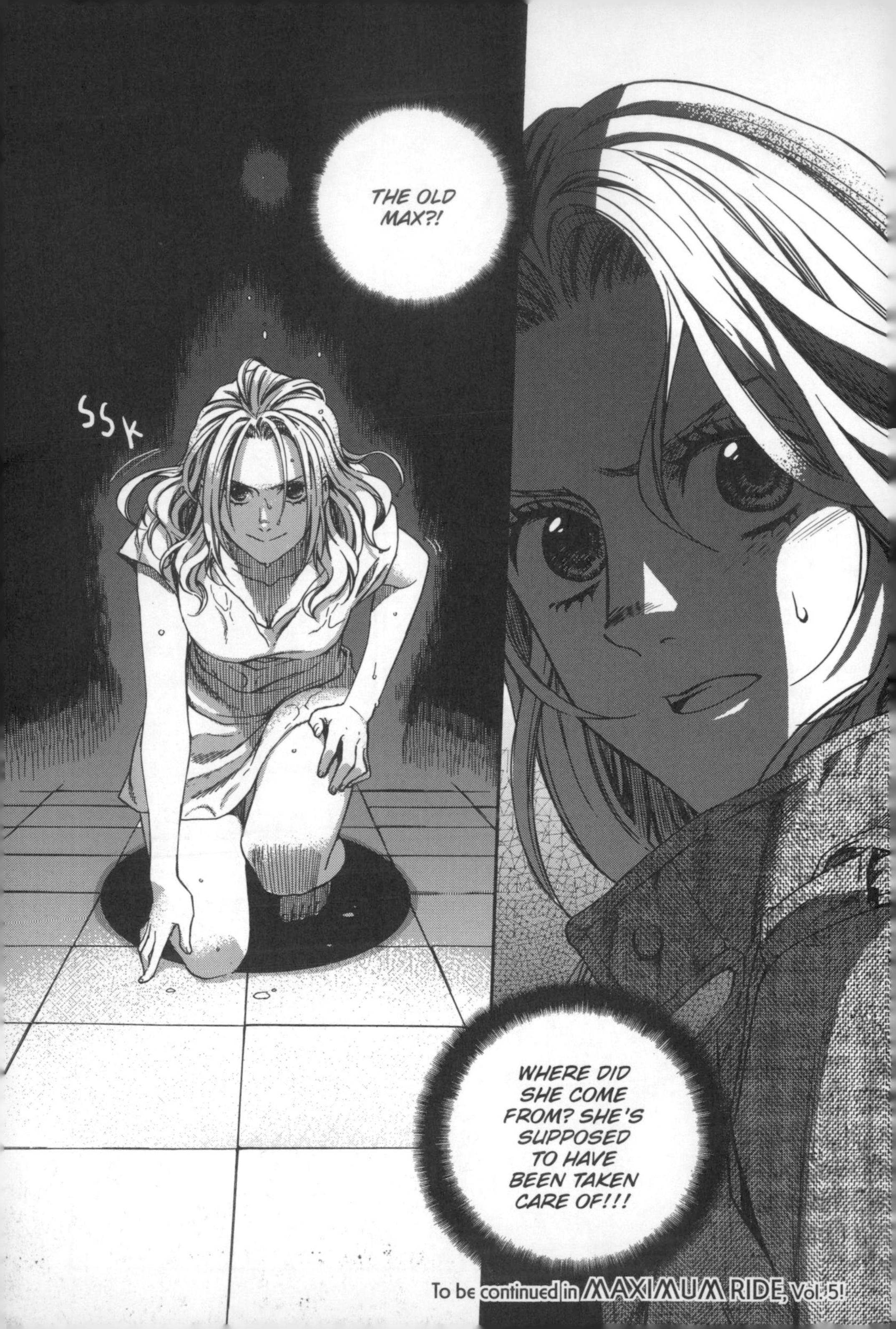
THE OLD MAX?!
SSK
WHERE DID SHE COME FROM? SHE'S SUPPOSED TO HAVE BEEN TAKEN CARE OF!!!
To be continued in MAXIMUM RIDE, Vol. 5!

YOU *WILL* CHECK OUT THE NEXT VOLUME, RIGHT?

MAXIMUM RIDE

For everything you need to know about the
bestselling Maximum Ride series, as well as
games, videos, competitions and much, much
more, go to the Maximum Ride website:

www.maximumride.co.uk

COMING JULY 2011

Middle School
The Worst Years of My Life

James Patterson
& Chris Tebbetts

Illustrated by Laura Park

Rafe Kane has enough problems at home without throwing his first year of middle school into the mix. Luckily, he's got an ace plan for the best year ever, if only he can pull it off. With his best friend Leonardo the Silent awarding him points, Rafe tries to break every rule in his school's Code of Conduct. Chewing gum in class – 5,000 points! Running in the hallway – 10,000 points! Pulling the fire alarm – 50,000 points! But when Rafe's game starts to catch up with him, he'll have to decide if winning is all that matters, or if he's finally ready to face the rules, bullies, and truths he's been avoiding.

Containing over 100 brilliant illustrations, *Middle School* is the hilarious story of Rafe's attempt to somehow survive the very worst year of his life!

A-

Turn the page for a sneak preview of

Middle School

CHAPTER 1

I'M RAFE KHATCHADORIAN, TRAGIC HERO

It feels as honest as the day is *crummy* that I begin this tale of total desperation and woe with me, my pukey sister, Georgia, and Leonardo the Silent sitting like rotting sardines in the back of a Hills Village Police Department cruiser.

Now, there's a pathetic family portrait you don't want to be a part of, believe me. More on the unfortunate Village Police incident later. I need to work myself up to tell you that disaster story.

So anyway, *ta-da,* here it is, book fans, and all of you in need of AR points at school, the true autobio of my life so far. The dreaded middle school years. If you've ever been a middle schooler, you understand already. If you're not in middle school yet, you'll understand soon enough.

But let's face it: Understanding *me* —I mean, really understanding me and my nutty life—isn't so easy. That's why it's so hard for me to find people I can trust. The truth is, I don't know who I can trust. So mostly I don't trust anybody. Except my mom, Jules. (Most of the time, anyway.)

So . . . let's see if I can trust you. First, some background.

That's me, by the way, arriving at "prison"—also known as Hills Village Middle School—in Jules's SUV. The picture credit goes to Leonardo the Silent.

Getting back to the story, though, I *do* trust one other person. That would actually be Leonardo.

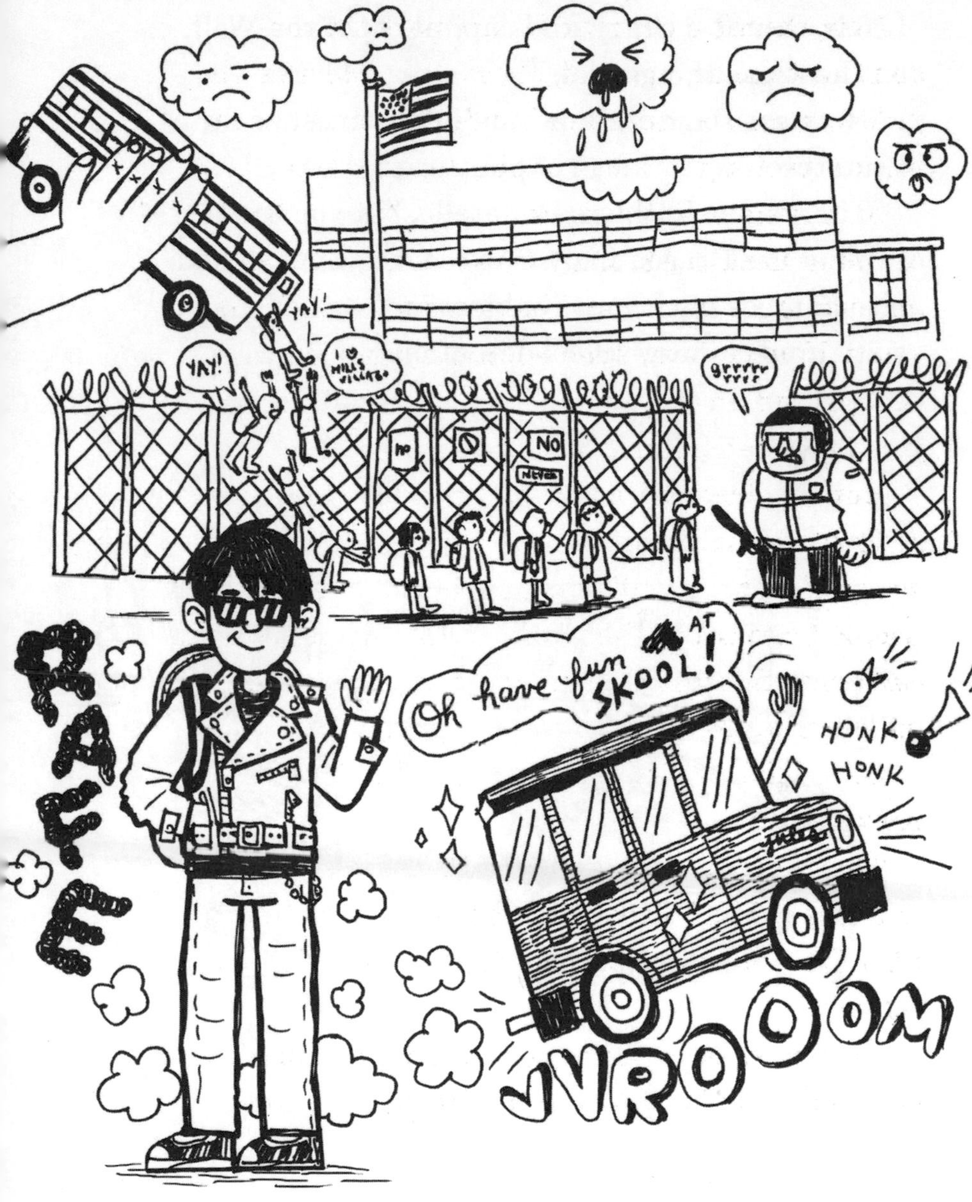
YAY!
YAY!
I ♥ HILLS VILLAGE
NO
NEVER
grrrrr rrrr
RAFE
Oh have fun AT SKOOL!
HONK HONK
VROOOOM

Leo is capital *C* Crazy, and capital *O* Off-the-Wall, but he keeps things real.

Here are some other people I don't trust as far as I can throw a truckload of pianos.

There's Ms. Ruthless Donatello, but you can just call her the Dragon Lady. She teaches English and also handles my favorite subject in sixth grade—after-school detention.

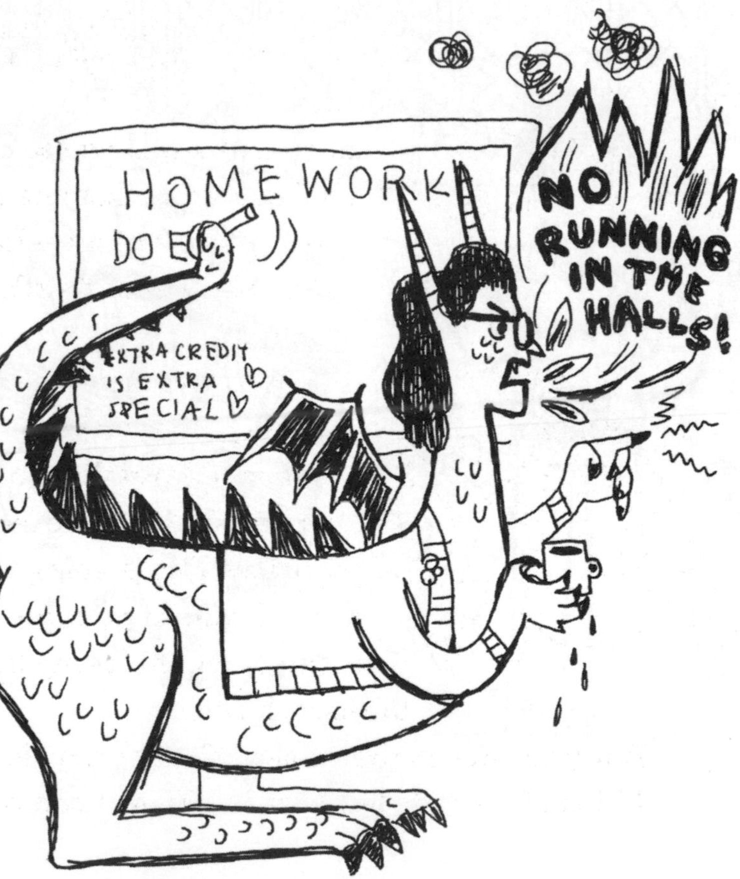
HOMEWORK
DO E
EXTRA CREDIT
IS EXTRA
SPECIAL
NO RUNNING IN THE HALLS!

SEES ALL!
HEARS ALL!
BEWARE!

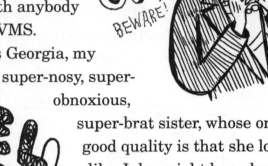

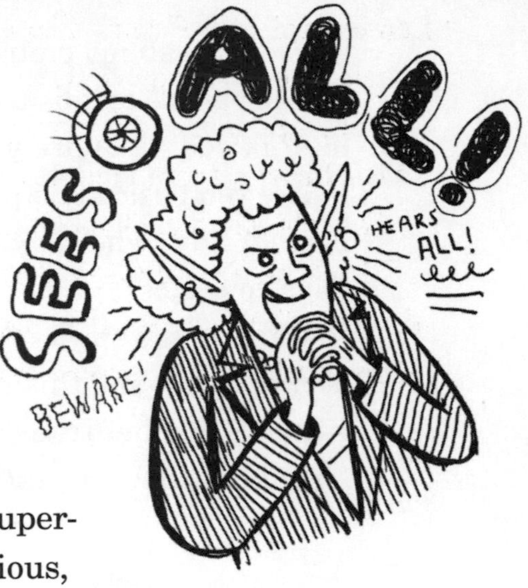

Also, Mrs. Ida Stricker, the vice principal. Ida's pretty much in charge of every breath anybody takes at HVMS.

That's Georgia, my super-nosy, super-obnoxious,

I'M TELLING!

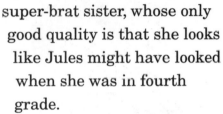

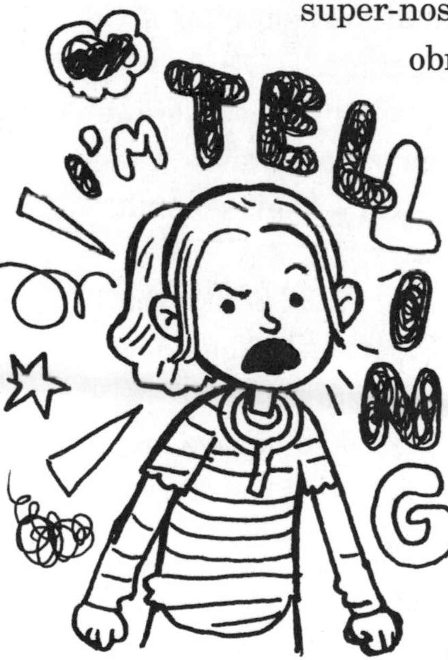

super-brat sister, whose only good quality is that she looks like Jules might have looked when she was in fourth grade.

There are more on my list, and we'll get to them eventually. Or maybe not. I'm not exactly sure how this is going to work out. As you can probably tell, this is my first full-length book.

But let's stay on the subject of *us* for a little bit. I kind of want to, but how do I know I can trust

you with all my embarrassing personal stuff—like the police car disaster story? What are you like? *Inside,* what are you like?

Are you basically a pretty good, pretty decent person? Says who? Says you? Says your 'rents? Says your sibs?

Okay, in the spirit of a possible friendship between us—and this is a huge big deal for me—here's another true confession.

This is what I *actually* looked like when I got to school that first morning of sixth grade.

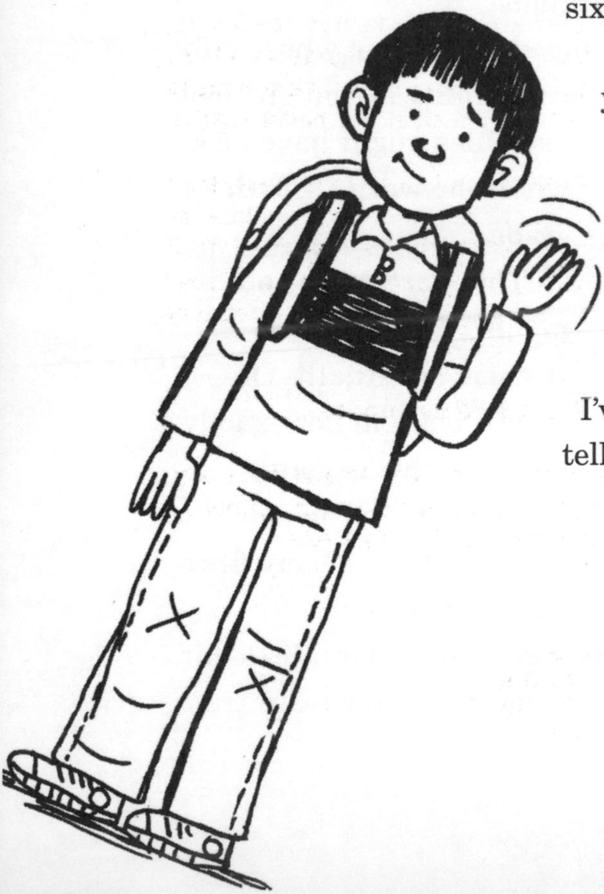

We still friends, or are you out of here?

Hey—don't go—all right?

I kind of like you. Seriously. You know how to listen, at least. And believe me, I've got quite the story to tell you.

THE NEW NOVEL IN THE BESTSELLING
WITCH & WIZARD SERIES,
AVAILABLE NOW!

Witch & Wizard
THE GIFT

James Patterson
& Ned Rust

Ever since Whit and Wisty Allgood were torn from their home and family in the middle of the night, the soldiers of the New Order government have relentlessly tried to capture and execute them for 'collusion, conspiracy, and experimentation with the dark and foul arts'. But this supremely skilled witch and wizard have instead boldly spearheaded the fight against the cruel and brutal regime.

The villainous leader of the New Order is just a breath away from the ability to control the forces of nature and to manipulate his citizens on the most profound level imaginable – through their minds. There is only one more thing he needs to triumph in his evil quest: the Gifts of Whit and Wisty Allgood. And he will stop at nothing to seize them.

Praise for the Witch & Wizard series

'A fast, exciting fantasy adventure . . . with wall-to-wall thrills and spills . . . page-turning suspense, pace and invention, street-smart irony and upbeat humour' *Books for Keeps*

ANGEL
A MAXIMUM RIDE NOVEL

James Patterson

HOW DO YOU SAVE EVERYTHING AND EVERYONE YOU LOVE . . .

Max Ride and her best friends have always had one another's backs. No matter what. Living on the edge as fugitives, they never had a choice. But now they're up against a mysterious and deadly force that's racing across the globe – and just when they need one another the most, Fang is gone. He's creating his own gang that will replace everyone – including Max.

WHEN YOU CAN'T BE TOGETHER . . .

Max is heartbroken over losing Fang, her soulmate, her closest friend. But with Dylan ready and willing to fight by her side, she can no longer deny that his incredible intensity draws her in.

BUT YOU CAN'T STAY APART?

Max, Dylan, and the rest of their friends must soon join with Fang and his new gang for an explosive showdown in Paris. It's unlike anything you've ever imagined . . . or read.

FANG
A MAXIMUM RIDE NOVEL

James Patterson

**A TERRIFYING PROPHECY. AN UNDYING LOVE.
THE ULTIMATE SACRIFICE.**

Maximum Ride is used to surviving – living constantly under threat from evil forces sabotaging her quest to save the world – but nothing has ever come as close to destroying her as the horrifying prophecy that Fang will be the first to die. Fang is Max's best friend, her soulmate, her partner in leadership of her flock of bird kids. A life without him is a life unimaginable.

Max's desperate desire to protect Fang brings the two closer together than ever. But when a newly created winged boy, the magnificent Dylan, is introduced into the flock, their world is upended yet again. Raised in a lab like the others, Dylan exists for only one reason: he was designed to be Max's perfect other half.

Thus unfolds a battle of science against soul, perfection versus passion, that terrifies, twists, and turns . . . and meanwhile, the apocalypse is coming.

THE NEW DANIEL X NOVEL,
AVAILABLE NOW!

DANIEL X: ***DEMONS AND DRUIDS***

James Patterson
& Adam Sadler

The Alien Hunter is playing with fire . . .

Daniel X is on an impossible mission: to eliminate every intergalactic criminal on the face of the Earth. Using his incredible superpower to create objects out of thin air, he's taken on some of the most fearsome and fiendish aliens in the universe. Now Daniel has travelled to England in search of his next target: the explosive demon of fire Phosphorius Beta and his army of flame-weaving henchmen.

But it's going to take a whole new level of mojo to destroy this villain. Beta's strength has been growing since he arrived on Earth more than a millennium ago, and he's finally ready to turn the blue planet into his own fiery wasteland. The only way to stop him is by jumping back in time to the Dark Ages to end Beta's blistering reign before it has a chance to begin. But can Daniel X take the heat? Or will the Alien Hunter finally get burned?

Join Daniel X on a wickedly wild ride – through space and time – for his most sizzling adventure yet!

We support

National Literacy Trust

I'm proud to be working with the National Literacy Trust, a great charity that wants to inspire a love of reading.

If you loved this book, don't keep it to yourself. Recommend it to a friend or family member who might enjoy it too. Sharing reading together can be more rewarding than just doing it alone, and is a great way to help other people to read.

Reading is a great way to let your imagination run riot – picking up a book gives you the chance to escape to a whole new world and make of it what you wish. If you're not sure what else to read, start with the things you love. Whether that's bikes, spies, animals, bugs, football, aliens or anything else besides. There'll always be something out there for you.

Could you inspire others to get reading? If so, then you might make a great Reading Champion. Reading Champions is a reading scheme run by the National Literacy Trust. Ask your school to sign up today by visiting www.readingchampions.org.uk.

Happy Reading!

James Patterson

MAXIMUM RIDE: THE MANGA④

JAMES PATTERSON
& NaRae Lee

Adaptation and Illustration: NaRae Lee

Lettering: JuYoun Lee

Published by Arrow Books in 2011

3 5 7 9 10 8 6 4 2

MAXIMUM RIDE, THE MANGA, Vol. 4 © James Patterson, 2011

Illustrations © Hachette Book Group, Inc., 2011

James Patterson has asserted his right under the Copyright, Designs and Patents Act, 1988 to be identified as the author of this work

First published in Great Britain in 2011 by
Arrow Books
Random House, 20 Vauxhall Bridge Road,
London SW1V 2SA

www.randomhouse.co.uk

Addresses for companies within The Random House Group Limited can be found at: www.randomhouse.co.uk/offices.htm

The Random House Group Limited Reg. No. 954009

A CIP catalogue record for this book is available from the British Library

ISBN 9780099538431

Printed and bound in Germany by GGP Media GMBH, Pößneck